Fearless

ALSO BY LAUREN ROBERTS

Fearless

LAUREN ROBERTS

SIMON & SCHUSTER
London   New York   Amsterdam/Antwerp
Sydney/Melbourne   Toronto   New Delhi

First published in Great Britain in 2025 by Simon & Schuster UK Ltd

Text copyright © 2025 Lauren Roberts
POWERLESS is a trademark of Lauren's Library LLC
Map copyright © 2024 Patrick Knowles
Crown image copyright © 2024 Tas Kyprianou
Crown designed by Howling Moon Headwear
Map designed by Patrick Knowles
Cover designed by Loren Catana

This book is copyright under the Berne Convention.
No reproduction without permission.
All rights reserved.

The right of Lauren Roberts to be identified as the author of this work has been
asserted by her in accordance with sections 77 and 78 of the Copyright, Designs and
Patents Act, 1988.

5 7 9 10 8 6

Simon & Schuster UK Ltd
1st Floor, 222 Gray's Inn Road
London
WC1X 8HB

www.simonandschuster.co.uk
www.simonandschuster.com.au
www.simonandschuster.co.in

Simon & Schuster Australia, Sydney
Simon & Schuster India, New Delhi

The authorised representative in the EEA is Simon & Schuster Netherlands BV,
Herculesplein 96, 3584 AA Utrecht, Netherlands. info@simonandschuster.nl

A CIP catalogue record for this book is available from the British Library.

HB ISBN 978-1-3985-3127-7
eBook ISBN 978-1-3985-3141-3
eAudio ISBN 978-1-3985-3140-6

This book is a work of fiction. Names, characters, places and
incidents are either the product of the author's imagination or are
used fictitiously. Any resemblance to actual people living or dead,
events or locales is entirely coincidental.

Typeset in the UK by Sorrel Packham

Printed and Bound in the UK using 100% Renewable Electricity at CPI Group (UK) Ltd

MIX
Paper | Supporting
responsible forestry
FSC
www.fsc.org   FSC® C013604

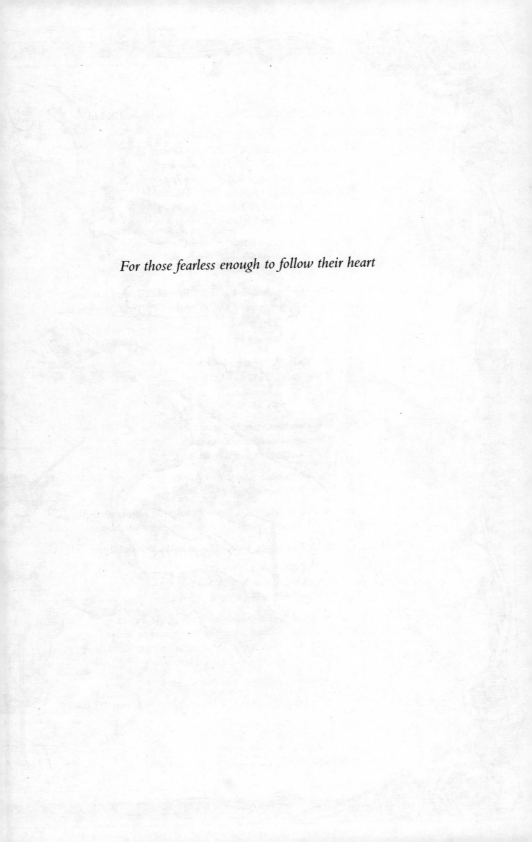

For those fearless enough to follow their heart

Prologue

There are very few reasons for a meeting between two cloaked figures in the dead of night.

Unsurprisingly, the list is as short as it is unseemly.

For some, it is love. For most, it is lust.

Lust for money. Lust for purpose. Lust for revenge.

But in some cases, it is love that first spurs these lusts. Or rather, the loss of it.

Though these odd contradictories are rare, they are consistently tragic.

A man leans against the wall, his stoic expression swallowed beneath the gaping hood.

It's been several minutes now, though the sudden wave of impatience seems to sneak up on him. Every wary glance begins to weigh heavily atop his cloaked shoulders. Because buried deep beneath that hood is a mind that screams at him to go through with this, persistently drowning out a much gentler, coaxing voice that tells him to walk away, a voice that makes him ache. Still, he leans heavier against the wall, as if to anchor himself to this moment, this

decision, before inevitably sinking with the consequences of it.

Moonlight slips between the slivers of crumbling stone surrounding the alleyway. It makes him uneasy for some unexplainable reason, as though the pale fingers are clawing their way towards him.

Yes, he much prefers the sun to its eerie opposite.

The cloaked figure straightens suddenly at the sight of a shadow slinking closer. It stops before him, morphing into something far more tangible, mortal. They stand, assumably, eye to eye, though their hoods shroud any hint of an identifying feature.

'Do you know what you have to do?'

This second shadowy figure speaks like gold, rich and soft. He has the practiced ability to spin words into something far prettier than the meaning behind them.

'To an extent,' returns the first man. His worn boots shift atop the crooked cobblestones, mind still screaming over that soft voice telling him to run away from this damning decision.

'Very good.' The second shadow shoves a hand into his pocket. 'I'm trusting you won't disappoint.'

'I can't make any promises.'

Pulling the hand from his cloak, the man presents a hefty coin purse to the cool air. 'This should be enough to ensure you make this worth everyone's while.'

The first man reaches for the pouch, swallowing at the sheer weight of silvers within. 'Yes, this should do.'

'Now—' the figure lowers his voice, '—it needs to look real, understand? Make *me* believe you.'

The first man's voice is low. 'I will.'

The battle within his mind roars louder still. But he has learned to ignore the constant din of chaos, just as he does now. Because nothing can save him from this fate. Not even that persuasive, gentle voice.

With a curt nod of his hooded head, the stranger begins that silent slip into a swarm of shadows.

'Why do you want this?'

Curiosity has the conflicted figure blurting the question. Awaiting an answer, he clutches the pouch against his chest, treasuring the feel of tangible security.

The shadows, shifty as ever and eager to eavesdrop, seem to lean in.

A soft string of words over a shoulder is all the man offers. 'Every brutal act is born of love.'

That understanding alone draws together even the most unlikely of allies. Even hooded and shrouded in shadows, these two strangers have never felt so seen.

CHAPTER 1

Paedyn

A drop of blood splatters onto the floor, marring the pristine marble beneath my shaking legs.

I stare at the scarlet splotch, ears ringing and vision blurring.

Honey. It's just honey.

Rivers of red twine down my leg, their currents swift enough to have me rocking on my heels. Or maybe it's the slow realization of my fate that has this throne room spinning like the band of steel that chokes my thumb. I blink at the shiny floor, staring at the shell of a girl reflected up at me. Her face is streaked with dirt, eyes haunted by a future she hasn't yet seen and never thought she would. Silver hair dusts her shoulders, as pale as the sweaty face it sticks to. She sways, like one might on the shoes of a loved one. Hands are cuffed behind her back, blood leaking from tattered skin.

She is shambles. She is haunted.

She is to be a bride.

But that can't be true. I took his everything from him. And he is going to kill me for it. He has to.

My chest is suddenly too tight, breath catching in my throat beside the flood of words I'm swallowing back. Because death is the fate

I've been preparing for my whole life – the destiny I deserve. I feel it on the stained fingertips that will forever drip with the blood of others, in the O carved atop my sputtering heart to brand me a weakness.

Death is the only constant in my life, like an old friend who hones every one of my dark secrets into a weapon. He calls me weak and all I hear is Ordinary. He calls me doomed and all I hear is an earnest promise. His is the hand my bloody fingers reach for because there is comfort in his imminence.

Now there is nothing but the ringing in my ears and this deafening quiet of the unknown.

'Paedyn.'

I stiffen at the same moment the looming figures around me do. He might as well have called me a traitor. A murderer. An Ordinary weakening our Elite kingdom. Because those are the only names this court knows me by. The only names the entirety of Ilya spit as I was paraded to their king. Simply, they sum up the insignificance of my short existence.

My eyes slowly climb from the pattern my blood has painted atop the floor.

Honey. It's only honey.

Polished shoes crowd my vision, their black shine bleeding into equally dark pant legs. My gaze slides up the slim-fitting stretch of fabric and every seam concealing the strong body beneath. Urging my perusal upward, my eyes collide with his belt buckle before skipping to the box resting innocently in his raised palm. I know what sits within that velvet case, can see it glinting out of the corner of my eye. And yet, I don't spare it a glance, as if that could stop the sparkling shackle from inevitably slipping onto my finger.

Higher still is his wrinkled shirt. I trail every button until my gaze settles at the base of his throat and the collar encircling it. I have yet to look him fully in the face since my sentence rolled off his tongue.

'You are to be my bride.'

It's as though I've been thrown back to the Trials and the equally challenging game of pretend that accompanied them. I couldn't bear to look at him then, not unless I wished to see the king staring back.

But I killed the man I once saw reflected in his son's green gaze. Edric Azer haunts me only in the fragments of my mind and the matching, broken heart he carved into. I made sure of that.

And yet, I still cannot bring myself to look at this Kitt.

My throat burns.

I may have created something far worse than his father.

'Paedyn.' His voice is startlingly soft, reminding me of a time when that wouldn't have been shocking. 'Look at me.'

This isn't the first time he's said those words in response to my pointed avoidance of his gaze. But there is now so much more keeping my eyes from his, a past far more ruinous than the resemblance to a king who had my father killed. There is betrayal. There is hurt. And history is not easily forgotten by the kings who write it.

But that hint of familiarity in his voice has my chin lifting, my eyes gliding from that crumpled collar to crash into his.

Green. Just as they were, and just as they always will be. He looks at me, and I look at him. A criminal without a father, and a son forever trying to please his. Just as we were, and just as we always will be.

And for the first time since that battle in the Bowl, we truly see each other.

His lips twitch into something too sinister for a smile, too soft for a scowl. As though he wears formidability itself. 'The future queen of Ilya bows her head to no one.'

My mouth dries at his words while the entire court leans in to hear them. Their disbelief is palpable, mingling with the collective cloud of confusion that hangs thickly over our heads. Dozens of eyes prickle my skin, tracing the scar down my neck and the blood staining my skin. They take in this new version of the Silver Savior, the one who cut off the very thing that gave her the title. My short hair does little to conceal the brokenness I now bear so blatantly on my body.

The court gawks at what it is they glean from my appearance. I am a Psychic who is nothing of the sort. An Ordinary who somehow survived their Purging Trials, committed treason, killed their king, and is still standing here before them, alive against all odds.

That is when I hear Death's whisper echoing from the darkest corner of my mind. The part of me that had accepted my imminent doom the moment I learned what it meant to be powerless in this kingdom. Now he calls me queen, and all I hear is laughter.

Because this fate may prove to be worse than Death himself.

'Uncuff her,' the king commands casually.

My breath catches at the brush of calluses against my skin.

Kai.

My head whips around, unable to stop myself. Unable to focus on anything but the burning need to look at him.

But it's not his gray gaze I crash into. No, this one is brown, murky with blatant hatred. These are not the eyes I search for in every crowd. Not the eyes that rake over me with a reverence I revel in. Not the eyes that have counted every freckle dotting my nose, every shiver of my body.

My breath grows shaky before the Imperial who had carelessly cut that cuff from my ankle in the poppy field. He is to blame for every drop of my tainted blood marring this marble floor. His movements are as rough as the hands that carelessly yank at the chain encircling my wrists, further tearing the skin beneath.

Tears prick my eyes, and I blink, forcing them back. I shake my head slightly in defiance to the growing weakness within me and bite the quivering lip that portrays it. My gaze scans the room, body shuddering in pain as I search for him. I'm frantic, eyes fumbling over unfamiliar faces.

Damn the pretending. Damn the hiding. Damn everything but him and us and this moment where I *need* him.

But he's nowhere to be found. And for the first time since stealing those silvers from him on Loot Alley, I feel utterly alone.

The lock clicks. The cuffs spring open.

They fall to the floor, clanking against stone and smearing blood. The sound rings through the ornate throne room, sounding of finality. Of freedom that comes at a price.

'Much better.'

I tear my eyes from the gaping crowd to find the king smiling pleasantly. Rubbing my raw wrists, I watch as Kitt extends the hand not currently cupped around that little black box I'm avoiding. I blink at his palm, his gesture of goodwill. This single touch separates a traitor from a future queen.

When my gaze flicks up to the king, he offers a single reassuring nod. But the look he wears is laced with a reminder – I have no say in any of this.

So, when my dirt-streaked hand meets his ink-stained one, I let him pull me closer.

I wonder if he can hardly bear to hold the hand that drove a sword through his beloved father's chest, let alone slip a ring onto the finger that once dripped with his blood. As if in response to my racing thoughts, he gives me a gentle squeeze. The action is meant to comfort, though it alarms me far more than any threat.

'We Ilyans believe to have conquered the Plague many decades ago.' Kitt's voice carries across the throne room, deliberate and domineering in that familiar way I know he learned from his father. 'Yes, our powers are a gift from the Plague, but they are also a spit in its face. Because it is Elites who came out stronger on the other side of a sickness meant to kill us. Elites who protected our weak kingdom from conquerors. Elites who showcase their strength in the Purging Trials.'

Murmurs of agreement flutter throughout the room, followed by a wave of prideful nods. I bite my tongue, anger rising until it stains my cheeks with a flush. I am nothing more than their Ordinary entertainment, their example of weakness. I've been put on a pedestal to be poked and prodded, degraded and shamed.

'But Elites weren't the only ones who survived the Plague, were we?'

His question has the rage cooling on my tongue, leaving my mouth dry. Time seems to slow as I turn my face to him and hang on every unspoken implication.

'No, there were also the Ordinaries,' he continues evenly. 'The Ilyans who managed to stay alive, and yet, did not obtain abilities. And after years of coexistence with the Elites, they were banished and continually hunted for their lack of power.'

My palm grows sweaty against his. My whole body stills, though

I'm unsure if it is my sentence or saving grace I'm waiting for.

The king – the Kitt I once knew – sweeps that green gaze over his court. Blond hair peeks between the swirling strands of his gilded crown, glowing like a halo atop his head. When he speaks, it is deliberate. It is calm. It is practiced. 'And if we wish for our great kingdom to remain, we will welcome Ordinaries back into it.'

My knees threaten to buckle, but Kitt holds me upright. It's as though he suspected as much and grabbed my hand, if only to keep me from collapsing at his words. Faces blur around me; mouths move; hands rise in protest. But I hear nothing, see nothing, know nothing but this moment and the hope for every one after.

Kitt's mouth is moving again, cutting through the roaring crowd and my ringing ears. 'I will address all your concerns in due time. But, for your peace of mind, I will elaborate quickly. Since sitting on my father's throne, I have come to realize the dire state Ilya is slipping towards. I've learned more about our kingdom in these past few weeks than I ever had before.' Inclining his head to a figure in the crowd, he continues, 'Calum was once a prisoner of mine. Once a Resistance leader who I thought was a radical.'

My heart stutters, my eyes searching until—

There he stands, swallowed within the crowd. It was his pale blond hair I found first, followed by those watchful blue eyes. Feeling my gaze, Calum offers me a slow nod. I press my lips together, fighting the radiant smile I ache to give him. Instead, I spell out the gratitude in my mind, knowing he's likely reading the whirlwind of thoughts within.

Kitt pushes on, smothering the murmurs rippling through the throne room. 'But the more I questioned him for his treasonous acts, the more he taught me about my own kingdom. Our resources run dangerously low, due to several decades of isolation. There is not enough room within our borders to hold the growing numbers of those in the slums, and records show that our food supply has dwindled alarmingly over the years.'

Ilya's impending doom slides calmly off the king's tongue, as if he's spent every second since I escaped staring at the list of failures his father left him to deal with. My mind flashes back to that moment

17

in the Scorches, when I had spat the truth of this kingdom's fragility at Kai's feet. My whole life has been spent in the slums, crowded and hungry. It's no shock that the records reflect a scarcity I know firsthand.

'Dor and Tando will not trade their livestock, crops, or knowledge of adapting to the Scorches.' Kitt flicks his gaze over the stunned crowd. 'We cannot expand, nor can we eat, without them. Izram's water, the Shallows, has grown far more treacherous over the years. Even the fish within it shy away from our shore.' His voice grows solemn while I hang on every word. 'If we do not open up our borders, and allow Ordinaries to live among us once again, this Elite kingdom will fall.'

There is a swelling of shouts before the king silences them with reason alone. 'Even still, our surrounding cities will not trade with us if we remain an Elite society. When my father began the Purging three decades past, Ilya cut ties with Dor, Tando, and Izram. They lost our recourses as much as we lost theirs, and this broken relationship will not be easily healed. These kingdoms now care very little for Elites.'

Warmth begins to pool in my chest, feeling so foreign I almost don't recognize it to be hope. But I have witnessed the animosity of Dor alone, shared their loathing for Elites. Not because they possess powers, but because of how they treat those without. And after decades of self-righteous shunning, it will take quite the gesture of goodwill from Ilya to prompt peace.

I'm swaying on my feet again.

That gesture of goodwill is me.

I feel hazy, numb to the fate set before me. As an Ordinary, a united Ilya was all I ever hoped for. My home, a place where I no longer needed to pretend to be something I wasn't in order to stay alive. But that skeptical, scrappy side of me says that Kitt couldn't possibly want this. Not when his father did everything in his power to eradicate the Ordinaries.

'As for Paedyn Gray . . .' The sound of my name startles me back to an unsettling reality. 'Her treason is not all that it seems. Our union will serve as a peace offering to the surrounding kingdoms. This show of faith will welcome Ordinaries back into Ilya, and therefore, entice our neighbors to reopen trade with welcoming Elites.' Kitt smiles tightly. 'Our marriage will mark the beginning of my reign, and the strongest Ilya there has ever been.'

I'm picking apart every word, pulling at the syllables to make sense of them all. Then he turns towards me, every thought vanishing when he plucks that ring from its velvet box. There is a dizzying moment in which I think he might hear me swallow, might see the panic welling in my eyes.

That is when his gaze softens, and I see myself reflected in it.

Every fear, every bit of unease. He wears all of it and more. Because that ring in his shaking hand represents everything he was taught to hate. And yet, here he stands, going against the wishes of his beloved father in order to save this kingdom.

So, I let him raise my left hand between us. Let him see the willingness that smothers every worry. It is my turn to become the difference I always dreamed of being, even if the king's reasonings do not resemble my own. He wishes only to salvage this kingdom by whatever means possible, while I offer him my hand for a united Ilya alone.

I am the sacrifice that Ordinaries have bled and died for.

I am the power they lack.

The ring trembles around my broken nail. His eyes flick to mine in quiet permission.

Every moment of my life has built up to this one. This one fleeting second of bravery.

I nod, and he pushes the ring down the length of my finger.

CHAPTER 2

Kai

I thought I'd known torment until it wrapped around her finger. No, torment is tangible, and it gleams atop her tanned skin.

I stare, unblinking, at the symbol my brother slid onto her finger. It is binding. It is infinite. It is my undoing.

A laugh threatens to slip past my numb lips. It's not as though she hadn't promised to be my ruin, hadn't already become my demise. She is the single most destructive thing I have ever desired, and yet, it is the diamond on her finger that will destroy me.

I watch Paedyn through the gaps of a gawking crowd, just as I will for the rest of my life. I'll be forced to spend my days at her service but never at her side. In her shadow but never truly seen. In love with a girl I'd bowed to long before she became my queen.

Kitt steps aside, allowing the court full view of his betrothed. Short hair whispers atop her shoulders with each slow turn of her head. Silver meets tanned skin, gliding across the scar trailing her neck until the torn skin gleams like the sharp end of a blade. Her blue eyes cut through the crowd, searching and swift and so unsure.

I step behind one of the many marble pillars framing the room, avoiding her piercing gaze for perhaps the first time. I've been

nothing but willing when it comes to drowning in those ocean eyes. But now, I can't fathom drowning if she is not the anchor I'm sinking with.

Questions fly around the room, each one teetering on an accusation. I blend into the chaos, listening as the court voices my very own confusion. Because this was the last decree I ever thought would form on Kitt's lips. And he hadn't even bothered to inform me of it.

I roll my neck, practically feeling that indifferent mask of the Enforcer melting away from the rage simmering beneath. The abilities of every person in this room begin to press down on me, begging to be unleashed. Anger is too dangerous an emotion to let myself feel. It dulls my senses and heightens my Wielder ability until all I know is the power pulsing beneath my skin.

But I have no one to blame but myself. I did this to her, to us, to each moment I spent hoping she would be the center of every one to follow.

I am the monster who hunted her down. I am the beast who delivered her to this doom. And I am afraid I'll become so much worse when I'm no longer striving to deserve her.

A man shouts beside my ear, waving a hand so obnoxiously that I contemplate breaking it. Better yet, maybe I'll borrow his Blazer ability and singe that wagging tongue from his mouth.

Fortunately for the man, Kitt's voice swells over the echoing shouts before I get the chance to do anything rash. 'I will answer all your questions in a formal meeting to come. Following that, we will announce our engagement to the surrounding kingdoms.'

Engagement.

It feels as though the ground is caving in beneath me. Why couldn't we have just stayed in that field of poppies? I would spend the rest of my days making her flower crowns if she wanted to be a queen. *My* queen. Not Kitt's. Not Ilya's. *Mine.*

My eyes trace over her, tracking each movement. Kitt dismisses the court, quieting every conversation with a wave of his hand. In that moment, that single movement, I see our father. It's as though he is the one standing before this court, and Kitt is nothing more than his shadow.

This king is not the same one I left a fortnight ago.

This king is collected and calm and conscious of every move he makes.

But just as it always does, my gaze trails back to Paedyn. She is making her way across the room now, spine stiff and eyes straight ahead, fixed on the maid awaiting her beside the towering doors still several yards away. Sneers follow her every step as she strides through the crowd. Dozens of disgusted faces close in on her, growing bolder by the second. And I'm already moving before a man steps into her path.

He leans close enough to subtly mutter his vile comment, but the spittle flying from his mouth to splatter her freckles doesn't go unnoticed. I shove the man away from her so forcefully that I vaguely wonder whether I let a Brawny ability slip to the surface. The reckless action has me suddenly standing between Paedyn and the man who so clearly has a death wish. Stepping forward, I tower over him, ignoring the gasping crowd surrounding the scene I've made. Because the truth is, I don't give a damn about what this court thinks of me. And my reputation sure as hell can't get any worse.

'So much as breathe on her again,' I snarl, 'and I'll ensure it's the last time you ever do.'

'No.'

Her voice cuts through every crazed thought, washing over me as though relief itself is nothing more than the mere presence of her. Paedyn steps beside me, her gaze unwaveringly set on the now ghostly pale man. 'No,' she repeats, voice lethal. '*I* will be the one to ensure that the next breath you take to insult me, or my people, will be the very last one you ever taste. And it will be me, an Ordinary, that ends your Elite life.'

She stares at him, looking as though formidability is woven into the very fiber of her being. My ears ring in the sudden silence smothering the throne room. Every eye is pinned on her, every jaw slackened by her words.

My future queen has just made her first decree.

That damn ring is going to slip off her finger with how terribly her hands are shaking.

I follow her out the double doors, fleeing the stifling throne room and gossiping court within. She quickens her pace down the plush halls, and I can only imagine how out of place we look among the emerald embellishments. The Enforcer – half-naked and wrapped in bandages – and the king's betrothed – bloody and dipped in a layer of grime.

'Paedyn,' I call, lengthening my strides.

That only has her skidding around another corner. I sigh, trying again. 'Pae, wait.'

She stops, suddenly. Shakily. Even at my distance, I see her shoulders tremble, hear the shuddering of her breath. She braces a steadying hand against the wall, and I'm about to call out again when a swarm of people spill into the hallway behind.

Shit.

I need to think fast, need to get Paedyn out of here before the entire court finds their future queen gasping for air in the hallway. Plague knows they would credit her panic to her weakened, Ordinary blood.

My eyes land on a door occupying the same wall Paedyn is currently slumped against before doing the only thing I can think of.

'All right, up you go,' I murmur before scooping her legs into my arms and slinging the rest of her over my shoulder.

This manages to get her attention. It's as though I've awakened a slumbering beast. 'What the hell—?' She wriggles in my hold, nails biting into the bare skin of my back. 'Put. Me. Down.'

I head for the door, a flood of voices following. 'Tempting, but I'm a bit busy saving your ass at the moment.' She can't see the smirk that twitches my lips, but I'm sure she hears it in my voice when I add, 'Speaking of ass, how's the view back there, Gray?'

'Nauseating,' she bites out.

I whip open the door and step inside. 'You know I can see your left foot twitch, yes?'

She grumbles incoherently in response to her betraying limb before nearly smacking her lolling head against the door I close.

Darkness swallows every inch of the small space.

I set her gently on the floor before me, feeling her breath tickle my heated skin. My hands linger over the shape of her. Calluses catch on the thin fabric of her shirt, dragging it up as my palms slide over her hips. I can't see the shape of her in this pressing darkness, so I'll simply have to settle with feeling every inch of it.

Her voice is breathy in a way that has me gripping her tighter. 'Where are we?'

'Likely a forgotten broom closet,' I mutter. 'Couldn't have the entire court seeing their future queen in shambles, now, could we?'

The words were intended to tease, but they tear through my teeth, biting and bitter. And I regret them the moment I feel her body tremble beneath my hands. 'Hey,' I amend gently, pulling at the hem of her shirt until she stumbles against me. 'Talk to me.'

I can feel each thundering beat of her heart against my chest. And just like that, the distraction I'd created for her dissolves. She's crumbling again, her voice cracking as her composed facade does the same. 'I . . . I can't do this. I don't want to do this.' I feel each vigorous shake of her head. 'I was ready to die. I was ready for you to be the last thing I saw and now—'

'Don't say that,' I choke out, cutting her off before any more of my fears can escape her mouth. 'I would have never let that happen. I promised to fix this, and I will.'

'Fix this?' Her laugh is little more than a rasp. 'Kai, this is no longer a matter of life or death. This is . . .' When her breath catches, I know it is the ring she runs trembling fingers over. 'This is until death do us part.'

There's that anger again, washing over me in waves. Because she was meant to be the death of me, not the life of another. It was her I was meant to adore in this world and crawl to in the one after. But now she's tethered to a king, and I am nothing more than her killer.

I fumble for her hands, desperate to hold on to her for as long as I can. 'Focus on this ring,' I urge, spinning the band on her thumb. 'Your father's, not my brother's. Until I figure this out, spin it like you always do. Distract yourself.'

I feel a weak scoff tremble through her body. 'But this doesn't belong to my father. Not truly.' Her voice quivers beneath the weight of each word. 'Everything I thought I knew about my life was a lie. And now I'm expected to live it alongside someone I thought wanted me dead?'

I shake my head, not knowing how to help her deal with the sudden discovery of how she became Adam Gray's daughter. It was not by blood, but by chance and neglect of a stranger. And I am useless when it comes to curing her of this confusion, this hurt.

'I don't understand any of this,' she continues in a rush. 'I should be dead by now. Every person in this Plague-forsaken kingdom *wants* to see me dead, not on a throne.' She sighs into the shadows, her breath skittering across my skin. 'But Kitt is right. The kingdoms won't open trade if Ilya does not welcome Ordinaries again. You saw how hated Elites were in Dor.' I feel the quick shake of her head. 'I've wanted a united Ilya more than anyone, even if the king does so begrudgingly. But . . .'

'But the Elites will not accept an Ordinary queen so easily,' I finish for her. 'Hell, even the idea of Ordinaries freely living in Ilya.'

There's a beat of silence before words are spilling from her mouth, the one I can't see but know the shape of by heart. 'I thought Kitt was spiraling. I thought he was grieving and angry.' A shaky breath. 'I thought he'd order you to drive a sword through my chest the moment I set foot in that throne room.'

'I thought he would too,' I murmur. 'And I was prepared to severely disappoint him.'

The ache in her voice makes me wince. 'Kai . . .'

'Pae. I had no idea that this is what he had planned.' Dirty fingers comb through the messy strands of my hair. 'I've known little of Ilya's disarray over the years. And that is simply because I was spending more time in the slums than anyone filling this castle. You confirmed my suspicions in the Scorches, about the lack of food and land. But I hadn't realized the situation was so dire.'

I can feel her spinning that ring on her thumb.

'You said he wasn't himself when you left,' Paedyn ventures softly. 'He was grieving. The people whispered about his madness.' The next words are a distant thought plucked from her head. 'So, what changed?'

'I don't know.' My mind wanders back to the plethora of paper that scattered his desk, and the stained hands rummaging through them. 'I don't know.'

The darkness speaks on our behalf for a long moment, swelling around us and filling our ears with a dull drone before I'm once again tugging at that fraying hem of her shirt. She melts against my body, and it feels like relief. That is, until she admits quietly, 'I don't know if I'll survive this.'

'You've already survived worse,' I remind her sternly. 'Besides, you seemed to have no problem handling that man in the throne room.'

'As did you,' she counters, and I can perfectly picture the steely look accompanying those words. 'I don't need you to fight my battles.'

'Oh, darling,' I murmur, 'I know you don't. But if I am to be your Enforcer, then you better get used to it.'

This shake of her head is imploring. 'I am no one's queen.'

'Is that so?' My fingers find her cheek before trailing down the smooth slope of her nose. 'Then you have no idea how much power you hold over me.'

'You seem to forget that I'm completely powerless, Prince.' Her words hold an edge, as though her breath has become a blade she drags along my neck.

'So be my weakness, then.'

'You know I'm betrothed to your brother,' she whispers, lips dangerously close to mine.

I swallow, voice stern. 'For now.'

'For *forever*,' she breathes harshly. 'I don't think there is a way out of this. And if what Kitt said in the throne room is real, then the future of Ilya and the Ordinaries within it rides on this.'

I tip my face until her forehead meets mine. 'I'm too selfish to let you go so easily.'

'Then pretend.'

My thumb drags lazily over her bottom lip. 'Does that mean I have to drag you into a closet every time I want to touch you?'

I'm toying with her, trying to ignore the bitter taste each word leaves in my mouth. I refuse to let this be her fate, and yet, fear twines around me, tightening my chest even as I tease her. Because if she truly becomes Kitt's, I will spend the rest of my life mourning her.

So I distract. Deflect. Desire her more than ever in case this is the last time I get to.

I can hear the weak smile beginning to creep into her voice. 'You're not supposed to touch me at all.'

'But you could command me to,' I drawl. 'Then I'd simply be following an order.'

Her laugh is breathy, and I memorize the sound.

Her arms twine around my neck, and I wonder if she will hold him like this.

Her nose nudges mine, and I silently beg that she will never flick another's.

Her lips have only just brushed mine when the door flies open.

CHAPTER 3

Paeдun

'That was not what it looked like.'

A soft sigh. A nod that bobs the messy bun atop her head. 'Like I said, I don't know what it looked like, because I didn't see a thing.'

'Ellie,' I blurt, exasperated. 'You know damn well what you saw.'

She tucks a strand of loose hair behind her ear, as if that could distract from the smile lifting her lips. 'I was just there to grab a broom, and that is exactly what I did.' As if to emphasize her innocence, she lifts said broom and continues down the hall while I trudge behind.

I'm thankful for the brisk pace she sets that blurs the faces we pass and cools the flush painting my cheeks. My mind refuses to do anything but replay the moment that door swung open to reveal the Enforcer and his future queen tangled in the dark. We'd sprung apart, but not before recognition widened Ellie's brown eyes.

And yet, a smile tempts the corner of my mouth. I stifle it with a hand before it has the chance to spread. Because the longer I mull over the mortifying moment, the funnier I find it. In fact, my entire life is in shambles and all I can do is stare at the jagged pieces in my

palm and laugh. I don't dare look in a mirror because what stares back is a mosaic of every mistake, every tragedy traced into my skin, and the looming shadow of each one to come.

Powerless. Fatherless. Adena-less. These were the things I was already struggling to survive. And yet, it's the ring on my finger that may be the death of me.

A choking laugh slips from beneath my palm, loud enough to have Ellie throwing a worried glance over her shoulder. I follow her blindly through the castle I only ever thought to be a prisoner within. My fingers fiddle with the intricate band now binding me to another. It glints in the light, harmless like a word not yet sharpened by a lashing tongue.

Of all the places I imagined sitting, a throne was the last of them. A dungeon, yes. At the edge of a blade, certainly.

Because Ordinaries don't rule. They cower.

The seriousness of my current situation seems to crash into me once again as we round another corner. Servants stare; Imperials leer; laughter dissolves in my throat. Happiness flees in the face of my future.

Because I am the very object of weakness. I am loathed by all of Ilya. And if I am to be put on a pedestal, even to save their kingdom, they will gladly push me off.

Ellie stops suddenly before a door, and I nearly skewer myself on the broom handle she holds. Forcing my mind to wander back to the present, I follow her into the pristine room.

It takes all of two steps to realize that this is most definitely not the chamber I stayed in during the Trials. No, sprawled before me is the sort of decadence I've only dreamed of.

My feet fumble atop the plush floors, eyes wide as they skim over the largest bedroom I've ever seen. Intricate molding climbs up the far wall to surround each arched window lining it. Warm light pours in as the sun stretches across the green carpet, as though reaching for me.

The bed itself takes up most of the wall to my right, its floral quilt shadowed by the sheer canopy hanging above it. A desk, vanity, wardrobe, and rug all decorate the space, each one a soft white and far larger than I'd imagine they could be.

My eyes slowly slide back to Ellie. 'What room is this, and why am I dirtying it?'

She presses her lips into a thin smile. 'It's the queen's quarters, of course. Well, the new ones. The memory of Her late Majesty, Queen Iris, still lives in the previous rooms.' Her words have my stomach dropping, skin paling. 'This is where you'll be living. I hope everything is . . . satisfactory?'

'Satis—' I take a deep breath before I've even finished echoing her word in confusion. 'Ellie, it has not been long enough for you to forget that I find everything about this castle to be far above my regular standards.'

The smile she gives me is far slyer than I thought her capable of. 'Yes, I do recall you informing me how you'd crawled out of garbage the day we first met.'

Swallowing my sudden sadness at her words, I manage a small smile.

My heart aches at the thought of our fort. Of the sanctuary Adena and I had scavenged for ourselves in the slums. To think I'd likened it to garbage makes me sick to my stomach. Though, to the naked eye, I'm sure that's precisely what it looked like – and why it managed to stay untouched for so many years.

Now, it likely lies empty. Cold without her warmth and dull without her brightness.

Sun and sand and her bloody, broken body in my lap suddenly flash before my eyes. I blink back the memory, forcing myself to forget the sound of her final rattling breath or the thundering feet of bloodthirsty Ilyans surrounding us in the Bowl.

'Paedyn?'

'Hmm?' My head snaps up to find a worried expression smothering Ellie's soft features. I hadn't even realized I'd been staring at the floor. 'Sorry, yes, everything is more than satisfactory.'

Clearing my throat, I step farther into the room. After ignoring what I'm sure is an equally exquisite washroom to my left, I find something far more enticing to stride towards.

I'm standing before the balcony within a matter of seconds. It's only after throwing Ellie a giddy smile over my shoulder that I push open the glass–paned doors and step out onto the large stretch of stone.

The crisp air combs its fingers through my hair as I take in the beauty spread beneath me. It's breathtaking, the gardens from this height. Rows of flowers weave around the circular cobblestone paths, colors colliding at every turn. The fountain where I'd thoroughly splashed Kitt lies at the center of it all . . .

Kitt.

That was all he was to me during those Trials. A prince, yes, and a replica of his father in face alone. But also, my friend. A friend I betrayed. And one I thought would surely kill me for that, and so much more.

But now *he* is so much more. First a friend, then a foe, and now my future.

I shudder at the thought and every implication behind it. Spinning on my heel, I head back into my – *the queen's* – chambers to find Ellie patiently awaiting my return.

Shutting the balcony doors, I lean against them with a nonchalance I don't feel and certainly haven't for a long while. 'Where is the queen? I mean, the . . . dowager queen.'

I wince at the words I've stumbled over, but Ellie – angel that she is – offers an answer before I have the chance to butcher an elaboration. 'She was moved to the west wing of the castle. That's where the infirmary is,' she clarifies quietly. 'But even if she wasn't ill, she wouldn't be occupying this chamber anymore. Because, as you know, these are the *queen's* rooms and . . .'

I brace myself against the doors. 'And I am to be queen.'

'Right.' She attempts a weak smile. 'And I'm honored to be your lady's maid. That is, if you'll have me, of course.'

I let out an exasperated laugh, and it feels good. Feels good to have my body shake with something other than pain. Make a sound other than a sob. 'Ellie, if I'm truly made queen, I'll ensure you don't have to work another day.'

'Oh, I don't mind the work. Keeps me busy,' she admits shyly. 'Besides, I want to serve you.'

31

Another laugh surprises my lips, this one more biting than before. 'Do you? After everything?' I take a few steps towards her. 'You've heard the rumors. Probably even the truth.'

'I'm sure you had your reasons,' she says softly, avoiding my gaze.

Her answer is jarring, like a sudden wave of relief. I swallow, scared of my own question. 'But why is it you don't hate me like the rest of Ilya?'

She studies me then, letting a long, silent moment stretch between us. 'The rest of Ilya doesn't know you.'

'And you do?' I ask, a little too quickly.

'Better than most. You learn a lot about someone when you're their maid.' Then she's walking over to the vanity, pulling out its matching stool, and beckoning me with a pat atop the plushy fabric. 'Now, come on over and let me get you cleaned up.'

I obey, stiff and unsure. Sinking into that cushioned seat feels like slipping into the past. A past where my only concerns were surviving the Trials ahead and the Ordinary blood in my veins. A simpler time, before I joined the Resistance and drove a sword through the corrupt king's chest.

And this is how I'm rewarded for it. With a crown on my head and a kingdom at my throat.

'You cut your hair,' Ellie says softly, her tone inquiring. Wetting a cloth with warm water, she begins dabbing at the hardened blood speckling my skin.

She's working on a particularly stubborn spot above my jaw as I murmur, 'It was getting difficult to run for my life with it so long.'

I say this instead of the pathetic truth of it all. Because I'd rather not reminisce on the feel of blood clinging to my hair so terribly that I begged Kai to cut it off. Because I still pale at the sight of it, feel it drenching my murderous palms, fear when I'll see it gushing from the next person I love. Though, there are very few left to choose from, and the thought is woefully relieving.

I watch her reach for a pair of thin clippers. 'Would you like me to even out the ends? It's a bit choppy—'

'No,' I blurt. Then I'm softly adding, 'Thank you. I'd like to leave it.'

Ellie nods, though I'm sure she aches to ask my reasonings. And if she had, I would have told her. I would have admitted why I cling to the crooked ends of my hair.

The bangs I continually cut for Adena looked the same.

Those jagged silver strands tether me to long nights in the Fort, snipping Adena's curly bangs with nothing but the stars to see by. She would giggle at the tickling sensation while I chopped a crooked line through her hair. And then we would laugh, both blaming each other for the unfortunate outcome.

Now I will never again get that privilege. So I hold on to her in the ends of my own hair.

'What was it like?' Ellie finally asks, eyes wide. 'Fleeing across the Scorches like that?'

'Lonely,' I murmur. 'Terrifying.'

Ellie nods slowly, tucking a stray hair behind my ear. 'Well, this length suits you. And I'm glad you're back. Safe.'

'Thank you,' I offer quietly. 'I'm just as shocked about that as the court.'

'Yes, I heard about that.' Her voice is the embodiment of a wince. 'And I can't say that the staff took the news much better.'

'I can only imagine,' I groan. 'In fact, I wouldn't be surprised if I'm poisoned by the kitchen crew before the end of the week.'

Ellie shakes her head, cloth persistently gliding over my skin. 'Oh, no, they wouldn't dare. Not with the king having claimed you as his bride-to-be.'

Claimed me.

Those are words I certainly never thought would be associated with Kitt. His brother, on the other hand . . . I know exactly what it feels like to be claimed by the Enforcer. And I've embraced it.

'Well, that's . . . reassuring,' I mutter.

'He's been doing much better, you know,' Ellie adds softly, her eyes trailing the scar down my neck. It's a struggle not to squirm beneath the weight of her obvious concern. But she continues, mercifully. 'After his coronation, he was rarely seen. Kept to himself, locked in that study of his.' She leans in, lowering her voice as though we aren't the only people occupying this room. 'He'd dump his food from the window. Some of us servants stumbled upon the pile of scraps beneath it in the courtyard.

'But it's to be expected, of course,' she continues with a sigh. 'He was grieving his father, after all.' Her eyes slide to mine before quickly darting away. 'And clearly Calum's visits seemed to help. His Majesty was able to hear firsthand what was happening in his kingdom, not just read it from the records.'

I nod slowly, still trying to piece this perplexing puzzle together. 'So, Calum would visit him? In his study?'

'Well, not at first,' she amends. 'He was in the dungeons for several days enduring Plague knows what. But I suppose Kitt saw something in him and decided to talk more civilly.' Ellie shrugs. 'That's really all I – and the staff – know on the matter.'

I've never been so completely shocked and unsurprised in the same moment. Such a contradiction is the only reasonable response to the past hour of my life. Because, despite my hope for him, I never truly believed Kitt would strive to make changes that contradicted everything his father told him to believe. And it seems I was right. This king does not care wholly for a united Ilya, only that this kingdom remains by whatever means necessary.

I almost find the courage to smile, because this is a start.

Kitt has every right to hate me after I killed his tyrant of a father, but he *needs* me. Together, we could save this kingdom from more than just ruin. We could liberate it from the segregation that has plagued this land for decades. Perhaps, without Edric here to feed his son lies and prey on that insatiable need for approval, Kitt will be able to think clearly for the first time.

And with Calum offering him council, helping him see the truth of this kingdom, there might just be hope. His eloquence combined with that intent way in which he listens help make the Mind Reader so persuasive. Or maybe he simply uses that ability of his to comb through our thoughts, picking apart how we feel and think before saying exactly what needs to be heard.

My eyes fall to the bed, where my only belonging lies slumped on the floor beside it. The dirty pack was likely brought to my chambers by a reluctant servant. But it's the journal residing inside that I itch to show Calum. Show Kitt.

That bound reminder of my father has me swallowing thickly. It's odd, how the man I once knew was merely a thread in the tangle of truth I'm only now beginning to unravel. Until recently, Adam Gray was simply a father, a Healer who taught me how to survive with tedious observance and training. Then I watched him die. And that one, devastating moment plunged me into a life I never thought I'd survive.

My father was the leader of the Resistance. Except, according to his journal, he wasn't really my father at all.

Having been trapped within my mind for far too long, I turn my attention back to Ellie. 'And the other Resistance members? I assumed some were taken as prisoners.'

She shakes her head solemnly. 'Last I heard, they were in the dungeons as well. But that was right after that final Trial, and it's been a while since then . . .'

She trails off, giving me time to imagine each cruel way they could have died. I wonder how many Resistance members — how many Ordinaries or the few Elites who supported them — were captured after that battle in the Bowl Arena. How many died brutally, because even after years of planning their uprise, it all went to shit.

Standing, I step out of Ellie's gentle reach. 'I need to speak with Kitt — the king.' I clear my throat. 'And Calum.'

She looks horrified by this idea. 'Not looking like that, you won't!' It takes mere seconds for the bashfulness to settle in once again. 'I mean, you've had a very long journey and must rest—'

'I thought I'd be dead long before this moment,' I cut in evenly. 'Thought I'd be skewered with a sword in that throne room. But I'm not, and I intend to find out exactly why.' My voice lowers into something far more solemn. 'I may not have much life left to live, so I won't spend it resting.'

'Okay, then,' Ellie says quietly. 'No rest. But you must bathe before you show yourself to the castle again.'

Right. My entire existence has been reduced to appearances.

I nod, suddenly unable to focus on anything but the blood crusted across my skin. It will be a relief to scrub away every remnant of the traitor running for her life. Every drop of blood, sweat, and tears shed on the treacherous journey.

Heading for the bathroom, I'm suddenly spinning on my heel and blurting, 'Have you heard from Lenny? I saw him during my . . . travels, but we got separated.'

'Right. About that.' Her gaze strays from my narrowing one. 'Um, he's here, actually.'

'What?' I choke. 'Where is he?'

She pads towards me, brown bun bobbing with every step. 'I'll tell you after that bath.'

'Ellie—'

'My *Lady*.' She emphasizes the title with a lifted brow.

'Fine,' I huff, turning once again towards the bathroom. Then I'm calling over my shoulder, falsely cheery and absurdly genuine, 'but only because the blood beneath my nails may drive me to insanity.'

CHAPTER 4

Paedyn

ater drips from the ends of my short hair, reflecting its silver color to mimic molten steel when sliding from the strands.

I'd scrubbed every inch of my body, spending extra time beneath my nails and around the many jagged cuts flecking my skin. It was only when I emerged from the rapidly cooling bath water, skin raw, that Ellie hesitantly broke the news to me.

All it took was a handful of rage-filled moments to throw on thin pants, pair them with a fitted tunic, and stalk to the door. Ellie was wise enough to stay out of my path, only stepping close enough to offer an apologetic smile and a set of slipperlike shoes. They now cling to my feet as I stride down the hallway, the silk soft against my blistered feet.

Faces blur past, but my gaze never strays from that door awaiting me at the end of the corridor. Through my tunneled vision, I see him leaning against it, emanating boredom as he stares pointedly at the shiny boots beneath him.

Several seconds pass before his head jerks up suddenly, having heard my thundering footsteps with that Hyper ability. His red hair stands out starkly against the crisp Imperial uniform fitted to his

body. Even with half of his face partially concealed by the white mask, I can still see those brown eyes widen when they land on me. That is when his gaze crinkles with a mingling of joy and relief.

He straightens, spreading his arms. 'Princess, glad to see you somehow made it back in one—'

My forearm meets the padded chest of his uniform, pushing him hard against the wall. My voice is a low growl that even I didn't know I was capable of until this very moment. 'What the *hell*, Lenny?'

'Woah,' he coos softly, hands raised in innocence. 'Look, if this is about losing you in Dor, I swear I was ready to turn that city inside out to find you, but—'

'You know damn well that is not what I'm talking about,' I seethe. This is most definitely not the manner in which a future queen would conduct herself, but fortunately for me, I doubt my reputation could get any worse.

I push away from him to turn towards the door and—

Lenny blocks my path.

'Move,' I bite out.

'Well, someone's already growing accustomed to giving orders,' he mutters, not budging an inch.

I blow out a breath. 'Get out of my way, Lenny.'

'I'm sorry, Princess.' He gives me a sympathetic shake of his head. 'You know I can't do that.'

I shove him again. 'Let me inside.'

'Paedyn, please. Just take a breath—'

'I promised,' I choke out, vision suddenly blurry with unshed tears. 'I promised to avenge Adena.' Another shove, this one weaker. 'So let me inside this damn room, Lenny.'

Sympathy smothers his face, crowding around his features like the freckles splattering his skin. 'I have strict orders from the king not to let you see her,' he whispers. 'I'm sorry. I'm so, so sorry.'

I grow suddenly numb, every thought muffled and feeling detached. My fingers uncurl from his uniform, slide from his chest. 'Blair tore a branch through Adena's chest during that final Trial.' My voice is distant, as though the words are falling from someone else's lips. 'And I'm going to kill her for it.'

Lenny reaches for me, hesitant. His hands cup my shoulders, steadying. 'I get it. Trust me, I do.' He sighs through his nose. 'But you can't kill her on my watch. And Kitt knows you won't kill me to get to her. At least,' he adds skeptically, 'I would hope not.'

A sound slips past my lips, something like a scoff. Of course Kitt knew I would come after Blair for what she did to Adena. What she did to *me*. It's genius, really, stationing Lenny as her guard. He knows how much I care for him – and he's used that against me. 'You can't be her shield forever.'

'And when I'm not,' he says slowly, 'you can do with her as you please. Though I don't recommend doing anything rash.'

'Rash?' I scoff, eyes ablaze. 'The thought of killing her is all that's kept me going. I've given my decision plenty of thought, I assure you.'

'Paedyn . . .' He shakes his head, red hair rippling with the movement. 'That was before all of this. Before you were betrothed to the king.'

I wince at his words, feeling the sudden weight of that ring on my finger. He runs a hand down his face before leaning in to murmur, 'You can't just . . . go around killing people anymore.'

'Anymore?' This time, he's the one wincing at the quiet hurt in my voice. 'I never wanted to kill anyone. I've only ever defended myself. But her . . .' I jab a finger towards the door beside us. 'She is to blame for what I've become.'

'I know,' he says softly, wrapping an arm around me. 'I know, Princess. I'm sorry.'

I step into his embrace, clutching him tightly. My face is buried against his uniform, nose stinging from the starchy scent. 'I'm scared, Lenny,' I admit, my voice muffled.

'You're allowed to be. You know that, right?' He ducks his head, resting his chin atop my hair. 'No one was expecting this. But I'm here to help you in any way I can.'

I lift my face, suddenly concerned. 'Why are you back? What about your mother? The Mixes? Finn and Leena?'

'They are all fine,' Lenny reassures me. 'Ma needed some help anyway, so Finn and Leena are staying with her. Besides, it's safer there for them.' Unraveling his long arms from our embrace, he gives me that sly look of his. 'I came back for you, Princess. And being slammed against the wall was certainly not how I figured I'd be thanked for it. But I suppose violence is one of your love languages.'

I smile sheepishly, warmed by his effort to find me. 'I didn't think you would come back to Ilya.'

'When you and the Enforcer were captured from the Mixes base, we didn't even know where to start looking for you.' He begins pacing then. 'So my mother, Leena, and Finn – shockingly enough – convinced me that I was more help to you here at the castle than I was aimlessly wandering Dor.' His eyes sweep over the hallway and each Imperial that marches through it. Voice low, he adds, 'We knew you would end up here at some point, and I'm not marked as one of the Resistance members, remember? I never even made it into the Bowl because I was down in those tunnels guiding people through.

'And with Calum in the king's good graces, he ensured that no one would bat an eye when I fell back into rank as an Imperial.' He grins, and I don't miss the triumphant gleam in his eyes. 'So, I'm here to help in any way I can. You, Ilya, and Calum.'

I nod. Smile. Try to grip the shambles of myself tight enough to sound okay. 'I'm glad you're here. I may need you to force me down the aisle.'

His grin fades. 'I know this is hard. But we are so close, P. So close to finally getting the freedom that the Resistance has fought so fiercely for, even if it is in a roundabout way. And I know that a marriage is not what you wanted. Hell, even becoming a queen. But . . .' He swallows. 'You're alive, Paedyn. And I didn't know if I'd make it back in time to ever see you again.'

I smile, sad and full of understanding. 'I thought I'd never get to see you again either.'

I'm just as surprised as he is when a laugh manages to escape me. His growing look of concern only spurs on the sound as I struggle to spit out, 'I can't seem to die, can I?' I wipe a loose tear from my eye. 'What was it you called me?'

I can see the exact moment recognition lights his face. 'A cockroach,' he chuckles, head shaking. 'You're a damn cockroach, Princess.'

CHAPTER 5

Rai

I've rehearsed this reunion, repeated practiced words over and over in my mind.

It's this conversation that has occupied my racing thoughts, forced my feet to tread the familiar path to his study. The one that was our father's before it belonged to the brother now resembling him.

Or maybe he doesn't. Maybe he is nothing like the man I loathed.

I'm not sure what to think after Kitt's dooming declaration in the throne room. And that is exactly why I find myself standing before that familiar wooden door – answers.

After three raps of my knuckle, I'm turning the handle and stepping into the room. The small space is stuffy, like that cellar where the Enforcer reunited with his Silver Savior. My gaze skims over the surrounding study, these four walls trapping so much of my past within. Embers endure a slow death at the bottom of the hearth, glowing faintly with the final remnants of warmth. Three plush chairs face the fireplace, one leather and worn and stealing my attention for a moment too long.

I clear my throat before striding towards the large desk at the center of the room. Kitt's head is bowed, eyes tracing the parchment

clutched between his fingers. It's only when I'm looming over him that his head lifts. 'Hello, Brother.'

I blink at the endearment in his voice. It sounds so foreign coming from the man I left to find our father's murderer. But this isn't that broken, crazed man the kingdom gossiped about. This is something else entirely.

'Hello, Kitt,' I return slowly. 'You seem . . . well.'

He chuckles slightly, setting his papers aside. 'I've definitely felt far worse. You would know.' The look he wears now is familiar, like a hint of the grin he used to give me so often. 'I'm sorry for being so . . . distant before you left. But I've grieved. I feel lighter, if that makes any sense.' A shake of his head, blond hair rippling. 'I've learned a lot in these past few weeks.'

I hum softly, unsure what it is I'm supposed to say. After a beat of silence, I settle with, 'I'm glad you're feeling better.'

'More like myself,' he adds with a small smile. 'Oh, and this . . .' He rifles through the assortment of parchment in search of something. 'This belongs to you.'

He sets that something on the only sliver of wood peeking out from beneath the blanket of paper. I stare at my Enforcer's ring and the large crest atop it. Two lions frame a bannered *A*, our family seal and sign of strength.

I wish that is all I see when looking at it.

No, I see every horrific thing I, and all the Enforcers before me, have done in the name of that crest. Every drop of blood spilled to secure our family's power. Every order obeyed because that banner has me bound for life.

But I slide it onto my finger anyway, feel the bite of cold steel against my skin. I flex my hand. Decades of death are wrapped into the band clutching my skin, and I don't dare to even flinch.

'So,' I mutter softly, eyes never straying from the ring. 'I earned it back.'

He shrugs slightly. 'You brought her to me, didn't you?'

'I did.'

And I regret it more than anything.

'I've got to hand it to you, Kai.' He slowly leans back in the chair, mimicking yet another one of Father's movements. 'I wasn't sure she would make it back here.'

Reading between the lines is rather difficult when they are blurred. I'm no longer sure if it is my brother speaking, or the king he's become. 'And you worried that would be my doing,' I say smoothly, voicing the words he avoids.

His smile is tinged with an amused sort of sadness. 'I thought you might let her go.'

'Why didn't you tell me of your plan with her?'

The question flies from my mouth, far harsher than I'd rehearsed in my mind. He blinks at me, bewildered for a moment before his newfound composure returns. 'I honestly wasn't sure what to do with her myself. Not until I started listening to Calum's counsel. Found the records with Father's letter.'

'So Calum told you to marry her?' My voice is low. Lethal. 'Better yet, why the hell are you listening to him in the first place?'

'Because he opened my eyes to so many things,' Kitt fires back. 'Suddenly, I was thrown into the role of king, ridden with grief and anger. And when Calum told me his story, what was really happening in the slums, I realized how little I knew of my own kingdom.' His chest heaves, though his voice is steady. 'So I listened. I learned. And for the first time in my life, I came to my own conclusions. So call me crazed like the rest of the kingdom, but—'

'I don't think you're insane.' My quiet words cut through his own. 'I think you're right. If Ilya is in danger, then you are doing what you must to save it. Hell—' I huff out a laugh, '—the Ordinaries should be welcomed back into this kingdom even if it wasn't needed to survive. Because I also learned quite a few things on my journey. Like the lies we were told and who it was that spread them.'

Kitt opens his mouth, but I push on. 'I'm not here to discuss politics or the Elite kingdom Father built atop decades of deception.' I brace my hands on the desk, leaning over the worn wood. 'I'm here to talk about her.'

He stands slowly to his feet, nearly leveling our gazes. 'Easy, Brother.'

'Marriage, Kitt?' I almost shout, shaking my head. 'What the hell are you thinking?'

'I'm thinking,' he says stiffly, 'that I don't have another option.'

'You're the king!' This time, I do yell. 'You will always have another option. Always have a way out, unlike the rest of us.'

'Fine, you want another option?' Challenge rings in his voice, smothering any sign of the composed king I returned home to. 'My way out is killing her. That is what I was going to do. How does that sound? Are you happy now?'

We stare at each other, chests heaving. Shock slackens my jaw; terror tightens my chest. His words are nearly as paralyzing as the unspoken ones hanging in the air between us. Because what is worse than her dying is me being the one forced to kill her.

'If I don't marry her,' Kitt breathes, begging me to understand, 'I have no choice but to kill her. She murdered our father, Kai. But as my bride, she can help restore Ilya.' He braces a hand on the desk, leaning in with each word. 'This is a mutually beneficial agreement. I would protect her. Twist the truth about what happened between Father and her. And in return, she would be my symbol of peace to the other kingdoms.'

I comb a hand through my hair. I'm not sure when I started pacing, but my feet now set a swift tempo up and down the worn rug. I laugh then, bitter and unable to stop the sound from bubbling out of me. 'Please help me understand, because when I left, you seemed plenty enraged and ready to have me plunge a sword through her chest.' My steely gaze searches his. 'So what changed?'

'Everything,' he breathes, quiet enough to have me regretting my harsh words. 'Everything changed. I was a son mourning the man I thought I loved. I see now that it was obsession because love was not an emotion Father taught me. But I was bitter, vengeful, unsteady without him here to guide me.' He takes a shaky breath. 'I grieved. I learned. I came to my senses. And you're right. I'm not the crazed boy you left. I'm a king.'

His words hit me hard, like a blow to the chest that's stolen the air from my lungs. I swallow. 'What happened to the son who would do anything to please his father? Because this decision goes against everything he wanted for Ilya, even if you're saving it in the process.'

He takes a deep breath, avoiding my gaze. 'Father only cared about eradicating the Ordinaries, not strengthening this kingdom. He hid under the Elite society he created, and yet, Ilya had never been weaker. I see now how small-minded he was.' Kitt finally meets my stare with a stern one of his own. 'And I want to make this kingdom truly great.'

I nod slowly. Kitt's zeal shines through each word, now no longer smothered by our father. It's admirable, his love for this kingdom and resolve to restore it. But pride swells in my chest, not for this king, but for the boy who dreamed only of approval. Now he wears Father's crown and forsakes the infatuation tethered to it.

I force a calming breath into my lungs.

Thoughts of Father are dangerous. They tend to lead me to *her*.

Escaping from the darkest corner of my mind, broken words slide off my tongue, barely more than a whisper. 'Don't you hate her?'

To my surprise, he forces a smile. It's a sharp, small gesture he's willing to share with me. 'Do you?'

We eye each other, and for the first time since setting that crown atop his head, I think we might just understand each other. Because suddenly, I see myself in him again. Paedyn is not a right or a wrong, not something as simple as a yes or a no. She is confusion itself, a feeling unplaced, a color between black and white. Hell, she is my Silver Savior. And hating her is not as simple as it may seem.

But for me, it is *not* loving her that has proven to be difficult.

'I don't want this to come between us,' Kitt ventures cautiously. 'I want things to be as they once were – us against every opposition. Brothers again.'

I open my mouth to tell him—

The door swings open.

I don't even need to turn around. The mere presence of her is familiar, branded into the hollow of my neck where her head rests, tethered to my ankle and forever tugging me towards her.

Kitt's gaze climbs over my shoulder before widening slightly in shock. I turn then, unable to keep my eyes from her any longer.

And there she is. Her stance is somehow stern, expression

45

unsurprisingly the same. Cropped hair dusts her jaw, tousled and wavy. Her father's leather journal is tucked beneath an arm, flush against the blouse clinging to her figure. Those blue eyes crash into mine like a wave, along with the sudden realization that I've been nearly deprived of drowning in them since our arrival to the castle. Only now do I have the privilege to drink her in. I watch her do the same, though the stoic expression she wears never slips.

Pretend.

She's far better at it than I am. Though, I would expect nothing less from the 'Psychic' before me. She has spent the entirety of her life practicing the art of pretending.

Her eyes tear from mine to land on Kitt. 'No need to catch me up to speed. I happened to . . . hear it all.'

My brows rise with a skeptical sort of amusement. 'So, it's safe to assume that your ear was pressed to the door.'

Her eyes flick to mine before offering me a deceptively pleasant smile. 'Only until the two of you started shouting. Then the entirety of the hall was eavesdropping as well.'

With a heavy sigh, Kitt lowers himself back into the seat beneath him. 'Paedyn, I had every intention of speaking with you about all of this—'

'Really?' Her voice is sharp, cutting through his words like a blade. 'Before or after we are married?'

I stiffen, eyes sliding down her arm to the shimmering ring choking her finger. It's so casually been carried into this room, this conversation. The sight of that symbol here, now, possibly *forever*, has my chest aching.

Maybe I'm even jealous of the ring. Jealous of the way it clings to her skin, feels every shiver of her body. Because that should be me.

'Before, of course.' Kitt's talking again, voice even. He avoids her gaze. 'I'm sure you have a lot of questions.'

'Oh, I sure do.' The words are little more than a laugh. 'Starting with the task you've assigned Lenny to.'

I lean against the desk, legs stretched atop the carpet and ankles crossed. My gaze finds Kitt. 'And what task might this be?'

Kitt opens his mouth, but it's Pae's voice I hear. 'He's been ordered to guard . . .' A bob of her throat. 'Blair's door. And likely every move she makes beyond it.'

Rage simmers in her eyes, and just like that, I understand what it is that fuels the fire burning within them.

Adena.

I'd watched that branch tear through every muscle and tendon in her chest. Watched Paedyn crumble in that sandy Pit, cry over the bloody body, and scream when it shuddered its last breath.

But behind that tragic scene stood the winner of the final Trial. Blair guided that branch through Adena's chest with her mind and a smile.

When my eyes slowly climb back to Paedyn's, it's revenge that reflects in them. And I have a feeling that Blair's blood will be the only she enjoys on her hands.

'I have to keep the peace,' Kitt says slowly. 'Her father is a trusted general, and I can't have my future queen picking fights within the castle. I knew you would go after her, and I figured that placing Lenny between you two was the safest option.' He runs a hand through his hair, tousling the blond strands. 'I need you on your best behavior if this . . . arrangement is going to work.'

'And you want this to work?' Paedyn asks with a sudden calmness that's begun to creep over her. 'Our *arrangement.* The uniting of the Ordinaries and Elites.'

'In order to save Ilya, yes,' Kitt clarifies. 'We must open trade again, and that is only possible if the surrounding kingdoms no longer despise us. I would elaborate further about our marriage, but it seems you already heard my reasonings through the other side of the door.'

Her silver hair swishes with a nod. 'I did . . . gather most of the information I was looking for. Except for the question you avoided.' She steps forward, tossing the journal before us. Her fingers curl around the edge of the desk, nearly brushing mine. 'Do you not hate me? After everything I've done?'

Kitt takes a long, trembling breath. My eyes flick between the two of them, nothing more than a witness of this civil standoff. 'It's not about hating or loving you. It's about what is best. And I cannot rule a kingdom that has fallen.'

'I killed your father,' she replies bluntly. 'And you forgive me for that?'

'You have yet to apologize.'

'I was protecting myself from him,' she whispers. 'I need you to know that. He came at me, and I barely made it out of that fight alive.' Her voice trembles, but she pushes on, head high. 'I'm sorry that I killed your father. But I will never apologize for killing a tyrant.'

Silence smothers the room, so loud it's nearly deafening.

I watch Kitt's face for any sort of shift and know that Pae is doing the same with that Psychic-like observance of hers. But he doesn't so much as blink, perhaps even breathe. When he does speak, his words sound slightly choked. 'You don't need my forgiveness. You only need my protection. And now—' Kitt's voice grows callous, so opposite his tone towards me, '—I've given you purpose.'

Her knuckles grow white around the desk's edge. She blinks, her face a canvas of shock and hurt and muted understanding. But Kitt has every right to harbor animosity towards the Ordinary who killed his father, so Paedyn simply nods in response to his earnestness. She pushes no further on the matter of forgiveness, not now.

'What about everything else? The disease you were told us Ordinaries possess?' She reaches for the journal then, tearing through worn pages until the hasty handwriting is on display. 'My father was Adam Gray, a Healer in the slums. And he recorded *everything*.'

I cross my arms over my chest. 'His journal entries state that Father was bribing the Healers, offering them their weight's worth in silvers if they backed the lie that Ordinaries were slowly dwindling our powers.' I blow out a breath. 'And as much as it pains me to admit it, everything written in that journal adds up. It's no wonder every Healer lives lavishly in the higher kingdom. They have all the means and no desire to help those in the slums.'

When my gaze lands on Pae, she nods in silent gratitude before continuing, 'Every Elite in this kingdom despises the Ordinaries. Getting paid to spread lies about them was only a bonus for the Healers. And the king,' she adds almost awkwardly, 'took advantage of that hatred. He tried to buy my father's silence, more than once.

But he was one of the only Healers who stayed in the slums, aware of the lies but unable to do anything about them.'

'So he started the Resistance,' Kitt sighs out, still avoiding Paedyn's wide gaze. 'Calum has filled me in on all the details. As did the letter Father left me.' He looks as tired as he sounds when his fingers begin massaging the crease between his brows. 'I know of the lies Healers have spread for decades.'

Paedyn swallows. 'And are you going to tell the kingdom this?'

Kitt waves a dismissive hand. 'Yes. Though, I'll spin the truth into something more appealing. I may have grown to despise my father in recent weeks, but that does not mean I wish to tarnish our family's name.' He leans forward then, eying the ring on her hand that I can't bring myself to look at. 'I will protect the Azer legacy. But . . .' His next words are reluctant. 'I will also protect you, Paedyn. The kingdom will be told a variation of what really happened outside that arena between you and the king.'

There is an edge to his voice, a bitterness I don't recognize from him. And it doesn't seem to be directed at me. Shoving the thought aside, I nod down towards the desk drenched in parchment. 'What of the records and Calum? They convinced you to change Ilya?'

Turning to me, Kitt's expression softens. 'It wasn't immediate. I had spoken to Calum several times, trying to glean information about the attack. Only, he spoke mostly of why there was a Resistance in the first place. I learned more about the slums and deprivation the kingdom – my kingdom – was heading towards.' His gaze drifts to Paedyn. 'Everything he said paired perfectly with what I had seen the day you snuck me from the castle. I know now how that was little more than a betrayal for the Resistance—' he nearly laughs then, '—but, nevertheless, it helped open my eyes.

'Calum, Mind Reader that he is, knew I was beginning to see the truth. He counseled me, suggested I marry Paedyn in order to save Ilya. I wasn't going to. Not at first.' The king looks up at me. 'But I visited the queen – your mother – and she told me of the letter Father had left for me. It was a plan, she said, for the future Edric wished Ilya to have. Something each king passes down to the next.'

He pauses to clear his throat. 'It was only after reading it that I realized what needed to be done. Father didn't care about Ilya – he hated Ordinaries. And the damning records of our dwindling food supply and overpopulation were proof of that. He failed to create an Elite society, and now we must face the consequences.'

Each word rings with disgust and betrayal. And I am glad of it. Finally, after all these years trying to please him, Kitt sees our father for what he is – was. Paedyn's expression reflects the king's, as though he's spat every bit of revulsion onto her face.

'His hopes for Ilya were crippling. Simpleminded. And he wanted me to continue them for him.' Kitt shakes his head in reminiscence of a time when he would have done anything for our father. 'He was destroying this kingdom for a futile cause. It was greatness he craved, and instead, he accomplished mediocrity.'

My brows lift, as if floated up by the wave of shock flooding through me. This certainly is not the brother I left mere weeks prior. Something has changed, stemming from something else as seemingly insignificant as disappointment.

'So,' Paedyn ventures skeptically, 'you no longer want to obey your father's wishes?'

She asks this knowing full well Kitt's reputation. His whole life has been spent aiming to please a single man who he has now defied with a single decree. My gaze flicks to the king seated before us, watching words fall from lips tinged with a smile. 'Why obey a man when I can be a far greater one? I once thought Father's plans for this kingdom were worth my unflinching loyalty, but now I see that they are not.'

It's difficult, trying to fight my smile.

Kitt has finally broken free from Father's choking grip.

'You're doing this solely to save Ilya.' It's not a question from the Silver Savior, but rather, a disappointed declaration.

Kitt laces his fingers atop the desk. 'I do this to make us great.'

'You don't care for a unified kingdom?' Paedyn counters.

'That is not why I am doing this.' The king's voice remains steady in the face of Pae's scrutiny. 'It is, for some, a positive outcome, though I don't much care for the Elites' powers dwindling due to repopulation with Ordinaries. Mundanes already make up half of our numbers. But we will deal with that at a later time.'

I hold my breath as Paedyn considers this for a moment. And when she leans in over the desk, so do I. 'I have dreamed of a free, united Ilya all my life, and if this is the only way to achieve that, then so be it.' Her voice grows hesitant. 'But it seems I have the rest of my life to change your perspective on Ordinaries.'

Kitt dips his head. 'Everything has changed. And now, I too wish for all of us to be united.'

My heart bangs against my chest, beating for her, beating for every moment we may never get to spend together. And when words finally spill from her lips, she might as well have plunged a dagger into my back like she promised so long ago.

'Then I will marry you, Kitt. To save this kingdom from itself.'

CHAPTER 6

Paedyn

'Remember to keep your back straight. Oh, and do try to look pleasant.'

I make a face behind the dressing curtain, fully aware that Ellie can't see it from where she stands on the other side. 'Pleasant?'

I can hear the hesitant smile in her voice. 'You know, maybe smile a bit. No scowling at court members.'

'But that is so much more pleasant for me,' I say wistfully. Because that is the truth, in more ways than one. It hurts less to scowl. There is no sharp, searing sensation that accompanies the downward turn of my lips. But a smile has quickly been associated with pain, leaving little joy to remain in the action.

My fingers deftly trail the jagged scar running down the side of my neck, stopping only when it reaches my collarbone and the carving beneath it. Like braille, the severed flesh tells a story. Each drag of the king's sword is traced along my skin, embedded into my very being.

'Are you all right back there?' Ellie's voice grows closer. 'Here, let me help you—'

'No,' I order, the word harsh enough to shock even me.

The command is met with a long, unbearable silence from the other side of the screen. Until finally, a soft 'Oh, okay' shyly meets my ears.

I take a deep breath, already regretting my clipped command. But I won't let her see my marred skin, the O branded above my heart. That piece of myself has only ever been shared with Kai. And I intend to keep it that way.

My fingers fiddle with the line of little buttons cascading down the dress's center. Mumbling under my breath, I finally manage to secure the last one. Only then, after ensuring that the square neckline thoroughly covers the branding of my weakness, I reveal myself to a fidgeting Ellie.

'Oh, it's lovely.' She moves to step behind me, hesitating slightly. 'Um, may I tighten this tie for you?'

I swallow, once again ashamed that I'd snapped at her. My apology takes the form of a slightly pained smile. 'Yes, of course.'

She makes quick work of the tie, stealing my breath with each tug. 'Do you think Adena would like this dress?'

Ellie's question makes me pause, and her sudden stillness tells me that she hadn't intended on asking it. But for the first time since her death, the sound of Adena's name doesn't feel like a twisted knife to the gut. No, I want to remember her like this. See her in the stitching of a dress or in the rays of the sun. Watch her shine through every second for as long as I remain breathing the air she no longer can.

I glance at the mirror beside me, studying the planes of the dress. 'She'd like the color,' I say softly. Ellie's relieved breath tickles the back of my neck. 'She would say that the deep blue brings out my eyes. But Plague knows she'd ensure the skirt was . . . ugh, what would she say?' I stare at the draping fabric until my eyes are crinkling with sudden recollection. 'Voluptuous. That's the word.'

Ellie giggles softly, stepping beside me to examine the dress fully. 'Yes, that does sound like her.'

I run my sweaty palms over the tight bodice, avoiding my own gaze in the mirror. 'Come,' Ellie says softly. 'Let's make those blue eyes pop even more.'

She ushers me to the vanity, where I sit stiffly atop the cushioned bench. My lashes are soon lined with coal, face powdered, and bruises concealed. She paints my lips a deep red, perhaps to match the blood forever coating my hands—

My breath catches at the comparison my muddled mind has made. I keep my gaze lowered after the jarring thought, hiding from my own reflection in the mirror. Because I'm scared of what I'll see there. Will it be the broken girl staring back, or the traitor queen I'll soon become?

'Paedyn?'

'Hmm?' My gaze lifts to Ellie, finding her staring at me in question. 'Sorry, did you say something?'

She smiles comfortingly. 'Yes, I asked what you wanted me to do with your hair.'

'Oh, um, just leave it.' I nod distractedly. 'It will help cover my scar.'

Another sad smile. It's not the first she's given me. 'Right.' Stepping away, she scans my face. 'You look . . .'

Ellie trails off, and that worries me greatly. 'What? If I look ridiculous, please tell me.'

'No. No, not at all.' Her gaze lingers over the length of me. 'You look . . . hardened, in a way.'

Those words don't surprise me. But her next ones do.

'In fact, you look like a queen.'

I spin my father's ring beneath the massive table, if only to distract myself from the foreign one now encircling a nearby finger.

Shifting in my plush chair, I sneak a glance down the length of wood to find that nearly every gaze is already pinned on me. I lift my chin slightly before mustering a cool facade as my only defense against so many prying eyes.

The colossal table sits in the center of the throne room, and even despite its impressive size, the court is thoroughly cramped around it. My gaze climbs from the expanse of dark wood until it lands on . . .

Comfort. Relief. Him.

Gray eyes flick between mine, soft in that way they only are when looking at me. That tether between us grows taut, heavy with the weight of so many unspoken words. But even the strongest of ties wear over time. It will be the slow death of us, spending every day alongside each other but never truly together.

Kai's gaze tears from mine when the looming doors swing open.

Every body clumped along the table's edge clambers to its feet when the king enters the room. Having spent my life learning how to blend in, I quickly stand alongside them. When my eyes lift to find Kitt, it's his brother they find their way back to – a repetition of the past I can't seem to escape. His black tunic is cut close to the body beneath, inky like the ebony waves that fall over his brow. As if feeling my gaze, he pulls those strong arms behind his back and tosses me a quick wink.

I dip my head, hiding the twitch of my lips. Then I tuck our moment into that quiet part of my mind, right alongside the others. Just in case we never get the chance to share another.

Kitt strides to the head of the long table, where Kai flanks his right and I his left. It's only after the king lowers himself into his extravagant seat that the court follows, numbly sitting back into their own.

'Good afternoon,' Kitt greets warmly. 'I'd like to first thank you all for joining me in this meeting. I know there is much to discuss and even more to answer.'

The sheer kingliness he exudes is still jarring, in a mournful sort of way. I miss the carefree boy he was before a crown was pushed onto his head. Before I pushed him to be like this.

But his very life has led up to this moment, this ruling of a kingdom. And it suits him more than I could have imagined. Or perhaps it's my revived hope for Ilya that has me suddenly looking at him with respect rather than revulsion.

Everything changed in that study, history unwritten and loyalties reformed. Kitt seems equally as unenthusiastic about our engagement, and I warily wonder about his feelings for me. How much does the king despise me for killing the father he once cared so dearly for? Our marriage will be nothing more than a political union, but if we are meant to spend the rest of our lives together, I hope to restore some semblance of the friendship we once had. That is, if he even wants it.

'To begin, I will first address the terrible misunderstandings we all believed to be true.' Kitt's gaze travels around the table. 'I hope then that the reasonings behind my decision will become clear.'

I take a deep breath, straightening my spine like Ellie suggested. But I don't, however, arrange my features into something that resembles pleasantry. Instead, I remain stern, feigning strength in the face of a kingdom so eager to cut me down.

'Decades ago, Healers claimed to have found an undetectable disease hidden within the blood of Ordinaries.' Kitt's voice carries, sounding so much like the king before him that I nearly flinch. 'With prolonged exposure, that disease was said to weaken the powers of Elites. And since becoming your king, I have discovered this story to be a lie.'

Chaos erupts around the table. I sit silently within it, my heart pounding as Kitt's liberating words hang in the air. I never thought I'd hear the truth from a king's lips.

I lean in slightly, searching his face. But he doesn't meet my gaze, doesn't glance in my direction at all as he states, 'Seeing that Ilya was such a weak kingdom before the Plague, King Edric did what he believed was best – banished the Ordinaries. He did this to preserve our Elite strength, offering a story that the Healers eagerly backed. You – the people – needed little convincing to rid our kingdom of those lacking power.'

Confused glances are thrown around the table, followed by hushed accusations. The king's voice cuts through them all. 'My father strengthened our kingdom greatly in the past, and for that, we should all be thankful. But now he has unwittingly weakened us by cutting off our resources, leaving me to do what I must to save us.' A long pause, a sinking in of words. 'So we will welcome the Ordinaries back into Ilya.'

My lips twitch into a smile.

After decades of lies, us Ordinaries deserve a far grander reveal, a proclamation across the kingdom. But this is the best apology an Elite king will give. So I revel in it.

Kitt's words spark an eruption that ripples down the table. Men and women of all ages push to their feet, shouting incoherently as the world they once ruled now shifts beneath them. Kitt raises a hand in a feeble attempt to regain control. But the chaos continues its destructive course, forcing me to dodge a flying elbow to my right.

'If you wish to lose your tongue, by all means, continue speaking over your king.'

Kai's casual threat carries across the room, clamping shut even the most eager of mouths. With one final glance at the court, the Enforcer gestures casually to his king, urging him to continue.

Kitt's green gaze brims with gratitude. He looks at Kai like he once had — like a brother. But the moment passes too quickly. Without warning, he's suddenly morphed back into a king addressing his court. 'I know this is an adjustment. I was shocked to learn of my father's deceit, though it benefitted us all. He was a harsh man who would happily kill for power — as do most kings. And after speaking with Calum, I realized that the Resistance was simply a voice for those harmless Ordinaries.' He lets the words sink in before uttering more. 'Banishing them, as my father once had, strengthened our city once. Allowing them back in now will do the same.'

My ears ring slightly as I release a shaky breath. I never thought this day would come, never imagined living in a world where I no longer had to hide what I wasn't. Kitt may only be allowing Ordinaries back in Ilya to appease the surrounding kingdoms, but it is a start.

A man shoves to his feet across the table, and my eyes fall to the pin of Ilya's crest that names him the court's spokesperson. His head of mint hair is next to draw my attention, followed by the words he utters evenly. 'Even without a disease, they'll dwindle our power if we reproduce with them.'

Them.

I hadn't realized my hands were curled into fists beneath the table until my nails threaten to draw blood. 'Over time, maybe,' Kitt was saying. 'For all we know, there may be benefits to mixing the blood of Elites and Ordinaries. But you will find that Ordinaries willing to procreate with an Elite are few and far between.'

Questions begin flying around the room, echoing off the many marble pillars framing it. 'And what about her?' My head snaps towards, the shouted accusation to find a bearded man pointing his thick finger at my face. 'What about your heirs? Will you taint your royal line with the blood of an Ordinary?'

My stomach twists, lungs suddenly too tight beneath the constricting fabric of my dress. Kai jerks to his feet and nearly topples the chair behind him. I stand too, readying myself to step between my Enforcer and the man testing his patience.

'Enough.' It's the king who says this, defusing Kai with the stern word. 'I will not have my judgment questioned, nor my future lineage. If the heir to my throne possesses less power, then so be it. That is a small price to pay for a thriving kingdom.'

His words should startle me more, but I've always known of Kitt's love for Ilya. That alone is why he's willing to sacrifice power. Not for the Ordinaries. Not for me.

A woman stands on heeled shoes, her gown pristine. She is the perfect picture of Offensive Elite privilege. 'None of this changes the fact that she is a criminal. A king killer!'

I can't help my wince at the uproar that follows her words. Hands rise in objection, their voices doing the same. My gaze slowly climbs to Kitt, awaiting what words he strings together. It's my life – or rather, my imminent death – that he now holds in the palm of his hand.

A terrifying realization courses through me, heating my cheeks with the blood Kitt likely wishes to spill. He must ache to grant these shouted requests for justice. After everything I did, he was going to kill me. That is, until I became useful to him.

Kitt's voice is even, eyes expertly avoiding mine. 'Paedyn was defending herself.' It's a simple, defiant explanation that no one will dare oppose. 'My father suffered a deep blow to the head during the chaos before stumbling into Paedyn. Due to his injuries, he was confused and not at all in his right mind. In his hazy state, he came after her, forcing Miss Gray to defend herself against him. Now, I will hear nothing more on the matter.'

The scar above my heart sears, as if to remind me what truly happened that day.

'. . . I will leave my mark upon your heart, lest you forget who's broken it.'

My eyes fall to the fisted hands in my lap. They shake slightly, rippling the blue fabric beneath. I can feel the imprint of the sword's hilt, remember the exact amount of pressure used to drive the blade through Edric Azer's chest. Feel the flick of a dagger, the release of a bowstring, the plunging of a sword.

Every death I've doled lives in the lines of these hands. And I fear who will find themselves beneath their next calloused touch.

'Fliers will be distributed throughout the city.' I blink back to the present, Kitt's words filling my muffled ears. 'They will announce our engagement to Ilya, but most importantly, to the surrounding cities. I will send messengers to Dor and Tando while searching for a way to deliver the news to Izram. On these scrolls will be what we spoke of today, every reasoning and explanation. In two days' time, we will host a parade in celebration. And any remaining Ordinaries within the kingdom, or anyone outside it, for that matter, are to be welcomed.'

Mouths open in unison around the table, but the king is speaking before sound is able to escape them. 'That will be all. Thank you for your time.'

I can practically hear jaws snapping shut at the dismissal. Kitt then stands, and after a moment of hesitation, extends a hand to me. My eyes slide to Kai, even as I slowly reach for his brother. But he doesn't look at me. No, the Enforcer's gaze is on the palm I've placed atop the king's, growing darker with every second our skin grazes.

And as we stride from the room, hand in hand, I will Kai to meet my eyes and read the message within them.

Pretend.

CHAPTER 7

Paedyn

She sleeps soundly to my right, just as she always does.

Shoulder to shoulder, fabric to face, gaze to stars.

Rough beneath my back lies the rug, piled with scraps of cloth that tickle my skin. The night is a comfort, combing cool fingers through my hair, tucking me in beneath a blanket of stars. They glint above while winking lazily down on the familiar pair of us.

This is home, however unconventional. However broken its inhabitants.

The bleak thought startles me into a sitting position.

Because I am the only bleak thing occupying this fort.

Adena is whole and bright and unbelievably unblemished. I turn to face her, my eyes heavy with the haze of sleep. Raising a sluggish hand, I brush aside the uneven bangs curling atop her brow. When my fingers meet her skin, I pull back sharply at the frigid feel of it.

She feels like death itself.

No, that can't be right.

Adena is the most alive person I know. She could never feel like anything less.

Hesitantly, I reach for her again. My finger traces the curve of her

cold cheekbone, right beneath the crescent of dark lashes fanning over her skin. The moon casts a sickly sheen over her once glowing skin. No, not the moon – it's Death's shadow she wears.

Eyes widening, I lean over her fully.

My mind grows foggy, focused wholly on the familiar figure who, at the moment, looks nothing like the girl I know. My palm finds her cheek, patting lightly at her icy skin.

Nothing.

I shake her unmoving shoulders.

A pleading whisper trips off my tongue.

'Adena, wake up. I need you.'

Then I shout at her death-drenched form to live. I might have even screamed.

'A, please!'

A dull thud meets my ears, sounding equally near and far.

My head swivels in search of the ominous repetition. I scan the darkened alley, squinting into the shifting shadows.

Another thud, this one louder than the last. The sound is crisp, clear enough to have me frantically whipping my head in every direction as I search for the source. And when I finally glimpse the gruesome picture that accompanies it—

A strangled gasp claws up my throat, tearing through the shuddering silence.

There's a bloody branch skewering Adena's chest.

I bite back a scream, my lungs too tight. Blood blooms beneath the lavender shirt, staining her favorite color with dwindling life.

I watch in horror as the branch lifts, as though being guided by some invisible hand, and begins a sickening plunge back into her chest. It sinks deep enough to pound against the hard carpet beneath, resulting in that horrific thud.

I scream again. Scream each time that branch lifts and lowers, over and over again.

I claw at it, fighting against every sickening beat. Rough bark bites into my palm, springing sticky blood from the torn skin. I tug at the branch and still it relentlessly sinks into her chest.

My hands shake, tears stream.

Thud. Thud. Thud.

It pierces through her, stopping only when it meets the rug. But still, it does not halt for my screams or pleading whimpers.

She's gone. She's gone. She's—

My eyes fly open, only to be greeted by shadow.

A figure looms over me, and I don't hesitate before slipping my hand beneath a pillow to find the knife I'd snatched from my dinner tray. Not my first weapon of choice, but it's probably sharp enough to provide a painful end to whoever it is that—

'Pae.'

His voice calms the sea of panic beginning to swell in my chest. A calloused hand catches the wrist I've raised towards his throat, halting the swift arc of my borrowed blade. 'Easy,' Kai breathes, body tense as it leans over mine.

Eyes adjusting to the dim light, I can just make out his fuzzy figure at the edge of my bed. I'm nearly teetering off it, skin sticky and chest heaving. His body shifts closer, one hand cupped around my lifted wrist while the other is braced beside my head, sinking into the plush pillow.

'It was just a nightmare,' he whispers, slowly lowering our joint hands until the blade tumbles onto the mattress. 'You're okay. I'm right here.'

A nightmare is an understatement. That . . . that was torture.

I blink up at the face I cannot see, and yet, I picture it all the same. 'How . . . how did you get in here?'

His fingers graze my forehead, sweeping away the sticky strands of hair there. 'I heard you scream. And nothing . . . *nothing* has terrified me more.' I hear him swallow. Feel a swipe of his thumb across my cheekbone. 'And it didn't stop. You just kept screaming. So . . .' A pause. 'We both know it will take more than a locked door to keep me from you.'

My eyes travel over his shadowed shoulder to find a gaping hole where my door once stood. Now it decorates the floor, having ungracefully toppled to the ground.

The thudding in my dream. That was real – that was this.

He had kicked the damn door down.

'Can I get no privacy around here?' I joke weakly, voice still shaky with the remnants of my nightmare.

'Privacy?' His chuckle skitters up my spine, awakening my sleepy senses. 'Darling, I'd be in this bed beside you if my brother hadn't slipped a ring onto your finger.'

His mouth hovers dangerously close to my own. Especially so considering the distraction I'm seeking – and every inch of him will most definitely do the trick. I want him desperately. Recklessly. And the embodiment of those feelings falls from my lips in the form of a single, traitorous sentence. 'So, slip it off.'

I feel his head shake above me, feel his nose rub against mine. He groans softly in a way that tells me he's restraining himself from happily obeying my command. The rough fingers that aren't currently cupping my jaw find their way to the band around my finger. 'I could,' he murmurs. 'So easily, I could.' His thumb slides over my knuckles. 'The problem wouldn't be taking that ring off. It would be getting me to put it back on.'

I shut my eyes, as though that could hide me from his words. From the reminder of my fate. I am betrothed to the king, and yet, my heart beats for his brother. 'I know,' I whisper, unable to muster anything more.

Several long, silent moments slip between us. His thumb brushes idle circles across the top of my hand – a delicate comfort, and yet, I might crumble beneath the feel of it. Then his touch shifts to stroke the short strands of hair behind my ear. I feel his following murmur on my skin, hear the smirk hidden between each syllable. 'A butter knife? Really?'

'It's all I have at the moment,' I grumble.

'Well, that just won't do.' He flicks my nose lightly. 'What if someone had broken into your rooms?'

I can't help the laugh that bubbles out of me. 'It seems someone already has. But don't worry, Prince.' My fingers fiddle with a lock of inky hair falling over his forehead. 'I can do plenty of damage with a shoe.'

'Oh, I'm well aware.' His words are a whisper against my lips. 'You are devastating, Pae.'

And then he's scooping me into his arms.

I squeal in surprise, having been swept from the mattress. Blankets slide off my skin, slipping away from the silky sleepwear Ellie had set out for me. A strong hand cups the back of my knees while the other is wrapped around my bare shoulders. The heat of his body seeps through my thin pants and accompanying tank as I sling a steadying arm around his neck. 'What—' He turns, causing me to pause my accusation as he casually steps across the fallen door. 'What are you doing?'

'Stealing you away,' he says simply.

I open my mouth to protest, but his whispered words against my ear have me falling silent.

'Tonight, we pretend.'

Branches drag along the ground, encircling us in a leafy embrace.

Kai's hand is firm around mine as he guides me beneath the weepy underside of the willow tree. Moonlight streams through thin branches, dappling the ground with slivers of silver light. At the center of it all lies a looming trunk, its roots clinging to the earth and rippling through the soft grass.

My palm slips from Kai's when he suddenly sinks to the ground, sprawling atop it with a sigh. He doesn't offer an explanation before sitting up and planting firm hands on my hips. I'm being pulled towards the grass before even getting the chance to protest.

Tangled in his arms, my body topples over him ungracefully. He embraces my clumsy descent, happily wrapping his arms tighter around me even after I've knocked the air from his lungs. I laugh, shoulders shaking from where I lie crookedly across his chest. At the rare sound, his calloused fingers tighten atop the thin fabric of my tank, catching on the silk.

My head leans against his. 'This is most definitely not allowed.' He hums in question, the sound vibrating against my back. 'Us being out here. Alone. In the dead of night.'

'It could be worse,' he murmurs. 'We could have stayed in the queen's quarters. Alone and in the dead of night.'

My cheeks flush. 'On second thought, I much prefer the night air.'

He chuckles beside my ear, forcing me to suppress a shiver. My fingers find one of the hands he's sprawled across my stomach, feeling the rough skin splattered with scars. It's only when I brush over his knuckles that I still in his hold.

'That's why you heard me scream.' I turn my face towards him, voice soft. 'You were up training.'

His skin is scabbed over, knuckles hardened with the remnants of blood. The sad smile he wears shines through his voice. 'Nothing gets past you, Little Psychic. I was heading to my room after being out in the training yard most of the night. Couldn't sleep,' he adds, the clarification an afterthought. 'That's when I heard you.'

I nod slowly, gathering my courage. 'I was dreaming about her.'

I feel his chest halt beneath me. He knows exactly who it is I'm referring to. 'I'm guessing it wasn't a pleasant dream.'

'No.' I almost laugh. 'It started that way, which somehow made it all so much worse.'

His voice is rough. 'I'm sorry you're forced to relive that moment every time you shut your eyes.'

'Not every time.' I shift, slipping off his chest to sit beside him. 'Not when I'm with you.'

He props himself up on an elbow, tugging at my tank until I'm leaning down towards him. 'Then I'll never leave your side.'

I give him a look. 'Don't make promises you can't keep.'

'It's not promises I care to keep – it's you.'

His words never fail to have my stomach flipping, heart fluttering, lips falling silent. So, I flick the tip of his nose with a soft, 'You're quite the poet, Prince.'

Moonlight pools in the dimple that accompanies his grin. 'And you the muse, darling.'

My silk-clad knees sink into the dew-kissed grass, growing damper by the second. 'Is this going to be our lives?' I whisper suddenly, avoiding his gaze. 'Forever pretending, sneaking away from reality to steal a few moments together?'

'You know,' he sighs, 'I pictured a different forever for us. One that took place far from here. But if this is all we get . . .' He pauses, eyes as silver as the moonbeams pouring down on us. 'Then we'll make the most of it. I will be your Enforcer. Your rival. Your secret waiting beneath the willow.'

Mention of the tree cocooning us has my gaze wandering down to its large base and the lapping grass there.

His sister is buried beneath this patch of earth, her body cradled by twining roots.

My voice is oddly hushed. 'Is it okay that I'm here? Under her willow?'

'I'm sure Ava won't mind the company.' His smile is bright against the darkness, unexpected within this moment. 'Besides, this isn't your first time here. I did nearly undress you beneath these very branches during the second ball.'

Memory of the seizing panic that night comes flooding back, along with the unforgettable feel of his fingers undoing the laces of my dress. 'Oh, yes, I remember.'

'Fondly, I hope.'

I scoff lightly before leaning closer. 'I also recall the game we played under this tree. And how I beat you at it.' He's shaking his head at me. 'Now *that* is a fond memory.'

'First,' he starts coolly, 'the game was a thumb war. Second, you're full of shit, Silver Savior.'

My mouth opens, appalled by his accusation. But it's a gasping giggle that escapes when he sits up suddenly to tug me closer by the waist. I'm pulled onto his lap within the next thundering beat of my heart. He wraps my legs behind his back, leaving me fully perched atop his crossed ones.

'Fine.' I smile. 'Rematch.'

'Oh, my pretty Pae.' His words are a murmur against my lips. 'For once, it is I who will be your undoing.'

And in this moment, I would beg him to be just that. Would give anything to live out the rest of my days under this willow and in his arms.

So, I memorize every shadow of his face, every shade of this vivid fantasy before me.

He kisses the pad of my thumb before the war begins.

CHAPTER 8

Rai

Their knees are touching.

The coach jostles again, only sliding them closer together. I'm sitting opposite the royal couple, knee bobbing and head tipped against the high back of my rumbling seat. This particular coach is open to the sky, as though the top half of it has been cut clean off. Several decorated carriages trail behind and before us, all draped in green banners wearing Ilya's swirling crest.

A soft breeze ruffles the hair falling over my forehead, forcing my fingers to continually comb through it. Sun pours over us to peer nosily at the uncomfortable, silent seating arrangement. Leaning an elbow on the shortened door, I lift a hand to shield my eyes.

And she is the first thing my gaze lands on.

The sun's golden rays intertwine with her silver hair, weaving down the short length of it to thoroughly blind me. Her body is wrapped in emerald, the fabric clinging to her hips, draping her legs—

And the knee that still touches his.

I look away, drumming fingers that wish to touch her on the ledge.

'It's a beautiful day,' she says, out of what sounds like discomfort. 'Perfect for the parade.'

'Yes, we couldn't have asked for better weather,' Kitt agrees distantly. 'Don't you think, Brother?'

His tone changes drastically when aimed at me, now light and cheery. My eyes lift to his, finding a familiar glint of mischief in them. 'Why, yes, I do love cooking beneath the sun.'

Kitt cracks a smile at that before murmuring dully towards Paedyn, 'Kai has never been good with heat, you know. When we were boys—'

'All right, that's enough,' I cut in, despite the smile beginning to stretch across my lips.

'No,' Paedyn says slyly. 'No, I'd very much like to hear this story. Do go on.'

'When we were boys,' Kitt continues, his grin aimed at me, 'he could barely stand to be outside for more than an hour. Any longer and he'd clutch his head, convinced that his hair was going to melt.'

Paedyn's laughter forces me to raise my voice. 'Do you know how hot my hair gets? It's like—'

'Tar sitting in the sun,' Kitt finishes, addressing his next words to Pae. 'Yes, that was the other bit he always used to say.'

I lean back, shaking my head at him in disbelief. 'Plagues, is there no secrecy amongst brothers anymore?'

The king resembles the boy I grew up with in this moment. 'Oh, there certainly is.'

My eyes flick to Paedyn's smile, and suddenly, it all seems very much worth it. 'That was very insightful. And entertaining.' Her smile widens wickedly. 'Please continue.'

Kitt opens his mouth, but it's my words filling the open air between us. 'Kitty here once shoved a playing die so far up his nose that the royal physician nearly gave up on retrieving it.'

Paedyn's hand flies up to cover her gaping mouth. Now it's Kitt's turn to shake his head at me. 'You seem to be forgetting the part where you dared me to do it.'

Pae laughs, eyes crinkling in the sun as the coach continues its rattling across the cobblestones. She points an accusing finger beside her. 'Didn't *you* dare Kai to climb the willow back by the gardens? And he fell, breaking his arm?'

Her smile turns on me as she awaits Kitt's answer. Except, there is none.

Kitt's expression grows subtly grim, shifting into something slightly sharper than the smile he once wore. 'I hadn't realized he told you about that.'

'Yes,' Paedyn says slowly, unsurely. 'In passing.'

'Hmm.' He turns away, looking out into the moving landscape beside us. 'Was that before or after the final Trial?'

I tense slightly. Not because his tone is threatening. No, quite the opposite. The words are heavy, weighed down by something far worse than anger. And that something tears at the part of me that betrays him. The part of my heart that beats for his betrothed behind his back.

He wants to know when I shared that intimate detail of myself. And if it was while I was meant to hate her.

'Before,' Paedyn answers softly, speaking the truth but only half of it.

Kitt nods, attempting to seem unruffled with a swift redirecting of the subject. His voice sounds suddenly tired. 'I see. Well, it's safe to say that Kai and I are likely equal in our stupidity over the years.'

I nod along, hoping my fading smile doesn't portray the sadness I suddenly feel. The Kitt I saw mere minutes ago was a glimpse of the boy I grew up with, the boy I loved before I'd even understood the meaning of the word. And I wish so badly to hold on to that familiar version of him, rip the crown from his head before it seeps into the body beneath.

Paedyn is the kink in our relationship that we can't quite iron out. Despite all that has happened, it seems that Kitt still feels something for her. Perhaps that is why he shies away, grows distant in our presence – because he knows I feel for her just the same. Our brotherly bond falters in the face of her.

The coach rumbles down the road as we return to a more comfortable silence. By now, the scenery surrounding us has shifted from an assortment of trees to a line of grand houses. We've entered the higher-class section of the city, an extravagant strip that most Offensive Elites call home.

Paedyn shifts uncomfortably as we turn down the first street. Looming mansions and well-manicured shops cast large shadows over us. Several marching Imperials join our procession as we slow our pace over the cobblestones.

At the echoing sounds of clopping hooves and stomping feet, Ilyans begin to spill out of their homes. They frame the road in their fine clothing, some even holding the fliers that were scattered across the city. It's mostly indifference on the faces we first roll past, though it quickly morphs into variations of disgust and betrayal at the sight of their future queen.

'It wouldn't hurt to smile, Paedyn,' Kitt murmurs as he raises a hand to wave at the growing crowd.

As if shaken from her stupor, Pae nods absentmindedly before mustering a small smile. The wave of her hand is sure, but I don't miss the trembling fingers she tries to still. I drum my own on the seat beside me; a distraction from the anger that surges whenever I see her panic. And she has every reason to.

As a traitor, she was paraded through this crowd, spit on by the mouths that now scowl at her. These were the same people who hatefully welcomed her back into Ilya on our way to the castle. She was humiliated on these very streets, degraded by Elites who loathed her the moment they discovered she was not one of them.

And, even now, they do the same. Though, this time looks different. Paedyn is not shuffling behind my horse, bound by rope, bloody and broken. No, she sits tall in the coach, cloaked in finery, and crowned with a shiny new title. Yet, silently, they sneer at her. They see nothing but what she was – a traitor – and what she will always be – an Ordinary.

As we continue our slow crawl down the street, I sit quietly within the chaos surrounding us. My eyes stray to Kitt, looking kingly as he waves and smiles at the crowd. Adoration still fills the gazes of those around us the moment they land on him. He has always been so loved by this kingdom.

But it's Paedyn who I study, helpless to keep from staring at her. She remains composed despite the occasional shout from the crowd. Harder still to stomach is the way Kitt continually leans against her – a show for his subjects. They are betrothed; now they must act like it.

And here I sit, unable to stop it. Unable to do anything but watch them slowly become each other's forever.

They wave. They smile. They look every bit the happy couple.

Kitt sighs, his following mutter a spilled thought that was likely not intended for us. 'So few . . .'

Eager to take a break from her stiff smile, Paedyn turns towards him. 'What?'

'Oh, it's nothing.' Kitt clears his throat. 'I just remember there being more Offensive Elites out here. Must be my mind playing tricks.'

'Or they would rather stay inside than see me,' Paedyn offers between the teeth she is baring at the crowd.

I blow out a breath when we round the final street corner, and the multitude of faces begin to blur behind us. Kitt relaxes in his seat. 'See, that wasn't so bad.'

I drag a hand down my face. 'Yes, it was riveting.'

Pae's eyes meet mine, stripping me bare with a single swipe of them. Shockingly enough, I find gratitude lingering in her gaze, thanking me for enduring this alongside her. And, suddenly, the look of relief she wears at my mere presence proves to be reward enough.

'You did well.'

At Kitt's clipped words, her eyes abandon mine to find his. 'I doubt they agree,' she says with a look over her shoulder at the mass of blurry bodies. 'Kitt, they will never accept me as their queen.'

I can't seem to tell whether he liked hearing his name from her lips. 'Yes, they will.' His tone is stern. 'It just takes time.'

'Time?' She almost laughs. 'This kingdom has been without Ordinaries for over three decades. From the looks of it, they will need much longer than that to *adjust*.'

Therein lies the truth of Paedyn's motivation – the Ordinaries. What point is saving Ilya if it remains segregated? Her purpose is freedom for those like her, not the saving of a hateful kingdom.

I lean forward, hands on bent knees. 'Why don't we discuss this back at the castle? In private.'

Paedyn's eyes lift to the procession in front of us and where exactly it's headed. 'We're going back? Now?' Her head whips towards Kitt, hair glinting in the sunlight. 'What about the slums?'

Kitt's gaze slides to mine, uncertain. 'Well, the parades always remain in the upper city . . .'

'But that is my home,' she says slowly. 'That is where any remaining Ordinaries will be. Is this not a celebration of the union that will unite Elites and Ordinaries?' Her voice grows firm. 'I took you to the slums, remember?'

'I remember you using me to discover the tunnels beneath our castle,' Kitt says coolly. 'And disguising your true intentions behind wanting to show me your home.'

She grabs his hand, and I nearly flinch at the genuine movement. 'And for that, I am sorry. I never wanted to use you like that, but helping the Resistance find a way into the Bowl was all I could do.' She shakes her head, voice suddenly soft. 'I wasn't a queen who could change this kingdom with the snap of her fingers. I was an Ordinary. I *am* an Ordinary. And I showed you a piece of myself that day. Before Calum's council, I *showed* you that the people in those slums are your people too.' She slides her hand from his. 'Or has power already made you forget that fact?'

I still at her words. There it is − that certain boldness only she possesses.

I didn't get the chance to learn exactly what had happened between them. Not before Kitt had locked himself away and sent me across the Scorches to find her. But I knew the betrayal ran deeper than the death of our father. And now I understand.

Kitt likely blames himself for that battle in the Bowl, for being fooled into showing a Resistance member exactly how to get into the arena unseen. He blames himself for getting swept up in her.

'You're right,' Kitt says slowly. A sort of placidness falls over his features. 'I should have known you would say that.'

My eyes flick between them, but he doesn't look at me.

His words have horses halting, men obeying, Pae's smile growing. 'Turn the coaches around. We are going to the slums.'

CHAPTER 9

Paedyn

The smell alone tells me that we have arrived at Loot Alley.

I never thought I'd miss the stench of fish, sweat, and bodily fluids, but here I am, smiling despite it. The wide market street hums with life and vibrance. Merchants haggle behind their carts while children weave around them, evading shouting mothers.

All of it is perfectly untouched. Perfectly as it was when I was struggling to survive within it.

At the sight of the long entourage, carts begin rolling out of the way while shoppers scuttle behind. The homeless that inhabit these slums begin to peer out from the many alleys branching off Loot, bored enough to let their curiosity drag them onto the street.

It is a flurry of color, this jostling parade. Bright, emerald banners flap against the belly of our coach and every one surrounding it. Ilya's flag is raised above a row of sleek horses, that swirling symbol rippling in the breeze. Shimmers manipulate the sunbeams to create a dazzling display of speckled light that drips down our coach and dances across the cobblestones.

My smile comes easily here, despite never doing so before. Perhaps some small part of me was homesick for this shithole I grew up in.

Or maybe it's because I understand these people. They are Elites, yes, but they are also outcasts. Here lie the Mundanes, the poor, and the few Ordinaries still left in this kingdom.

And one of them has just returned.

I wave at the shocked faces sliding by. They don't look at me with disgust like the Elites outside the slums do. The most emotion I'm offered is confusion or indifference. When looking at me, they likely see themselves. I was living right beside them, stealing from right under their noses, not too long ago.

My eyes scan the packed crowd of tired faces staring back blankly. There are so many of them, all fighting for the same food and shelter. I wonder how many Ordinaries are hidden among them, blending in with hunched shoulders and a broken will.

I hope they see me now. Every smile, every wave, every sacrifice I've made for them.

My eyes light up at the sight of a crumbling building. 'That's Maria's shop there.' I point, directing the boys' attention to my sudden enthusiasm. 'I used to steal her sticky buns and fabric before climbing up the chimney to escape.' I smile at the memory. 'The sticky buns were for both of us, but the fabric was obviously for . . . Adena . . .'

I trail off, but the feel of watchful eyes on me forces more words from my mouth. 'So, I've had a lot of practice climbing up chimneys, even when I hate small spaces.' I shoot a pointed look at Kai. 'Which is why I didn't burn to death when you lit my house on fire.'

'My search had to be thorough, darling,' he muses. 'Don't take it too personally.' His words are casual, perfectly playing the part of dutiful Enforcer. But I see the apology hidden in the gaze he keeps pinned on mine, see the promise we share.

Pretend.

With a realistic rolling of my eyes, I turn my attention back on the gawking crowd. I continue my routine of waving and—

My smile falls slightly.

I know we are halfway down the street when the bloody post comes into sight. The wooden block is stained a sickening shade of red, drenched in the blood of dozens. It stands as an example, or rather, whipping practice for the Imperials.

The faint scars flecking my lower back seem to sting at the sight of it. My clumsy fingers were the cause of many slashes across my skin. That is, until I got good enough to steal from the very Imperials who made me bleed.

'Paedyn?'

I turn towards the voice, finding Kai's concerned gaze on me. 'Are you all right?'

'Yes,' I say calmly. 'Just reminiscing.'

His eyes climb over my shoulder then, and I can see the exact moment he realizes what it is I'm talking about. A cool mask slips over his features, concealing what I know to be that terrifying, icy rage simmering beneath. His mouth opens, perhaps to ask who it was that stood over my crumpled body and let the whip crack. Perhaps the Enforcer will demand to know how many times I found myself at that post or, better yet, admit how he never noticed the scars on my back despite running his hands over them plenty of times, damn the king sitting beside me.

But I never find out what it was he meant to say.

Instead, he dives over me when the explosions erupt.

I'm thrown against the floor of the coach, Kitt toppling beside me as Kai's body shields the both of us. My ears ring from the impact, drowning out the screams I know echo all around. Lifting my cheek from the dirty floor, I blink blurry, watering eyes. The burst of light momentarily blinded me, but as my vision slowly returns, muffled sound follows.

Screams. Pained, guttural screams rip through the ringing in my ears. I bolt upward, pushing at the limbs pinning me down. I know it's his calloused hand that wraps around my wrist even before the order leaves his lips. 'Stay down!'

I barely hear his shout over the chaos consuming us, over the deafening panic rising within me.

What the hell is happening?

I must have croaked these words aloud because Kai is suddenly answering, 'Bombs. Man-made.' Then he's barking orders once again, morphing back into the Enforcer he was created to be.

My head pounds, whether from the impact or from my racing thoughts, I'm not sure. Each breath comes in quick, shallow pants.

Who is behind this?

Kai's orders, once muffled and distant, grow clearer. 'On me!' I can see nothing but the billowing black smoke wafting above the coach, but know enough to determine he's just assigned a group of Imperials to surround the king and his future bride.

He looks down at me then, eyes flicking between my wide ones. 'Stay here. You're going to be fine.' He doesn't let himself linger any longer before jumping from the coach and into the thick smoke.

I shudder when another explosion shakes the coach, followed by an eruption of screams all around. Horses bolt past in a panicked trance, free to weave through the chaos without their riders. Sitting up suddenly, I meet Kitt's worried gaze. Imperials surround us, acting as a shield against the horrors beyond. Kitt remains stiffly on the floor, following the orders of his Enforcer. And rightfully so. He is the king, after all.

But I am no queen. Not yet.

All I can smell is burning flesh and thick smoke. All I can hear are terrified screams and the thudding of my heart. All I can think is that *this is my home.* These were my people long before I was told to rule over them. These screaming Slummers chose me to go into the Purging Trials, because they saw hope for one of them to become something more.

And I have become so much more.

I offer one last look at my betrothed. He must see it in my eyes – the hurt, the determination, the tangible need to do something other than sit here.

'Paedyn, don't—'

I jump from the coach before his hand is able to grasp my own.

The circle of Imperials have their backs to us, and I don't hesitate before sweeping the feet out from under one blocking my path. He falls with a thud, allowing me to bolt past despite the shouts ringing out behind.

I skid to a stop at the horror surrounding me.

Chunks of stone careen from crumbling buildings lining the

street, shattering atop the cobblestones, and tearing screams from the throats of scuttling figures. Flames lick over dozens of carts to melt coins and burn the livelihoods atop them.

I spin slowly, taking in the street I once called home. Bodies scatter the ground, some twitching while others lie stone-still. A shaky hand rises to cover my mouth and the sob growing within it. Blood paints the street, blending with the fire to create a horrific depiction of death itself.

I don't know what to do, how to help—

A soft whimper sounds beside me.

I whirl, finding a bloody boy staring up at me mere steps away. I'm skidding to his side, sinking to my knees in the pool of blood surrounding him. His pale skin is sheened with sweat, breaths shallow beneath the crimson bubbling from his chest.

A shard from a nearby building is wedged between his ribs.

I swallow my sob and place shaking hands around the wound, trying to stall the blood as best I can. 'I'm sorry,' I whisper, tears stinging my eyes. 'I'm so sorry. You're . . . you're going to be okay.'

The boy's honey eyes simply stare into mine. He doesn't cry out, doesn't beg for life. He only stares, preparing to meet his bloody end.

Honey.

Those eyes are like honey. So similar to her sweet gaze. Suddenly, it's Adena dying before me all over again. And all over again, I cannot save her.

A tear slides down my dirty cheek. Blood oozes between my fingers, nausea swelling with every second the sticky liquid stains my skin. But I don't dare move my hands. And just like I had with Adena, I tell this boy that he is going to be fine. I spew lies, spin a happy ending into existence even as tears slip from my burning eyes.

And when he takes his final breath – gaze trained on the sky – it's as though I'm back in that Pit, cradling her dead body. Death steals the boy from my incapable hands, oddly gentle in the way he halts this straining heart. My mouth opens, a cry on the tip of my tongue—

But my arms are being yanked back, fingers sliding from his wound. I feel numb in the rough hands that wrap around me. My dress is soaked in blood, the drenched hem dripping a path behind my dragged body.

'Dammit, Pae. You never follow orders, do you?'

His voice is harsh, but I hear the tinge of sorrow lacing every word. I let the familiar arms cling to my waist, let Kai nearly carry me back to the coach. My unfocused gaze sweeps over the still-scrambling bodies tripping over those littering the ground.

Loot is in shambles.

My *home* is in shambles.

And so is my heart.

Edric Azer

For every end, there is always a beginning.

The king would come to realize, many years later and thousands of steps beyond the ones he currently takes, that this was the start to his impending demise.

Edric sets a formidable pace through the twisting gut of his pristine castle. As a child, the coiling corridors used to taunt him, trap the princeling in a confusing loop with every corner he rounded. Even now, it reminds him horribly of the maze that is his mind, and how any word that enters through the shifting gate – his gaze – will meet a stony wall before breaking into a series of jumbled syllables – or rather, what his father liked to call 'a disgraceful lack of competency'.

But his father is no longer here, leaving behind only the memory of a sniffling boy who struggled to read.

Edric's polished shoes tread swiftly past the servants who slave over them every evening, the feet within navigating him confidently through the castle.

A distant memory indeed.

It was long after ridding his son of this 'shameful illness' that Landan

Azer finally met his end, though, it was regrettably far more pleasant than Edric's cruel journey to literacy. His soul drifted peacefully from the frail body it had inhabited, which seemed entirely too gentle a death for such a harsh man. But with the kingdom now squirming in the palm of his hand, Edric thinks fondly of that fruitful time with his father, feeling a growing sort of gratitude for the man who pushed him along this path towards power.

Cruelty molded him into a king, where kindness would have only crippled him.

The crown curls atop his head, burrowing into the blond strands of hair like a drowsy mutt. Each gaping hallway drips with the honeyed rays of sunset, seemingly slowing his pace as if they were clinging to his shoes. But the king pushes past every oozing puddle of light. Because there is little in this life that Edric loves more than power – and he is heading right for it.

The queen is rarely seen outside her quarters this late into the pregnancy. Even still, Iris was hidden away long before the growing of a spare in her womb. Love and paranoia are quite fond of each other, habitually mingling into a suffocating protection.

Edric pauses before the familiar slab of wood that separates them. He often finds this moment to feel like the end of a maze he's been stumbling through since he was a boy. Here, there is no taunting castle or befuddled mind. It all falls away at her feet.

It takes four beats of the king's fluttering heart for the door to swing open.

Iris has always been the type of beautiful that can only be inarticulately described as breathtaking. As a descendant of an Izrami queen, she bears their tanned, freckled skin and bright eyes. And yet, Iris Moyra had never stepped foot on the seaside kingdom's rocky soil.

Over a century ago, a family feud had divided the royals of Izram, forcing several of Iris's ancestors – whose claim to the throne was nearly as weak as their relationship with the woman who sat upon it – to settle in Ilya. A handful of years had passed before the Plague swept through, isolated the kingdom, and gifted the descendants of those bickering royals more power than they could have ever earned with a crown on their head.

Edric, with his lust for power, married the woman before him nearly a decade after the Purging. With every Elite being contained to Ilya, no powerless princess beyond the border would be allowed to taint the king's line further. But the pairing of Iris's royal blood and rare ability was shocking enough to finally entice him into settling down.

Iris was stunning like the sea, as though her skin were seeped in salt water until it shimmered. Edric tells her as much, smiling when the words draw out a warm flush atop her cheekbones. That golden hair cascades down her body and over the large swelling of her belly, like water carving a trickling path around a stone. She gently tugs the king towards her, pressing soft lips against his with a lingering sigh.

Once released from his wife's captivating clutches, Edric begrudgingly glances around the room. 'Did you dismiss the servants again?'

Iris rests a delicate hand atop her stomach. 'I'm fine, Ed. They don't need to be swarming me every waking moment.'

'Iris—' Edric smooths a hand across the fabric draping her rounded belly, '—you know they are needed for your safety. This baby is coming any day now, and for your protection . . .'

The king stops talking then, because he recognizes the look on her face. Iris is gentle, in soul and body. But her expressions are less so.

'What?' Edric insists at the narrowing of those brilliant, blue eyes.

She takes a breath, the type that sounds like loving someone despite their flaws. 'All you do is protect me. And, of course, I am grateful for that, but . . .' Iris raises a hand, somehow encapsulating the entire kingdom with a single gesture. 'But it has been years since the people have heard about me. Seen me. For all they know, I died shortly after giving birth to Kitt.'

'And I would rather them think that,' the king utters slowly, 'than use you against me. I won't risk an enraged Ordinary putting you in danger to hurt me.'

Iris pads slowly atop the carpet, her loose nightgown dragging green fabric behind her feet. 'The Purging was over a decade ago. Your paranoia cannot keep me trapped here forever.' She grasps his

81

face, cupping him in the warmth of her presence. 'In our five years of marriage, I have done little more than hide away.'

Edric rubs a hand behind his neck, a habit his father plagued him with. It's as though every prickle of agitation builds beneath the skin there and chips away at his sanity.

Ordinaries remain in his kingdom out of spite, hiding until their swelling anger has them committing some final act of violence. They all die in the end, as the weak always do. But it is the defiance of it, the constant worry that his queen may get caught in the cross fire.

'Soon,' the king sighs. He pulls Iris's soft hands into his own. 'I will free you of these walls shortly. Once I've disposed of these lingering Ordinaries, you will be safe. They are a mistake I am remedying. And the Elites are just as eager to be rid of them.'

The gentle queen ponders this for a long moment. 'Good. Because I would like very much to show our child to the kingdom.' She guides her husband's hand along the swollen curve of her belly. 'The castle may be good at keeping secrets, but I am—'

'Not,' Edric finishes for her, knowing his wife more than he has ever wanted to know anyone. 'I know, Ri.'

'But despite it all, I love you.' She draws a circle above the king's thumping heart as she says it, just as she has so many times before.

'Thank the Plague for that,' Edric responds earnestly.

Iris's soft laugh morphs into a hiss when she clutches her belly. The king shudders at the sight of his wife in pain, shifting suddenly from stoic royal to concerned spouse. Threading an arm around her waist, he guides his groaning queen onto her bed. It is only after adjusting her legs and propping a pillow behind Iris's back that Edric allows himself a long breath.

'Are you all right?' The question is laced with his own terror for her.

'Yes, I will be fine.' Sweat glistens on her brow. 'Just labor pains, dear.'

The king nods in an attempt to expel that lingering fear within him. His father always hated when he showed any sign of weakness – and Iris is exactly that. Clearing his throat and smoothing the worry between his brows, Edric lets his gaze fall to the bedside table. Her beloved jewelry box sits there, filled with each of the queen's coveted pieces. Iris has a passion for beauty, and despite her confinement to the castle, she has never missed an opportunity to sparkle in even the dullest of halls.

But that pristine box is not what holds the king's attention. No, it is the pink rose sprawled peacefully atop the wooden lid, and its accompanying folded piece of parchment.

Iris notes every emotion that crawls across her husband's face. First, interest. Second, curiosity. These are both followed by a tumble of more sinister feelings: Scrutiny. Concern. Jealousy.

'A gift from one of my handmaids,' the queen answers flippantly, though no question was voiced. 'I rarely get to walk the gardens, so she thought to bring a bit of the gardens to me.'

With her belly wrapped in one arm, Iris uses the other to toss the gift beneath the jewelry box's lid. She traps the flower within the wooden walls so simply that Edric won't spare it another thought. Instead, he will continue on until met with the end that begins in this very moment.

So, when Iris cries out in pain, and a dampness spreads the covers beneath her, the end is very near for Edric Azer. At least, for that dwindling bit of warmth within him.

CHAPTER 10
Paedyn

I sit numbly beside the fire, enveloped in its heat.

The blood coating my dress and hands is nearly dry now, as are the tears that streamed down my face. Now there is nothing left but a slow, simmering rage as I sit silently in this study.

Hushed voices seep around the cracked door, stealing my attention from the trapped flames. 'Where is she?' I sit up slightly at that voice. 'I want to see her. I haven't even been able to since—'

I move quickly, tripping over fumbling feet. I'm suddenly standing before the door, cutting off his words with nothing more than the mere sight of me. The smile that slides to his lips is a sad one, filled with an abundance of apologies while looking like a sigh of relief.

I fling myself into Calum's arms without a second thought. He holds me tight, cradling the broken pieces of me with gentle care. 'It's good to see you, too,' he whispers into my hair, making me smile against his shoulder.

I pull away, looking him over. His pale eyes shine, searching mine and likely the mind behind them. This theory is only confirmed when he nods slowly, blond hair dull in the dim light. 'You're

welcome. It was Kitt that discovered the truth. I simply helped him get there.'

I smile, relieved to know that he heard every echo of gratitude bouncing around my skull. Because I'm not sure I could put it into words at the moment. He has helped change everything, helped turn my father's hope into a reality.

Well, not quite my father. Just the man who raised me.

At that sudden thought, Calum's brows rise slightly in surprise. I sigh, shaking my head. 'I'll explain later. But for now . . . thank you. For everything.' I return his nod with another small smile. 'I just wanted you to hear me say it out loud.'

My eyes trail over Calum's shoulder, finding Kitt and Kai conversing softly. I step aside, gesturing for them to continue their murmuring in the study behind me. Kitt nods in silent agreement, striding past to take a seat behind his desk. Calum follows quietly, leaving only Kai standing before the doorway.

He had carried me up into the castle, started the fire that warmed my numb limbs. Then he'd kissed my forehead and slipped out the door, likely dealing with more pressing Enforcer duties than the crumbling queen-to-be.

He watches me now, an ache in his gaze that mirrors my own. I want nothing more than to be held by him, enveloped in the comfort of his arms. He is a weakness I am not supposed to indulge in. Not in this life, at least.

I can't imagine what he sees in this moment. Likely running makeup and dirt-stained cheeks. Tangled hair and blood-drenched skin I'm struggling to ignore. And yet, he looks at me with a relieved sort of adoration, ensuring I'm all right with a lingering swipe of his gaze.

Our fingers brush as he steps past, leaving me standing in the doorway. I take a long, steadying breath before turning to retake my seat beside the fire. Only then do I allow my thoughts to stray back to the horrors I'd seen. My sharp words cut through the men's conversation with ease. 'What the hell happened out there?'

Kai leans against the desk, shaking his head. 'The explosions came from man-made bombs. Six of them. I haven't seen those since—'

'The first Trial ball,' I finish for him. My gaze lands on Calum. 'Only the Resistance had use for those. Why go through all the trouble of making bombs when an Ignite could do just as much damage?'

Lowering himself into a chair, Calum sighs. 'If I had to guess, I would say that this attack was meant to be a message more than anything.'

'All that for a message?' I hiss. 'Innocent people died.'

Kitt coughs into his fist, likely due to the inhaled smoke. 'How many casualties, Kai?'

'Nine. So far.' My eyes fall shut as he adds a low, 'But dozens are injured and being tended to by Healers.'

My eyes flutter open to the sight of Kitt rubbing a hand down his face. 'Do continue, Calum. I'd like to hear this theory.'

'Well, it wasn't an attack on the royals themselves.' Calum gestures around the room to our very much alive bodies. 'Which leads me to believe that this was an attack on the meaning behind the parade. On . . . well, the future of this kingdom.'

'There won't *be* a future if our borders remain closed, and Ordinaries remain banished,' Kitt huffs under his breath.

'The people don't want Paedyn as their queen.'

I swivel towards the foreign voice, finding a minty head of hair in the doorway. The court's spokesman steps into the room, his clothing finely pressed against dark skin.

'Ah, Easel, welcome.' Kitt gestures towards him while addressing the rest of us. 'As head of my court, I figured it best to hear what he has to say on the matter. Or rather, what the people are saying.'

'Your Majesty.' Easel tips his head towards the king. 'The people are in a state of unrest.'

'They don't want an Ordinary as their queen,' I say bitterly.

'Well, you did kill the king that ensured an Elite society,' Kitt mutters.

Calum, his voice distant, adds, 'And that is not the only royal you have killed.'

My eyes dart to his. 'What are you talking about?'

He opens his mouth quickly, folding stiff arms behind his back. 'A piece of Kitt died that day, did it not?' Gesturing in the direction of the west tower, he adds solemnly, 'Along with the king's wife, now sick with grief.'

Guilt sinks its teeth into my chest, gnawing at my conscience. For the first time, I feel a twinge of shame for bestowing death upon the king. Not for his sake, but for those around him.

'You're right.' Swallowing, I glance over at the brothers, having wounded them both in very different ways. 'I am sorry, again. For the hurt I caused you, Kitt.' My gaze flicks to the Enforcer beside him. 'And for the grief that has sickened your mother.'

There is a long, contemplative pause from the three of them. Kai nods his forgiveness as Kitt breaks the unbearable silence. 'Thank you, Paedyn.' The words are stiff, but spoken, nonetheless. And within the next breath, he's returned diligently to the conversation at hand. 'So, why not go after Paedyn if she is what they see as the problem?'

It's Easel who answers. 'This is now much bigger than her, my King. The whole kingdom has been suddenly told to welcome Ordinaries when they now barely tolerate the multiplying Mundanes. No matter the reasoning, most refuse to accept this.'

'Do they not realize what is at stake here?' I scoff. 'Ilya will fall without resources.'

'They realize.' Easel nods slowly. 'But ignorance was their bliss. Some admired the late king's persistence in ridding Ilya of Ordinaries rather than saving it from collapsing.'

Kai crosses his arms, the sleeves hugging them dried with blood. 'The Defensive and Offensive Elites are turning against the entirety of the slums. I've seen the shift over the past few years. It's not just Ordinaries they want out of the city.' His eyes meet mine. 'The entirety of the slums is beneath them now.'

'Well, that is no surprise to me,' I breathe. 'Anyone in the slums has known that for years. My father even wrote about it – how the Mundanes will soon become the new Ordinaries.'

Calum's eyes meet mine, seeing right through me to learn of my father's journal. I've never been more thankful for his mind reading ability than in this moment. I don't even have to address the questioning look in his eyes – he can go right ahead and find the answer within my mind.

'They already are.' Kitt states this evenly. 'Their numbers are growing and the rest of the Elites only see them as a weakness—'

'Just like the Ordinaries,' I finish for him.

Easel nods. Kai stiffens. Calum remains stoic as ever.

'So,' Kitt says slowly, 'do we have any idea who exactly is behind this?'

'Likely a group of Elites who think they're doing the kingdom a favor.' Kai's tone is dry. 'And also think they have a sense of humor by copying the Resistance bombs.'

'Handmade bombs are harder to trace than an Ignite,' I realize softly. 'There is no one to interrogate. No way to know who threw them.'

The study fills with silence until Kitt dares to break it. 'What does the court want us to do about this? How do we get the people to accept Paedyn as their queen?'

A lock of Easel's long hair slips over a broad shoulder. 'Paedyn must prove herself to all of Ilya. Prove she is strong enough to rule, even as an Ordinary. That is the only way we believe they will accept her.'

I almost laugh. 'And how do we plan on doing that?'

His silence is ominous. And when he finally speaks, I understand why. 'The people want to send you back into your own Trials.'

CHAPTER 11

Kai

I know Death. There is something intimate about the ending of a life.

Over the years, Death and I have come to share a special bond. But fear is a far less familiar feeling. One that has never gripped me as tightly as it had in that study.

Calum agreed with Easel's proposition and urged Kitt to do the same. But my focus was wholly on her. I watched Paedyn ponder this deadly decision, watch the agreement form on those pretty lips of hers. Rage was a rumble in my chest that rose to my tongue, shouting that she can't be serious. I stood before her, fought the urge to cup her face, and told her she cannot enter another set of Trials. I simply wouldn't let her risk everything for a kingdom that would rather see her die.

But I should know better than to give Paedyn Gray an order. She is not one of my soldiers, after all. No, she is so much more.

That was when she looked me in the eyes, took Death by the hand, and declared once again that she would enter herself into these new Trials.

'It's the only way,' she had said sternly, though her face was pale.

'I have to prove myself to them.'

'And if you die?' I'd shot back, chest heaving.

Her next words still plague my thoughts, more than a day later.

'Then they will have been right about me. I'm a weakness.'

The ring feels foreign on my finger.

I pull my hands behind my back, hiding them from the sea of prying eyes beneath the dais. Fidgeting with the thick Enforcer's ring, I can practically feel the blood that has been spilled by those who wore it before me. I blow out a breath, keeping my gaze on the large throne room doors ahead.

I – and the rest of the court, for that matter – have been begrudgingly awaiting our king to grace us with his presence. The minutes drag by, leaving me alone atop the dais and very much on display for the entire court. By the time I've considered borrowing a Veil's power from the crowd to simply vanish from this unfortunate situation, the doors swing open.

In steps the king. The golden crown glitters atop his head, bleeding into the hair beneath. His outfit is simple at first glance, refined at second. The buttoned shirt he wears is pressed perfectly, tucked into equally pristine green pants. But every feature is enhanced by what he carries on his arm.

Her hand is threaded through his bent elbow, tan skin glowing against the white dress hugging her closely. The neckline encircles her throat, hiding what I know to be a branding of my father's doing above her heart. Shoulders exposed, waist cinched tightly, hair waving around her ears.

She looks equally youthful and thoroughly weathered by the world. It's a contradiction she wears confidently.

But the draping white fabric is a message to this court, a reminder piercing my heart. She is a bride-to-be. But not mine.

I swallow at the sight.

Her eyes are on mine as she steps up onto the dais beside me. I stare too long, too desperately to be nothing more than her Enforcer. With more than a little effort, I pry my attention from her, returning it to the door even as Kitt begins speaking.

'Ladies and gentlemen of the court, thank you for your patience. I'm sure you are all very curious as to why I've called you here today.' His voice carries over the intrigued faces filling the room. 'As you all now know, there was an attack in the slums during our parade. Most of you will likely not find this to be grievous news. But you should.'

At the sound of his deep breath, my eyes flick to him. Exhaustion smothers his features. 'I know that my engagement to Paedyn Gray, along with the sudden acceptance of Ordinaries, will be difficult to adjust to. But I will not tolerate outright acts of defiance against my decrees. Especially those I make for all our sakes.' His voice softens slightly. 'But I do understand how difficult this change is, and how this kingdom does not wish to accept Paedyn as their queen. Despite the necessity of this arrangement, I offer you the opportunity to judge her strength and see for yourself if she is capable of becoming a ruler.'

Murmurs ripple throughout the room, forcing Kitt to raise his voice. 'Paedyn Gray will once again compete in a series of Trials.'

Giddy gasps ring out at his words, followed by bloodthirsty nods of approval. This is what they wanted – and their king provides.

'These Trials,' Kitt continues, 'will be for the future queen alone. They will be structured around the three *B*'s you all know my father to have lived by. It is bravery, benevolence, and brutality that make a great ruler. These events will test each of those qualities. This will allow Paedyn to prove herself worthy of the throne – and your loyalty.'

The court is thrilled to find their proposition becoming a reality, likely because the outcome will mean certain death for an Ordinary. Paedyn barely survived the first set of Trials she was thrown into. Even still, Ilya may not deign to accept her if she makes it out of these ones alive.

'Once again, we will be posting fliers all across the city,' Kitt states over the whispering crowd. 'This test is for Ilyans alone. As far as the surrounding kingdoms know, we have gracefully accepted our Ordinary queen. And I hope that will prove to be true in due time. For all our sakes.' There is a pause before his next damning declaration. 'The first Trial will take place in three days' time.'

This solution seems to satisfy the court. They will happily sit back and watch her die, smile if she meets the death they think she deserves. But I will only survive this life if she does.

She steps forward then, every gaze snapping to her. The dress clings to her in a way I long to, eyes sweep over the crowd that I now desperately wish I was in. She is striking in the most formidable of ways. Sharp like the pointed stare she gives, the tongue I've tasted, the end of her dagger that's worn my blood.

The words that leave her lips are stern, possessing the subtlety that anger lacks. 'I know I am not who you want as your queen. In fact, I did not ask for this. I've dreamed of nothing in this life except to survive it.' Her gaze travels around the room, bright and bold. 'But I do this for the hope of a kingdom far better than this one. One where Ordinaries and every ranking of Elites live side by side. One where we still have a kingdom to call home.'

She takes another step forward, forcing me to fight the awe beginning to slip through my mask of indifference. 'I will show you my bravery, my benevolence, my brutality. I will survive these Trials and so much more. Still, you will likely hate me.' She lifts her chin, expression deceitfully calm. 'So bow at my feet with a sneer, if you must. I won't see it with your face to the ground.'

My lips twitch, utterly amazed by her. Looping her arm back through Kitt's, she turns one last time towards the crowd. 'If it is power you seek from me, then so be it.'

Kitt wears an expression of muted surprise as he nods slowly to the court in silent dismissal. But they don't move, nor do the loose lips they all possess. No, they are all too busy staring at her.

And so am I as she strides, arm hooked within the king's, out of the throne room.

CHAPTER 12

Paedyn

I stare at the shadows clinging to the canopy above me.

Despite the impressive comfort of the bed beneath my back, I can't seem to let sleep claim me. Thoughts swirl behind my eyes, making it impossible to shut them even as tiredness tugs at my body.

I can think of nothing but my reunion with doom.

My future haunts my present — and it is grim.

I have to endure another set of Trials.

Only, this time, I'll be facing Death alone. Fear twists in my gut, tugging at the heart I'm not sure will still be beating after this. I nearly died in the Purging Trials, more than once. The thought of willingly stepping back into an awaiting grave has me panicking.

Worse than the imminent danger is the constant reminder of Adena's death. I may have survived the last set of Trials, but my light did not. My A left me to decorate the sky. And I don't know how to live, how to survive, without her at my side.

Sweat dampens my brow as panic swells within me. I can't go back. I can't lose any more of that warmth Adena planted within me.

What if I'm forced to kill? Coat my hands with more blood?

I don't know what I'm capable of without Adena's light to scatter my darkness.

These Trials could ask anything of me. Though, it is fitting that the three B's I'll be tested on belonged to the king I killed. Ironic that they have now become the way I will prove myself to rule the kingdom he built – or rather, rebuild it.

I roll over, spitting stray strands of hair from my mouth. My eyes squeeze shut as I attempt to find sleep one last time.

Ten lazy beats of my heart, and I'm crawling out of bed.

My mind aches for a distraction from the deafening thoughts. And my body, tired as it is, itches to move. Or maybe I'm tired of feeling useless, feeling trapped in this life I don't know how to live. Plagues, I was just beginning to figure out how to live the unfortunate one I had before everything went to shit.

I'm suddenly striding down a dark hall, arms crossed over the thin sleeping shirt I wear. The most I'd done before stepping out of my room was slip on my boots. Changing before this impulsive escapade might have been a good idea, but I'm already nearing the door I know leads to the training yard beyond.

The guards stationed there shift on tired feet at the sight of me, their masks doing nothing to conceal the clear disdain beneath. They know better than to stand in my way, not with the ring that glitters on my finger. So, with my head raised stubbornly high, I stride past and push through the door.

The night is cooler than I'd anticipated, each whisper of wind pebbling the skin on my bare arms. Moonlight pools on the path long worn into the ground. Following it, I lift my gaze to the black sky draped above and speckled with stars. They seem to blink back at me, leaning in to help guide my steps.

The first circle of dirt comes into view, blanketed in shadows. I follow the path, letting it lead me between each training ring. Flickering flame floods the farthest circle of dirt to illuminate a formidable shadow, sharp like the sword he holds. I know who stands within that halo of light.

But when a second figure flickers into focus beside him, I falter.

'. . . couldn't sleep, but it seems you can't either.'

Kitt.

My breath catches.

I would rather not let my betrothed know I came out here to meet his brother.

With that in mind, I crouch low to the ground and creep silently to a ring beside the brothers. Shadows clothe me from sight until I've slipped behind the weapons' rack. Blowing out a breath, I peek through one of the many gnarled holes in this wall of wood, my gaze narrowing on the king and his Enforcer.

'I thought I might find you out here,' Kitt was saying. 'It's good to be back in this training yard with you. Just like old times.'

'If it were really like old times,' Kai muses, 'you would be sprawled in the dirt already.'

Kitt laughs, a sound so genuine I nearly startle. It's as though I'm suddenly back beside that fountain in the gardens, splashing a boyish prince unashamedly. 'You think you could still take me, Brother? We haven't sparred since you found a better partner.'

The tips of my ears burn.

'Come on, Kitt.' The Enforcer's tone is deceptively casual. 'That was during the Purging Trials. Things haven't been like that for a long while.' Despite knowing the truth of our relationship, Kai's nonchalance still manages to sting me. 'Besides,' he sighs. 'You're the one who's marrying her.'

And there is that twinge of jealousy.

'It is what needs to be done. You understand that.' Kitt runs a hand through his hair, looking younger beside his brother. 'For the kingdom. And for us.'

Kai stifles his scoff. 'For us?'

'Yes.' It's a simple word, yet it holds so much defiance from the king. 'I know your relationship with Father was strained. More than strained,' he amends quickly. 'I don't want that for us. What I want is to be brothers again, without orders you detest shoved between us. And with the Ilya I am rebuilding, you won't need to hunt down Ordinaries anymore.' Knowing his brother more than most, he reassures, 'I won't make you hurt anyone.'

I can't make out Kai's face in the flickering torchlight, but I know gratitude paints the planes of it. 'Thank you, Brother.'

Kitt nods earnestly, waiting a long moment before speaking again. 'But after this bombing at the parade, I've been advised to ensure our army is ready for whatever threats may arise. Especially now that our borders have opened. You know how Father grew a bit lax with training over the years.'

'He didn't believe we would need to fight very many battles,' Kai recalls.

My legs ache from kneeling on the hard ground, but I don't dare shift this close to the keen Enforcer. I watch as Kitt absentmindedly crushes clumps of dirt beneath his shoe. 'Now anything could happen. So I need you to focus your attention on rebuilding our forces and training new recruits.'

'New recruits?' Kai echoes.

I can just make out the smile that transforms the king's tired face. 'I want you to train Ordinaries.'

My heart stalls its rhythmic beat.

'After the bombing,' Kitt continues, 'it became clear to me how vulnerable Ordinaries really are in this kingdom . . .'

'No shit,' I breathe recklessly into the darkness.

'. . . so I want to offer them the chance to defend themselves.' The king takes a breath. 'They will train with you alongside the other Imperials.'

'Are . . . are you serious?' Kai stumbles over the string of words, holding in his shocked laugh. 'Don't mess with me, Kitty.'

'I wouldn't dream of it.' Kitt's chuckle seems to light the darkness. 'And I already have some Ordinaries for you. The few we captured from the Bowl after that third Trial.'

Shock sweeps over me.

He didn't kill them.

Kai echoes my surprise. 'They are still in the dungeons?'

'I wasn't sure what to do with them,' Kitt says, sounding as though there is a shrug lodged in his throat. 'But after that bombing, it seems time they are freed and trained.'

The Enforcer shakes his head. 'You're really going to do this? Let them go after what happened?'

'Huh.' Kitt huffs out a dull laugh. 'I suppose I am.'

Clapping a hand on his brother's shoulder, Kai murmurs, 'I'm proud of you. And I'm honored to help rebuild and protect this kingdom by your side.'

They look at each other, seemingly untouched since the day I met them. In this moment, their bond resembles the one I thought I had broken. And the realization that they are stronger than my vengeance makes me smile.

'You and me, Brother.' Kitt takes a slow step back. 'Always.'

When he strides back onto the path, I'm forced to press my back against the weapons' rack and silently beg that shadows cloak me from the corner of his sight. I don't breathe as my betrothed walks past, not even when Kai's words have him halting.

'Try to get some sleep.'

Kitt flashes his Enforcer a smile. 'You first, Kai Pie.'

I wait there until long after the king has vanished and my heartbeat has slowed. Standing on sore legs, I watch Kai rotate a sword in his hand, the motion fluid and precise. His back is to me, bare and slithering with strands of darkness as I step to the ring's edge. When he turns to face me, I'm slightly offended by the lack of surprise at my presence.

'Couldn't sleep without me?' he muses, sword glinting in the flickering light.

I frown. 'How did you know I was here?'

'I knew you couldn't stay away from me for much longer.'

'Don't flatter yourself.' My arms cross over the thin shirt I'm suddenly all too aware of. 'How did you know?'

He gives me an unsure tilt of his head. 'I guess I can sense you, in a way. It sounds odd, but the darkness helps me focus. Everything is heightened.' Kai waves a hand, as if to slash through the words he's just spoken. 'I just knew.'

'Hmm. Yet another perk of being Elite,' I say, my tone bittersweet.

He shakes his head. 'Well, I'm assuming you heard everything, then?'

'I did. Thought it best he didn't see me out here with you.' My foot taps a steady beat atop the dirt. 'This is good, right? I thought he had killed those Ordinaries from the Bowl.'

Kai runs a hand through his tousled hair. 'It seems good. *He* seems good. Wanting to train Ordinaries is not something I expected from him.'

I nod distantly, my mind a mess of fractured pieces. Lost among my thoughts, I nearly miss Kai's sly words. 'Did the burning desire to see me wake you?'

I slowly steal the space between us, stepping quietly into the ring. My smile is sharp. 'No. But the sudden urge to hit you did.'

He looms over me, his bare chest nearly brushing mine. 'If you want to put your hands on me, just say that.'

A bead of water falls from the dark sky, splattering my bare shoulder. He watches it roll down my skin before swiping it away with his thumb. His rough palm grazes my arm, leaving a trail of goose bumps behind.

I lift a hand, my fingers boldly skimming across his stomach. This seems to startle him enough to suck in a quick breath, and the sound has a satisfied smile curling my lips. The tips of my fingers trail higher, tracing every dip and groove of muscle. He seems to have stopped breathing.

My eyes lift to his, and whatever it is he sees within them has the Enforcer looking at me as though I've already become his queen. And some possessive part of myself aches to command him to never look away.

My touch travels lazily up his chest, fingers outlining the swirling tattoo etched above his pounding heart. The sky cries steadily above, speckling us with water. But Kai barely seems to notice, his attention fully on my hand now twining around his neck.

His sword clatters to the ground. Strong arms wrap suddenly around my waist before another drop of rain can fall from the sky. I'm being pulled closer, pressed flush against his solid body. With a tilt of my chin, he murmurs against my lips. 'My pretty Pae. Tell me you missed me.'

Our lips brush, and I can taste his desperation for me. I smile.

My response is a swift hook of my foot behind his. With a firm tug, I accomplish something few have ever done.

I send the Enforcer sprawling into the dirt.

My voice drifts into the night like the cloud of dust between us. 'I missed kicking your ass.'

'Oddly enough—' his smile is crooked, '—so did I.'

He attempts to pull me down with him, but I dance away from his grasp with a laugh. 'I have more Trials to train for. So no more distractions.'

'You started it, Gray.' He seems content to stare up at the starry sky, even as it cries steadily. 'I was trying to keep my hands to myself.'

'Well, don't,' I offer. 'Fight me.'

My words have him sitting up solemnly, ignoring my request. 'I hate that you're being thrown back into this.' I feel his head shake. 'You should have never agreed to these Trials.'

'Well, it was nice to have a choice this time.' I swallow my bitterness. 'Besides, it was the only way. I mean, you saw how the court reacted—'

'Yes, because they want to watch you die.' He tears himself off the ground, standing swiftly to his feet.

'So I won't,' I say, with much more confidence than I feel. 'I need to do this. And if I die, then make me a martyr.'

'A *martyr*, Paedyn?' His laugh is void of humor. 'Do you even hear yourself? Part of you has already given up before even starting.'

'I'm not giving up; I'm being realistic.' My words are clipped. I'm stunned by how suddenly this conversation escalated. 'I could die—'

He closes the distance between us, pressing rough palms against my cheeks. 'So damn the Trials. Pae, let me force every person in this kingdom to their knees for you.'

'This is so much bigger than me now.' I shake my head in his hold. 'I have to do this.'

His hands slip from my face, wet with rain. 'Just like you have to marry Kitt?'

The words hit me hard, as if we were fighting with our fists. It pains me, that look in his eyes. The one that pleads for a different, happier ending to our story. 'Yes,' I whisper. 'Just like I have to marry Kitt.'

He lets out a slow, steadying breath. I watch him regain his slipping composure. His next words are blunt, laced with defeat. 'Fine. It seems you've already decided your fate. And I won't be in it.'

'But I want you in it,' I force out. 'We just need to be careful. Kitt can't see us together. It . . . it will only make everything more complicated.'

'Right.' He stiffens slightly. 'Pretend.'

'And if I want to survive this, I should train,' I add quickly.

Kai takes a step back, his head shaking. The movement is more terrifying than him swinging a sword at me. 'If you want me to fight you, I won't, Paedyn. I told you in that field of poppies how I would never do that again. That when I lay a hand on you, it would only ever be in a caress.' Raindrops drip from his lashes, but he doesn't dare blink as he murmurs, 'And I plan to keep that vow.'

A long moment passes between us, in which I attempt to fathom just how much he cares for me. And nothing has ever felt so right, vowing to never fight the Enforcer again. So I smile up at him, a bead of water sliding down my nose as I attempt to tease. 'If you were sick of getting your ass kicked, just say that.'

The corner of his mouth lifts begrudgingly. 'Oh, is that what you think?'

'Let's just say I can sense it.' I lean in, whispering, 'I'm kind of a Psychic.'

The last thing I see is a shake of his head before the world flips upside down. I squeal when he throws me over his shoulder, hair dangling and face angled towards the now-muddy ring.

'Did you sense that coming, Little Psychic?' he calls over the shoulder I'm currently slung over. I laugh despite myself, body swaying with each one of his steps.

'Where are you taking me?' I'm breathless and gripping the waist of his pants for dear life.

He's quiet for several steps. 'Somewhere even the future can't find us.'

I smile sadly. 'The willow tree?'

'The willow tree.'

CHAPTER 13
Paedyn

'So, how exactly did this happen, again?'

I look up from where I'm perched on the edge of the bed, struggling to slip my shoes on. She's staring at the door currently occupying the floor before her, wine-red hair falling into her eyes. And when that skeptical, honey gaze flicks up to mine, thin brows quirk above it.

'There was . . .' I scramble to come up with a convincing string of words. 'An emergency. Of sorts.'

'I see,' she muses, placing a hand on the belt of tools around her waist. 'Well, the door should be back on its hinges before you get back from dinner.'

I smile, relieved. 'Thank you, Andy.'

Ellie scurries about the room behind me, gathering the scattered clothing that litters the floor. It had taken us an unbearably long time to pick something out for my dinner with the king. In truth, the outrageous amount of nerves fluttering in my stomach had me stalling in the form of sudden pickiness over my appearance.

I stand at the thought, smoothing out the green fabric clinging to me. The dress is flowy and laced up the back in a way that makes

it rather difficult to suck in a full breath. Attempting to avoid that concerning thought, I make my way over to where Andy now crouches beside the doorframe.

I watch her fiddle with the loose hinges, twisting various tools around the bolts. She lets me observe, fully knowing I should be halfway to the throne room by now to dine with her cousin. Instead, I ask, 'Do you enjoy doing this? Being a Handy around the castle?'

She tucks a strand of wine-colored hair behind an ear. 'I can't imagine doing anything else. It's . . . rewarding, in a way.' She flashes a smile over her shoulder. 'Fixing something that was broken.'

I hum quietly, the sound unsure. The silver ring hugging her nose glints as she turns to give me a questioning look. 'What? Does that surprise you?'

'No.' I shrug. 'It's just . . . you have so much power.' My eyes flick to her hair, remembering every burgundy creature I've witnessed her transform into. 'And yet, you're content with . . .'

'Being a lowly Handy?' she finishes with a laugh. 'Most people are shocked. Then again, most people don't realize there is more to life than power.'

My scoff is weak. 'Is there?'

She tilts her head, the mannerism so like her dark-haired cousin. 'I figured you of all people would understand that.'

I shake my head, smile sad. 'For you, there is more to life than power. That is because you have it.' My eyes drift up the walls while her own remain pinned on me. 'But for me . . . my life has always been about power. And trying to survive without it.'

When my gaze finds its way back to her, I catch the slight nod she offers. 'Well, you sure had all of us fooled.' She offers a wry smile. 'I'm impressed.'

'Don't be.' A weak laugh falls from my scarlet-stained lips. 'I was only trying to make it out of the Trials. And now I'm back in them.'

She stands, inspecting the other set of hinges. 'You'll be fine. Survive these Trials . . .' Her amber eyes meet mine, mischievous. 'And you'll get your power. You'll be queen of Ilya.'

I study her, searching for any kind of distrust or bitterness lingering after those words. But I see nothing except factual indifference painting the sharp planes of her face. It's relieving, looking at someone and not seeing hatred staring back.

I nod a thanks I can't seem to voice, before my feet find their way past her and into the hall. 'It's good to see you again, Andy.'

'You too.' She's searching for another tool on her belt when I turn away. 'Oh, Paedyn?' I whip around, dress swishing against my ankles. Her brows lower slightly over suddenly stern eyes. 'Don't hurt him. He can't afford to break again.'

I swallow. Nod slowly. 'I'm not planning on it.'

She seems satisfied with this answer, turning away with a small smile. I do the same and head down the hallway, my chest tight beneath the confines of this dress. I smooth a hand down the wavy hair curling around my ear, steps quick across the plush carpet.

A familiar head of red hair rounds the corner before easily stepping in time beside me. I barely glance at the masked Imperial. 'Aren't you supposed to be guarding a certain murderer?'

'Yeah,' he scoffs, 'so *you* can't murder *her*.'

My eyes find his. 'Well, she's alone right now.'

'But you're not.'

I turn down another long hall. 'What are you doing here, anyway?'

He presses a palm to his chest, putting on a show of offense. 'Am I not allowed to visit you, Princess? I missed you dearly.' I give him a look that forces the truth from his mouth. 'All right, so I had to take a piss. Doesn't mean I wouldn't have come and found you.'

I halfheartedly fight my smile. 'Well, I'm on my way to dine with the king, so no need to worry about any murders from me tonight.'

'How reassuring,' he says dryly. 'And don't you mean dinner with your *betrothed*?'

'Right,' I mumble. 'I forget what a happy couple we are.'

'Play nice, Princess,' he warns, leading me towards the towering doors of the throne room. 'You're not his queen yet.'

I smooth the skirt of my dress with hands that refuse to still. 'And I may never be.' We slow beside the doors, and before he can convince me all will be fine, I pull him into a hug. He only hesitates for a moment, then folds his arms tightly around me. 'I'll see you after the Trial,' I whisper, if only to convince myself of that fact.

After several long seconds, I step out of his embrace. And at my nod to the awaiting guards, the doors swing open.

The throne room stretches out before me, outlined with the same white pillars I've been paraded between more than once. I lift my chin, walking alone towards the large table at the center of the room.

For once, I am here of my own free will, and there is power in choice.

The king takes a seat at the end of the sprawling table, blond hair tousled and green eyes smudged with fatigue. He offers a small smile as I approach. 'Good evening, Paedyn.'

'Good evening,' I return, eyes drifting to the spread of parchment he shuffles into a pile beside his plate. 'Am I pulling you away from your work?'

'No, it's nothing pressing,' he answers dismissively. I watch him hand the stack of paper to a nearby servant who scurries away. 'I came from a meeting with the Scholars.'

'Scholars?' I stop before the yawning table. 'I'm sure they are aching to advise you on how this kingdom should be run.'

'They certainly are,' the king scoffs.

I can't help but take a moment to admire his resilience in the face of those who mock it. Kitt has changed since I tore his life at the seams. Now, selfishly, I'm hoping he will allow me back into this carefully mended one.

My gaze falls to the food laid before us. The plate awaiting me sits at the opposite end of the table, shoving several feet of distance between us.

I must have let the confusion spill into my expression because Kitt sighs, 'This is how royal meals are typically conducted.'

Nothing about his tone implies he wishes things to be any different. And that realization has my chest tightening. I don't want our lives to be distant conversations and avoidant glances. If we are meant to rebuild the kingdom a tyrant king destroyed, I want us to do so together, not begrudgingly.

'This is ridiculous,' I say simply before picking up my chair and carrying it over to him. His expression shifts slightly, enough to portray a shade of unsurety.

I made us this way. I marred the relationship he meticulously cultivated. So it is I who will meekly extend an olive branch, raise a white flag between us.

When I've reached the space beside him, I let the wooden legs of my chair hit the marble floor with an echoing thump.

Kitt raises a brow. 'What are you doing?'

'That—' I gesture to the opposite end of the table, '—was how things used to be done. But we are changing things, yes?'

'We are.' Impressively, Kitt changes the subject with a gesture towards the piles of food before us. 'Please, help me eat some of this.'

I blow out a breath.

He is not going to make this easy for me.

When the king reaches for a spoon partially buried within the bowl of green beans, a servant scurries from the wall to assist me. I hadn't even noticed the several pairs of eyes lining the room until he politely waves her off.

Having left my plate and utensils on the other side of this absurdly long table, I stand to retrieve them before a servant beats me to it. She resets my spot without a word, offering a slight nod in response to my gratitude.

'Thank you, Mandy,' Kitt murmurs. 'We will serve ourselves for the rest of the evening.'

The sound of her name rolling so easily from his tongue has my chest tightening. I had forgotten how well he knew the staff, how much he cared for every servant within the castle. Sitting beside him, I can almost see the friend I once knew. The one I betrayed.

I attempt a casual lightness that is now foreign to my voice. 'This looks delicious.'

It seems I'm incapable of carrying on a conversation with substance.

Kitt scoops a generous portion of mashed potatoes onto his plate. 'Gail knows this is my favorite food and has been making it for weeks.' He takes a bite that is quickly followed by a pleased nod of his head. 'But I'm definitely not complaining.'

I pick at my own food, even while my eyes are stubbornly set on him. 'She must have been so worried about you,' I say quietly. 'I heard you were . . . not doing well.' When he meets my gaze, I hurry to add, 'Which is completely understandable and most definitely my fault, but—'

His laugh cuts through my words.

He's laughing.

It's not quite a positive sound, but rather, one that is made at another's expense. This is nothing like the laugh I witnessed between him and Kai. The sound quiets with a slight cough. 'Take a breath, Paedyn. I've put it behind me.'

I still my fidgeting hands. 'But you don't forgive me.'

Silence swells between us.

His fork clatters against porcelain. I straighten at the sound, watching the king brace elbows atop the table that have him leaning closer. 'I want this to work,' he finally murmurs, gaze pinned on the sparkling diamond. 'This needs to work – for Ilya. For everyone. But that doesn't mean we need to be anything more to one another than what we are now.'

My resolve hardens in the face of his disregard for this stagnant relationship. 'No. No, I won't accept that.' His brow quirks as I continue with a defiant, 'I want to fix this. Us. We used to be . . . close. And I know it's my fault we no longer are, but if we're to spend the rest of our lives together, we might as well try to enjoy it.'

Kitt sits back in his chair, stretching the embarrassing silence further with a long swig from his glass. Finally, he deigns to mutter a chilling string of words. 'You already have Kai. Why bother furthering our relationship?'

My heart thuds against a constricted chest. Silently cursing this damn dress, I manage a breathy, 'Kai is not who I'm marrying.'

'But he wishes you were.'

I open my mouth. Close it. Try again. 'Is that what this is about? Whatever . . . closeness you believe me to have with Kai?'

'I know him, Paedyn.' Kitt's words are clipped. 'Better than I have ever known anyone. Don't think I haven't noticed his smothered feelings for you. Even after everything.'

There is a bitterness in his voice that makes me pause. It's the type that typically accompanies jealousy and quiet longing.

The king's gaze travels over me, and my throat goes dry.

Thoughts swirl around my head, each one more absurd than the last. Kitt couldn't still have feelings for me. Not after what I've done. But his words, his piercing look that strips me bare, say differently.

'Is that why you push me away?' I breathe. 'For Kai?'

He almost laughs again. 'Something like that.'

'You don't want to hurt him by . . . being with me.' With a shake of my head, I scramble to gather the pieces of this dangerous game Kai and I pretend to play. 'But there is no need to worry, Kitt. Whatever was between the Enforcer and me ended when he dragged me back here. On your orders.'

The king takes a breath at that, perhaps relieved by the reminder of an obeyed command. 'Yes, I can't say I wasn't a little surprised when he brought you back to me.' His green gaze grows pointed. 'He was yours, entirely.'

I swallow. 'Not anymore.'

Pretend.

Pretend that the Enforcer hadn't tried to free me before our trek to the castle. Pretend our time spent together didn't bring us impossibly closer. Pretend he isn't the fate I foolishly hoped to earn.

Kitt smiles, more freely than he has since my arrival. 'Time will tell.'

'I want to earn your forgiveness. Your trust.' My hand finds his, surprising the both of us. I hadn't planned the movement, but here I was, fingers splayed across his skin. 'Let me try to do that.'

His eyes are still on our linked hands when he nods. 'I suppose it's only fair I give you the chance.'

'Thank you,' I sigh out.

With a small smile, he returns his gaze to the plate of cooling food in front of me. 'Now eat. Please. You need all the energy you can get for your Trial tomorrow.'

Relieved to be speaking less formally, I groan while shoveling a forkful of mashed potatoes into my mouth. 'Don't remind me.'

'Everything will fine.' He takes a bite of ham. 'Ilya will be wowed.'

I snort. 'Only if I die. Perhaps they will even clap.'

'Even if you did, no one would be there to clap for it.'

The fork hovers in front of my mouth. 'What do you mean?'

'Just like the Purging Trials, these ones won't take place in the Bowl,' he offers graciously. 'Well, not all of them, at least.'

'Really?' My stomach twists into knots. 'Will there be Sights dragging at my heels?'

He lifts a glass of wine to his lips. 'Maybe. Maybe not.'

'Well, if the court came up with these Trials for me, I can't imagine they'd be anything short of perilous.'

Those green eyes roam over my face, and when I finally meet them, it's a contradicting mixture of emotions I see within. 'The two landmarks you haven't yet had a Trial at,' he finally says. 'That is where you will be.'

My gaze falls to his chest, where I know Ilya's crest lies inked into the skin beneath his collared shirt. The sideways diamond represents the four landmarks surrounding us — two of which I have already survived in the Purging Trials. That leaves—

'The Scorches and the Shallows.'

He nods slowly. 'The desert and the sea.'

'Great,' I say cheerily. 'I barely survived the Scorches the first time.'

Crossing lean arms over his chest, Kitt adds, 'This first Trial is all about bravery. And fears come in many different forms.'

I study his stoic expression. Then, a hurried question surprises my tongue. 'What fear would test you in this Trial of bravery?'

'That is a bit personal.' He says this accusingly despite his expression being tinged with amusement.

'That's the point,' I counter.

'Failure,' he says finally, simply. 'Insignificance.'

I don't tell him that this makes perfect sense considering the way he was raised. Instead, I extend that olive branch in the form of understanding. 'That is an admirable fear to have.'

Kitt huffs, and I think it might have been a laugh in disguise. 'And yours?'

I shrug. 'Too many to count.'

'It doesn't seem that way.' He takes a sip of wine. 'Not even when you were in the Purging Trials.'

'I'm good at pretending.'

'I've gathered that.'

Words spill from my mouth in response to his own. 'But I'm not pretending to be your friend. I've never had to. Not even when I needed to find that tunnel. And I will keep trying to prove that until you tell me you believe it.'

There is a long pause. 'Okay.'

'Okay,' I repeat sternly.

He cracks a smile. I smile back.

I feel young. Hopeful. Anew.

In this moment, I see the future we could have – a glimpse of the boy who threw chocolates into my mouth and helped clean each one I missed off the floor.

I see a friendship, not love.

No, love is what I see when I look at his brother.

I run my fork through the pile of mashed potatoes on my plate. 'Is this a horrible time to tell you that I've never much liked your favorite food?' His raised eyebrows have me attempting to amend with a weak, 'It's a texture thing.'

He leans back, head shaking. 'You're not helping your case, Paedyn.'

I don't stifle my laugh in time. 'Oh, so my dislike for mashed potatoes is what's unforgivable?'

'I'm afraid so.'

With a shake of my head, I lift a forkful of potatoes between us. 'Fine. To my dislike for mashed potatoes. May it be our biggest problem.'

This earns me a slight smile. He clinks his fork against mine and echoes, 'May it be our biggest problem.'

CHAPTER 14

Kai

I weave between the training rings, hands tucked casually behind my back.

Sweaty bodies pack the yard, some sparring while others groan through the set of exercises I've forced upon them. I scan the crowded expanse of dirt and torn grass, tracing the movements of those around me. My hand shoots out, lifting a Brawny's elbow as I pass. 'Keep your back straight. Carry the sword higher.'

The Imperial nods before I continue down the path, catching a Flash before he runs into a loaded crossbow or a Bloom keen on uprooting my training yard.

It seems my soldiers are out of practice.

Father ensured that most of my time was spent hunting down Ordinaries. But, seeing that Kitt freed me from that gruesome task, I can now focus on whipping my men into shape.

'I don't care if you are the strongest Elite out here,' I call, standing in the center of chaos. 'I want you to learn how to fight without ability.' I point to a particularly filthy Imperial. 'Widen your stance. And you—' I step into a ring, pulling a Shell's forearm higher. 'Guard your face, always. You're not made of stone right now.'

I've spent the entire day shouting variations of the same thing. Every two hours a new rotation of soldiers stepped into the yard, replacing the ones I'd worn out. Ordinaries are sprinkled among the Elites and instantly recognized by the group. They are timid, unsure of every movement, as if terrified to make a wrong one. I've learned over the past several hours that it is best to separate those Ordinaries from the taunting Elites. At least, until I'm confident they can swing a sword correctly.

Darkness has bled across the sky before I finally stride back into the castle.

I'm tired and hungry, but most of all, I'm thinking of her.

My feet are quick to find their way towards the queen's quarters. It feels wrong, and yet, so entirely fitting that she is occupying them. The halls are quiet, the shadows are thick, and—

Her door is fixed.

I shouldn't be surprised, considering I'm the one who told Andy it was in need of repair. With her hard work in mind, I gently rap my knuckles against the wood rather than kicking it off the hinges.

Her footsteps grow closer on the other side of the door. I've gotten rather good at memorizing every sound she makes. Every laugh from her throat, every shuffle of her feet, every sigh against my mouth.

The door swings open, and there she is. A large shirt hangs off her tan shoulder, the hem of it nearly covering the silk shorts exposing the length of her legs. Her short hair is damp, skin sweet with the remnants of bathing oils. I breathe her in as my eyes roam over the familiar figure before me.

She peeks her head out the door, expression suddenly anxious. 'You shouldn't be here,' she hisses into the silence. Then, without another word, I'm being tugged into her room.

I kick the door shut behind me. 'Where else would I be?'

'Your own room, maybe?'

'My room doesn't have you in it.' My lips twitch. 'Hence why I'm in yours.'

She shakes her head at me in disbelief. 'Insufferable, cocky bastard.'

I wrap an arm around her waist to pull her against me. My fingers flick the tip of her nose, voice softening to a whisper. 'And my

111

pretty—' I kiss her gently, feel her mouth melt against mine. 'Pretty Pae.'

She tugs at my shirt, pressing her lips against mine. I shove away from the door before pushing her farther into the room. This kiss is greedy and aching. This kiss is made up of every moment I wasn't able to touch her, every moment I wanted her but willed myself not to.

Her lips are as soft as the skin beneath my roaming hands. I feel a shiver snake down her spine when my fingers curl into her damp hair. 'You shouldn't be here,' she reminds again, barely managing to get the words out.

My response is a whisper against her lips. 'I know.'

'Someone could have seen you,' she pants.

'I know.'

Her hands grasp at my hair. 'I'm an engaged woman.'

My voice is low. 'Oh, I know.' My fingers find that damning ring, slipping it off even as my mouth moves against hers. She makes a sound of protest against my lips that has my heartbeat quickening, but I manage to grab her other wrist from where it's buried in my hair. Before she can stop me, I've pushed the band onto the finger of her right hand. 'There. Now it's just a ring. No vows attached.'

She pulls away with a smile that has my breath catching. 'Oh, it's that simple?'

'It could be,' I say too quickly, too desperately.

The heated moment fizzles out between us, leaving only panted breaths and the grim reminder of our future. Paedyn takes a step away, then a dozen more as she begins pacing the plush carpet. Lifting wet hair off her neck, she clears her throat. 'Kitt is . . . suspicious of our relationship. I think that is why he pushes me away.'

I force myself to scoff, knowing that the alternative is far more dangerous. 'Because he still cares for you.'

'We just need to be careful,' Paedyn says calmly. 'I don't want to make things more difficult than they already are.'

I turn away, shoving hands into my pockets. I'm suddenly very interested in the molding that decorates her door. 'So, I take it you spoke to Kitt?'

'We had dinner together.' She waits for a reaction I don't give her. 'We're going to start doing that regularly.'

'Of course,' I bite out. 'Kings and queens dine together, after all.'

Jealousy weighs heavy on my words, straining my voice enough to have Paedyn sighing. Her hands cup my face to turn it towards her. 'Please don't push me away too. I don't want this any more than you do.'

I manage a nod before she's flicking the tip of my nose weakly. I'm momentarily stunned by the action, as I always am. But it never gets easier, adjusting to the joy that swells within me when her fingers flick my nose. To feel her endearment so physically is a privilege I don't deserve.

'Don't do that,' I breathe.

'Do what?'

I duck my head. 'Ruin me.'

'I thought that is what you wanted?' she reminds me slyly.

'Not like this.' I tuck a damp strand of hair behind her ear. 'Not with him.'

A slow ache begins its inevitable build in my chest. I will always love my brother, but I'm not sure I can bear to watch him grow old with her. Loyalty and love are damning enough when apart from each other. Now, they are dangerously tangled together.

A lingering, sympathetic look is the only answer she offers.

'So, did you come to say goodbye?' Pae's voice is soft, her change of topic less so. 'Just in case.'

'I don't need to say goodbye,' I answer blandly. 'Because I will see you after the Trial.'

Her gaze is distant. 'I'm going to the Scorches. Or the Shallows.' I still at her words, prepared to ask how she knows this when the answer spills from her mouth. 'Kitt told me. Two of the Trials will take place at the remaining landmarks I haven't yet survived.'

I shake my head. 'Of course they will. I shouldn't be surprised that the court would throw you somewhere you've never been before.' She opens her mouth, urging me to add, 'But, no, I won't say goodbye, because you're going to be fine. Bravery is the least of your worries.'

She's quiet for a troublesome amount of time. Then, a soft smile finds its way to her lips. 'When I left for the Purging Trials, Adena reassured me that it wasn't a goodbye, simply a good way to say bye until I saw her again.' She swallows thickly. 'It was the most ridiculous line, but she said it so many times over the years.'

She makes a pained sound that slightly resembles a laugh. I look down at her, finding a mingling of grief and anger harshening her features. My fingers lift her chin. 'So, in the wise words of Adena, this is simply a good way to say bye until . . . whatever the hell.'

She was laughing before I'd even begun trailing off. But this time, it's the kind of sound that has my breath catching, eyes unblinking so I don't miss a single second of it. 'Until whatever the hell,' Paedyn repeats with a nod.

I smile until the one she wears fades, and even then, I grin again in the hopes hers will return. After a moment too long, I finally admit why it is I'm here in the first place. 'I have something for you.'

A shadow of skepticism falls over her face. 'Should I be worried?'

Reaching into my boot, I carefully slide the gift from it. '*I* should be worried. It will likely find its way to my neck again.'

The silver dagger gleams, as if calling to her.

Her eyes widen, roaming up the sharp blade and over the swirling pattern dressing the hilt. Reaching out slowly, she grabs hold of her father's knife. And for this one, single moment, all is right in the world.

There she is, the Silver Savior, standing before me – dagger in hand and a smile spreading across her face.

'Thank you.' She can hardly get the words out. 'I thought I would never see it again.'

I smile. 'Just try your best not to slice me open, yes?'

'You first, Prince.'

Her words are meant to tease, but instead my eyes drift to the scar crawling across her thigh. The smile fades from my face at the reminder of what I'd done to her while trying to fulfill my mission. She takes a step closer, sensing my sudden seriousness with a slight look of concern. My gaze trails up to the letter I know to be carved above her heart.

Her palm finds my face in a gentle caress. 'You're not him.'

Those three words threaten to shatter me to pieces.

I can't bring myself to look at her. It's a sudden, deafening relief that follows in the wake of her reassurance. I hadn't even realized how terribly I'd needed to hear that from her lips. The symmetries between my father and the monster he made of me have haunted every corner of my mind for as long as I can remember.

'Kai.' Her voice is delicate enough to refocus my fragile mind. 'You're not him,' she whispers again, tears pricking those beautiful blue eyes. 'I need you to know that. For me.'

I nod, not knowing where all my words went. She holds my face in her hands, holds me together with a touch I wish would belong to only me. 'You're not him,' she repeats with a soft smile. 'But you have both left very different marks on my heart. One an O, and the other something even more damning.'

Her unspoken words hang in the air between us.

'Paedyn.' I tip my forehead against hers, aching to say what she is so scared of. In that field of poppies, I told her how impossible it was to stop myself from falling in love with her. And yet, the three damning words have yet to fall from my lips.

I love you.

I open my mouth, but it's her strained voice I hear. 'Don't. Not yet.' She blows out a breath, her fingers brushing down the length of my cheek. 'Every person who has ever said that to me is gone. And I . . . I need you more than I need those words.'

I smile, pressing a kiss to her forehead. 'It will take far more than mere words to drag me from you, darling.'

'It better,' she breathes.

Her dagger hangs loosely from the hand she's twined around my neck. Odd, that there was once a time I feared her burying it into my back. Now I readily bare my weaknesses before her.

It's as though she is whole again in my arms, reunited with the ghost of her father and held in the arms of her Enforcer. And when she kisses me, long and fierce, I realize how happily I'd live the rest of my life at the end of a blade. So long as she is the one holding it.

115

CHAPTER 15

Paedyn

I step in time to the steady beat of my heart.

Sunlight streams through the worn buildings, following me like a spotlight across the crowded street. The familiar dagger strapped to my thigh is a comfort I cling to, along with the memory of his hands fastening it there.

'Impress me today, darling,' he had whispered, kneeling before me. The words were so similar to the ones I had uttered after we sparred for the first time. And with his hands gripping my thigh, gray eyes meeting mine through dark lashes, I realized, terrifyingly, that I would do anything to earn his praise. Least of all, survive this Trial.

So I keep my head high, even as hundreds of eyes scrutinize every inch of me. The entourage of Imperials leading me through the city do nothing to quiet the occasional shouts as I pass. And if it weren't for the king walking beside me, I'm quite sure there would be nothing but curses flying from the mouths surrounding me.

I lean towards Kitt, though my gaze never leaves the broad shoulders of the Enforcer a few paces in front of me. 'So, I'll be in the Scorches.' I say this flatly, knowing we are heading east through the city.

The shoulder he shrugs brushes against mine. 'Sort of.'

My eyes flick to him, confusion crinkling my brow. The movement has a bead of sweat rolling down my temple, forcing my focus to how insufferably hot I already am. My dark pants are tight against my legs, tunic slicked with sweat beneath the blistering sun.

A small crowd has gathered behind us, trailing our steps to the city's edge. The hope that they will witness my death firsthand keeps them marching on in the heat. I almost admire their devoted detestation for me.

By the time we halt at the outskirts of the city, it's not the warmth that has my palms slicking with sweat. My heart pounds as I take in the vast expanse of desert sprawled before me. I barely survived that sea of sand last time I dared to cross it.

And if that is the bravery this Trial is testing, I'm not sure I can muster the strength to do it again. Terror hugs me tightly as I await my inevitable return to another set of Trials. I have yet to fully address the abundance of lingering pain and fear that accompanied the last ones I endured.

As if hearing my racing thoughts, Kitt turns to face the expectant crowd. A familiar face stands beside the king with a hand on his shoulder. Tealah uses her Amplifier ability to project his voice down the street, just as she had done during each Purging Trials interview. 'Today, Paedyn Gray will be tested for her bravery – the first of the three *B*'s my father ruled this kingdom by. Once the Trials are completed, you – people of Ilya – will accept her as your queen.'

I have never felt so many gazes sweep over me. Their silent scrutiny has my skin crawling, but I force myself not to turn away. 'As you all know,' Kitt continues, 'the first queen of Ilya was laid to rest in the Sanctuary of Souls when the barren land was intended as a burial ground for royals. Today, Paedyn's Trial will consist of retrieving her crown from the crypt she is buried in.'

Breath catches in my dry throat.

When Kai's eyes find mine for a brief moment, I know he is thinking of the time we spent together on that dangerous road. He had told me how the first queen was buried there before the bandits claimed the land as their own. Now she lies all alone, her only

117

company those who hope to steal from her grave.

'Bandits have wished to find her crown for decades,' Kitt adds, 'but even they have been scared away from the crypt for reasons that are unknown.' His eyes slowly find mine, brimming with encouragement despite his next words. 'This is truly a test of bravery. First, she will cut through the Scorches before finding the crypt within the Sanctuary of Souls. To retrieve the crown, Paedyn will be met with all manner of danger. Worst of all, her mind will likely conjure up fears all on its own.'

I take a deep breath, trying to pretend as though that wasn't absurdly ominous. And to conclude his comforting speech, Kitt adds, 'If the crown is presented to the court before midnight, Paedyn Gray will pass this first Trial. If she does not, however . . .' He scans the crowd, expression unreadable. 'She is not fit to be your queen.'

I barely spare a glance at the nodding crowd before turning towards the awaiting Scorches. His words have an icy anger spreading through me, cooling my sticky skin. This Trial proves nothing of my ability to rule a kingdom, and he knows it. But to be an Ordinary is to prove myself in ways that even Elites cannot.

It's not the Trials themselves I fear – it's what they will take from me. What will I be forced to survive this time? The breaking of my will? The flickering of that light within me?

My heart pounds in muffled ears.

If I return from these Trials, it will be as less of myself. I'm running out of loved ones to watch die in my arms, so perhaps it will be me this time around. And maybe it's better that way – to die before this life steals the warmth Adena sewed into my soul.

This kingdom has done its best to set me up for death. Or worse – failure.

So when Kitt offers a slight nod of his head, and Kai a familiar twitch of his lips, I set off into the desert.

My boots shift in the sand, reminding me of the torturous days spent trekking through it. Voices grow more distant with each step, but every gaze on my back is just as tangible as the sun beating down on it. I've only just begun my diagonal path through the Scorches, and yet, my body feels heavy. It betrays me with each step, as though my very legs ache to carry me away from this place.

Perhaps the fear began the moment I stepped onto this sand.

But it was not bravery that brought me back out here. It was necessity. Hope.

Sweat slicks my neck, trickling down my back. Attempting to pull up my hair into a strap, I quickly discover that only half of the short strands will stay tucked in the knot.

With a frustrated huff, I squint in the blinding sun and fix my attention on the cluster of rocks far ahead. I have to fight the absurd urge to smile at the memory of running past those stones and into the field of poppies beyond, Kai nipping at my heels. He was my enemy then, and yet, we had never been closer.

I turn, shielding my eyes, to see a familiar figure watching me from the edge of the city. Now, the Enforcer is something far more devastating than a lover, yet we have never been further apart. Keeping my distance from him is a Trial of its own.

It is cruel, not being able to call him mine after everything we've endured.

Perhaps in another life, I am strong enough to never need proof of it. Perhaps in another life, I am brave enough to confess that I love him. Perhaps in another life, I learn to love him from afar. And that is the most fearless thing of them all.

So I look away, letting my feet carry me even farther from him.

CHAPTER 16

Paedyn

My throat is dry, tasting of déjà vu.

With every shuffling step I take, history repeats itself. Yet again, here I am — sand slipping into my boots and sun stinging my skin. At least this time, the end is in sight.

I trudge towards the rocky path, desperately wishing this Trial took place in the welcoming field of poppies beside it. The sun has tiptoed across the sky, sneaking up on the horizon. Not only have I been tasked with finding the first queen's coveted crown, but I'm also racing against time itself.

I pick up my sluggish pace, spinning the steel ring around my thumb.

If Father could see me now . . .

A pang of my heart hits me hard in the chest. Not the typical sadness that seizes me when I think of him and the death he met, but the type of hurt that tends to accompany truth. Because he's not my father.

The words sound cruel, even from where they echo in my skull. And in most ways, it's unfair of me to think that. I have been unwanted in this kingdom from the moment I was born. But not to

the man who found me on his doorstep after losing a wife and child of his own. I became his everything. And maybe that is all you need to earn the title of 'father'.

It's only when gravel crunches beneath my boots that I realize I've stepped into the Sanctuary of Souls. Clearing my thoughts and gathering my vigilance, I head down the wide path that eventually leads to Dor. My pace quickens without the sand to slow me, leaving a wall of stones on each side.

The sheath strapped to my thigh has grown hot in the sun, but habit has me resting a hand on the hilt of my dagger. It's eerily quiet on the stony path, putting me on edge. Bandits have claimed this land, stolen it from the souls themselves. And I know firsthand how cutthroat they can be.

I scan the towering stones beside me, looking for any sign of movement. Worry quickly creeps its way into my thoughts, doubt following soon after. I haven't the slightest idea which cave hidden among the rocks contains the lonely queen within it. 'So I'll have to search all of them,' I mutter under my breath.

The sun has dipped behind a cluster of looming boulders, and I'm left oddly cold without its consistent comfort. My tired gaze stumbles over the sight of a cave to my left. Pace quickening, I head for the gaping entrance.

I'm swallowed in darkness after several slow steps beneath the arching stone. My hands grope for the wall, palms flat against cool rock in an attempt to guide. Jagged creases of stone slice at my skin to spring blood from thin cuts.

I bite my tongue against the stinging pain and accompanying stickiness that now coats my palm. Forcing myself to focus on feeling what I cannot see, I drop to my knees. My hands roam over the cold floor of the cave, searching for any sort of clue.

'What the hell am I doing?' I whisper, already losing my patience. Father may have trained me to be hyper observant, but the key to my 'psychic' ability is sight. And that is precisely what I am missing at the moment.

As I crawl farther into the cave, darkness weighs down on me like a smothering blanket. I blink, unable to fathom the nothingness in front of me. After several minutes of fumbling fingers, panting breaths, and nothing to show for it, I turn and head for the ring of light at the tunnel's opening.

I stumble out of the cave, nearly blinded by the setting sunlight. Sucking in a deep breath, I rest shaking hands on my knees. It is only then that I allow myself to acknowledge how terrified I had been. The absence of light is the absence of knowledge. I have no idea what it is that awaits me in these caves, and that is a foolishness I fear.

Squeezing my eyes shut, I take a deep breath, willing myself to calm. After a long, steadying moment, I set off again down the path. My mind races to conjure up a plan that helps me see within the caves. But I hardly have the time to build a fire, let alone scrounge up the wood for it. I shake my head at nothing but my circumstance, angered that the only tool at my disposal is a dagger.

Again and again, I've been set up for failure.

It is that bitter thought alone that has me charging into the next cave.

This one is taller, allowing me to maintain my straight spine as I step farther into the blackness. With one hand dragging along the wall beside me, I extend the other in the hopes of finding—

My palm collides with a stubbornly solid wall.

I let out a grunt of pain, shaking out my wrist. With an aching hand, I search the slab of stone before concluding that I've truly met a dead end. I can't say I'm not thrilled to be leaving the cave, but when I'm bathed in sunlight once again, it's a struggle to force my feet down the path.

The next two caves I venture into follow the same disappointing routine. I stumble inside, run my hands along the walls and floors, panic in the small space, and eventually give up to scramble back towards the rapidly setting sun.

Now I stand at the mouth of the next taunting cave, mustering my courage. A golden ray stretches across the stone floor, as though the sun itself is pointing a finger. I follow the beam's path, my heart stuttering at what lies glinting within it.

I drop to my knees beside the scattered silver strands, eyes wide as I take in the pieces of a girl I left behind. Blood coats each sliver of severed hair, dulling the silver braid beneath. Tears prick my eyes for the version of me that still lingers in this cave where Kai held the broken shards of me together.

So much hurt had lived within the strands of something so unsuspecting. And when I could no longer handle the weight of blood coating my hair, my very body and being, I begged my captor to free me of it.

The one person meant to be my undoing saved me from it.

I gather the scattered pieces, ignoring the feel of dried blood that paints them. It feels symbolic in a way, like gripping a tangible moment in time. My gaze lifts to the small cave curved around me. The crypt is not here, but it feels like a tomb, nonetheless.

I gently lay the long pieces of my past self back onto the stone floor, leaving them to rest.

The sun has abandoned me for the night.

I squint in the growing shadows, only to be met with the yawning darkness of a cave before me. A shiver skitters down my spine when I take a step inside. My eyes widen in a futile attempt to see while my hands reach for something solid in this place of nothingness.

My palms find a wall, and I cling to it with each shaking step. The sound of my quick breaths echoes around me, accompanied only by the pounding of my heart.

This cave feels different. Unwelcoming. Occupied.

My mind reels, picturing every menacing thing that could be a single step away. Trying to calm my unhelpful thoughts, I crouch to the floor. But it's not stone I find beneath my palms, but packed dirt. I suck in a surprised breath, feeling hope bloom in my chest.

This could be it.

I continue my slow crawl, hands dragging through the dirt in front of me. The air is thick and damp in my lungs as I force myself deeper into the cave. Reaching to my right, I find the wall now far closer than it had been when I entered. Panic swells in my chest as I turn to my left, nearly cracking my skull against the rock.

It's as though the stone is shrinking in on me.

My breaths grow shallow in the narrow place. All I can feel is the grimy dirt clinging to my hands and knees, see nothing but a thick blackness blanketing my eyes. I hear nothing but my thundering heart and—

A soft squeak echoes above me.

My breath catches. My body stills.

Something rustles over my head, forcing me to clamp a dirty hand over my mouth to keep from making a sound. My whole body shakes in anticipation of meeting what it is that dwells in this cave with me. I can't move freely in the cramped space, and that alone terrifies me into stillness.

A flutter of wings sounds beside my head. I jerk away instinctually, slamming the side of my temple against a jagged wall. The dirty palm pressed to my mouth falls away as I let out a yelp of pain.

I feel the first bead of blood roll down my face when all hell breaks loose above me.

A symphony of screeches echoes off the walls. I feel dazed, unable to determine up from down or fear from confusion. My head aches as a flurry of wings rain down on my crumpled frame.

I think I may be screaming.

Bats – hundreds of them. The creatures rush past me, claws tearing at my skin from the ends of leathery wings that beat against my body. They feel far larger than they should be, pelting me persistently with a strength I doubted they could possess.

Amid the terror and chaos, I manage to pull my dagger from its sheath. My palms are sweaty, eyes squeezed shut in the already smothering darkness. The scream that rips from my throat is rabid, the accompanying swipe of my dagger even more so. I slice wildly through the air, managing to hit several of the bloodthirsty beasts. Their screeches mingle with the pounding heartbeat in my ears.

Fear and pain course through me to create a daunting concoction of desperation. I can see nothing, but I feel the demons that dwell in this darkness. They swarm around me as I blindly brandish my blade. Countless cuts sting my skin, blood bubbling to the surface with nauseating quickness.

Another bat meets the wrath of my dagger and careens to the ground with a soft thud. I don't know what to do, or how to breathe, or if I ever will again. Terror grips me tightly, squeezing tears from my eyes and screams from my throat until—

They dart past my head.

Like a gust of wind, there one moment and gone the next, the swarm of bats rush out of the cave. I'm panting, turning towards the mouth of the tunnel as I tuck my dagger back into its sheath. I can barely make out the outlines of their huge bodies as they fly into the night.

With palms pressed into the dirt behind me, I shuffle back several feet, attempting to put distance between me and the creatures beyond the cave's mouth. The night sky awaiting me looks bright compared to the darkness within this swallowing stone. My eyes strain, body scrambling back, back, back—

The dirt caves in beneath me.

Wood snaps loudly before my scream drowns out the sound. I fall through what feels to be a decaying trapdoor, arms flailing as clumps of dirt and splintering pieces of wood plummet with me.

My back slams against something solid, my head following shortly after. I groan, unable to stop my body from rolling off the object and onto the ground beside it. Cool stone meets my cheek as I lie there on my aching ribs, panting and numb with pain.

My palms press into the uneven rock as I struggle to lift myself into a sitting position. Blood leaks from the many slices I've earned, making me acutely aware of each sticky path staining my skin. I lean against the large something I fell onto, back aching nearly as much as my head.

I open my eyes and—

No, my eyes are open. They have been this whole time.

Now they dart around the darkness, wide with panic. The blackness that stares back is so thick that I thought it belonged to the back of my eyelids. For a single, blissful moment, I had forgotten the fear that gripped me. Forgotten how suffocatingly *dark* it is.

This is the complete and utter absence of light. And for all I know, the presence of something far more terrifying.

I scramble to my feet, fear spurring my aching body into action. My hands fumble blindly, hoping to collide with that solid something in the center of this cavern. Empty air slips between my shaking fingers.

I'm panting now, claustrophobic in this space I cannot see.

I don't remember falling far, but with my head throbbing this persistently, I'm not sure what to think. With a trembling step, I manage to stumble into that large expanse of what I now realize to be smooth wood. My hands flatten atop it to steady myself, but slow recognition has them running down the long length of it.

Head spinning and palms sweating, I feel each intricate groove of wood outlining the rectangle box.

My heart stutters in my chest, breath catching in my throat.

It's a coffin.

It's *her* coffin.

The first queen, Mareena of Dor, lies beside me.

I've found the crypt – fallen into it, really – and I am very much not alone. A chill skitters down my spine at the thought, feeling a sudden eeriness twine around my stiff body. The shadows seem to slither around me, like a snake assessing its prey before choking the life from it. I now understand why the bandits never dared look for her – they are smart enough not to disturb the dead.

Because Death protects his own.

My hands wander over the coffin, searching for some sort of opening. The lid is latched tightly enough to withstand my shoves against it. Fumbling for my dagger, I manage to wedge the blade beneath its stubborn lid.

Blood trickles from my temple and nearly every patch of exposed skin. My head aches so fiercely that I'm sure my vision would be swimming if given the opportunity to see a damn thing. Mustering what is left of my strength, I push down on the hilt of my dagger until a loud crack echoes through the crypt.

I've just broken into the queen's coffin.

I stand there for a long moment, gripped with terror and the anticipation of something even worse. But it is only my own quivering breaths that fill the space as I curl trembling hands around the lid and throw the creaking wood open.

I shut my eyes, as if to convince myself that this stifling darkness is my choice. As if I have control over this petrifying situation.

Splayed, shaking fingers reach for what lies before me.

I know what I'll find within the cushioned box. So when my skin brushes against the cold length of a bone, it's not shock that has me gasping. It's regret.

This was a human. This was a woman who lived and loved and was left to rot. The dead deserve more than respect from the living. They deserve peace. And I've disturbed her rest to steal what rightfully belongs to her.

Something eerily vast fills the space behind me, chilling enough to pebble bare flesh. I've never felt Death so tangibly, and yet, I recognize his presence all the same. The cold breath on my neck can only belong to the Death I have nearly met so many times before.

Terror sinks its teeth into my very soul.

I need to get out of here. But not without that crown.

Panicking, I run my hands up what is left of the once-beautiful queen. Decaying bones flake beneath my swift fingers and crumble against my touch. I choke on my next breath, forcing my hands to climb higher still.

Pelvis. Spine. Ribs.

It's been decades since the body was placed in this crypt, and now there is nothing left of her. The very essence of what she once was crumbles in my hands, fragile in death. My fingers meet her skull, fractured and caved in with the weight of time. I bite my tongue and continue up, up, up—

Something cold meets the tips of my fingers.

I can just make out the raised jewels and jagged points beneath the caking of dirt.

A smile pulls at my cracked lips. I may not be able to see what it is I've found, but I know this symbol of power by feel alone.

With a steadying breath, I pull that coveted crown from the queen's body.

CHAPTER 17

Rai

𝕴 would have stood at the edge of that desert until she walked back into my arms.

That is, if I weren't the damn Enforcer of Ilya.

I pace atop the familiar path I've worn into the carpet. My desk sits to the right, patiently waiting to be relieved of the piled paperwork decorating its chipped wood. Guard rotations, training schedules, and safety precautions beg for my attention, but only one thing holds it – her.

I have thought of nothing else since watching Paedyn stride into that sinister stretch of sand. Hair glinting like a blade and legs swift like one who's spent their whole life running, the Silver Savior began her first Trial. And I stood there, watching her form slowly shrink into the horizon.

It was Kitt's insistence that had me reluctantly returning to the castle. He needed me to 'be the Enforcer, even when she is not around.' The words had stunned me for a moment, had me glimpsing that suspicion Pae spoke of. Perhaps the king really does know how tragically in love I am with his betrothed. Perhaps he is as well.

We haven't spoken since our journey back to the castle – him

returning quietly to his study, and me to the training yard. Only after hours of shouted corrections and tedious demonstrations, I find myself pacing the weathered carpet blanketing my bedchamber. She has less than three hours to walk into the throne room with that crown in hand. And some selfish part of me hopes that she won't.

As if that were a solution.

'If I don't marry her, I have no choice but to kill her.'

Kitt's words haunt my thoughts, dash my hopes. Because if Paedyn fails any of these Trials, her fate will be worse than marriage. It will be death.

As much as I want her to be mine, I want her to be Death's far less.

I rake a hand through my hair, feet still treading their familiar path across the carpet. I've never felt so completely useless. Every fiber of my being begs to find hers, despite duty trapping me within these castle walls. Though, it's comforting to know that she doesn't need my help — the Silver Savior has made that abundantly clear since the day she earned the title.

And yet, one day I hope she does. Just to show her the extent of what I'm willing to do if only she asks.

Unable to pace my bedroom any longer, I throw open the door and stride out into the dim hallway. Imperials don't hesitate to move out of my path, skittering servants doing the same. My steps quicken and faces blur as I pass. The plush carpet beneath my shoes is something I had never taken the time to notice until Adena — Paedyn's other half — had brought it to my attention before that final Trial ball. And with each step towards the west tower, I focus on the feel of it to distract from my reeling thoughts.

My quick pace through the castle has each dark hall slipping swiftly past. I'm draped comfortably in shadows until a puddle of light laps at my shoes, rippling around my faltering steps. It pours from beneath a door that hasn't been opened in years. At least, not by anyone other than Father.

I reach hesitantly for the handle, feeling suddenly like a disobeying child. I've spent my whole life avoiding this room due to the king's orders. But he is not here anymore to punish me for my defiance.

The door creaks open on hinges unaccustomed to serving their purpose. A lamp spills dull light into the room, old enough to have the Volt power slowly flickering from it. I sweep my gaze over the preserved chamber, landing on a tarp-covered bed adorned with royalty. Kitt sits stiffly on the dusty sheet with a jewelry box clutched between inky fingers.

His tired gaze flicks to mine, only slightly surprised to see me standing uncomfortably in the doorway. 'It's weird, being in here, huh? After all those years of wondering what was behind that door.' Setting the wooden box aside, he stands with a pained laugh. 'All that waiting, just for it to be a regular old bedroom.'

I feel oddly trapped beneath the doorframe. It seems wrong to step into a piece of a past that doesn't belong to me. Iris Moyra was Kitt's mother, not mine. And I alone have known just how desperately he wished to know her, even at a glimpse.

'Father shouldn't have kept this from you,' I say quietly.

'Among other things. But he knew he could, because I would always come back to him.' His gaze grows distant. 'Always obey.'

I slip my hands into the pockets at my sides. 'So, what changed?'

He contemplates this for a moment. 'Power. When you have nothing, you live only for those who promise you everything.'

'You lived for Father,' I reiterate.

'Now I live for legacy.' He smiles. 'For us.'

I dip my head, offering the pale carpet my grin. 'I can't say it isn't nice to serve a king that actually gives a shit about me.'

'You're my little brother,' Kitt teases. 'I've been forced to give a shit about you my whole life.'

I chuckle softly. 'Sorry to be an inconvenience.'

He shrugs. 'It was pretty annoying when you started being able to kick my ass.'

'Well, you should be used to it by now.'

'Easy, Brother.' Kitt's boyish grin has returned to his face after far too long. 'Let's not start a brawl in the one room we haven't yet.'

I let this moment soak in, relishing every laugh that passes between us. Alone with him, I don't think of the future ahead, or the ring wrapped around Paedyn's finger. And I'm grateful for that. Grateful to just be brothers.

'I'll leave you to your thoughts,' I say after a long while of talking like we used to. 'I didn't mean to interrupt. Just saw the light under the door and figured I'd check it out.'

'Nothing special, huh?' Kitt muses.

My expression softens. 'It is for you.'

He nods, thanking me for my understanding. I nod back.

The door screeches shut, leaving my brother alone with what is left of the mother he never knew.

It's not long before I'm making my way up the spiral staircase of the west tower. I remember a time when a trip to the rickety turret felt hopeful. Now, my heart pounds faster with each step higher. The air grows cold and damp in a way I've now come to associate with the presence of Death.

I swore to never set foot in the infirmary again.

Though, I've been here several times since making that vow. And each time I stare blankly at the wooden door atop the stairs, allowing myself a split second of hesitation before pushing it open and stepping into the large room behind.

It looks exactly as it had the day Ava died.

Cots line the walls, though my gaze avoids one in particular. The room is just as plain and dreary as it had been all those years ago. Heading for the only occupied bed, I nod at the Healer who hurries past, more than happy to give us some privacy in exchange for a moment beyond this dreary tower.

I walk towards my mother slowly, taking in the dark circles below her eyes and the frail shoulders peeking above crisp covers. My throat tightens at the sight. She looks worse than when I last left her.

'My sweet boy.' Her tired eyes brighten when they land on me. 'You're home. I was so worried.'

A wave of guilt hits me in the gut like a blow. 'I should have come to see you sooner.' I take a seat in the chair beside her. 'These past few days have been . . . difficult.'

The look she gives cuts right through me. 'I know that. But you can also admit how hard it is for you to be up here. See the cot she used to occupy.' Mother glances around the infirmary, gaze haunted. 'I understand your pain.'

I duck my head. Of course, she understands. It was her daughter she grieved.

'I thought I was broken after losing Ava,' she continues softly. 'But it seems that the loss of your father will be the death of me.'

My teeth grind together at her words and every one I wish to say in return. I could never imagine Father deserving more of my grief than Ava. And when I look at my mother in this moment, I'm angry that she ever let her daughter be a secret – die a secret.

But I say none of this to the woman on her deathbed.

I study her pale face and distant gray eyes. 'How are you feeling?'

'Kai, it's not long now,' she says simply.

'Don't talk like that.'

'Bury me as close to him as possible.'

'Mother, please—'

'I want to reach out and grab his hand.'

At those whispered words, it's I who grabs her hand, pulling it close to my chest. 'You will be close to him. I promise.' Swallowing, I add, 'But that won't be for a long while.'

She shakes her head with a sad smile. 'I'll miss you, my pretty boy. Keep taking care of Kitt for me.' Her dark lashes flutter. 'I regret not being there for him.'

'It's not your fault,' I murmur. 'Kitt has always been . . . stubborn when it comes to you.'

'Because I'm not really his mother.' A long pause. 'I know.'

I squeeze her hand. 'He loves you. I know he does.'

'In his own way, yes. He even came to visit me while you were gone on your mission.'

'He mentioned that,' I say softly.

'It was brief.' Her bottom lip trembles slightly. It's a sight I never thought I'd see from a woman of such power and grace. 'Kitt misses him dearly.'

'I know,' I whisper, because I do. I know exactly how much Father's death affected my brother, even when he didn't wish to show it. 'Have you heard about what is happening in the kingdom?'

'Yes,' she says evenly. 'Your father always was more occupied with the Ordinaries than the affairs of Ilya.'

I wait patiently for an elaboration worth the trouble Father left for Kitt. But she says nothing more on the matter, which is unsurprisingly disappointing. Queen Myla was nothing if not loyal and loving towards her husband, though she has told the occasional story of the days in which she once despised her king. These moments of reminiscence were only prompted by several cups of wine and told with hazy memory. But even now, Mother refuses to speak ill of the man she loved.

It's stubbornly admirable.

'And Paedyn?' I ask slowly. 'You know of his engagement to the Ordinary?'

'The Ordinary,' she muses, gaze sharp. 'That is not all she is. Especially to you.'

I drop her hand, securing a mask of indifference onto my face despite the quickening beat of my heart. 'I don't know what you've heard, but—'

'Oh, don't go denying it, Kai.' Her laugh morphs into a harsh cough. I reach for the glass of water atop the bedside table. Pressing it to her cracked lips, she swallows greedily before managing, 'I knew from that first dinner – the one with all the Purging Trial contestants – that there was something between you two.'

I blow out a breath. 'Mother—'

'And then she went and killed your father, and things got complicated.'

She says this so bluntly that I nearly laugh. After another dry cough, she adds, 'Though, that might not have been enough for you to hate her. I know how you felt about him.'

'He never really was much of a father to me,' I state. 'So, no, I can't say I was terribly grieved by his death.'

The words are harsh and laced with an anger I rarely let myself feel for him anymore. But it is his wife I spit them at. And for that reason, I open my mouth to apologize.

Instead, her hand grips mine, gaze pleading. 'I'm sorry for what he did to you. And I'm sorry that I never stopped him.' Tears brim beneath the gray eyes we share. 'I just wanted you to be strong. And look at you – you're formidable. But that is no excuse. I shouldn't have stayed quiet about your training sessions with him—'

'Shh.' I cut off her words with the single sound. 'It's okay. You made me strong.' A tear rolls down her cheek, and I wipe it away with a knuckle. 'You made me strong,' I whisper again.

Equal parts sob and laughter slips past her lips. 'Not strong enough to stay away from her, it seems.'

I shake my head, smiling slightly. 'No, not strong enough to stay away from her.'

'Kai,' she murmurs, suddenly serious. 'She is your brother's.'

I look away. 'I know.'

'Don't let her come between the two of you.' Her tone is stern. 'Promise me, Kai.'

A shake of my head. 'It's a little late to be making that promise, Mother.'

'Then make me a different one.' She struggles to lift her head from the pillow, words strong in a way her body is not. 'Don't let her be your weakness.'

Some time later, when I eventually stand to leave the infirmary, she reminds me of that promise I have yet to make.

In return, I remind her that Paedyn Gray has been my weakness since that very first dinner before the Purging Trials.

CHAPTER 18

Paedyn

I'm teetering atop the coffin.

The dirty crown rests in the crook of my elbow, sliding to my shoulder when I lift my arms again. I reach up into the darkness, desperate to find the hole I'd fallen through. The wooden lid caves beneath my weight, having nothing better to do than rot after decades spent in this crypt.

My head pounds, and the blood oozing from my body is only aiding the dizziness. Only the promise of moonlight on my skin has me pushing through every bit of pain. And when my fingers brush a jagged piece of wood dangling above, I nearly laugh in relief.

Hands searching blindly, I manage to find what feels like the remaining frame of the trapdoor. With a deep breath, I curl my bleeding fingers around the wooden lip and tug. This time, I do let out a hysterical laugh when it holds. I don't bother testing its strength again before pulling myself upward with a grunt.

Two things happen within the span of a single moment. The first being that my head collides with a splintered piece of what used to be the trapdoor above. After letting out a gasp of pain and surprise, the second thing follows soon after.

I have the eeriest feeling that I am no longer alone.

A sudden chill pebbles my skin as I drag myself up onto the cave floor. I haven't even taken a full breath before I'm scrambling to my feet and heading for the splotch of night sky beyond the tunnel.

An icy sort of fear grips me at the thought of what it is I may have just done. The crown around my arm grows heavy, as if being pulled back to its owner. A panicked sound finds its way out of me at the thought. The dead are not meant to be disturbed. And I may have awakened something that no one else has dared to.

I shake my head at the absurdity of it all. 'Mind tricks,' I whisper, stumbling forward. 'This is all in my head.'

As the mouth of the cave grows closer, I find myself looking over my shoulder and into the yawning darkness behind. It is all-consuming, that lightless expanse. And I am nearly petrified by it.

I force myself to turn back towards that awaiting night and push on. Blood spills into my eye, demanding I use the back of my filthy hand to wipe it from my vision. That swarm of oversized bats has thoroughly torn open my skin and left claw-shaped slivers to decorate my body in their absence.

Beyond, the starry sky awaits me, mere steps away. My pace quickens, heart racing in anticipation of my reunion with the night. I brace a hand against the wall, feel the last stretch of cold stone before—

Shadows slither across the ground, lapping at my feet.

Three figures step into the entrance of the cave, blocking me from freedom. Moonlight illuminates their backs to outline their broad figures. I take a slow step back, swallowing a scream of fear and frustration.

Bandits.

'Thanks for getting that crown for us. Now hand it over,' one of them grumbles, voice like gravel beneath the bandanna covering his mouth. 'And if you're quick about it, we might not even take that shiny ring from your finger.'

My wounds ache, but I force myself to muster whatever strength I have left. Fingers flexing at my side, I focus on the feel of my dagger while mapping out my next moves. Only when I've gathered every bit of brutality that lurks within me, I speak. My voice is scared and small, and if the men bothered to listen closely, they might just hear the danger lacing it. 'Take it all – I don't care. Just . . . just please don't hurt me.'

I extend my hand, presenting the ring to them. The dirty diamond glints enticingly enough to have a man stepping forward. I can practically feel the sly grin beneath his bandanna as he reaches for my hand, intent on pulling the band from my finger.

I calm my mind. Shut out my soft heart. And stain my soul once again.

My fingers close around the man's wrist before I'm pulling him into the awaiting dagger now gripped tightly in my other hand. The blade sinks into his stomach with a sickening sound. Blood pours from the wound as the bandit grunts weakly.

I ignore the dull ache in my chest. This is precisely what I feared – myself.

Adena's light within me sputters out.

Pulling the dagger from his gut, I watch him fall to my feet.

I stand over the dying body, chest heaving and hand bloody. The men gawk as I slip the crown off my arm to clutch it in my fist. My voice is ragged, hand beckoning in challenge. 'If you want this, come and take it.'

The larger of the two remaining men charges at me, seemingly awakened from his stupor. He swings a massive arm that I easily duck under. After spending so much time in complete darkness, my eyes seem suddenly sharper than before. Crown in hand, I stand to my full height before sending its pointed jewels careening towards his skull.

He yelps as blood gushes from his temple, stumbling back to let the final man have a go at me. I dance on the balls of my feet, ignoring every wince of pain at the movement. When the last bandit pulls a long dagger from his belt, I let the crown clatter to the cave floor, tightening my hold on the hilt of my own weapon.

He lunges, blade flashing. I manage to rotate my body before he can stab me in the chest, but the sudden, searing pain shooting from my shoulder tells me I wasn't fast enough. He swipes at me again, forcing my feet farther back into the cave. Analyzing each one of his movements, I let him jab at me again. Arm extended and chest open, he's made himself an easy target.

Holding my dagger by its blade, I cock my arm and let the weapon fly. It pierces his chest, has him staggering back before eventually slumping against the cave wall. I watch his body slide down the stone, staining it with a streak of scarlet.

I blink at the two bodies sprawled before me. Blink again when a very much alive one comes barreling towards me. Blood runs down his face from the gash I'd given him with a century-old crown. I don't have the chance to move my leaden feet before large arms are wrapped around my middle.

He shoves me against the wall, my skull meeting stone. Spots swim before my eyes to blot out what little vision I have. My cry of pain is weak, the tired body it crawls from unable to muster anything more.

A rough hand has found its way around my throat. Fingers squeeze until I can no longer breathe.

He watches me choke, smiling at the sight. I claw at his hand, kick at his legs. With blurry vision, I find whatever fight is left inside me. Whatever sliver of my soul begs to stay in this life. And with that last wrinkle of resolve, folded deep inside my crumpled being, I drive my knee into his groin.

His hand slips from my throat as he doubles over, allowing me time to slide away from the wall. My own bloody hand closes around the back of his bowed neck. I don't let myself think as I slam his head against the cave wall, again and again.

Blood sprays from the impact, splattering my face in that sickly warmth of another's life. It's animalistic, this need to stay alive, to tear apart anything that stands between me and my next breath. The growl in my throat does not belong to me, nor do the hands that repeatedly sink a skull into stone.

When the red fades from my vision, I let his limp body fall to my feet.

Adena's warmth returns shyly, as though her very memory does not recognize the creature I've become. I'm shaking, every part of me trembling in fear of what I've done. In fear of *myself*.

A sort of numbness creeps over me as I step around the still bodies. The crown sits innocently on the ground, despite some of the gems being coated with blood. It glitters beside the body adorning my dagger. My stomach churns at his vacant gaze, wide with the shock of Death's swift arrival.

I look away before yanking the blade from his chest. And with the crown's sharp points fitted between my fingers, I turn towards my awaiting freedom.

Keeping my gaze forward, I don't dare look down at the stone floor now slicked with blood. Instead, I focus on that starry night, ahead and beckoning. I trip over my own feet in anticipation of the open sky.

Scrambling from the cave's gaping mouth, I fall to my knees on the rocky path. A crazed laugh bubbles out of me as I tilt my head to the sky. Moonbeams stroke my face as a soft breeze tangles my filthy hair. I swipe a hand over my face, smearing mud, blood, and the sticky residue of guilt.

But I'm laughing again, strained yet relieved.

Adena's light, however dim, is returning to my soul.

I am alive. I, an Ordinary, survived a Trial. Again.

My eyes fall to the long path ahead, and the comforting field of poppies beyond. Farther still is the city I'll have to trudge through before marching into the castle, crown in hand. I lift my crazed gaze to the moon, unsure how much time I have before midnight.

With that sense of urgency returning to my weary mind, I force shaking legs to stand beneath me. Soon after, I'm quickening my pace – body sore, but hope swelling.

With every step, I grow closer to becoming a queen.

With every step, I grow closer to a united Ilya.

CHAPTER 19

Rai

My foot taps a steady beat against the marble floor.

Members of the court mill about the throne room, having used the last three hours as an excuse to drink and sloppily trade gossip among themselves. The countdown to midnight has become nothing more than an exclusive party of Elites.

Forgotten goblets of wine litter every flat surface, while others can be found sloshing in the hands of noble men and women. Scanning the room and what obvious boredom fills it, I take a sip of my own wine, savoring the biting sweetness on the back of my tongue. I've been leaning against a towering pillar for more than an hour now, content to stay tucked within the chaos.

After my visit with Mother, I reluctantly joined the court to restlessly await Paedyn's arrival. My wandering gaze continually returns to the large doors at the opposite end of the throne room in the hopes she will stride through them. Because the alternative would mean that something happened to her, and I simply refuse to entertain that spiraling thought.

I will her to walk through those doors. If not for this kingdom, then for me. I need her to come back to *me*. She is willingly my

weakness, and yet, nothing has ever made me stronger. And I fear what I will become if—

'You've been staring at the doors since you got here.'

I turn to face a grinning Jax, his hands shoved into the pockets of too-short pants. 'Not the whole time,' I state smoothly. 'I've managed to catch you sneaking sips of wine from Andy's glass.'

His grin shifts, suddenly sheepish. 'I don't know what you're talking about.'

I cross fidgeting arms over my chest, chuckling. 'Really? Why don't you go ahead and walk in a straight line for me, then?'

The mere question has him swaying on his feet. 'Because . . . maybe I don't want to.' He leans against the pillar in a comical attempt at nonchalance .

'At least one of us is having a good time.' I sigh out the words, my gaze straying back to the doors.

'I could finish that for you,' Jax says, pointing to the cup in my hand. 'I mean, if you're not going to . . .'

I tilt my head against the cool marble. 'What the hell,' I mumble, handing the goblet to him. 'It's not doing me any good—' He's tipped his head back, greedily gulping the wine despite a ribbon of it dribbling down his chin to stain the dark skin beneath.

'Easy, J!' It's a struggle not to laugh as I tug the cup from his sticky hands. 'I better not have to carry you out of here tonight.'

He gives me a toothy grin. 'Hey, I've helped Kitt ca—' A hiccup interrupts the word. '. . . carry you from a party more than once.'

I can't exactly argue on behalf of nights I don't remember. So, instead, I settle with a simple, 'If her life weren't at stake right now, I guarantee I'd be much more fun tonight.'

His confused look is only exaggerated by the alcohol that's loosening his features. 'But why are *you* so worried about Paedyn? Isn't that Kitt's job? They're engaged, after all.'

I open my mouth before promptly shutting it.

My gaze travels across the room, skipping between the several circles of gossiping court members. I wonder how many of them whisper the same question. Why does the future Enforcer worry for his brother's betrothed? Is it simply due to loyalty and protection over the king? Or perhaps something far more scandalous?

I suppose the truth leans more towards the latter, but reducing my feelings for Paedyn to something as juvenile as a scandal is absurdity. Only, it does not matter that every beat of my heart belongs to her. Because she does not belong to me.

Turning my attention back towards an awaiting Jax, I open my mouth to spew an answer he likely won't remember in the morning.

That is when the doors swing open.

Everything fades away, forgotten in her presence.

The future queen of Ilya strides into the throne room, and every Elite falls silent. She is covered in dirt, streaked with blood. It freckles her face in a gruesome addition to the twenty-eight ones I know stretch across the bridge of her nose. Large tears in her clothing reveal jagged cuts beneath, softened only by the mud accompanying them.

My eyes trail down the length of her, knowing just how much that blood must be affecting her. It's coating her temple, her shoulder, her hands . . .

Her hands.

There, gripped between scarlet-stained fingers, hangs a crown.

The rest of the court seems to recognize her achievement at the same moment, resulting in a collective gasp that ripples across the room. I push off the pillar, eyes wide as I study the lost relic from afar. A crack crawls up one of the sides where a splotch of blood stains the large gem there. The rest of it remains covered in mud, just like the woman holding it.

Paedyn's piercing gaze travels over the crowd as she watches them take her in. No one dares speak, dares move beneath her commanding stare. But when that blood-splattered face turns in my direction, I nearly smile. This formidability is not unfamiliar to me. I've seen it within her since the moment she saved my life.

Her eyes meet mine, and it feels like relief.

She reflects my sentiment with a slight softening of her expression. But it doesn't last long. It can't — not with this audience.

So I let her go. Let her pretend. Let her morph back into the queen she will become.

All it takes is a single slow nod of my head.

She understands — and meets the king's gaze with a newfound fortitude.

My eyes flick to the dais, seeing something akin to awe settle on Kitt's features, and I can only assume that my expression looks the same. She takes another step into the throne room, pushing aside her pain for the portrayal of what is far more potent — power.

Every wound is on display. She wears them proudly, allowing each pair of eyes to sweep over her. Blood drips from the gash at her temple, staining her hair and spilling a trail of crimson into her eye. With strides never slowing and face unflinching, she wipes at the blood with the back of an already stained hand.

I push slowly through the crowd, my gaze unable to stray from such eminence. But watching isn't nearly enough. I could fall to my knees, beg to be the only one worthy of witnessing her.

Clothes torn and body bloody, she slows before the dais. I shift on my feet, knowing the weight of those piercing eyes now pinned on my brother. Kitt clears his throat, blinking at the scene before him. When he finally finds his voice, it's to declare, 'Ladies and gentlemen of the court, it seems Paedyn Gray has successfully completed her first Trial.'

And with that, Paedyn's lips lift. She raises the crown then, matching its bloody and mud-streaked appearance. I smile before she's even done it. Wide enough to show those damn dimples she loves to hate.

Yes, I smile when she pushes the crown onto her head.

It sits atop her blood-streaked hair, drawing gasps from the gaping court. My breath catches as she stands before the king, every bit his queen-to-be.

With a slight nod to Kitt, she turns slowly towards the court. Her sudden smile catches even me by surprise, the flash of her teeth white against that dirt-streaked face framing it. She inclines her head then, dipping it towards each side of the throne room. The movement is nearly taunting, as if daring any Elite to try to tear the crown from her head. Her gaze is a challenge that travels around the room. But with one final dip of her head, she turns back to Kitt.

He stands, accepting her silent invitation. Stepping from the dais, he offers Paedyn an arm she readily takes. I feel suddenly hollowed out as the happy couple stride down the aisle.

I'm stunned by the sinking bite of bitterness. This shock of envy is quickly swallowed by my resolve, focused only on being rid of this crowd. Seeing her. I push through the shifting bodies, unburdened by the need to be polite.

Murmurs grow into a gentle roar even before the royal couple steps from the throne room. It's difficult to shove against the shocked sea of people now milling mindlessly about. But I'm nearly at the door now and—

A hand tugs at my arm.

I turn to find Andy looking alarmingly serious. 'Don't steal her away from him when they finally get a moment together.'

Unspoken words hang in the air between us. The corner of my mouth twitches. 'I don't need to steal her away.'

'No,' she says smoothly. 'You just kick down her door when she isn't answering you.'

My voice is low. 'Don't start, Andy.'

She shakes her head at me, saddened by what she sees. 'They're engaged, Kai. You can't have her.'

'Yes, and I'll spend the rest of my life trying to accept that fact.'

I turn away and push through the doors.

They are standing in the hallway, bodies close and voices hushed.

Her eyes meet mine over Kitt's shoulder.

I quicken my pace. Smother my jealousy. And open my damn mouth.

CHAPTER 20

Paedyn

The crown grows heavy on my head.

I can't imagine the neck pain royals must endure. Though, it seems I'll find out firsthand.

My arm is pressed tightly within Kitt's, but he doesn't seem to shy away from the blood and dirt I mar his pristine tunic with.

Eyes, so many of them, skimming over my disheveled body.

I've never let myself bleed in front of so many Elites. Never let them see me so weak. And for that reason, I keep my head high and gaze forward.

Pain laces every movement, slows each step. I force my aching body to keep up its charade until I've made it out the doors. My legs shake, barely able to support me after my long trek through the city. But Kitt's arm is a comfort, a disguised source of support that I lean on heavily.

The doors loom, as does the prospect of relief. Every head turns to follow us out of the throne room, and it's only when the countless pairs of eyes are sealed from sight that I slump fully against Kitt.

'Just a little further,' he murmurs, his arm now wrapped around me. 'Let's get you to the wall.'

I let him guide me, and even more difficult, let him see me struggle. His hold is hesitant and hovering, as if unsure how much he wishes to help. It's unfamiliar, his touch. So unlike the claiming feel of his brother's.

The crown slips atop my bloody strands of hair, the ones I'm trying very hard to ignore. Kitt's face ducks towards mine when I slump against the wall. He sounds as unsure as he looks. 'Are you all right?'

I nearly rasp out a laugh. 'You know, I've been better.'

He almost smiles at that. 'You were . . .' He clears his throat, rebuilding that indifferent distance between us. 'You did well in there.'

'I was just trying not to fall on my face,' I pant.

'No need for that.' He glances over my battered form. 'You're wearing enough blood as it is.'

I swallow. 'You have no idea.'

Despite the heavy feel of his gaze roaming my face, I avoid it. Understanding my unspoken desire for a change of topic, he states, 'You retrieved the crown.'

At the mention of it, I happily pull the heavy accessory from my head. 'Here. My body aches enough without this thing trying to snap my neck.'

'Well—' Kitt takes the crown slowly, '—I'm sure you will be used to it soon enough.'

'Right,' I say awkwardly.

Thought of our engagement has his gaze dropping to the ring still clinging to my finger. Emotion flits from ear to ear as he gently lifts my hand. The clearing of his throat turns into a slight cough. 'We will have to get this cleaned.'

He runs a thumb over the muddy diamond. Then his gaze lifts to mine, calculating in a way that surprises me. But his next words are far more startling. 'After that, we'll ensure the ring finds its way back onto the correct finger.'

My heart stutters against bruised ribs.

I look down, eyes snapping to the ring still decorating my right hand. Still exactly where Kai had left it the night before my Trial.

I never put it back.

146

My mouth opens, ready to spew an excuse, spin the truth into something less damning. Kitt has already expressed his concern for my relationship with Kai, and this has all but confirmed it. I can feel the panic that pushes against my blood-splattered face, slowly rearranging my features into something all too incriminating.

That is when my eyes wander over the king's shoulder, as if pulled there by a tether I can't seem to untangle myself from.

A gray gaze locks with mine, and I can read the relief within it at the sight of me. My body trembles; my throat burns. I ache to fall into his arms.

I made it back to him. I lived to spend another day pretending I'm not in love with him.

Kai's long strides carry him towards us to spare me from spewing a lie to the king. Only then does the Enforcer tear his attention from me, pinning it on Kitt. 'The court seems a bit restless, Brother. You might want to go back in there and say a few words.'

One moment, the king's gaze is flicking between the two of us, seeming to piece together our puzzle of pretend. And in the next, he directs cheery words towards his brother. 'Yes, I suppose I should. I'll also announce the ball we'll be hosting tomorrow night in honor of this remarkable achievement.'

I force a smile, though he wasn't speaking to me. 'Thank you. But I'm not sure I'll be up for dancing.'

His gaze meets mine after a long moment. 'I'll have a Healer sent to your rooms.' The shake of my head is interrupted by his stern words. 'Let him help you. That is an order from your king.' With that, he backs away, lifting the crown slightly. 'I look forward to hearing the story behind this. But for now, rest.'

I sag against the wall when he strides back into the throne room.

Kai is on me in an instant. His arm is sure around my waist, breath warm against my ear. 'I've got you. I've got you, Pae.'

I feel willingly weak with him to hold me, as if strength is a facade only needed when he is not near. And it's that realization that has every moment of the Trial flooding back. My eyes fall to the trembling, bloody hands I hold out to him. 'I've . . . I've stained my soul again.'

'Shh.' He grabs my wrists, pressing those bloody palms against his black tunic. 'There. Now it's my soul that is stained.'

I laugh weakly for him, though it sounds more like a sob. Still holding my wrists, he guides those crimson hands around his neck. My eyelids flutter closed when his arms encircle me, warm and comforting. But when my feet leave the ground, they fly open.

'Easy,' he murmurs, hearing the protests I don't say. 'It would be your wedding day before you made it to your rooms.'

My head lolls against his shoulder with each step he takes down the hall. 'I didn't think you would ever speak of my wedding.'

He swallows. 'I thought you might not walk through those doors tonight. And it made me realize that I'd much rather spend the rest of my life apart from you, watching at a distance, than without you.'

I swallow. My throat is dry. 'You shouldn't be doing this. We are supposed to keep our distance. Now more than ever.'

'Yes,' he says simply. 'Which is why I'm selfishly stealing this moment.'

I'm too tired to formulate a response, let alone a coherent thought. He turns a corner, holding me close. I let my eyes wander over his stubbled jaw, over the worry creased between those dark eyebrows. I'm lulled by his even steps, hypnotized by the rhythmic beat of his heart beneath my ear.

'Turn the handle for me, would you, darling?'

I must have dozed off because when I pry open my eyes, we're standing before my bedroom door.

'I'd rather not kick it down this time,' Kai continues. 'No need to give Andy yet another reason to be pissed with me.'

Dropping a heavy hand from his shoulder, I fumble for the knob. As soon as I've managed to twist it, Kai is stepping into the room and alarming a distracted Ellie.

'Oh, Paedyn!' Her voice is as soft as always, though filled with far more concern than I anticipated.

'Do I really look that bad?' I practically croak.

Kai sets me gently on the bed, treating me like I'm as fragile as I feel. His hand cups the back of my neck to ensure my swaying body remains upright on the edge of the mattress. 'You look like someone who has just done the impossible,' he murmurs, face close.

I smile, tasting blood on my cracked lips. 'So I look like hell?'

'If you look like hell,' he whispers with a sly grin, 'then I'm fortunate to be going there.'

My strained laugh is cut short by the sudden movement over his shoulder. Pulling back, I'm reminded, horrifyingly, that we are not alone. At the color staining my cheeks, Kai turns to find Ellie wide-eyed and paralyzed in the center of the room.

Crouching down before me, the Enforcer clears his throat in preparation of the soft command about to spew from it. 'Ellie, get me a pail of warm water and a cloth, please.' He says this as if she hasn't just seen what passed between us mere moments ago. As my maid – I suppose it doesn't matter. But as my friend – I'll have some explaining to do.

She nods curtly, hurrying towards the bathroom as Kai adds, 'Soap, too.'

I sit there awkwardly with his hands now braced on either side of my legs. Our eyes meet, mine concerned and his far too content. I give him a look that I hope screams, *Keep your hands to yourself until she leaves*, which I'm quite certain he understands because it's the complete opposite he does next.

With a smirk that makes me want to simultaneously kiss and hit him, he slides calloused palms down my thighs. My weak warning look doesn't stop his slow search of my legs. I can't help but smile back at him, and he seems to take that as a sign of encouragement.

I'm so distracted by the feel of Kai's hands that I hardly notice Ellie place the pail of water beside him. After setting down a cloth and bar of soap, she straightens with a clearing of her throat.

Kai's eyes are locked on mine. 'That will be all, Ellie. Thank you. I'll let you know when to send in the Healer.'

With a quick curtsy and glance in my direction, Ellie swiftly strides from the room, shutting the door behind her. Turning my attention back on the smirking boy before me, I give his chest a good shove. 'So much for pretending, Prince.'

He dips the cloth into the pail, shrugging at my words. 'I'll have the rest of my life to pretend with you. But for now, I needed to keep you alert.'

'You were distracting me,' I breathe, eyes dropping to the blood coating my hands.

My stained palms are quickly covered by the damp cloth he places over them. 'And I will happily be your distraction from pain. For as long as you need.'

The bar of soap is rough against my hands, but I welcome the discomfort. Kai wipes at the scarlet now swirling atop my skin, leaving the towel stained with the blood of strangers.

I attempt to swallow the emotion clogging my throat. 'It's not the pain I need a distraction from. It's the memory of what I did.'

He threads the cloth between my fingers, ridding my skin of any trace this Trial left behind. 'I know.' His voice is saddened with the weight of understanding. 'It just all starts to feel the same after a while.'

I'm blissfully numb as he guides my hands into the pail of water, letting the warmth wash over them. 'I didn't think I'd walk into that throne room tonight either,' I whisper. 'I was ready to die beside Mareena in that crypt I fell into. I have never been so terrified – and I've spent my whole life in fear.'

He's moved to my arms now, guiding the cloth over every speck of dirt and blood splattered there. 'Pae, we don't have to talk about this now—'

'It was so dark,' I breathe, because part of me desperately wants to be free of what haunts the confines of my mind. 'I've never seen such complete and utter blackness. And the bats . . .'

My visible shudder has Kai placing a comforting hand against the small of my back. I watch him clean every claw mark, every nick the beasts gifted me. When the stained cloth reaches the slash across my shoulder, I hiss in pain. He does his best to mop up the blood surrounding it as he murmurs, 'But you got out. You got the crown. And then you cracked it against a man's skull.' When my eyes flick up, they land on his wry smile. 'I'm assuming.'

I shake my head at him. 'How did you . . . ?'

'You're not the only one who's observant, Little Psychic.'

When his smile only grows, I huff, 'Well, I didn't enjoy doing it.'

'I know.' His gaze softens. 'I wish I could have done it for you.'

My voice is tired, reflecting the current state of my body. 'Does it ever get easier? The bad that supposedly justifies the hope of something good?'

'It hasn't yet,' he says with a sigh. 'But your bad will belong to me when I become your Enforcer. And maybe then, when I know you are reaping the good, things will get easier.'

I shake my head, gaze lingering on the splotch of blood soiling his chest, the place where he had pressed my palms. 'I don't want to stain your soul further.'

His smile is sad. 'There's not much left to stain, darling.'

It takes all of three swipes with the cloth before he's changing the subject. His words hold a certain challenge as he says, 'What about striding across the throne room? Seeing the looks on all those faces when you put that crown on your head?' The gaze he flicks over me is heavy. 'Did you enjoy that?'

'I . . .'

I loved it.

What I settle on instead is 'I didn't mind it.'

He wipes a streak of mud from my jaw, brushing the jagged scar below it. 'Come on, don't be modest, Gray.'

'Fine.' My gaze settles on his. 'Powerful. It made me feel powerful.'

'Good,' he breathes. 'Focus on that feeling. Not what it took to get to it.'

My fingers find his free hand. 'I don't want to gain power if it means I lose myself in the process.'

He wipes the cloth down my nose, freeing it of blood before flicking the tip with his finger. 'Everyone loses themselves to something. So make it worthwhile.'

I let him tilt my head in the dim light. He dabs gently at the bead of dried blood clinging to my temple. 'And what did you lose yourself to?'

'Duty. Loyalty.' His lips quirk. 'A silver-haired pain in the ass.'

I lean back on my palms, studying him. 'And you think that's worth it? Losing yourself to an Ordinary?'

As he drops the cloth from my face, I can't quite read his mixture of emotions. 'Between the two of us, you're the only one who seems to care about that fact.'

I straighten swiftly, enough to have Kai's hands flattening on my thighs to ensure I stay on the bed. 'Of course I care.' My voice is rough, raw with emotion. 'I'm weak. I nearly died today and—' I place a hand to his cheek, turning his face towards me. 'Look at me, Kai. Look at what you chose to lose yourself to. I may have seemed strong in that throne room, but I will always been an impostor among the truly powerful.'

He's shaking his head, hiding his gaze from me. Both of my hands are cupping his face now. 'I worry about you, Malakai.' The sound of his full name has those gray eyes fluttering closed. 'If I die—'

'Stop.'

'If I die,' I repeat sternly, 'I need you to find something else worth losing yourself to. I won't let my impending death be yours as well.' I press my forehead to his, voice breaking as I say, 'Promise me that. Please.'

'Pae.' His voice is ragged. 'I would lose my life for you before finding something else worth living for.' His fingers weave into my hair, slide along the back of my neck. 'You are my inevitable. In life and in death.'

Tears cloud my vision, one of them slipping down my cheek when our mouths meet. He holds me gently, his kiss soft enough to shatter every wall within me. I crumble in his arms. Nothing has ever tasted as sweet as the silent promise on his lips.

You are my inevitable.

The kiss deepens, and with it, a plea with each press of my mouth.

I love you.

I tell him in the sigh he draws from my lips. In every slow caress across his skin. In every pounding beat of the heart that belongs to him.

I love you.

He smells of pine and spice and long nights under the willow.

I love you.

He tastes like a secret I wish to scream; a word on the tip of my tongue that will never be mine to utter. So I say his name instead, as if I could claim him so easily. As if I'm not thinking of three damning words when I say it.

I love you.

152

Edric

E dric's arms are covered in blood.

That should not bother him. He is a king, after all. History itself is bathed in blood, and it is the kings who shed it. He should be indifferent, stony like his father raised him to be.

But this is not some necessary battle or worthless Ordinary. This is . . .

Voices muffle around him, blurring together into one frantic string of words.

The queen is dead.

Iris's lifeless body lies on the bed. Blood stains once-white covers, mars once-warm skin.

Advisers bicker, Healers hover, Fatals stand solemnly beside him.

Edric hears none of it. There is a steady ringing in his ears, and for that, he is thankful.

His wife is dead. The life has been drained from her body by a mere infant, and there was nothing his Healers could do to save her. Now, there is nothing left but a still shell of the woman Edric loved.

Well, that isn't entirely true.

There is a baby girl in his arms.

Her lungs are filled with shrill cries that slip from a small mouth. Again, the king does not mind such a distraction. He shuts bleary eyes, unable to lower them to his daughter below. Only further remnants of his lifeless love lie there.

This child shares her mother's piercing gaze, or rather, stole it. Those eyes belong to Iris, not the infant who killed her.

When the ringing quiets in Edric's ears, and the floor threatens to cave in beneath him, there is only one question the king cares to ask. The child is quickly shoved into his Silencer's arms. 'How much power?'

The three words are born of greed, of an unquenchable ache for strength. Because nothing is more important to Edric than power – not anymore.

The Silencer stutters.

'What is it, Damion?' the king pants.

All eyes fall to the three Fatals under Edric's care. A crease of concentration forms between Damion's brows, followed by a concerning flurry of blinks. He opens his mouth. Shuts it.

'Out with it!'

The king's command rings about the chamber, cutting through even the thick stench of death. It is the anger and grief in his voice that pushes the Silencer to whisper what may be his own death sentence. Kings have a way of killing the messenger.

'She is powerless.'

CHAPTER 21

Paedyn

I flinch at the tingling sensation in my temple.

Not because it's painful to have a wound close beneath the hands of a Healer.

No, it's the familiarity that hurts most.

The feel of my skin stitching back together only reminds me of when it was my father on the other end of that ability. Once, his nimble fingers were the ones to run over every ache and gash earned during my long training sessions. And after he had healed me, or I'd helped him heal another, we would share a butterscotch to celebrate another day survived.

Until he was gone. And now I've forgotten what the sweet tastes like.

I shift on the bed, my body tingling with each pass of the Healer's swift hands. Attempting to distract myself from the familiar feel of it, I stare instead at the late afternoon light spilling through so many surrounding windows. Kai hadn't left my bedroom until the early hours of the morning, leaving me to sleep most of the day away.

He had tried to convince me to see a Healer up until the moment I watched him slip out the door. But I was far too tired to entertain

the idea until this very moment, having stumbled out of the bath in a tremendous amount of pain. And with the ball looming only a handful of hours away, I force myself to endure the ache of being healed by unfamiliar hands.

Ellie bustles around the room, readying herself for the great deal of work that awaits. Having slept so late, I've left her with little time to make my damp hair and raw skin look presentable. I watch her quick movements, unnerved by the fact that we have yet to speak since Kai's late arrival in my rooms.

'You're all set, miss.'

I startle at the man's deep voice beside me. 'Yes, thank you,' I manage to the Healer, adding a quick nod in emphasis. He returns the gesture before making his way out of the room, leaving my healed body behind.

With a sigh of relief, I stand to my feet, stretching out stiff limbs. 'It no longer feels like I nearly died yesterday,' I say cheerily. 'In fact, I think I may actually be in the mood for dancing.'

'Someone seems happy.' Ellie pats the vanity chair with a smile, beckoning me to her.

I sit before her, letting my eyelids flutter shut as she begins powdering my skin. 'I feel good. Hopeful.'

'I'm glad.'

Something about her tone has my eyes snapping open. 'And this good mood has nothing to do with K—' I take a breath. 'With the Enforcer.'

'Mm-hmm,' she hums, lips tucked into a thin smile.

'Ellie, there is nothing going on between me and . . .' I trail off when she shakes her head at me.

'Paedyn, I don't need to know about you and the prince. I just . . .' She chews on her bottom lip. 'I just hope you're being careful. Queens are not as easily forgiven as their kings.'

Her words are a much-needed reminder. My eyes fall on the ring still residing on my right hand – a detail Kitt will not soon forget. The warm bath water has thoroughly cleaned it of the mud, leaving the promise to glint in my lap.

With a deep breath, I slip it onto the correct finger.

Ellie doesn't seem to notice as she continues with that soft smile of hers. 'But I enjoy seeing you giddy like this. It reminds me of Adena and her boy from Loot.'

My whole body stiffens beneath her hand currently dragging a dark line of kohl atop my lashes. 'What are you talking about?'

I hear the hesitance in her voice, the quiet sadness that remains there. 'That's right. She never told you, did she?' She lets the words linger. 'There was this boy she would sneak off to see while you were in the Trials.'

My heart pounds in time with her words, aching like it has since the day Adena died. 'Why . . . why didn't she tell me?'

Ellie pulls back, allowing me to open the eyes now welling with tears. 'She didn't want to distract you from the Trials.' Her lips pull into a thin smile. 'She said you wouldn't rest until you met him and approved. So the plan was to tell you after. But then . . .'

'There was no after,' I whisper, turning away with a shuddering breath. 'She was always too damn selfless.'

We fall silent as Ellie hesitantly returns to the task at hand. After a long while in which I dwell only within my thoughts, I manage to gather enough courage to peek at my reflection. But I don't recognize the girl within it. Her lashes are darkened, her lips tinted the color of blood. She looks like the sharpness that piercing grief hones one into. Like fearlessness carved out of necessity, not courage.

'I want her with me tonight. Adena,' I say quietly, breaking the silence that has long stretched between us.

Ellie nods in understanding and swings open the closet doors.

Silver pools at my feet, cascading down the body above.

Cool air brushes the low dip of my bare back. The dagger strapped to my thigh is more of a comfort than anything, as is the steel ring I spin on my thumb.

So much has changed since the first time I wore this dress. And yet, here I am again, walking towards a ball in honor of the Trials I'm competing in. Only, I've now gained a ring on my hand. Cut the hair falling down my back. Earned more scars I'm ashamed of. Lost the girl who made this very dress for me.

I pull at the elegant shawl around my shoulders, ensuring it covers the O carved above my heart. Thankfully, Ellie hadn't questioned me when I requested to wear the silver wrapping. It ties elegantly beneath my breasts, draping over my shoulders while still covering the maimed skin I wish to hide.

Kitt nods as I approach the closed door to the ballroom. There is no denying how handsome he looks in a black suit. It's perfectly tailored to his body, contrasting against the blond hair and golden crown atop his head.

'You look lovely,' he says evenly.

I smile, trying to warm this frigid indifference between us. 'Thank you, Kitt. You look very handsome.'

He nods his thanks before offering me a stiff arm. I accept it, feeling more than a little awkward as I do. Kitt doesn't waste a moment before tilting his chin towards the Imperials beside us. Understanding his silent request, they begin to open the massive doors.

We wait, loosely joined at the elbows.

The king looks down at our linked arms then, examining the bare fingers that fan around the crook of his elbow. 'I see your ring made it back to the correct hand.'

The doors groan on their hinges. My heartbeat quickens its pace.

I lift my free hand, flashing the diamond at him.

This is the hand Ilya needs this ring to be on. The finger Ordinaries need it to be on.

'Of course,' I say evenly. 'After hiding it from the bandits, I must have slipped it onto the wrong finger in my delirious state.'

The slightest bite in my voice has him studying me curiously until the doors fall open.

'Ready?' he murmurs.

'Not in the slightest.'

And with that, we step out onto the balcony that overlooks the ballroom. Kitt guides me to the railing, our bodies close. A sea of people stand below us, all staring up expectantly. I haven't seen this view since my entrance to the final Purging Trial's ball. And I can't say I've missed looking down on every cold expression.

'Good evening!' Kitt welcomes, his voice carrying across the long length of the room. It's suddenly warmer when not directed at me. 'Tonight we celebrate the success of Paedyn Gray's first Trial. She has achieved what few dared to do, bringing Mareena Azer's crown back to its rightful home. And if Paedyn continues to complete these Trials, she will soon be wearing that crown herself.'

I struggle to stop from startling at the servant who suddenly appears beside me. Hesitantly, I accept the flute of champagne he offers and watch as Kitt does the same.

'A toast,' the king declares, lifting the glass out towards the crowd. They respond with a raising of their own champagne. He seems to clear a cough from his throat before finishing, 'To Paedyn Gray, and the completing of this first Trial.'

My murmured words are swallowed in the echoing crowd. But they are meant for no ears but my own. 'To surviving long enough to see a united Ilya.' I lift the glass to my lips, swallowing the champagne in time with everyone else. The bubbles fizz their way down my throat, crisp and sweet.

Life resumes on the dance floor as we make our way down one of the emerald-padded staircases that lead to the marble below. Spirited music accompanies each of my steps, Kitt's arm an anchor to keep me from taking a tumble down the stairs.

When my heels hit the floor, I'm surrounded by a swarm of bodies. Not for me, of course, but for the grinning king. Women of all ages flock to us, rambling about Plague knows what while batting their lashes at him. I'm quickly shoved from his side, left to sip my champagne alone while Kitt occupies his entourage.

Annoyance quickly crawls across my features to redden my cheeks. I'm not upset by the women attempting to woo my betrothed, only that they were bold enough to do it in front of me. With that thought in mind, I begin to push my way through the gaggle to claim what is mine – not out of jealousy, but as an act of power that I clearly need to establish.

I reach for Kitt, looping my arm through his. 'Let's dance. I want to dance.'

The women seem to deflate at my words, Kitt nearly as surprised as they are. 'You do?'

I flash him a bright smile, as though it could mend the relationship I left in shambles. 'We are engaged, yes? It seems only right that we dance for the court.'

Kitt contemplates this for a moment before deciding he doesn't have much of a choice. In silent agreement, we stride towards the dance floor. I throw back the rest of my champagne and set the empty flute on a nearby servant's tray, stomach warming from the alcohol. As I turn back to smile at the begrudging king I've dragged along, my gaze snags on a familiar shade of purple.

Kitt nearly slams into me with how abruptly I plant my feet.

An emotion more potent than rage begins to boil within me at the sight of that lilac hair. Kitt's mouth is moving, but I don't hear a word that falls from it. Instead, I'm standing at the edge of the dance floor, staring at Adena's murderer.

It's as though I'm back in the center of that Pit, cradling her broken body with my eyes locked on the culprit, just as they are now.

My feet are suddenly moving. I push through the clustered bodies and swaying couples, not caring that I'm striding through a dance. With each step, her features grow clearer. The long lilac hair that was tied in a strap for that final Trial in the Bowl. The brown eyes that had watched the branch plunge through Adena's chest. The painted lips that curled into a smile as she guided it there with a single murderous thought.

And I am going to tear her apart for it.

I've nearly reached Blair by the time her gaze finally deigns to land on me. And I smile when it widens with an emotion that might just be fear.

I lunge, teeth bared, and arms outstretched—

Arms wrap around my waist, tugging me back from her.

I let out a cry of frustration as I fight against the familiar hold. Kai's lips are at my ear before my feet have even met the floor. 'Easy, Pae. You need to calm down.'

I claw at his arms, anger clouding my vision. It's not until another figure blocks my view of Blair that I still. Lenny's face hovers in front of me, free of its usual Imperial's mask. Without the leather obscuring it, I can see the worry that clearly crinkles his brow.

'Paedyn, you can't touch her, all right?' His voice is part plea and part command. 'This isn't worth it. You're going to be queen. Think of what would happen if you tried to kill the general's daughter in front of your entire court?'

Kai's arms slacken around my waist, leaving me panting up at Lenny. 'It's not worth it,' he says quietly. 'Please, don't make me stand between the two of you. Because I will.'

His words have me taking a staggering step back. I shake my head at him. He must see every bit of hurt and hatred on my face because his falls into an equally torn expression. And yet, he chooses to return to his spot at Blair's side. Her brown gaze flicks to mine, face placid in a way that makes it difficult not to shatter the facade with my fist.

'Keep her out of my sight,' I order evenly. 'Because you won't be able to stop me, Lenny. You know that.'

I'm walking away before a reaction can form on their faces. I hear Kai's long strides behind me, likely following to ensure I behave myself.

But that is the last thing I want to do tonight.

I grab a flute of champagne from a servant's tray and gulp down the liquid in a matter of seconds. Then I exchange that empty glass for a full one and do the same. Warmth spills into my stomach, coating my body in an intoxicating fuzzy feeling.

That is all I want to feel tonight. Not anger. Not hurt. Not queenly. Just this contentment beginning to thrum through me.

'Do I even want to know what you're planning?' Kai sighs from where he towers over me.

I give him a smile, noting the way it affects him. Then I shove my empty glass into his hand. 'I'm planning on having fun.'

CHAPTER 22

Rai

She's lost her shoes.

Well, she had.

That was before I'd scoured the ballroom for them, knowing Paedyn would not. Seeing that she flung them off her feet with a declaration of discomfort, I'm sure she was quite content to never find them.

Now, swaying in time to the music, she hardly notices the heels hanging from my fingers. I lean against the pillar, watching her with a smile that has rarely left my lips all evening.

Her familiar silver dress clings to the body beneath, rippling with each of her movements. She's hypnotizing – every laugh, every smile, every sway of her hips. Her cheeks are flushed pink beneath the strands of silver hair falling over her face. But despite her glistening skin, Paedyn doesn't remove the thin shawl around her shoulders.

And I may be the only one in this room that knows why.

Lifting my eyes from where I know Father's parting gift to her lies beneath the fabric, I find her lifting yet another glass of alcohol to those distracting red lips. I push off the pillar, halting her arm before the liquid can slip down her pretty throat. 'I can't believe I'm saying

this, but I may need to cut you off for the night.'

Her eyebrows rise comically, every movement exaggerated. '*You* cutting *me* off?' She leans closer, tilting her head at me. 'That seems a bit ironic.'

'Trust me, darling.' I sigh. 'I'm well aware.'

She waves her glass at me, sloshing champagne over the brim of it. 'Aren't you the one who loves to get drunk at these boring balls?' With her free hand, she shoves a finger into my chest. 'Then you'd beg for a dance with me. And occasionally unlace my dress afterward.'

I chuckle at her sly grin. 'You know why I did that.'

'Yes, but what I don't know,' she says innocently, 'is why you haven't since.'

'Are you . . .' I shake my head at her in disbelief. 'Are you flirting with me, Gray?'

She giggles in a way I've never heard before but would beg to again. 'I'm simply thinking out loud.'

Now it's my turn to tilt my head at her. 'Then I would certainly like to hear what else it is you are thinking.'

'Why aren't you drinking with me?' she shoots back with a mischievous grin.

'Someone has to look after you.'

She takes a step closer. 'I have a fiancé.'

'And yet . . .' I dangle the heels in front of her. 'I'm the one carrying your shoes. Though, I am worried about what it is you'll be taking off next.'

This has Pae laughing, loudly. Her teeth are bright against red lips, and I can do nothing but study the unbridled brilliance of that smile. 'Why, because I won't let you help?'

I shrug a shoulder, my eyes darting across the packed room. 'Because I don't like to share.'

This seems to still her for a moment. At least, long enough to take a slow swig of champagne. Then her eyes are pinned on that sparkling ring, even while returning my shrug. 'Well, you'll have plenty of time to get used to it.'

I'm not even drunk, but her words are sobering. They cut right through me, the reminder a slap to the face. Because I will forever be sharing her in secret, in the shadow of her marriage to my brother. That thought alone has me dropping her forgotten shoes and snatching the glass from her hands. In one swift movement, I down the stolen liquid, savoring its sweetness on my tongue.

Her eyebrows rise as a laugh tumbles from her mouth. 'Changed your mind about keeping an eye on me, hmm?'

I wave over a servant, grabbing two more flutes of champagne from his tray. 'Oh, I'll still have my eyes on you when I'm drunk, darling. And that is exactly the problem.'

Taking the glass I extend, she gives me a wry look. 'And why would that be a problem?'

I lean towards her to murmur, 'We are supposed to be keeping our distance, remember? I have enough trouble doing that when I'm sober.'

Something about the way she's looking up at me has already made it difficult to think straight. This version of Paedyn seems to be even more dangerous than the one who unflinchingly holds a blade to my throat. Alcohol emboldens, loosening her lips to spew sober thoughts. And, truthfully, I'm not sure how to hold myself back from a Paedyn who so brazenly pursues me.

In fact, she might even be making me nervous. I'm unused to the feeling.

'In that case . . .' Her voice is a lazy drawl as she presses her fingers to the bottom of my glass, lifting it to my mouth. Even as she tips the glass against my lips, our gazes never roam from each other. 'Let's test that self-control of yours, Enforcer,' she croons, handing her own champagne to me.

I sigh before sipping generously from her glass. 'Is that not what you've been doing since the day we met?'

She clicks her tongue. 'I won't be charmed by your pretty words, Prince.'

The corner of my mouth curls into a wicked smile. 'Seems a bit late for that, doesn't it?'

'Cocky bastard,' she whispers.

'Pretty Pae.'

I admire her for a long moment, desperately wishing we were the only ones in this room. Wishing there was no audience, no rules to follow. She seems to be thinking the same thing, because with a huff, she grabs the glass from my hand and finishes off the champagne.

'I want to dance,' she declares, face flushed.

I slip my hands into the pockets of my dark pants. 'Well, you'll have to ask me properly.'

'And what makes you think I want to dance with you?'

'I can't think of a reason you wouldn't want to, actually.'

Her smirk sharpens before she turns her back on me and calls, 'Jax!'

A lanky figure across the room whips around at the sound of his name. When his gaze lands on a waving Paedyn, his face splits into a grin. He hurries over, his long strides carrying him quickly through the crowd.

'Hi, Paedyn!' He says this cheerily enough to disguise the nerves rattling his voice.

'Hello, Jax.' When she smiles at him, I catch the nervous bob of Jax's throat. 'I've missed you.'

'R–really?'

'Of course.' She extends her hand. 'Now, let's dance.'

Jax's eyes widen. Paedyn, on the other hand, shoves her empty glass into my palm. Then she's throwing a smug look over her shoulder while pulling my little brother onto the dance floor. I shake my head at her bare back, watching that silver dress ripple behind, Jax in tow.

It's not long before I'm chuckling at the two of them attempting a dance. They have barely managed a series of steps without stumbling, and Pae can't stop laughing long enough to even try. Instead, she seems to have abandoned the choreography accompanying this song and is now doing whatever the hell she wants.

Picking up her shoes, I return to my spot against the pillar, leaning there as I watch them spin around the room. As they smile brightly, their laughter cuts through the commotion of the room, reaching even my ears. It reminds me of a time when—

'We used to laugh like that all the time.'

Kitt brushes my shoulder as he rounds the pillar. I glance over at him with a shake of my head. 'You read my mind.'

He sounds tired. 'I miss enjoying these balls.'

'As do I.' I stare out onto the dance floor. 'At least someone is having a good time.'

He takes a sip of his drink, eyes following Paedyn's spinning figure. 'She seems so . . . happy.'

'Well,' I sigh, 'half a dozen glasses of champagne will do that to a person.'

Kitt snorts. 'So she's taking a page out of your book for the night?'

'It would seem so.' I crack a smile. 'But she's definitely doing it better. I would have stolen a bottle of something stronger and staggered off to my room by now.'

'And I would follow,' Kitt adds, 'because I refuse to endure a ball if you aren't suffering with me.'

I shake my head, smiling at the floor. 'The good old days, huh?'

'Oh, yes.' He blows out a breath. 'I wish these balls were our biggest concern now.'

I'm not sure what compels me to say it. Even the words taste bitter. 'I wish they were my biggest concern then, too. But I was busy being cut open by our father.'

I can feel his shocked gaze roaming my face. 'Kai, I . . . I can't tell you how sorry I am about that. What he was to you, what he put you through, was just so . . . different from the man I knew.'

Guilt twines its way around me as I immediately regret the words. Taking a breath, I look him in the eyes. Father's eyes. 'I only say that to remind you of how much better you can be. How much better you've already become.'

His eyes light with an emotion I can't quite make out. 'I want to be better. Hell, I want to be great.'

'And you will be.' My hand meets his shoulder, shaking it slightly. 'I'm with you until the very end.'

His voice is a murmur, earnest as the gaze he pins on me. 'You and me, Brother.'

'You and me,' I repeat.

We share something then. A smile. A moment of understanding. A repairing of a bond once strained.

It's taken much grief and anger to get here, but I'm proud to say that my brother has returned to me. This is the Kitt I know and love.

This is the friend I'll spend the rest of my life with.

This is the man who is marrying the woman I love.

I push the thought away. 'That was too depressing a topic for a ball. We should be attempting to have fun.'

Kitt nods to the dance floor. 'I think the two of them are having enough fun for the both of us.'

Indeed, they were. Jax and Paedyn had yet to stop causing a scene with their incessant spinning. 'Has it been three dances? If they have any more, the court may begin to think our little brother is trying to steal away your betrothed.'

'Oh, I doubt that's the brother they're worried about,' Kitt says evenly.

Here we go.

I have rehearsed my rebuttal to this touchy topic. Clearing my throat, I ensure it is only those soft, practiced words that fill the air between us. 'I don't want to get in the way of you two.'

It is the truth. I have no desire to be the wedge driven between them. But that is what I am, and I will not stop loving her because of it.

Kitt chuckles, and I'm slightly startled by the sound. 'It is not you who's getting in the way.'

I don't have the chance to ponder his words. He moves on quickly, avoiding any further discussion on the matter. And some cowardly part of myself is thankful for it. 'Andy seems to be enjoying the show.'

Scanning the crowd, I find her familiar wine hair among the throng of bodies. I can see her body shaking with laughter from here, one hand pressed to her mouth while the other curls around her pretty dance partner.

My eyes quickly flick over the crowd to land on a shock of lilac hair. Pressed close to Blair is the tall redhead I know to be Paedyn's friend. 'It was risky having Blair here, you know. The queen-to-be nearly tore her head off in front of the whole court.'

The words have Kitt taking a drink. 'Oh, I know. But I need to somehow . . . acclimate the two of them.' He coughs quickly into a curled fist. 'I can't keep them separated forever. And I certainly can't have my queen attacking the people in this castle.'

My queen.

It's the way he says the words that has me tensing. And that is precisely the reaction he was looking for. Aside from my subtle flinch, I keep my expression blank and gaze forward. 'No, you can't have that.' Turning to face him, I lower my voice, adding, 'But if I know anything about your queen, it's that she will always find a way. To survive or to kill. And I'm not sure anyone can outlive Paedyn's wrath.' My eyes flick to the dancing couple, a lilac-haired girl in the arms of my Imperial.

Kitt nods. 'I don't doubt that. You know her better than I do. Better than you once knew me.'

'I would know you in every life, Brother.' My words are hurried. I step in front of him, facing my other half fully. 'More than any other soul. Believe that.'

He smiles – a slow, relieved movement. His hand clutches my arm as he ducks his head, hiding the emotion shining in those green eyes. 'And I you.'

I loose a breath, feeling the tension flee from my body. This is the brother I know, the bond I know to have with him. And I cannot bear to lose that.

'Are those her shoes?'

I follow Kitt's gaze to where the heels dangle from my hooked fingers. My laugh is muffled by the hand I run down my face. 'She took them off about two glasses of champagne ago.'

The king's gaze crawls over my shoulder. 'Speak of the devil.'

I turn slowly towards the dance floor, and there she is, striding towards us with a dazzling smile between rosy cheeks. I'm breathless at the sight of her, doomed by the hope of having her. It's a beautiful ruin, a devastating devotion. This girl holds my heart in her hands, could crush it between her fingers and still have me thanking her for the touch.

And I hold her shoes.

CHAPTER 23
Paedyn

My blood feels bubbly.

I'm light and heavy all at once, the spreading warmth beneath my skin hypnotizing. I've never felt so carefree, so unbothered by life and rules and hopes and failures . . .

What was I thinking? My head is spinning. Not in a particularly unpleasant way. But fast enough to routinely dump the thoughts from my head.

It doesn't help that the rest of me has been spinning for . . . a length of time I don't care to determine at the moment. I've finally untangled myself from Jax's long legs after dancing — or something loosely resembling that — between the staring court members.

Because I've set my sights on something equally as fun.

The boys lean against a pillar, black suits stark beside the marble stone and—

And I can't focus on anything else because, *holy shit*, they look good. I can feel my smile growing as I walk towards them in as straight of a line as I can manage. They are a pretty pair, the Azer brothers. And I have the rest of my life to spend with them. Married to one and in love with the other.

That bleak thought is one of the many I'd hoped the numerous glasses of champagne would ward off. But like all the others, the thought is fleeting. As is the urge to rip Blair's head off. For now.

I'm suddenly standing before the king and his Enforcer. Kitt and Kai. Betrothed and regrettably not betrothed.

My tongue feels loose and dry and where the hell are my shoes? I ignore all of this to say, 'Why aren't you two having fun?'

It's Kai who answers, voice enticing in a way I certainly wouldn't refuse at the moment. 'Are we supposed to dance with Jax as well?'

Kitt chuckles while I smile loosely, tilting my heavy head. I want him to laugh at my words like that. I want him to want to spend time with me. Or something like that. 'No, I'm sure you've already done that. So, I've come to ask you to dance.'

Well, that's an interesting idea. I'm scared what words will fall from my mouth next. Whatever I say is a shock to even myself.

Kai shakes his head. 'And I thought you couldn't surprise me any further tonight.'

When the Enforcer's gaze meets mine, the king returns to his frustrating stoicism. Yes, I would very much like for us to be friends again. His words are clipped. 'Me? Or Kai?'

I think I hear myself giggle. 'Yes.'

And with that, I'm grabbing them both by the arm. I don't bother trying to comprehend their persistent protests as I drag them towards the dance floor. The sea of people parts for us, amused enough to turn to their neighbor and gossip.

When I halt in the center of the dance floor, I turn to the boys. 'As future queen, I hereby instate a new tradition.'

I might have yelled the words. Oops.

Kai is now pinching the bridge of his nose, swallowing the laugh in his throat. 'Plagues, I hope you remember this tomorrow.'

'Shh, I'm making a decree,' I scold.

Kitt might have smiled. 'We're listening, Paedyn.'

I like that he said my name. That feels like progress.

I clear my throat, ignoring the many wide gazes surrounding, and—

Hmm. I feel like I should be taller for this. Establish my strength and such. So where the hell are my heels when I actually need them?

'I declare,' I say slowly, my spine straightening, 'a dance between the three of us. Unified as one.'

I don't even give them the chance to argue. How very queenly of me.

I'm wrapping an arm around each of them and swaying to the lively music. This is the fun I wanted. This will bring us together. What better way to force the king into friendship with me?

I laugh and laugh and, Plagues, have I ever laughed so much? A safe bet would be, no, I have never laughed so much. And I think it may be that very reason that gets the boys' feet to move with me.

They share a single glance. It's that brotherly bond that can never be broken – except by perhaps me, but what a grim thought – that has them communicating in a language I can't hear. And the silent conclusion they come to is clearly for my benefit. Not rooted in pity, no, but in caring. Kai for me, and Kitt for Kai.

Soon enough, their arms weave around my back, wrapping around each other. We spin in our makeshift circle with any series of steps we desire. I'm pulled and spun and laughing louder by the minute. They laugh with me, at me, maybe, but I don't care. This is a happiness I'm willing to sacrifice my dignity for.

We break out of our circle, dancing however we please. I'm spun between them, passed from arm to arm. I barely even notice the groups of people beginning to dance beside us, all following our lead. Clusters of bodies spin and dance among themselves, laughing at the informality of it all.

And I dare say it's the most fun this court has ever seen.

Teetering on my toes, I throw both arms over the king and his Enforcer's shoulders, beaming at the room around us. There is such beauty in chaos and I—

I'm being lifted off the ground.

I squeal when arms wrap around my waist and hoist my feet off the floor. I'm now a foot taller than the boys holding me up, and this is exactly the height I wished to be when making my impulsive decree.

I look down to my left. Kitt – crown crooked atop blond hair, smile shockingly wide, demeanor that of the boy I befriended so long ago, not the one I'd betrayed. I see hope when I look at him in this moment. A blooming companionship.

I look down to my right. Kai – black hair curling over his brow, eyes bright, and dimples that I curse beneath my breath. But above all, love. It lingers in his gaze, in his touch, down to the very curve of that smile I know belongs to me alone.

The room spins around me, but it's him I focus on. Him I cling to.

Long after our dance and long into the next life.

The night passes in the form of hazy flashes.

My mouth hurts from smiling. My feet ache from dancing.

But I'm not on my feet in this flashing moment.

No.

I'm in strong arms, pressed against a broad chest, smiling up at a handsome face.

He tells me to stop looking at him like that.

My voice sounds far away. 'And how am I looking at you?'

He says I'm looking at him like a promise I can't keep.

This confuses me. Or maybe it doesn't. Maybe it makes perfect sense.

'I want to tell you a secret, but I'm scared of it.'

He offers to say it for me.

I nod.

I notice what is hooked around his fingers, dangling from the hand beneath my knees.

'You found my shoes!'

He whispers the three-worded secret.

'You found my shoes for me.'

Another murmured declaration of devotion.

Tears prick my eyes. '. . . you found my shoes for me.'

He says he loves me. Again and again.

I cover my face with a pillow, smothering out the light.

Groaning, I roll over, nearly slipping off the side of my bed. My head pounds as I dare to peek open an eye and instantly regret it.

Sunlight has long since poured into my room to bathe the bed in warmth, as if the rays wish to caress my cheek.

Throwing the covers over my aching head, I happily hide from the world beyond. Except, the world beyond begins to speak.

'You know, I bet noon, but Kai was confident on two hours past that,' says the familiar voice. 'He was right. I suppose I should have listened. He does know you far better.'

'I wouldn't give him too much credit,' I grumble from beneath the sheets. 'It'll go to his head.'

Gathering my courage, I slowly peel back the fort I've buried myself beneath and squint in the painful light. I know by voice alone who occupies this room with me. But that doesn't make it any less shocking when I see his green eyes and tousled blond hair.

He is in my room. Shocking still, he came to see me. I don't remember much of last night, but I must have done something right. Now, I just need to ensure I don't ruin this progress.

I scramble into a sitting position as Kitt so obviously points out, 'Champagne is not nearly as fun in the morning.'

My heavy eyes land on where he sits beside my bed. The king is watching me closely and all I can manage is a weak, 'My head is pounding.'

'That,' he says slowly, 'I expected. So I had Gail mix this up for you.'

He grabs a glass from my bedside table, swirling the murky liquid within it. I try my best not to seem shocked by his kind gesture. But it's difficult to ignore the hope swelling in my chest. 'That looks . . . terrifying,' I finally croak. 'What even is it?'

His smile is worrisome. 'It's best if you don't know. But it will make you feel better. Trust me.'

I cut him a skeptical glance after peering at the liquid. He inclines his head, urging me to drink. But as soon as I press the glass to my lips and tip my throbbing head back, I immediately regret it. The taste can only be described as foul, and I'm momentarily considering spitting the grainy texture out.

'No, don't give up yet.' The corner of Kitt's mouth kicks up, and that alone keeps me going.

Hastily gulping down the rest of the vile liquid, I push the cup into his hand with a sputtering cough. 'That was . . .' I physically shudder. 'That was awful.'

'Gail's hangover remedy is not for the weak, let me tell you.' His gaze grows distant. 'Kai and I have endured it many times over the years.'

I'm handed a glass of water next, which I eagerly drain in the hopes it will rid me of the horrid taste in my mouth. The king watches me closely, looking far from the title with how casually he sits beside me. 'How are you feeling?'

I assess myself before determining, 'Better, actually. Thank you. I didn't . . .' I'm feeling annoyingly awkward. 'I didn't think you would come and see me.'

'Someone had to ensure you were still alive up here,' he says simply.

'I'm glad you cared to check.'

There is a long pause. It's as though he hadn't considered that to be true. Then comes his curt change of subject. 'I'm addressing the court today about your next Trial.'

I straighten. 'Already?'

Kitt nods. 'Testing your benevolence will take longer than your bravery, so I'm getting you started sooner.'

'I'll be in another Trial within the next few days.'

The words are deafening, and yet, I had hardly whispered them. A familiar sense of panic eats away at my composure. I may have completed the first Trial, but that does not guarantee I'll make it out of this one alive. And just as I have been my entire life, I'm afraid.

'At least you're plenty rested,' Kitt offers.

I lean my head against the wall where it continues to ache dully. 'When did I get back to my room last night?'

'Nearly five in the morning,' he states. 'Kai carried you up here.'

I practically wince at his words. There is no bite to them, and that almost makes it worse. Talk of Kai has always been, and always will be, unbearably awkward. So I attempt to avoid it. 'Plagues, how much did I drink?'

'Enough to not remember much, I assume?'

I blow out a breath. 'Yes, it's all very . . . blurry. I remember bits and pieces of the ball.' Cutting him a glance, I add, 'Well, I certainly remember why I started drinking in the first place.'

The sight of Blair flashes in my mind, managing to boil my blood even now.

'I'm sorry that her being there was so upsetting,' Kitt states, not sounding too torn up about it. 'But I need you to get used to her being around. I can't simply make her disappear.'

'Oh, I could.' There is not a hint of a smile on my face. 'Allow me. Please.'

'You know that's not possible, Paedyn.' He runs a hand down the back of his neck. 'But you seemed to be having fun despite her being there. Even managed to get the court to have a good time, and that is no simple feat.'

'Yes, the dancing,' I say slowly. 'My feet are sore.'

'Well, I hear you discarded your shoes rather quickly.' He nods to the heels that were hastily strewn beside my bed.

I stare at them, a memory struggling to surface at the sight. But before I have a chance to recall, Kitt is standing to his feet. 'You made another decree as well. Very impressive.'

I laugh. 'Don't mock me.'

That almost manages to earn me a smile before he clears his raspy throat and stands. 'I'll send Ellie in to get you ready. I have a meeting to get to.' He points to the bedside table, drawing my attention to what sits there, steaming in the sunlight. I hadn't noticed the bowl in my foggy state. 'Kai said you might want some of that. Again, he knows you rather well, so I took his word for it.'

Despite myself, I smile at the porridge decorated with fruit. Fruit that Kai despises. Blueberries sit among the steaming oats, reminding me of that long night under the willow. 'Thank you,' I murmur, lifting my eyes to his. 'For bringing it for me.'

He gives me a quick nod of his head. Then he coughs into an ink-stained fist. 'You have two hours. I'll see you at the throne room then.'

Stepping out the door, he's quickly replaced with Ellie. I scarf down the porridge while she readies the room, eying me from afar.

'What is it, Ellie?' I finally ask between bites.

'Nothing,' she answers quickly. 'I'm just happy you're feeling better. You were very out of it when Prince Kai dropped you off last night.'

I feel my cheeks redden. 'Yes, not my finest moment.'

'He insisted on staying in here with you.' She glances over at me bashfully. 'Said he would sit in that chair until he was sure you were asleep.'

I swallow. 'And did he?'

'Yes.' Her voice is quiet. 'And long after.'

We fall silent soon after that, setting our focus on the task at hand. After a cool bath that further wakes me, Ellie ensures I look presentable in record time. She's pinned half of my damp hair up with the exception of a few pieces that fall around my powdered face.

Next, I step into an elegant green gown behind the screen. The drooping sleeves and high neckline cover my scars, following the requirements I'd given Ellie for any future dresses. Shoving on my heels, I'm hit once again with that fleeting memory at the sight of them.

But Ellie is pushing me out the doors before I have the chance to ponder it further. I set a steady pace down the hall, passing the many emotionless Imperials lining it. They stare, and I stare back.

Soon enough, I'm threading my arm through Kitt's and watching the large doors swing open. When I look over at him, he nods slowly. And then we're stepping into the throne room.

The same eyes that watched me last night are watching me now. We walk between the throng of people on either side, faces forward. Reaching the dais, Kitt guides me up before we turn as one towards the court. His fingers reach for mine, lacking all the hesitancy he shows in private. But this is for show, not feelings.

'Ladies and gentlemen of the court, today we gather in honor of Paedyn Gray's second Trial,' Kitt announces, voice steady. 'As you and the rest of Ilya know, she successfully retrieved Mareena Azer's lost crown. After proving her bravery, she will now prove her benevolence.

'As second of the three *B*'s,' Kitt continues, 'benevolence has proven difficult in the past, due to our isolation from neighboring cities. But with our borders now open, we must extend peace to the kingdoms. This will take more than a letter detailing Ilya's changes. It will require action.'

My eyes skim over the crowd, finding Calum among the unfamiliar faces. He's smiling slightly at Kitt's words, pleased with every one that leaves his mouth. Beside him stands a girl I haven't seen since the Resistance meetings at my old home. Her hair is the same blond as her father's, eyes nearly as blue.

Mira.

When she catches me staring, I'm barely offered a nod, let alone a smile. This is hardly surprising. We weren't particularly close, and I'm not sure she would give me a grin even if we were.

I turn my attention back to the king when he glances over at me. It's a fleeting look that just might resemble an apology. 'For that reason,' Kitt declares, 'Paedyn will be traveling across the Shallows Sea to befriend the city of Izram and open future trade between us.'

My sharp inhale is drowned out by the clapping crowd.

Of course they're clapping. No one has crossed the treacherous stretch of water in years. And I may not make it back if I dare test the unforgiving sea.

That is why they cheer.

'Paedyn will inform Izram of our opened borders and negotiate peace . . .'

Kitt continues his speech, but I hear none of it.

No, my eyes land on Kai's before running over his rigid body.

Fear pulls at his features, and when he dares to meet my gaze, I'm forced to once again wonder why I ever bother looking at anyone else. Those icy eyes drag over my body, feeling heavier than a touch, more meaningful than a word. I revel in his reverence. That is, until it lands on the fingers I've laced between his brother's.

A muscle feathers in his jaw. I can see the anger seeping out from beneath the unbothered mask he's slipped on.

So he looks away. He turns. He strides from the throne room.

And I can feel myself beginning to drift without him to anchor me.

177

CHAPTER 24

Rai

I pace the worn rug, doing the same thing I'd done when it was Father sitting behind that desk.

Kitt leans back in his chair with a sharp clearing of his throat. Sensing the tension, Easel steps forward to offer, 'There is no alternative. This is what the court wants.'

'This is a death wish,' I bite out. 'That is why they want her to do it. Not to prove her benevolence but to die trying.'

It's Calum who speaks next, though I don't bother looking at the Mind Reader. 'I have faith that Paedyn can do this. And traveling to Izram will impress the people far more than even finding that crown.'

I shake my head, failing to hide my frustration. Damn pretending. Damn these Trials. Kitt already suspects that my allegiance to Paedyn runs far deeper than me being her Enforcer. 'All of this for what? To deliver some damn roses?'

Easel draws a breath. 'Izram struggles to grow them due to their sandy soil. And—'

'Roses are used to treat illnesses.'

It's the first thing she's said since striding into this study and taking

a seat beside the fireplace. At the sound of Paedyn's voice, I turn to look at her, finding those blue eyes already pinned on me.

'I was the daughter of a Healer once,' she continues simply. 'I know of the benefits and high demand for the flower.'

Kitt nods in agreement to her words. 'This gift would be beneficial to Izram – a physical peace offering for shutting off trade with them. Queen Zailah has yet to hear of our opened borders, so it would be Paedyn who reintroduces Ilya as an ally.'

'And the Shallows?' I ask, exasperated. 'The things that lurk within it?' I'm suddenly bracing my palms on the desk, leaning forward as I say, 'Kitt, you know that Jax's parents died in a shipwreck over that sea. That was the very last time anyone has publicly tried to make the trek.'

'I know.' Kitt's voice is suddenly stern. 'Of course I remember what happened to Jax's parents. But times have changed. Ships have evolved. Teles and Hydros will be on board. Extra precautions have been made.' He pauses. 'Paedyn will be safe.'

Easel's long mint hair comes into view beside Kitt's desk. 'As for what supposedly lurks within the Shallows, we have no way of knowing if those myths are true or not. But, rest assured, the ship will be equipped with weapons and plenty of Elites.'

That finally has Paedyn standing from her seat, unsurety slanting her brows. 'What myth?'

I gesture to the court's spokesman. 'You're the one sending her on this journey, so why don't you tell her?'

He obliges, though, slightly hesitant. 'It has been said that the Plague may have even altered . . . animals. There are stories of enhanced creatures – bigger, faster, stronger than before. Because of that, many believe there to be some creature living in the Shallows.'

'A beast that belongs to the sea,' I finish for him, turning my attention back to Paedyn.

My words seem to have hit her with a sudden realization. Her eyes are pinned on the carpet, her head shaking slightly. 'The bats . . .'

'What?' Calum asks, stealing the question from my lips.

'The bats,' she repeats distractedly. 'There were these massive bats in the cave above that crypt. I remember thinking there was something unnatural about them.' Her eyes find Calum's. 'Do you think they were . . . ?'

'Genetically mutated?' He inhales deeply, tucking tanned arms behind his back. 'It is definitely possible. The Scholars have collected evidence themselves, though they don't publicly speak on it. But that doesn't mean this sea creature is anything more than a bedtime story.'

'Yet another thing I never got the chance to learn on the streets of Loot.' Paedyn huffs out a laugh, the sound cutting. 'I really am Ordinary. Even to animals.'

I catch the slight hardening of Calum's face, likely in response to the bitter way she speaks about herself. 'Are you up for this journey, Paedyn?'

'I didn't realize I had a choice,' she answers earnestly. 'But if this is what the people need from me . . .'

Easel nods solemnly at her words.

'Then I will do it,' she finishes.

'I'm going with her.'

There is not a hint of hesitancy in my voice. It's a demand, a compromise I won't negotiate. Even worse, I don't care if my worry for her seeps into the words. I will follow her to the bottom of the sea if I must.

'Kai, you can't be serious—' Kitt starts, sounding betrayed.

'I'm not just your Enforcer,' I state. 'I'm now Paedyn's as well. And if there is one thing Father ensured I had learned, it was to never let my king and queen face danger unless I was between it and them.'

I can feel Paedyn's wide gaze roaming over me, but I don't dare let my stare stray from Kitt. He studies me long enough to have Calum begin filling the silence. 'The king needs his Enforcer here—'

Cutting him off, it's Kitt I speak to. 'What do you think that crew will do to their Ordinary queen?' My voice drops as I murmur, 'It wouldn't surprise me if they tried to throw her overboard the second that ship reaches open water. Call it a freak accident.' I shake my head. 'But not if I'm there. No one will dare touch her. And if you weren't so damn important, Brother, I know you would be on that ship with her. But we can't risk losing you. So risk me instead.'

'I'll ensure the crew behaves,' Kitt challenges.

'Threats won't stop them from throwing her overboard and returning with a tale about how the future queen ran off in Izram,' I counter quietly.

'Kitt.' Paedyn is suddenly beside me, her palms pressed against the wood desk. 'I wish it was you coming with me.'

The words sting more than I suspected they would. Even knowing this is another moment of pretend, I feel a twinge of hurt in the heart I've so readily given her.

'But you have a kingdom to rule,' she continues steadily. 'And if you want me to return to it, I need some protection.'

After a long moment of scrutinizing, Kitt finally tears his eyes away. 'All right,' he says, voice hushed. 'Kai will go with you.'

I nod curtly despite my sudden relief at his words. 'I'll ensure she makes it back to you.'

'I'm sure you will.'

'When do we leave?' Pae cuts in, sensing the slight tension.

It's Easel who answers. 'Day after tomorrow. Early.'

'You're making the right decision, Kitt.' I swallow. 'For your future bride.'

Everything inside me recoils at the words, but I utter them all the same. He seems to notice how much it pains me. But he plays along, giving a slow nod to the door. 'You two have some packing to do.'

Not a very subtle dismissal, but I can't say I'm surprised. So I take the hint along with my leave. Reaching the curved staircase, I climb the steps two at a time, following the familiar route towards my room.

My pace is even, hopes oddly high for one who may be sailing to their death. But I am no stranger to drowning. I've been doing just that since the day I looked into her ocean eyes.

A power shifts beneath my skin, growing stronger with each step. It feels familiar, harsh in the same way it has been since we were children.

I know who awaits me even before I round the corner.

Her lilac hair is braided loosely down the back of her simple blouse. It's jarring, seeing Blair look anything but lethal. Yet, here she stands, face free of its usual dark makeup and clothes surprisingly plain.

'What are you doing here?' I ask as way of greeting.

She raises a dark brow. 'What am I doing outside my door?'

My smile is sharp. 'Why aren't you behind it?'

'Oh, I see!' She says this with more than a hint of disdain. 'You're asking because, apparently, I'm no longer allowed to step foot outside of my own room.' A slight pout forms on her lips. 'We can't have our future queen hurting herself trying to kill me.'

I run a hand down my face, already exhausted by this conversation. 'What are you doing out here, Blair? I thought Lenny gets you everything you need.'

'Not everything, unfortunately.' She sighs. 'If you must know, I was sharpening my knives. You know, for throwing at little children outside my window.' Her eyes roll. 'Or whatever other twisted hobbies you think I enjoy.'

'Just . . .' I gesture lazily to the door. 'Get back in there. Please.'

'Hmm.' Her gaze travels over me. 'It seems the Slummer taught you some manners. How ironic.'

'Don't, Blair,' I warn.

'So will you share her with Kitt the rest of your life? Or find another Ordinary on the streets?'

The words have barely left her mouth before I snap.

I throw her back against the wall with nothing but my mind and the use of her borrowed Tele power. She gasps in surprise, straining slightly beneath my hold on her body. No Elite appreciates their own power being used against them, but I have little concern for her feelings at the moment.

Each step towards her pinned body is slow, deliberate. The glare she gives me is dull, seemingly unconcerned by her current situation. But when I loom over her, she fights to tilt her head up and meet my icy stare.

'Talk about her like that again,' I murmur slowly, 'and you will be begging to stay locked in that room, safe from me.'

Something about her gaze gradually softens in the seconds after my threat. And that concerns me. 'Shit,' she breathes, mouth gaping.

Her lashes flutter as she stares up at me, equally shocked and amused. 'You're in love with her.'

I step back abruptly, releasing my hold on her and the power I'd clutched tightly in my mind. She slumps against the wall, free to move her slackened limbs. And the first thing she does is shake her head at me in disbelief. 'I always knew there was something between you, but . . .' Her laugh is slightly crazed. 'You're completely in love with her.'

My eyes wander to the floor, chest heaving with each breath. I can't even find a convincing enough lie to spew. I'm not even sure I could bring myself to deny it if I had to. So I stand there like an open wound, letting her examine the weakness she's discovered.

Blair takes a single slow step towards me. When my gaze finally climbs up to her awaiting one, the shake of her head is pitying. A sharp smile settles on her lips to mirror the one I've seen her give since we were children. 'Oh, you are fuc—'

'Prince Kai!'

Looking up, I find an Imperial standing in the center of the hall with a plate of food in each hand. Identifying his red hair immediately, I watch Lenny's eyes flick between his Enforcer and the girl he's meant to be guarding. He clears his throat, hurrying over with an equally rushed, 'Hello, sir, it's great to see you. Um, Blair, sweetheart, you're meant to be *in* the room. Not loitering outside of it, yes?'

Her eyes roll before she's spewing falsely sweet words, thoroughly mocking him. 'Um, Lenny, my little gingersnap that I could quite literally snap in half with a single thought, Kai spotted me before I had the chance to enter the room and send my sharpened knives flying towards those who pass beneath the window.' She turns to me then, smiling sarcastically. 'He loves that game. Don't let him tell you otherwise.'

Laughing uncomfortably, Lenny shoos her towards the door. 'Quite the sense of humor she's got. Never a dull moment with this one!'

'Oh, please,' she huffs. 'Don't pretend that you like me; it will only make me work harder to—'

Lenny kicks the door shut behind her with a smile.

'—ensure you don't,' Blair calls from the other side, voice muffled.

Alone in the hall, we stare at each other for a long moment. With a sigh, I mutter, 'Keep her out of sight, all right? It could have been Paedyn that walked down this hall, and we all know what she would have done.'

Lenny nods in agreement. 'Yes, sir.' He steps closer then, casting a weary glance at the door. 'She can't stay locked up forever, though. It's not right.'

I run a hand through my hair. 'I know. But Paedyn needs time.'

That's the only explanation I offer before turning away and beginning down the hall once again. 'Good luck with her.'

His response is quiet, lost to the growing gap between us as I round another corner.

CHAPTER 25

Paedyn

Water drips from the ends of my hair, pelting my shoulders as I swirl a finger in the warm bath.

I bask in the luxury of it all, lathering sweet-smelling soap onto my skin. Leaning my head over the edge of the porcelain tub, I shut my eyes and focus on this last bit of calm I feel. Because the water I'll be venturing out onto tomorrow will not be so peaceful and contained. It terrifies me, the unknown and uncontrollable, nearly as much as it inspires.

After a long day of packing and silently gathering my courage, I've approached dusk with much fear of the day that follows. So, as the night yawned on and sleep evaded, I decided to drown my sorrows in a bath.

I'd been buried beneath bubbles for so long that Ellie came to check on me. It took several attempts to convince her that I was, in fact, capable of getting to bed without her being there. After finally giving in and hesitantly wishing me good night, she left to get the rest I desperately wished I could.

Dipping my head beneath the water, I'm reminded how easily something so warm and soothing can swallow me whole. Even this

bath is dangerously unassuming. But the sea is far less enticing.

I'm running out of air.

I don't even know how to swim. If I end up overboard, the sea will claim me quickly.

My lungs tighten.

There would be no fighting my way out of Death's clutches.

Now they burn.

I'll be completely vulnerable.

I break through the surface, gulping down the damp air. I allow myself another moment to sit within the water, feeling every ripple and lap of it against my skin. Then I'm combing my wet hair back from my face and standing.

Throwing on the silken robe Ellie set out for me – only after smiling at the bag of chocolates she left beside it – I pad into the bedroom, intent on flopping face-first onto my mattress. Not that I expect to get much sleep. No, it's a combination of nerves and boredom that has me wishing to do nothing at all but rot with my thoughts.

This may be my last night on solid ground.

I feel queasy.

A gnawing worry grows within the pit of my stomach. I think vaguely of how I might leave this world. Fighting? Regretful? At peace?

No, peace implies that all is well in my life. But there are wrongs to be righted and forgiveness to be earned. I refuse to die until I'm satisfied with the way I lived.

I groan.

In the end, it is the imminence of death that manages to drag me from my bed.

I knock hesitantly on his door.

My heart pounds wildly in anticipation. I'm not normally the one to do this, and I doubt I'll ever do it again because of how annoyingly nervous I—

The handle turns.

And when the door opens, I almost expect to be met with a cocky smile, a mess of black hair, or a familiar set of lips that have tasted mine.

But everything before me is unsurety.

This mouth is slackened with surprise, and one I've never met. The hair atop his head is blond and neat and the opposite of his brother's. *He* is opposite of his brother.

I stand in the doorway, blinking up at the shocked Kitt.

'Hi,' I say, if only to fill the silence.

His response is equally awkward. 'Hi.'

'Sorry, did I wake you?'

'Oh, no.' Kitt rubs the back of his neck, an action he frequents. He looks over his shoulder, seeming slightly surprised to find the air unoccupied. 'No, I don't sleep much anymore.'

My gaze dips to his stained hands. 'Are you writing something?'

'Just . . . notes. It helps me think.' He clears his throat. Mumbles something under his breath. For a moment, I think he's forgotten my presence.

My eyes narrow at his strange behavior. "Are you—?'

'Is there a reason you're here at this hour?' He's blinked the bleariness from his distant gaze.

I'm momentarily startled by his sudden composure. 'Right, yes.' I lift a bundled blanket between us, one I'd ripped off my bed after quickly dressing. 'I thought we could have a . . . picnic?' I wince. 'I'm not sure, really, but I have chocolate?'

We stare at each other, both of us knowing precisely what this is – a peace offering. Kitt glances over his shoulder again, as if weighing whether this is worth a pause in his writing. I'm beginning to believe the king will turn me away when he finally steps aside. 'I can't say no to chocolate.'

With a relieved smile, I creep into the room. The folded blanket hangs limply from my fingers while I try not to look so intrigued by his bedchamber. It's surprisingly plain for a king, at least compared to the lavish lifestyle I assumed one would have. But it is not void of character. Potted plants litter the room, dotting each corner with color and twining around anything in reach. My eyes skip over the crumpled bed to find books piled on either side. Their broken spines pile to dangerous heights around the room, never far from a strewn map or scribbled document.

'I would have tidied up had I known you were visiting,' Kitt says, sounding only slightly self-conscious. He sweeps aside a cluster of inky parchment as I set the blanket on the ground.

'No need to clean on my behalf.' I unfold the fabric to reveal that bag of sweets Ellie left me. 'You've seen where I lived.'

'I have.' He sounds regretful.

Taking a seat on the stretched blanket, I fold my legs beneath me and beckon for Kitt to follow. He obeys, sitting stiffly to my right with all the comfortability of an acquaintance, not the man meant to be my husband. And that lack of progress is exactly why I'm here.

I offer him a chocolate before unwrapping my own. 'I haven't had one of these since our game of catch in the kitchens.'

Popping the sweet into his mouth, Kitt mumbles, 'I was the only one catching. You were dropping.'

'All right.' I sigh out the words. 'No need to gloat.'

He smiles, and *that* is progress. 'So, why did you really want to have this makeshift picnic with me?'

'Do I need a reason to eat chocolate with you?'

'No,' he says slowly, 'but you likely have one.'

'So you do know me, after all,' I tease.

'I thought I did.' Another chocolate disappears into his mouth. 'Once.'

A frown pulls at my mouth. 'I haven't changed. I'm still that girl you knew during the Purging Trials.'

'No,' he counters. 'You're hardened.'

I stop chewing. Our eyes lock in silent scrutiny. 'I have to be. That is the only way Ordinaries can survive in Ilya.'

'Well, soon you won't be Ordinary.' The king sounds ruffled. 'You'll be royalty.'

My laugh is humorless enough to draw a look of surprise from Kitt's stoic features. 'Maybe. But your father ensured I would never forget who I really was.'

Maybe it's habit, or anger, or a cruel mixture of both that has my gaze falling to the top button of his crumpled shirt. It seems history refuses to go unrepeated. Once again, I'm avoiding the gaze of a man who nearly killed me. And despite the reminder that these green eyes do not belong to Edric Azer, I still find it difficult to meet them. Even in death, the late king tortures me.

'There you go again,' Kitt murmurs.

I will my stare to meet the speculating one he's pinned on me. 'Hmm?'

'There was a time when you couldn't look me in the eyes,' he says evenly. 'Just as you're doing now. And in the gardens, you told me it was because I reminded you of someone. It was my father, wasn't it?'

I lean back, slightly startled by his question. But if I want to restore that relationship between us, I need to be honest. 'I thought your father killed mine,' I explain softly. 'And, well, in a way, he did. It was Kai he gave the order to. Kai I watched bury a sword in my father's chest. But I didn't know that until the king taunted me outside the Bowl.'

Kitt's voice is numb. 'And that is when you killed him.'

'Barely,' I murmur, remembering every blow the king rained down on me. 'It was like he had been waiting for that day. Like every blow was planned. It's all become such a blur now but . . .' I glance over at his stiff form. 'But, yes, I avoided your gaze, your company, because you look so much like him.'

The chocolates sit forgotten on the floor, now little more than witnesses to our hushed conversation. 'And when you did seek out my company,' Kitt says dryly, 'it was because you needed to find a way into those tunnels.'

'No.' My explanation is a flurry of rushed words. 'Well, maybe at first. Yes, I needed a way into those tunnels, but it became so much more than that. I *wanted* to spend that time with you, be honest about what I was doing. But I wanted to make a difference more. And I knew how close you were with your father . . .'

'So you assumed I was against the Resistance, against Ordinaries, as well,' he finishes for me. This is followed by an indifferent shrug. 'To be honest, I never much cared what happened to the Ordinaries. Banished or not, it didn't matter. But my father was obsessed with ridding Ilya of them, and it was his undoing. His greatest failure.'

I fiddle with an empty wrapper, rolling it between my fingers. 'And now you're marrying the one thing he hated. Better yet, the one thing that killed him.' My whole body tenses in anticipation of my next question. 'And you're okay with that?'

'I don't really have a choice,' he mutters. 'You know, I didn't think I would be able to look at you, either. Not after what you did. But I quickly realized that my father wasn't worth pleasing. His praise wasn't worth obsessing over.' He mindlessly gathers the chocolates in a tight circle. 'Now, I will be the one to make Ilya great. My own way.'

I nod slowly. 'I'm glad to hear he doesn't still control you.'

He lets the words hang between us. My fingers take advantage of the tense moment and lift a chocolate to my lips. I savor it, tasting nostalgia between each nutty bite. This is the chocolate I used to steal for Adena on special occasions. The last of which was her birthday, though we hadn't known it would be her last at the time.

'I can't say the same about you.'

I'm pulled from my thoughts and back onto the king's plush floor. 'What do you mean?'

'He clearly has control over you. My father,' Kitt clarifies. 'Otherwise, you would have no issue looking me in the eyes.'

I'm doing it again. My gaze snaps up from his throat to crash into the familiar gaze above. It is heavy atop the purple smudges of restlessness.

It's time he knows.

Kitt opens his mouth again, but I'm already moving, already gathering my courage alongside the folds of my shirt. Determination overrules my sudden desperation to hide this marred piece of myself. But if this man is to be my husband, he will soon see every bit of brokenness that makes up my being.

So I might as well start with the scars on my heart.

I shift in front of him, forcing the tremble from my voice. 'He doesn't control me. He haunts me.'

My hand lifts to tug the collar of my shirt down, down, down . . .

I know the brand is visible when his face pales.

'Is that . . .' He swallows. 'Is that an *O*?'

I don't bother looking down at the jagged letter that defines me. 'For Ordinary.'

Kitt is shaking his head now. 'I . . . I don't . . .'

'After trailing his blade down my neck,' I say flatly, 'he promised to leave his mark on my heart, so I never forget who broke it.'

He raises his hand, as if wishing to run his fingers over the scar before thinking better of it. 'This is not the man I knew.'

'The man you knew didn't exist.'

His eyes trace that mangled circle of flesh. 'I'm sorry.'

My voice is hoarse. 'I am too.'

'You're not the girl I knew during those Purging Trials,' he says softly. 'Not anymore.'

His words don't startle me like I thought they would. Because he's right. I've already mourned the girl who died alongside Adena in that Pit. Something broken staggered out of the Bowl Arena that day. And I have only been stronger for it.

'And you are not the boy I knew either.' My throat is dry, but I scrape the words off my tongue. 'Now, I want to know this king you've become.'

Kitt's voice is light despite the weight of his words. 'I worry for what you will find.'

CHAPTER 26

Paedyn

Wind whips at my hair and stings my cheeks.

It's biting in a way that's oddly refreshing after the stuffy coach ride between the uncharacteristically quiet brothers.

I've never been so close to the sea. Never dared.

Now I'll be sailing over it.

We stand at the edge of the only rickety dock left in Ilya. Inky water slaps against the long posts supporting each wood slab we stand on. I breathe in the salty air, scan the ever-stretching horizon. It's terrifyingly exhilarating, this something that finds such strength in the ever-changing.

But what floats atop the water is nearly as breathtaking.

The ship looms to our left, casting an ominous shadow over us. The dark wood spans several hundred feet long, coming to a slight point at one end. Two large sails are bunched tightly against the tall masts, readying to be reunited with the wind.

My gaze travels over the expanse of wood before falling back to the waves lapping beneath. 'Is the water always this choppy?' I ask, looking over at the brothers.

'No,' Kai answers dully.

I let out a sigh of relief. 'Well, that's good.'

'It's usually worse.'

And just like that, my chest is tightening once again.

Kitt claps his Enforcer on the shoulder. 'Ever the optimist, Brother.'

The king seems to be in higher spirits this morning, despite our heavy conversation last night. Or perhaps it's simply Kai who brightens his mood.

'Yes,' I muse, 'very comforting.'

The sound of approaching footsteps has us turning. It's Calum striding down the uneven dock, clutching a small stack of books beneath his arm. To his right, the court's spokesman resides with a tight smile. Easel steps forward before curtly relaying information. 'Your trunks have been loaded onto the boat and brought to your cabins. The crew is ready to depart when you are.'

My stomach churns at the thought of abandoning solid ground, but I force myself to nod convincingly. Noticing my worry, or rather, reading my anxious thoughts, Calum asks, 'May I have a moment with Paedyn?'

The brothers oblige, conversing quietly as they head down the dock. Tucking his hands, and the books within them, behind his back, Calum leads me slowly to the end of the dock. 'You're doing well, you know.'

I kick a rock off the wood plank and hear it hit the water with a soft plunk. 'It doesn't feel like it.'

'Respect is earned,' he says softly. 'It takes much time. But once you finish these Trials, things will begin to move very quickly.'

I nod, gaze lingering on the crashing waves below. 'I'll be married.'

'You'll be a queen,' he adds.

'And I'll still be Ordinary.'

The words have him turning to look at me, blond hair catching in the light. At the feel of his piercing gaze, I wonder briefly what it is he's gleaning from my thoughts. 'Yes, you always have been and always will be. Even with a crown on your head.'

We stand in silence at the edge of the dock, watching the sun shimmer against the water as it tiptoes slowly into the sky. I glance over at him, committing this peaceful moment to memory. 'Thank you,' I breathe into the crisp air. 'For everything. But mostly for being here with me. You're a comfort in the castle.' I laugh sadly. 'And in this whole new life I've been thrown into.'

His smile is reserved. 'I am here to help in any way.' He pulls the books from behind his back, presenting the worn covers to me. 'In fact, I brought these for your journey. They may help pass the time.'

Reaching out, I run a hesitant finger over a familiar burgundy spine. 'Thank you. But I'd hate to ruin your things if we somehow end up in the sea—'

'You don't have to worry about that,' he cuts in softly. 'Well, ruining my books that is. These belong to you.'

My eyes snap to his. 'What?'

'When your father died, and you disappeared,' he starts slowly, 'I grabbed some of your favorite stories for safekeeping. And I hoped to give them back to you one day.'

With every word, the books seem to familiarize before my eyes. Each faded cover holds a distant memory, a fleeting image of a man in his reading chair, and a little girl sitting at his feet. 'He used to read these to me.'

'He did.' Calum gently hands me the four thin books. 'I believe you even wrote a few notes in there as a child.'

'I can't imagine I had anything important to add,' I say, laughing lightly. Quickly flipping through one of the books, I find a small rose sketched onto the inside cover. The words 'For Paedyn' are scrolled beneath it in vaguely familiar, looping handwriting.

He eyes me carefully. 'You'd be surprised.' With a small smile, he adds, 'I'll have them brought to your cabin.'

I suppose he can likely hear the gratitude in my thoughts, but that doesn't seem like quite enough. So I emphasize the unspoken words with an impulsive throwing of my arms around him. This makes him hesitate for a moment, stutter in confusion, and finally return the sentiment.

With his arms circling my shoulders, I whisper one last 'Thank you.'

We stand in the ship's shadow, all staring at the vessel meant to carry us across the treacherous water.

A crowd has formed on the rocky shore where hundreds of eyes hope to get their last glimpse of the hated Ordinary. Imperials barricade the dock, halting anyone who dares push their way towards us. But no one makes a move, content on letting the Shallows have their way with me.

In their eyes, I'm as good as dead.

The king glances over at his Enforcer. 'Changed your mind yet, Kai?'

'Unfortunately not,' he sighs. 'But do try not to miss me too much. I've stationed extra Imperials with you while I'm gone, so you certainly won't be feeling lonely.'

'Oh, yes, I look forward to not a single moment of privacy.' The humor in Kitt's voice dissolves quickly. 'Please come home, Kai. I can't have you dying on me too.'

I look away, as if that could save me from this awkward intrusion of their conversation. Still, I hear the Enforcer's earnest response. 'I'll be back. Death fears me, remember?' I can hear an inkling of that cocky bastard slipping into his voice when he says, 'And when I return, we'll celebrate with another dance between the three of us. So long as Paedyn doesn't purposely step on my toes this time.'

'I have no recollection of that,' I state defensively. 'It must have been subconscious.'

Kitt laughs, and the sound bleeds into his next words, all of them aimed at his brother. 'Well, she kept trying to jump onto my back, remember?'

'And then blamed her failed attempts on the "constricting dress",' Kai adds with a punch-worthy smile. 'Trust me, I remember. The moment replays every time I close my eyes—'

'All right, that's enough,' I huff. 'Remember this conversation when I suddenly push you overboard.'

'Oh, you can try, Gray,' Kai mocks with a crooked grin. 'But don't blame your constrictive sleeves when you aren't able to.'

Kitt's laugh nearly drowns out my words. 'That's it. I'm getting on this damn boat.'

I step out onto the plank, forcing my gaze ahead and not on the raging water beneath me. The voices behind grow muffled by the lapping waves, but Kai's stands out, even among the sea. 'Take care of yourself while I'm gone. Get some rest. Promise me.'

'I promise,' Kitt returns quietly. 'I would ask you to ensure Paedyn does the same, but I already know you will.'

My heart quickens its pace as I step onto the ship's deck. Several seconds pass before the Enforcer follows, wood groaning beneath his boots. As I lean over the rail, Kitt's gaze finds mine from the dock below before he offers a mouthed 'Good luck.'

'Kai!'

The shout rings through the air, carried on the wind. Kai whips around, scanning the wall of Imperials on the other end of the dock where a tangle of limbs attempts to break through.

'Kai! Wait!'

But he does nothing of the sort. Instead, he's striding towards that familiar voice, shoving Imperials aside to reach the lanky boy.

Even from this distance, I can see the tears brimming in Jax's eyes. He stands there, panting before his brother. And when he opens his mouth, the choked sob that escapes it makes my breath catch.

'Don't go,' he begs Kai. 'Please don't go. I might never see you again—'

A hiccup cuts off his words at the same moment Kai wraps his arms around the boy, holding him tight. He's saying something I can't hear, something that is likely meant to be a comfort.

Jax squeezes his eyes shut as he grips the back of Kai's shirt in his fists. 'My parents never came back,' I hear him say, voice breaking.

A piece of me shatters at the sound of it, at the grief already filling his voice. Jax has lost so much, so young. And I am watching him beg Kai not to be the next person he mourns.

Sniffling, Jax lets himself be pried away from his big brother. More hushed words are exchanged before Kai ruffles the boy's hair for what may be the last time. Then he turns slowly, solemnly, and strides back to the ship.

Shoulders tight and silence heavy, Kai joins me on board.

The Enforcer nods to the awaiting crew while I manage to muster up a smile. Chaos ensues shortly after our acknowledgment of them, as men and women begin bustling around the ship. Orders are shouted suddenly, setting every person into motion with a different task to complete.

With a subtle hand at my lower back, Kai guides me to the head of the ship where we watch the sails unfurl above us. Just the sheer amount of cloth would have Adena gawking. And I cling to that thought, that image of my smiling A.

My gaze travels to the large man at the helm, his hand gripping one of the many spokes adorning the massive wheel. His hat, attire, and shouted commands tell me that this is our captain for the journey to come. He looks weathered by the sea, and that alone is a comfort. Perhaps we have a chance at survival after all.

Thick ropes dangle from every corner of the ship, swaying from the masts towering over us. I'm in awe of such structured mayhem. It takes every scuttling crew member and their seemingly unimportant tasks to persuade the vessel into gliding across the water.

Of course, the Gusts on board certainly aid in the ship's quick pace. They guide chilling blasts of air into the sails, all while Teles hold down ropes and rigging with nothing but their minds. My gaze wanders over each soul attempting to coax the sea into something tamer, right down to the Hydros leaning over the railings, trying to smother what waves crash into the hull.

When the ship starts moving, my attention falls to the dock that slowly begins slipping away from us. My knuckles grow white around the wooden railing with each second the wind takes me farther from solid ground.

'You're going to be fine, Pae,' Kai murmurs beside me.

'Right,' I say distractedly. 'I know.'

'Is that why you're giving yourself splinters?'

Dragging my gaze from the distancing dock, I look down at the hand I've clamped around the railing. 'I'm just . . . nervous.'

He leans his forearms on the rail. 'You usually are around me. Don't hurt yourself over it, darling.'

I turn to face him with a scoff. 'I'm nervous about the journey, you prick.'

'Not even twenty minutes on the sea and you've already come up with a new nickname for me.'

'I'm sure many more will come to mind in the days ahead.'

His eyes roam over me, and I'm reminded how much I enjoy the feel of it. 'I missed you,' he finally murmurs, voice low.

Something flutters in my chest, and it might just be those nerves he determined I feel around him. 'I never left.'

A shake of his head. 'And yet, I felt the absence of you all the same.' He looks out at the water, his gray eyes mirroring the sea before us. 'I suppose that is my sentence for the rest of this life.'

I scramble for words, fight for the strength to speak them once they're found. But the moment shatters when a figure approaches.

The captain extends a hand to Kai, shaking it sternly. 'Enforcer, sir. It's an honor to be sailing with you.' When he turns to me, his greeting is far less enthusiastic. With a nod of his head, he offers a soft 'My Lady.'

I nearly jump when he claps his large hands together. 'Now, I'm Captain Torri, and this beauty—' he smacks the railing beside me, '—is the *Reckoning.*'

The long brown hair beneath his hat ripples when he shakes a thick finger at us. 'I haven't sailed in nearly a decade because of that damned decree to stay out of these damned waters.' His dark eyes flick to me. 'Excuse my language, miss. But, shit, if you ask me, this voyage is long overdue. We need to take back the Shallows.' He all but caresses the railing. 'And she is our reckoning.'

'Of course.' My tone has Kai's lips twitching. 'Now, what was that about not sailing for nearly a decade?'

'Well,' Torri stutters, 'the Shallows has been legally off-limits, so this will be my first crossing in some time. But I assure you,' he booms, 'that the crew and I are up to the challenge.'

Kai nods to the captain. 'Well, we greatly appreciate your willingness. It's not easy to find sailors in Ilya anymore.'

My stomach churns at the reminder. Ilya's experience with the Shallows is as limited as it is alarming, and the countless shipwrecks are a testament to that. No one of sane mind has set sail on this sea in nearly a decade, which would make this crew incredibly out of practice.

Any hope of survival has severely dwindled.

'Well, you won't see me running from these waters, sir,' the captain practically yells with a puff of his chest. 'Not even the creatures could keep me away.' He points to a thin scar slashing across his weathered cheek. 'Oi, but the devils have tried!'

He laughs, belly shaking beneath his buttoned coat. An uncomfortable sound climbs from my throat while Kai manages a polite laugh with the man. After taking a moment to recover, Torri continues with a wheezing cough. 'Now, let's get you acquainted with the *Reckoning*, eh?'

After an incoherent shout from the captain that makes me flinch, a man hurries over to his side. 'This,' Torri says nonchalantly, 'is my first mate, Leon. He will be showin' you to your rooms and around the ship.'

Leon nods curtly, his dark skin glistened with sweat beneath the bandanna tied around his head. The loose, white blouse he wears catches the wind like a sail of its own, the fabric flapping against him. Warm, brown eyes fall to me, and for once, it's not hatred I see within a gaze. Rather, curiosity.

'If you need anything,' the captain continues, 'it will be Leon here you go to. I'll be busy ensuring this damn ship makes it to shore.' He laughs deeply at his own words, even while stepping away with a toothy grin. 'Leon will give you a nice little tour of our lovely lady. But don't get too comfortable. We'll be docking at Izram in six days' time. Hopefully.'

With another bellowing laugh, he's heading for the helm, coat billowing behind him. I glance at Kai before obeying Leon's gesture to follow him. He leads us towards the stern of the ship, where a pair of wooden doors sit beneath the quarter deck at the rear. I'm forced to dodge bustling crew members as we walk, though they make an effort to steer clear of the Enforcer in front of me.

Two sets of wooden staircases lead to the deck above where Torri now stands at the wheel, conversing with the man who is likely his navigator. Gaze falling back to the doors before us, I watch as Leon shoves them open to reveal a slim hallway. He points to the particularly large doorway at the end of the corridor. 'Captain's quarters. If he invites you to dine with him one evening, you'll get the chance to see it.' His voice is deep, tone dry in a way that makes me assume he'd rather be doing anything else. 'And these are your rooms,' he informs, turning to the left and opening a pair of doors.

I peek inside one, finding a small bed crowding most of it. My packed trunk lies on a rickety dresser that creaks with every rock of the ship. A small porthole allows foggy light to stream in and drape the cot beneath. And there, on a small bedside table, sits the stack of books Calum brought for me.

Leon doesn't allow much time to examine the cabin before we are walking again. Leading us back onto the bustling deck, I blink in the searing sunlight as he lifts a large grate from the wood floor. 'This is the cargo access,' he says simply before stepping down the steep stairs that lead to the ship's underbelly.

With a reassuring glance, Kai descends first into the dim room below. I'm halfway down the steps when the ship rocks, forcing me to wrap my fingers around the wobbly railing beside me. Leon is talking again before I've even reached the floor. 'This is the berth deck. Otherwise known as the gun deck.' To emphasize, he gestures to the several cannons that innocently line the room. 'This is also where the crew sleeps.'

I stare at the dozens of swinging hammocks, most of which are haphazardly hung between the ominous cannons. 'All of them?' I blurt, unable to help myself. 'In this one room?'

'Yes, miss,' Leon responds plainly. 'Only the higher officers receive cabins. The rest of the crew live and sleep here.'

I swallow at the thought, already feeling nauseous at the sight of each swinging hammock. But the first mate pries my gaze from the assortment of hanging fabric when he points to the right. 'The gun port lies that way, along with the caskets of rum and water.' He swivels in the other direction. 'Some officers' quarters and the infirmary lie that way.'

Leon then points down at the deck beneath our feet where another grate rests. 'Ship's stores, cargo hold, spare sails, rigging, and your crate of roses. Oh, and the galley.' At my look of confusion, Leon adds, 'The kitchen. That's all down there where you will never need to go.'

With that, he starts up the stairs again, saying over his shoulder, 'That's about it. Not much of a tour.' Once again, I find myself blinking in the sudden brightness when we reach the main deck. 'You're free to head to your rooms or stay on the main deck. At the front of the ship—' he points towards the pointed bow, '—you'll find the head, or simply put, a place to relieve yourself.' With a glance at me, he continues, 'For you, miss, and the other women on board, we've added a bit of privacy to one of the toilets.'

I smile thinly. 'That is much appreciated.'

He nods, looking slightly apologetic before continuing. 'Your meals will be brought to your cabins. Where you eat them is up to you.' Deliberating, Leon seems to find nothing else of importance and concludes the tour with a reassuring string of words. 'If you need anything at all, find me. And trust that I will find you in case of an emergency.'

Before I can question what emergency that might be, the first mate is walking away. My doubt forms into a single sentence. 'What are the odds we survive this journey?'

Kai runs a hand through his windblown hair. 'You tell me, Little Psychic.'

I roll my eyes. 'I'm sensing that we may end up in the sea before even spotting land.'

He smiles, and suddenly, the frigid water starts to seem like a good idea. 'Then I'll swim for the both of us.'

CHAPTER 27

Kai

The ship rocks beneath me, lulling my body into a quiet place that isn't quite sleep.

Lacing my hands beneath my head, I stretch out on the cot, listening to the muffled waves outside my porthole. The sea is kind today, perhaps only to lure us into a false sense of security. Water is fickle, and man is foolish enough to think we can tame it.

The sun is setting beyond my small window, casting the cabin in an orange hue. I stare idly at the slatted ceiling above, unsure what to do with myself. I've never been so useless on a mission. One might find this dullness relaxing, but it's restlessness I feel.

My dinner plate sits atop the bedside table, now empty of the potatoes and beef that once filled the chipped dish. Reaching over it, I grab the bottle of rum that was graciously brought to my room and lift it to my lips. I sit up from the rough pillow, grimacing as the alcohol burns down my throat.

'Shit.' I cough out the curse before deciding it's a good idea to take another sip. This may be some of the strongest liquor I've had in years. Likely since Ava died.

The thought leaves a bitter taste in my mouth that has nothing

to do with the rum. My grip is tight around the bottle's neck. Since boarding this ship, I've been continuously reminded of just how dangerous it is to be alone with my own thoughts.

So I have no choice but to be with her.

That is what I tell myself as I stride out into the hall and rap my knuckles against her door.

Paedyn's voice is muffled behind the wood. 'Yes?'

'Would you like some company?' I call back.

'Is it yours?'

'I'm afraid so, darling.'

'All right, come in,' she says, sounding amused. 'By turning the handle, not kicking down the door.'

Smiling, I do as I'm told and step into the room. She's sitting on the bed, ankles crossed in front of her and back propped against the cabin wall. The dying sunlight streams far brighter through this porthole, splashing color and warmth over her. A worn book is held loosely between her fingers when those blue eyes flick up to mine.

'See,' she says sweetly, 'that wasn't so hard.'

I give her a look before sprawling onto her bed, my head in her lap.

'Are you drinking away your boredom?' she muses, looking down at me.

I shake the bottle still clutched in my hand. 'I was. And then I remembered that you are a far more appealing distraction.'

She rolls those bright eyes at me. 'Did you come in here just to flirt, Azer?'

'Darling, I haven't even started.'

Groaning dramatically, she snatches the bottle from my hand. 'Then I'm going to need this.'

'Don't act like you don't love it.'

She takes a swig of rum, twisting her face at the taste. I'm laughing before her lips have even left the bottle. She coughs and sputters and shoves the liquor back into my palm. Composing herself, Pae looks down at me with watery eyes that may just be a drop of the sea itself. 'There are a lot of things I pretend not to love.'

I still at her words. My gaze wanders over the face she tilts towards me, over every strand of silver hair falling around it. I reach up slowly, running my fingers through the shining, sun-drenched pieces. My voice is a murmur, a quiet confession. 'You're far better at pretending than I am.'

Her smile is sad. 'I've just had more practice at it.'

I shut my eyes for a long moment, reminded of the wearisome life she's endured. 'I know.'

She manages a smile, her fingers suddenly closing around the bottle once again. As soon as it's pried from my hand, she's lifting it into the air. 'But we don't need to pretend in here.'

After taking another sip, she hands the rum to me between coughs. 'I'll drink to that,' I mutter before sitting up and swallowing a mouthful.

She wags a finger at me. 'But that means we have to be on our best behavior when and if we make it back to Ilya.' Her gaze drops to the ring hugging her finger. 'Kitt noticed that this was on the wrong finger from the night you came to my rooms. So no more sneaking around. Let's just . . . enjoy this time together.'

Because we won't get it again.

I hear the unspoken words hanging between us. They mock me, just like that glinting diamond she wears. Every moment with her is spent mourning the next, awaiting the day we speak for the last time.

She glances up at me. Clears her throat. 'I went to his rooms last night.'

My blood chills. 'Did you?'

Words spill from her mouth, sounding more and more like a confession. 'I'm just trying to fix this . . . awkwardness between us. If we are supposed to spend the rest of our lives together, I want to at least enjoy being around one another. He is so stoic with me, and that is certainly not the Kitt I once knew, nor is that the brother he is towards you. So . . . I will keep befriending him in the hopes he will eventually reciprocate.'

She looks back at me expectantly, brows raised. I let her words sink in before washing them down with another swig of rum. It burns in my throat as I reach for the little purple book beside her. 'What are you reading?'

My hand is quickly halted by her quick snatching of my wrist.

'Did you even hear anything I just said?'

'I heard you.' My hands cup her face. 'I did. I do. And if you want me to tell you the sheer extent of my jealousy, then I will. But I'd rather not waste what little time we have together talking about my brother. Especially while I sit on your bed and try to stop myself from doing something rash with my future queen.' My eyes flick between her wide ones. 'But when we are back in that palace, I will let you see just how much I hate that you are not mine.'

Paedyn's mouth parts. 'Okay. I . . . um . . .' It seems I've rendered her speechless. She clears her throat before trying again. 'What was it you asked?'

My smile is wicked. 'Your book, darling.'

'Right.' She takes a deep breath. 'It's one I loved as a child. Calum brought a few for me.'

I place a hand on her thigh, leaning in to watch her flip open the cover. Faded illustrations are scattered throughout the pages, as are several pencil markings I can't quite make out.

'My father used to read them to me,' she says softly. 'This one was my favorite.'

'Tell me about it,' I murmur.

My request makes her smile. 'It's about phoenixes and other mystical creatures I always wished to meet. But it was the girl in this story that I liked most.'

She pauses on a random page, running her finger over a faint message scribbled there in crooked handwriting.

I want to be powerful like her.

Paedyn shakes her head at the words before closing the book. 'It's just a silly story.'

I watch her for a long moment, though she avoids my gaze. 'And the other books?'

'Mostly magic and worlds I wanted to escape to.' She sounds oddly bashful. 'Worlds where I might have fit in.'

I shift, laying my head back onto her lap. 'So which one will you be reading to me?'

Her whole face lights up, and it is a beautiful thing to behold. 'Really?'

'I'm all ears, Gray.'

Beaming, she flips to the front of that purple book. 'Phoenixes it is, then.'

My eyes fall shut when soft words begin spilling from her mouth. I'm quickly lost in the story, in the hypnotic voice that strings it together. The rocking ship lulls me into that fleeting sense of peace while her fingers comb through my hair, tickle my skin.

I picture this version of us, far in a future that will never come to pass. A happy ending in which I lie on Paedyn's lap, listening to her read until the day I fade into a distant memory.

But that is nothing more than a silly story of my making.

So I revel in the present, in the moments where we hide from the inevitable. She reads until the sun tires and dips beneath the waves. Until darkness drapes the room and smothers each word on the page.

Paedyn quiets, brushing a strand of hair from my brow. At the sound of her book snapping shut, I lift my gaze to her shadowed one above me. 'Do you—?'

Muffled stomping from beyond the door has me swiftly sitting up. Glancing at each other, we strain to hear the commotion coming from the main deck. Clapping follows the pounding of boots, creating a symphony of chaos.

'Is that . . . ?' Paedyn quiets at the growing sound of music.

'That,' I say, grinning into the darkness, 'is the sound of a poorly played fiddle.'

I don't give her a chance to reply before I'm pulling her off the bed. Sputtering, she manages, 'What are you doing?'

I turn to face her, lifting the hand that isn't wearing my brother's ring. My lips find the pad of her thumb. She sucks in a breath at the intimacy of it, at the meaning buried beneath. 'My pretty Pae, would you like to dance?'

Her smile seems to brighten the darkness. 'I would never pass up the chance to stomp on your toes, Malakai.'

I tug her close, hold her tight. She knows exactly what she's doing. My name means nothing to me until she speaks it. Nothing until she claims it as her own.

I kiss it off her lips, taste the very power she holds over me. My hand cups the back of her neck, fingers tangling in her short hair. She's clutching my shirt and pulling me against her—

Another chorus of stomps has us breaking apart and breathing heavy. Paedyn laughs in that intoxicating way that makes me want to pull her mouth back to mine. But she's grabbing my hand and swinging the door open before I get the chance. I'm being tugged out into the hall and towards the double doors ahead. With a quick smile over her shoulder, she drops my hand and pushes them open.

The deck sprawls before us, bathed in moonlight. Men and women of all ages dance in time to the fiddle's melody, linking arms to spin around the wood. The crew claps and stomps and crudely sings along to a song that belongs out at sea.

Paedyn steps forward, seeming unsure even as she smiles at the scene. Spotting us from the makeshift circle of bellowing men, Leon strides over, looking less stoic than he had this morning, though the bottle of rum in his hand is likely to thank for that.

As way of greeting, he answers the questioning look Paedyn wears. 'The crew always celebrates a tame day at sea. Today has been especially smooth sailing considering the Shallows' reputation.'

The ship rocks slightly in agreement, its hull cutting easily through lazy waves. Leon nods to the rowdy group. 'You're welcome to join. Have some rum. Dance. Oh, and Sam's fiddle is out of tune, but believe me, it's been worse.'

I offer an arm to Paedyn. 'Should I hold your shoes now, or wait for you to lose them?'

'Maybe I'll just throw them at you.' She smiles sweetly. 'So you can find them easier.'

My gaze lazily explores her face. 'Vicious little thing.'

When we step into the circle, Paedyn wastes no time before clapping to the beat. I watch her smile at the dancing before us, but more importantly, I watch those eying her closely. Some scowl at her presence while others barely notice the future queen among them. And before I'm dragged into a dance, I memorize the faces of those glaring men.

Paedyn hooks her arm through mine before we are stepping in a circle. She laughs, picking up our pace and flipping around to take my other arm. We do this until I'm out of breath, until my mouth hurts from smiling at her.

Rum is passed between us, as are the dance partners we link elbows with. The fiddle's quick melodies have us stomping long into the night, clapping when our feet get sore. Before long, Paedyn is swaying beside a sailor, singing a ballad to the sea crashing around us.

I do this for her. Every dance. Every smile. She seems so much more alive away from Ilya, away from the reminder of everything she is not. But out here, even surrounded by Elites, we are all at the mercy of the sea. I think she finds comfort in that.

So I spin her in the moonlight. Smile when she laughs at my expense. And let her step on my toes.

Edric

There is little that King Edric, ruler of the first Elite kingdom, fears.

But this child is a tangible nightmare in his arms.

'You are wrong.'

Those are the first words out of Edric's mouth, aimed sharply at his Silencer. Damion has curtly handed the king his daughter before stepping away, now holding tightly to that stoic expression plastering his features. There is a slow shake of his head, the action regretful. 'I can silence no power from her, Your Majesty. I could be mistaken, but . . .'

The king has heard enough. See, the mere prospect of a powerless child sharing his name is sufficiently damning.

Whispers slither their way into the silence, and with them, the ringing in Edric's ears. He looks down at the baby girl, seeing little more than her lack of power. How could he, a Brawny and king of gods, produce something so *weak*?

This is an embarrassment. This is a mockery of everything the king is and believes.

His green eyes grow colder with each passing moment as they

drift towards Iris's dead body. She was a rarity, one that Edric had not known before her – a Soul. This ability allowed her to sense and manipulate another's emotions. More than once, Iris had used it on the king to turn the pressures of ruling into a spark of happiness that he only ever felt when she was around.

The child cries in Edric's trembling arms, its skin still sticky with blood.

How could this nothing come from something so strong and rare?

An Ordinary born of two powerful Elites is unheard of. Yet, here she is, this weak excuse for life.

Each scream has the infant's bloody chest rising and falling, the action so frail. It's almost impressive, the pathetic little heart pumping beneath her skin. The king thinks this with disgust, reminded only of the fact that his wife no longer has a pulse – but this weakness does.

Edric looks down at his own daughter, hate in his heart and sorrow welling in his eyes.

Iris is dead, and it was all for an Ordinary. For this embarrassment. For *nothing*.

The king gives a command, cutting through the silence. It's even and deliberate, as though the words tumbling from his mouth don't steal the breath from every pair of surrounding lungs. 'Get rid of it.'

Feet shift. Throats clear.

A Healer, her hands stained scarlet, can think of nothing to say but the king's title posed as a question. 'Your Majesty?'

'It killed my wife,' Edric says coolly. 'An Ordinary killed my wife. Get rid of it.'

'Your Majesty,' an adviser protests, 'it's merely an infant—'

'Get. Rid. Of. It.'

The king extends the child into the open air, pushing as much space between them as possible. His gaze is sharp enough to draw blood, and that is precisely what will happen if his demands are not met.

'I'll dispose of . . . it.'

Edric's Mind Reader steps forward, extending his hands towards the crying princess, who only has these fleeting moments to be so.

The king smiles tightly before handing his daughter over to the trusted Fatal.

This is the last time he will ever hold her. All this child will ever know is his violence and hatred before the end.

'See that you do,' Edric orders, holding the Mind Reader's gaze before turning to address every other stunned stare. 'What you saw today did not happen. Your queen did not die giving birth to an Ordinary, because she passed two years ago when delivering me my son and heir. That is what the kingdom will know. That is what history will know.'

He glances over at his wailing daughter, expression void of any sympathy. 'This Ordinary does not belong to me. It is already forgotten.'

As the Mind Reader steps from the room, a lost princess in his arms, the king barks a command at his advisers. 'Seal the records. Ensure that today never happened.'

Then he storms from the room, having rid the world of one more useless Ordinary.

CHAPTER 28
Paedyn

A clap of thunder jolts me awake.

I sit up, blinking in the darkness that surrounds me. The ship shakes violently, nearly tipping me from the cot. Rain pelts the porthole, the sound echoing off the glass.

I sit there, stunned by how quickly the weather turned. Our second day at sea had been eerily peaceful, dragging on as I read to Kai and milled about the deck.

Another sharp turn of the ship has my books toppling to the floor with a soft thud I hardly hear over the roll of thunder. Another crack of lightning follows a beat after, illuminating the room with a fleeting flash of light. I can feel each angry wave against the boat, hear the roar of rushing water so close beyond these wooden walls.

Muffled shouts echo from the main deck. I stand, legs shaking atop the unsteady floor. The ship dips into a crashing wave, pitching me forward before I can find my footing. I collide with the wall, bracing my arms against it until I trust myself to take another step.

Managing to stumble towards the door, I reach for the handle, fingers slipping as I'm flung forward once again. The dresser creaks behind me, mimicking each chilling groan from the ship.

When I finally throw open the door, I screech at the figure standing behind it.

'Kai!' I'm forced to yell over the storm despite my relief at seeing him. 'What is—'

My eyes fall to the dark shadow spilling slowly down the hallway. It takes me a moment to realize what it is I'm looking at. And what it means.

Water.

The waves are crashing over the ship, readying to swallow us all—

His hands are suddenly on my hips, pushing me back. 'You need to stay in this room!'

Thunder growls all around us, shaking the very floors we stand on. Kai is kicking the door shut, closing us in this room, this watery grave. I shake my head at him, at the feel of panic rising up my throat. 'No. No, I can't be locked in here, Kai! Not now!'

A crack of lightning shadows his stern features. He cups my face, holding me steady when the ship lurches. 'Do you trust me?'

A trickle of water seeps beneath the door. Like Death's cold finger, it reaches for me.

'Pae?'

His shout forces my gaze back to him. I nod shakily. 'I do. I did even when I shouldn't have.'

'I know the feeling.' He presses his forehead to mine, breathing soft words across my skin. 'So I need you to stay in this room with me until we are told otherwise.'

My pounding heart drowns out every crashing wave, every desperate shout from the crew who wrestles them. The cabin seems to close in on me, growing smaller with the echoing thought that I can no longer leave it. The sea rages all around me, and yet it may be my own claustrophobia that drags me into death.

The room is growing smaller, the ocean yawning larger. I'm going to suffocate in this cabin before the water even rushes into my lungs.

My lungs.

They can't seem to find air. I'm choking on a different type of sea. It's this shallow space, this ever-shrinking cabin come to crush me.

My knees buckle beneath me before I'm sinking to the floor. Ears

213

ringing, I can barely hear Kai's shouted concern behind me. He's holding my crumpled body against his as we rock back and forth with the churning waves.

Something cold laps against my leg. Hazily, I look down to find Death's icy finger grazing my skin. A caress and reunion all at once. He's found me once again. The last time we met he brushed sandy fingers against my cheek in the Scorches. Now, it's the raging sea he commands to drag me back to him.

A muffled shout against my ear has me stirring. I place a palm in the puddle of water as if to shake Death's hand. Commend him for his resilience.

'Pae!'

Lightning flashes across the room at the same moment my name rings out into it. His head is tucked into my shoulder, breath warm against the bare skin there. 'We are going to be fine,' he reassures sternly. 'You've survived the Scorches more than once. Now you'll do the same for the Shallows.'

I nod, forcing my breath to slow. We sit on the floor, holding each other while the boat tries to throw us apart. I cling to him, every finger fisted into his crumpled shirt. He strokes my hair, whispers words of comfort.

My anchor in the storm.

'I have something for you,' he murmurs.

Still struggling to swallow my panic, I croak, 'A distraction, I hope.'

'Something like that.' He unwraps an arm from me, never fully letting me go as he struggles to shrug something from his shoulders. It's only when he sets the pack atop the damp floor that I notice it for the first time. Reaching inside, he pulls out a thinly wrapped sphere.

I don't even have to ask what it is. I know that shape. Know that smell.

Honey.

Tears prick my eyes. 'You brought that from Ilya?'

Another streak of lightning allows me to see the slight smile gracing his features. 'Just for you.'

Kai lets me do the honors of unraveling the sweet dough. The honey coating my fingers has a smile tipping my lips. I forget every chilling wave that tries to tear the ship apart, every fear lodged deep in my throat. It's this sticky bun I focus on instead, and the memory of every one I've shared before.

My eyes flutter shut when I finally take a bite. This dough holds every happy moment I've had in this life, and if I am to die tonight, I want it to be with this honey on my tongue. This reminder of my home – Adena.

'It might be a bit stale by now,' Kai starts softly.

'No,' I choke out. 'It's perfect. That's exactly how I always ate them. How *we* always ate them.'

Thunder roars as we sway on the floor with each roll of the ship. I sink my fingers into the sticky bun, pulling it in half. Kai looks surprised when I offer him a piece. 'This is for you. Your distraction,' he says firmly.

'I want you to share it with me. Please.' I wave the dough in front of him in that way Adena always used to do. 'I don't know how to eat one of these alone.'

Graciously, he nods in understanding before plucking the piece from between my fingers. I flinch at the echoing shouts that are quickly carried away on the whipping wind. 'You deserve a distraction too,' I say as softly as the stormy sea will allow.

He brushes cool knuckles down the side of my cheek. 'You are forever my distraction, darling.'

Water pools around my ankles, and yet, I sit here with my head against his chest. We eat this sticky bun on the floor of my cabin, in the middle of a raging sea, and somehow find tranquility in the violence.

As if I've found the eye of the storm within him, and he in me.

I wake to a soft pillow beneath my head.

I certainly didn't put it there. Nor did I lift my body onto the bed last night. But here I lie, snuggled beneath the covers with hands that are clean of honey.

Blinking my tired eyes into focus, I sweep them over the damp floor and the spot we had occupied last night. We sat there for hours, talking over the storm and bracing ourselves against each shuddering wave. I must have dozed off in his arms before they lifted me onto the cot.

Beyond the porthole is a sky of gray, and beneath is a riled sea, likely embittered by this ship still being afloat.

The ship is still afloat.

A relieved smile settles on my lips as I sit up. I've survived my first storm on the Shallows. Whether I live to see the next is a worry for another time.

Standing to my feet, I pad across the damp floor and unlatch my trunk. A heap of neatly folded clothes greets me, though I'm quick to rummage through them in search of something comfortable to wear. I settle for a pair of fitted black pants beneath a loose blouse.

Pulling my olive vest on, I run my fingers down the fraying seams and stretched pockets. It feels as though I've barely worn the gift since returning to Ilya. Instead, I've been shoved into gowns that make me think of Adena and how she can no longer make them, even in death, with those broken fingers.

Dipping my hands into the fresh water basin atop the dresser, I banish the thought from my head with a cool splash across the face. With a slight shiver, I pat my skin dry and—

And my books are on the floor.

'No, no, no,' I murmur, rushing over to collect the delicate stories. The ship still rocks enough to have me struggling with my footing, so I drop to my knees before the waves send me sprawling.

I quickly gather the books into my arm, noting their rippled pages from the seawater. Cursing under my breath, I stand and head for the door. The damp spines stick to my palm as I march out onto the deck and greet the dreary sky above.

Wind whips at my unbound hair, sending silver strands to obscure my vision. I fight to free my gaze, only to stop suddenly at the devastation I see. Large chunks have been torn from the railing where the sea has sunk its icy teeth into the wood. Tangled ropes lie strewn across the deck, littering the floor alongside other miscellaneous debris.

The captain's bellowed commands ensure that no crew member stands idly. The ship teeters beneath me, and I stumble on legs not accustomed to the sea. The sailors surrounding me sneer at the sight before continuing to stride utterly unfazed across the slippery dock.

I straighten my vest and gather what is left of my dignity as I walk carefully towards an unmarred section of railing. The wind cuts through me, stinging and salty. I lean over the railing, watching the water rush below. Its light blue and green coloring is deceitfully inviting, despite the great depth beneath its surface. And that is precisely how it earned the name Shallows for itself.

Clutching three of the books tightly beneath my arm, I lift one into the air, letting the pages flutter in the wind. It's not the most ideal way to dry them, but it will certainly be the fastest.

Snickers behind my back tell me that the crew have taken a liking to laughing at my expense. I ignore them, as I've done with every haughty Elite I've been forced to live alongside, and switch books.

That is when the boat dips into a wave, spraying water across the deck to thoroughly drench me. More laughter fills the air as I stand there, shivering and clutching the last piece of my childhood against a constricting chest.

'Need some help, darling?'

I spin on my heel, nearly tipping over when the ship bucks beneath us. But there he stands, hands shoved into pockets nearly as deep as the dimple peeking out at me. Damn him.

Damn him.

With the way he's looking at me, I might have just mumbled the words out loud. Nothing and no one has ever devastated me more. Not the sand, the sea, the slow brush of Death's hand. Because maybe, just maybe, he is the most ruinous thing of them all.

He shrugs off his coat to reveal a fitted black shirt. 'Don't look at me like that.'

Those words seem to stir something within me, a fleeting memory muffled by several glasses of champagne. The fragile thought shatters with the chattering of my teeth. 'And h-how am I looking at you?'

His responding grin has blood rushing to my numb cheeks. He steps close, swinging the coat around my shoulders before tugging it closed. I watch his mouth form a response I never get to hear.

'Oi, that was quite the storm last night!'

I barely know the man, and yet, I recognize his voice from across the ship. Turning, I find Torri trudging towards us, long hair knotted at the base of his neck. 'But she pulled through,' he continues, running a hand over the chipped railing. 'Though, I fear this is only the beginning. The Shallows will not continue to be so kind.'

I clutch my books tightly beneath Kai's draped coat. If it was kindness the sea showed us last night, I'm not sure I'll live long enough to see land.

'Cheer up, girl!' The captain laughs at whatever it is he sees on my face. 'You only need to last four more days. And then, well, the trip back, but we won't concern ourselves with that just yet.'

He finds that funny as well and continues his chuckling all the way to the helm. I turn back towards Kai, giving him an exasperated look that never fails to make him smile.

'What was it you were about to say?' I ask, curiosity momentarily grabbing hold of my tongue.

He seems to ponder this as his gaze drifts out over the water. 'Nothing I haven't said before.'

And that is the only answer he offers before extending a hand to me. 'Now, put me to work. These books need to dry before you read one to me tonight.'

I huff in amusement before placing one of the damp covers in his awaiting palm. Flipping open to a particularly crinkled page, Kai holds the book into the wind. I do the same, my teeth chattering beside him.

We must look ridiculous, leaning against the rail and holding literature in the air. I almost laugh at the odd picture we paint, but the view of rushing water around us steals my frigid breath away. The horizon stretches in every direction, nothing but a rippling blanket of blue.

'Do you ever wonder if there is anything else out there?' I ask, my words nearly snatched away by the wind's cold fist.

Kai flips to another page. 'Well, other than the myths?' He shrugs. 'I'm not sure.'

'The myths?'

His brows lift. 'Have you never heard of Astrum? The birthplace of shadows and the death of a great love?' He recites this as though I should know the phrase by heart.

'My father—' I nearly stumble over the word, now knowing the truth and mystery behind it, '—didn't waste his time teaching me myths. In fact, he barely had time to educate me on things that actually do exist,' I finish with a pointed look at the prince.

'Of course. Yet, he had time to read you a story about . . .' He thumbs through several pages of the book between his fingers. 'A horse with fangs and—'

'That's enough,' I laugh, snatching the book from him.

'Shit, no wonder you're afraid of horses, Gray.'

I roll my eyes. 'You were saying? About Astrum?'

Kai throws me a grin before flipping open another damp book. 'Well, many people believe Astrum existed long before Ilya. There, they live in a constant state between dawn and dusk, thanks to the separated lovers – the sun, Solis, and the moon, Luna.' He continues despite the skeptical look I give him. 'Shadows are precious there. They are a power that can be stolen.' I startle when he snaps the book shut. 'You know what, I bet the captain has a copy.'

A hoarse laugh falls from my mouth. 'There's a book about this?'

Kai's already set a steady pace towards the captain's quarters. 'Of course there is. Torri likely has one because every sailor does. They are always looking for the city, hoping they can be the first to find it.'

I shake my head at his back. 'This is absurd.'

'You live in Ilya, home of Elites, and you think this is absurd?'

I hum in agreement. It is the most I will do to acknowledge that he may be right.

Before pushing through the double doors that lead to our rooms, Kai turns to face me. 'It's called *Shadow and Soul*.' The corner of his mouth twitches. 'And I'm looking forward to hearing you read it tonight.'

CHAPTER 29

Kai

My chest rises and falls beneath her back.

Paedyn sits between my legs atop the bed, her spine pressed against my beating heart. I can feel every vibration of her soothing voice as she reads a piece of her past self to me.

It's no wonder she grew up to be so formidable if the women in these stories helped raise her. They are fearless, their stories thrilling.

She tore through *Shadow and Soul*, despite claiming it was only to appease me. A terrible defense, seeing that she would never do anything that she didn't already want to do. So, her disguised interest in the tale had us reading long into the night. We spent longer still discussing the story after she'd snapped the book shut, unable to contain her annoyance at wanting more.

Now, she reads yet another one of her own books, and I am more than content to listen to the words falling from those familiar lips. I wrap an arm around her waist, letting my eyes flutter shut. This is how we have occupied ourselves over the last two days. It has become our distraction during the never-ending storm that is the Shallows. The sea has yet to stop raging since early yesterday morning, and

with night now falling on our fourth day at sea, Paedyn has nearly read me three books.

The ship grows more nauseating with each violent roll and dip. In fact, when I'm not in the presence of Pae, I can likely be found emptying the contents of my stomach over the boat's railing. But it's her voice that seems to keep the stale biscuits and salty beef down.

The lantern on my bedside table teeters on the edge, readying to careen towards the wet floor after a particularly rough rocking of the ship. My free hand reaches out to steady it at the same moment Paedyn quiets.

'What?' I ask, clutching her closely when lightning flashes into the room.

'That was the end of the chapter.'

I rest my chin against her shoulder, pointing to the page. 'Well, there is another one beside it. So, go on.'

'Kai,' she laughs out my name, and I wonder if she knows what it does to me. 'It's getting late.'

I tilt my head to study her profile. 'Are you implying that you're tired?'

'Of you?' She smiles. 'Very.'

My mouth twists. 'If you're going to continually lie about wanting me, at least try to make it believable.'

'You know,' she says calmly, 'there is still plenty of time for me to throw you overboard.'

'See, I knew you couldn't go more than a couple days without threatening me.'

She turns to face me then, folding her legs so they rest against mine. 'Because I know how much you like it.'

'How very thoughtful of you.'

Thunder shakes the very bed we sit on while waves pound against the ship. She presses a startled hand to my thigh, fingernails digging into the flesh beneath my pants. I can still see the terror that flashes in her gaze, but it's lessened into something far more tolerable. Something like numbness.

Without a story to distract her, without words to form on the lips she chews with worry, Paedyn fiddles with the steel ring on her thumb. 'I should get back to my room.'

I tilt my head. 'And why is that?'

'Because,' she sighs, 'the crew has already seen enough to gossip about when we get back to Ilya.' She flinches at a sudden flash of lightning. 'If we make it back.'

'All the more reason to stay with me tonight.'

'Hmm.' She untangles her legs from mine to slide from the cot. 'Still not convinced.'

'And if I said please?'

She stills beside the bed, her body swaying with the rolling waves. Pae's eyes meet mine and suddenly I'm back in the palace, back to that night when I begged her to stay with me after watching her die in my nightmare. I'm reliving that moment, only this time, it's my own selfish desires that have me needing her beside me.

Swallowing, she crosses her arms. 'Well, go on then.'

I chuckle at her insistence before standing to my feet right as the ship bucks violently. Caught off guard, Paedyn comes careening towards me with a gasp. I catch her against my chest, feel her body melt against mine. My head dips until our noses brush. 'Stay with me. Please.'

Her head shakes, but she's wearing a smile. I nudge her nose again as I murmur, 'My pretty, pretty Pae.' She laughs breathlessly. 'Stay with me.' I press my forehead to her own. 'Stay with me. Stay with me.'

'Fine!' She laughs out the word while offering a gentle flick to the tip of my nose. 'Fine, I'll stay.'

I smile for her, only her, always her. 'I was prepared to plead.'

She gives me a look. 'You would not.'

'Oh, darling, I would do so much worse if only you asked.' I tuck a strand of hair behind her ear with a smile. 'Or, even more difficult, so much better.'

'You know,' she says slowly, 'you're not nearly as terrifying as you seem.'

'Not to you. Never to you.'

I sit down beside her, feeling the ship rock viciously all around us. She looks at me, eyes as bright as the sea itself. I stare into them, memorizing the multitude of hues they hold in the flickering lantern light. My favorite color is a shade of her, a sliver of the vibrance she exudes. And I will gladly drown, gladly burn, gladly fall into those blue eyes until the day she looks at me for the last time.

'Don't look at me like that,' she breathes.

My lips twitch. 'This is the only way I've ever looked at you, darling.'

Her smile grows uncharacteristically timid. I lean forward, grabbing our book to flip deftly through the pages. 'Well, you might as well keep reading since you're here.'

'So, that's why you wanted me to stay.' Her scoff is accompanied by a shake of her head. 'So I'll read to you.'

'Among many other reasons—' she hits me with the pillow, '—including your wonderful company.'

'You're unbelievable, Azer.'

My eyes flick to the dimly lit bed we occupy. 'Not the first time I've been told that in a setting like this—'

The pillow collides with my face, muffling her laugh behind it.

I'm jolted awake to the rumbling of thunder.

I lift my head off the pillow to—

Shit.

Pain pounds beneath my skull, growing sharper by the second. I vaguely wonder if my temple had met the bedside table during the night to cause this current throbbing.

My head feels heavy as I turn to face her.

Dull moonlight creeps over Paedyn to mingle with her silver hair. It's fanned across the pillow, surrounding the placid face she wears in sleep. The covers have been kicked down below her feet, and I'm shocked to see she isn't shivering without them.

My head aches as I sit up to grab the forgotten quilt. I'm about to throw it over her when I lean in close, my mouth mere inches from meeting her forehead.

I stop suddenly, my eyes scanning her face, the bridge of her nose—

There can't be more than ten.

I jerk back, staring at the body beside me.

This is not my Pae.

I still my mind and focus on the distant thrum of powers beneath my skin. Flash, Tele, Hydro—

And that is when I feel it. Close and strong and to blame for this.

Staring at those ten freckles, I throw the blanket over her.

It meets nothing but air as Paedyn's body vanishes.

Illusion.

I jump from the bed, my pounding head clearing enough to realize that I have been drugged. All so someone could rip her from my bed.

Boots are suddenly on my feet before I'm buckling a sword around my waist. I shove open the door and do the same to those awaiting me at the end of the hall.

It's as though I've stepped out into the sea itself.

Wind whips at my thin shirt, instantly numbing every inch of me. Water pours from the sky to pelt my skin and soak me to the bone. I can barely keep my footing on the drenched deck as waves continually crash over the railing. The ship groans with each dip into the water, leaving me swaying like a drunk as I try to keep my balance.

I stride out farther onto the deck, struggling to see anything through the sheets of rain. 'Where is she?!' I shout the words into the storm, hoping the whipping wind will carry them towards the scattered crew members.

It's the sea that responds with a towering wave, drawing my attention to the far end of the boat. I squint through the rain, watching water curl over the railing to drench the three figures huddled there.

The Illusionist's ability burns hot beneath my skin, growing stronger with every step I take towards the group of men. I feel for the other powers, finding a Tele and Gust awaiting me.

My heart beats wildly against my soaking shirt as I stride towards them. When the ship pitches violently, I drop to a knee until I'm able to get my feet beneath me. The men grow closer, clearer against the rain. The three of them—

No. Not three.

The world goes quiet. The storm fades. Lightning dulls.

There are four figures beside that railing.

One of them is gagged and bound, her arms tucked tightly behind her back. She still wears that green vest, having fallen asleep with the comfort wrapped around her. The men have her raised in the air, two of them clutching her roped ankles while the other sinks his fingers into her shoulders.

I've found her.

Lifting Paedyn towards the rail, they grin as she thrashes in their hold, desperately trying to free herself.

And something snaps in me at the sight.

I unleash that piece of myself that Father carved into me. That lethal sliver of darkness he once commanded at will, having known it by name. Created it in the depths of his dungeons, in every one of my fears, in a shadowed home with my sword through an innocent man's chest.

It's a piece of Death himself that lives within me.

And now, I command it.

I grip the Tele's power in my hand, feeling the ability course through me. My steps don't falter or slow. Nor does my soul repent for what I'm about to do to theirs.

With little more than a vengeful thought, I throw the Gust over the ship's edge. It's a lazy toss that has his head cracking against the wood before he's plummeting into icy water.

After watching a wave swallow their friend, the other two men whip around to find me steadily striding towards them. Paedyn's legs drop to the ground, her frantic gaze widening when it lands on me. The men react the same, though it's fear filling their eyes, not relief.

And I smile at it.

Paedyn struggles against the Illusionist's grip while the Tele steps towards me. Even through the pouring rain, I recognize his blurry face. This is one of the men who was watching Paedyn dance that first night on the ship.

He throws out a strand of power, wrapping it around my neck. It feels as though a phantom noose has been knotted against my throat, squeezing hard enough to have black creeping in at the corners of my vision.

He's choking me with his ability.

Pathetic. All that power, and this is how he thinks I'll meet my end?

I can no longer breathe, but I've faced far worse from my own father. Closing the distance between us, I throw a punch at his face. And when he dodges like I knew he would, it's already too late. My left hand is drawing my sword from its sheath and slicing the blade across his stomach within one swift movement.

His choking hold on my throat drops at the same moment he does. I suck in a breath before rolling my tight neck. The man sprawls onto the wood before me, blood gushing from the deep gash, even as water pelts the wound. A stream of scarlet quickly seeps out beneath him, staining the deck before the rain can wash it away.

I step over his body, not offering him another glance. Pushing dripping hair from my brow, I turn back to Paedyn and the Illusionist. With his eyes locked on mine, he lifts her bound body into his arms.

The tip of my blade is pressed to his heart within the next beat of it. I shake my head, panting, 'Put her down, and I won't make you suffer.'

He holds my gaze, body rigid beneath my blade. 'I'll die before seein' an Ordinary sit on Ilya's throne.'

My sword plunges into his heart at the same moment he throws Paedyn over the railing.

A scream rips from my throat, lost in the raging storm.

I don't think. I don't breathe. I don't hesitate to leave my sword buried in the sailor and dive towards the railing.

She's falling to her death.

The gag has slipped from her mouth to allow a chilling scream. Those blue eyes are locked on mine as she plummets farther and farther and—

The Tele's power grows weak beneath my skin. He's barely alive, but barely is all I need. Tugging at that power, I hurl it towards her bound body.

The ability grows taut, like an invisible rope has wrapped itself around her waist. I grit my teeth as her falling weight slams against my mind, and her body hangs suspended above the waves.

Her head falls back, silver hair brushing the hungry water awaiting her. I strain to lift her towards me even as piercing pain cuts through my mind. When the ship threatens to tip from a vengeful wave, I'm nearly thrown over the splintered railing. Urging myself to focus, I will her towards me, commanding my tired mind to obey.

A wave crashes over the ship, soaking Paedyn's hanging body before meeting my own. The force of the water nearly pulls her down, but I fight to keep her rising upward. Grunting against the pain in my head, I reach towards her, stretching my dripping arms over the rail.

Her head lifts then, our eyes locking in a moment that even time cannot contain. She stares at me with a sort of fear I've never seen her wear. And maybe I'm looking at her the same, like nothing has ever terrified me more than losing her.

And that is when the Tele's power flickers and dies beneath my skin.

CHAPTER 30

Paedyn

The last thing I see is the terror on his face.

Then I'm falling again.

I am going to drown.

Death will meet me in this watery grave, grinning as he snatches my soul from the sea.

When I felt that Tele ability release me, I wouldn't let my eyes leave his. I wanted Kai's gray gaze to be the last thing to take my breath away, not the ravenous waves.

But something happened.

I didn't hit the water.

Kai lunged forward, nearly falling after me, and grabbed hold of the only thing he could.

Adena's vest.

I'm halted in the air once again, heart in my throat.

Waves crash angrily below as Kai grunts, using every bit of his own strength to pull me upward. I hear the seams rip as my beloved vest begins splitting apart from my weight. Hands bound behind my back, I can do nothing but stare at the popping thread as Kai strains to lift me.

Water drips from my drenched body, making the tearing vest slippery. Kai cries out, his arm bulging beneath a soaked sleeve. Another sharp tear from the thick fabric has me accepting my watery fate.

Then an arm wraps around my waist.

Kai grits his teeth, pulling me up and over the railing. I'm pressed to his chest, my legs dragging over the wood railing.

Blood rushes to my head. Knees buckle. Kai guides me to the soaking deck with arms that dragged my soul from Death's clutches. 'I've got you,' he pants against my ear. 'I've got you, Pae.'

I press my head into his chest, tears leaking from my eyes. The storm rages around us and still he holds me. His body quivers against mine, likely from exhaustion, but perhaps from the fading fear. I feel him shift, lifting an arm from around me. I'm too tired to track the movement, but when the rope is suddenly cut from my wrists, I realize that he's pulled his sword from the sailor's chest.

Kai then gently stretches out my legs, cutting them free with a precise swipe of his blade. My dazed stare lands on the bodies littering the deck beside us. Both are covered in blood, their gazes glassily turned to the stormy sky. The realization that I'm likely sitting in their blood doesn't torment me as much as I thought it would. In fact, I believe I could bathe in their remains for being the reason my last piece of Adena is destroyed.

And just like that, I'm one step closer to overcoming this choking fear of blood.

Kai is suddenly crouching before me, turning my face from the dead bodies with a gentle press of his fingers against my jaw. 'Are you all right?' As if unable to restrain himself, he cups my face in his hands before running swift fingers down my body to check for wounds.

'I'm okay.' My whisper is nearly lost in the howling wind, but I know he hears it when his eyes snap to mine. 'I'm okay. I'm alive.' Tears are pricking my eyes again. 'Because of you.'

Water drips from his lashes, but it's the slight indent of his right dimple that my eyes fall to. 'I promised to save your life again and again. And I will, whether you allow me to stay in it or not.'

I nod at him, vision blurry from my tears and the sky's. 'Now, let's get you inside,' he says, scooping me into his arms.

I let him carry me into my cabin. Let him convince me to stay put. Let him retrieve my dagger from under the pillow and shove it into my hand. 'This would have been useful tonight,' I say weakly.

He shakes his head, and I see the shade of anger that falls over his face. 'They drugged me in my sleep. Then that Illusionist cast you sleeping beside me so I'd see you when I woke up.'

'What?' I could almost laugh. 'They hardly seemed like the calculating type.' My gaze drops to the dagger I wish I'd had with me. 'But after they drugged you, I woke to the three of them dragging me from the room. I couldn't break free, couldn't move . . .' I swallow at the reminder of my panic. 'I was screaming, but no one heard me. Or no one *wanted* to hear me. Then they tied me up, gagged me, and . . . well, you know the rest.'

Rage rolls off him in waves as deadly as the ones colliding with this ship. 'You're not safe here. I told Kitt that. And where was the rest of the crew?' He begins pacing, fists clenched beside his drenched pants. 'They were likely in on this in some way. And if I'm right, I will deal with them when we return to Ilya. But for now, we need them to get us back there in one piece.'

I offer him a nod. 'That sounds like a good plan.'

'What,' he muses, 'you're okay with the spilling of so much blood?'

I run a finger down my blade before flicking my eyes up to his. 'It depends on whose blood.'

He's never kissed me so thoroughly.

<hr/>

'Paedyn, miss, I cannot tell you how shocked I was to hear what some of my men tried to do last night.'

I stare at the captain, my face blank as I await an apology. Kai had already charged into Torri's quarters last night to fill him in on the eventful evening. By the time he returned to the cabin, I was fast asleep, my dagger clutched in a fist.

Now I sit in the captain's cushy dining area, my fingers laced atop the wooden table and expression unamused. The sleepy sun fights to peek around the thick blanket of clouds, occasionally slipping a ray of light through one of the many windows. The room is larger than I'd expected with wide shelves that line the walls, all filled with toppled-over trinkets and maps.

A particularly worn piece of parchment curls against the wall opposite me, snagging my attention. It's decorated with an assortment of sketched cities and their accompanying flags. Well aware of what kingdoms live on our map, I begin to steer my gaze away before it stumbles over splotches of unfamiliarity.

The scribbled world I'm staring at extends beyond Izram.

My eyes narrow on the foreign masses of land bubbling from the Shallows. No map I've ever studied has looked like this. I can't make out the names of these supposed kingdoms from where I'm sitting, but after reading about that mythical city of shadows, I'd bet Astrum has been wistfully scrawled atop an inky landmass.

I almost smile.

So this is what keeps sailors setting off for a horizon they likely won't meet before their doom. Adventure. The hope of a discovery thrilling enough to risk their mundane lives. They navigate from a different map, one inked in myths and legends.

I admire their resilience in finding something to live for.

I turn my attention back to where Torri sits at the head of the table, his splotchy face wearing an uncomfortable expression. Kai stands beside me, looking every bit my Enforcer as he leans against the back of my chair. 'So, you knew nothing of your crew's plan to murder their future queen?' he asks smoothly.

'Crew?' Torri bellows. 'No, sir, as we discussed last night in private, these three men acted alone. There were only a handful of sailors on that deck last night and most of them were at the helm. We could hardly see a damn thing through that rain.'

He says this all rather quickly, as if forced to spit out the words before they are forgotten. I incline my head towards the captain. 'Why were so few of your men on the deck during such a storm?'

Torri's large hands wave with each of his words. 'My crew had been battling that storm for two days straight. They needed sleep, miss.' He laughs uncomfortably. 'I had them on shifts to conserve their strength and—'

'Forgive me for interrupting, Captain—' Kai says this in a tone that suggests he's certainly not asking for forgiveness, '—but I still haven't heard an apology for Miss Gray.'

I have to fight the grin that wishes to form on my lips. Torri clears his throat and flicks his gaze down to where I sit. 'Miss Gray,' he says slowly, 'I am deeply sorry for the distress this must have caused you. And, rest assured, I will not let it happen again.'

Leaning forward, I offer him a thin smile. 'No, it won't happen again. And rest assured that I am not distressed.' My eyes narrow slightly. 'I'm disappointed.'

I stand then, letting the chair scrape loudly against the wooden floorboards. As way of goodbye, I add, 'I trust we will be making it safely to Izram tomorrow?'

It takes Torri a moment to gather his words. 'Um, yes. Yes, that is correct. We should be docking no later than midday.'

I flash him a smile before turning to leave. 'Good.'

Kai trails behind, stopping only to throw a question over his shoulder at the captain. 'Why was an Illusionist on board? They aren't easy to come by, especially not one with sailing experience.'

'Well, I requested one from the king,' Torri explains with a slight shrug. 'He would have come in handy if we encounter the beast that lurks in these waters. Created an illusion for it to chase after rather than us.'

The Enforcer seems to be mulling this over. 'And what is it you do, Captain?'

Torri looks confused before a loud laugh escapes him. 'Well, exactly what you said, Highness. I captain.'

'Ah, yes.' Kai nods slowly, and I study his face, unsure where this is going. 'So you're the one who was fearlessly steering the ship during that storm?'

'Aye, sir! Right up until you charged into my quarters.' The captain laughs again, slapping a hand to the table. 'The Shallows are a bitch that I intend to tame.'

I can only muster an annoyed sigh at his words before Kai is heading for the door once again. 'Sorry for killing your men, Torri. But I'm afraid they deserved it, so I'm really not.'

'Of course,' the captain calls after us.

'And do keep a watchful eye on your men, Captain.' Kai is halfway out the door when he turns one last time. 'I know you're capable of it.'

I follow him quickly into the hall beyond, trying to keep up with his long strides. When we turn into his cabin, I finally blurt, 'What just happened in there?'

Kai shakes his head. 'He knew you needed help last night and did nothing.'

'But the storm. He said—'

'No one at the helm could see or hear anything on the other side of the ship with that rain,' he finishes for me. 'But that bastard was the only one who could.'

The pieces suddenly click into place, leaving me murmuring under my breath. 'The captain's a Hyper.'

Kai rakes a hand through his disheveled hair. 'He could see and hear you just fine. He just chose not to.'

I scoff. 'That shouldn't even surprise me.'

'I'll deal with him when we get back to Ilya. But until then—' he pats the dagger strapped to my thigh '—this doesn't leave your side. Even when you're with me.'

I step closer with a teasing smile. 'Oh, especially not when I'm with you. What if I wish to threaten your life?'

'Even after I just saved yours?' He says this fondly.

I trace a finger down his thin white shirt. 'Perhaps I have yet to forgive you for chasing me across the Scorches.'

He pulls me close, his fingers tipping my chin up towards him. 'And I would do it all again just to hear you threaten my life.'

'That seems foolish,' I breathe.

'Then it's fitting.' He runs a thumb over my bottom lip. 'Seeing that I am a fool.'

I raise my eyebrows at him. 'You told me you weren't anymore.'

His lips brush my cheek. I smile when they meet my nose. Gasp when they graze my neck.

'That was pretend, darling.'

CHAPTER 31

Paedyn

I've been staring at a speck in the distance for hours.

Only now, it's grown into a city that stretches before us.

A maze of docks splatters the horizon, sitting within the bright blue water. Dozens of boats bob beside them, some larger like the mangled one we're arriving on, though most are small and sturdy. Squinting, I can just make out the large fishing nets that hang from their sides.

I breathe in the sea's scent, willing the ship to move faster. With the storm having subsided, Gusts now litter the deck, pushing wind into the large sails. I tap a foot impatiently, my eyes skipping over the crew. They avoid my gaze, focusing instead on their duties and the difficult task of ensuring the crumbling ship makes it to land.

With the torn sails, missing railings, and splintered boards across the deck, it's a miracle we aren't sitting at the bottom of the Shallows. And that is just the damage I can see.

'Raise the flag!'

The captain's bellow has a sailor pulling at the rigging, obeying the command. I watch as a white flag rises into the sky, halting beside Ilya's swirling crest that has now been thoroughly tattered.

My wandering gaze falls back to the deck before landing on that familiar figure stepping out onto it. Kai lifts a hand to shade his eyes from the sudden brightness, and I can't help but take the moment to stare unabashedly at him. His clothes ripple in the wind, pressing to the strong body beneath. Black hair splashes over his brow like the unruly waves beneath us. And gray eyes—

They are suddenly on me.

He smiles in a way that suggests he knows exactly how much I was admiring him. Even after striding towards me, the smug look never leaves his face. 'Enjoying the view, Gray?'

'Of Izram?' I shoot back with a smile of my own. 'Why, yes, I am, Azer.'

He leans his forearms against the splintered railing, grinning enough to have those dimples on display. I look away before he can catch me staring yet again. 'Why did we raise a white flag?' I ask quietly.

'Izram hasn't seen a ship with our crest on it in nearly a decade.' He nods to a large watchtower that looms over the bay. 'We don't want them thinking we have ill intentions. Just like in Dor and Tando, they won't be too happy with Elites showing up.'

I lean against the railing beside him, our arms brushing. 'Then it's a good thing a benevolent Ordinary will be greeting them.'

'Yes, with a crew of Elites,' he muses. 'And the Enforcer.'

'And a crate of coveted roses,' I add, sounding hopeful. 'Now, I vaguely remember reading about Izram's queen, Zailah, as a child. But I'm not sure what I should expect.'

'It's been said,' Kai recalls, 'that she is ruthless. Some say she killed her husband for the throne, others believe he died of natural causes.' He lifts a shoulder in a lazy shrug. 'Either way, she's helped Izram thrive. They rely on the sea and its fish to survive, and from the moment Zailah sat on that throne, their harvest has been nothing but plentiful.'

'Hmm.' I spin the ring on my thumb distractedly. 'And it's been several years since she became queen, yes?'

Kai's eyes meet mine. 'Nearly a decade ago.'

I tuck that bit of interesting information away and turn my

attention towards the dock we are heading for. A throng of guards stand atop the weathered wood, dressed in royal blue and holding spears. The sharp tips glint in the sun, forcing me to look away from the odd sight.

It's strange, seeing such obvious weapons on a guard. Most Imperials don't even bother carrying a sword when they can rely fully on an ability. But the people of Izram don't possess powers. They depend on their own might, their own will. And I admire that far more than unearned strength.

The shining points of the guards' spears seem to sharpen as the ship drifts closer. They stand stiffly along the wooden planks, lining the creaking dock with solemn expressions and a tightening grip on their weapons.

They are afraid of us.

I lurch forward into the railing when the ship groans. We slide against the dock, drawing a long screech from the hull. When we finally come to a stop within the port, my wide eyes manage to make their way to Kai's. He wears a familiar expression, one that creeps onto the corners of his features.

It's a slight smugness that touches his lips, I realize. A brightening of his eyes and relaxing of the body beneath.

He enjoys being feared.

I suppose I would too if even an inkling of his power dwelled beneath my skin. But I am something less than fear and power and Elite. For that reason, I step cautiously behind the Enforcer as he strides across the deck.

A teetering, wooden ramp sprawls between the ship and dock beneath. Sparkling water sways beneath us, lapping at the hull and reaching for the bridge we step out onto. Without hesitation, Kai strides down the creaking wood to greet the gaggle of guards.

But he doesn't even make it to the dock.

Dozens of spears are swiftly pointed at his chest, gleaming ominously as they inch towards the sliver of bare skin beneath his loosely buttoned shirt. I tense, heart stalling as I take in every long weapon aimed at the Enforcer.

Though, the lack of tension clutching his shoulders tells me he doesn't seem to mind. Still standing behind him, I can just make out the lifted corner of that cocky grin he's wearing. I shouldn't be surprised by this, and yet, I want to hit him over the head all the same.

Kai lifts his hands slowly, showing his seemingly harmless palms to the guards. Yes, he does enjoy this. Fear is power. And where there is power, there is something for him to wield.

'State your business here, Elites,' booms a steady voice belonging to a particularly gilded guard. Glancing over the golden buttons adorning his uniform, I catch the small pin above his heart.

Ilya's Enforcer has just met Izram's captain of the guard.

'Easy, gentlemen,' Kai says smoothly, lowering the tip of a prodding spear with his palm. 'I'm sure this is quite the surprise, but we come in peace. Things are changing in Ilya, so I'm here to escort our future queen to meet with yours. She will explain everything.' Kai gestures behind him to where I stand, stiff and unsure. 'This is Paedyn Gray. The Ordinary.'

Astonished blinks are the only response to his words. I watch the captain and his guards take me in, eying the silver hair I earned from the Plague. I clear my throat, uncomfortable. 'We brought a gift,' I blurt quickly. 'As a gesture of goodwill.'

The captain meets my eyes, his own skeptical. They are a warm brown, crowded by the lines that a life of laughter carves into one's skin. But that stern expression solidified onto his face smothers the happiness that once came so easily. And yet, even as a middle-aged man, he's quite handsome.

'You're telling me,' the captain says slowly, 'that a crew from Ilya braved the Shallows just to reintroduce themselves to the kingdom they shut out?'

His question spurs me forward until I've stepped beside Kai and planted my feet before the multitude of spears. 'Yes,' I say, voice even. 'I've fought to survive every day. Just like all of you. And I will do anything to see Ilya become free and welcoming again.'

A long stretch of silence stifles everything but the sound of sloshing water around us. The captain keeps his gaze pinned on mine, though not in a way that tells me he's scrutinizing every disheveled piece of me.

I believe it might even be hope I hear in his voice when he orders, 'Lower your weapons, men. We're taking our guests to the castle.'

☙

We have been walking for nearly an hour, cocooned within a constricting circle of guards.

They barely bother glancing at me when the Enforcer strides among them. Every eye is trained on him, every weapon at the ready to defend themselves from the Elite that stepped straight out of a bedtime story they tell their children.

Captain Torri walks beside me, surprisingly silent. I was only allowed the company of two Elites on this hike to the castle. The rest of the crew was left to patch up what is left of the *Reckoning* that currently bobs sadly beside the dock.

I've had plenty of time to take in the surrounding city. It's filled with a quieter sort of bustle than Ilya. The cobblestone streets are even and neat, filled with mindful men and women. Bright blue banners hang from roofs and stretch between wide alleyways. Merchants are kind, children are well-behaved, and smiles are shared regularly.

It's an anomaly I find both comforting and concerning.

I breathe in the salty air and grant myself a moment to acknowledge the warmth coating my face. The sun seems to shine only for me, painting my skin in a soft glow and wrapping its rays around me. A cool breeze ruffles my short hair, and I shut my eyes, relishing the feel of a sturdy ground beneath my feet.

People stop and stare at the spectacle I don't doubt we are. I'm swallowed by guards, forced to dodge the piercing tips of their spears. They herd us up another hilly path that has me panting before my eyes lift to the towering castle.

I step into its shadow, feeling so small beside the mass of stone. The castle is encased in a pearly white stone that winks in the dripping sunlight. Tall towers spring up into the sky, casting ribbons of shadow across the path. Billowing blue flags sprout from the highest spires to display what I recognize as Izram's crest.

I lift a hand to shield my gaze from the peering sun and scan the flapping fabric. A pair of swirling fish create a perfect circle within the sea of blue. Atop the rippling flag, it seems as though they are forever swimming around each other, creating a constant balance.

A barked order from the captain of the guard has us coming to a halt at the base of several pristine stairs. They ascend towards a milky set of doors that match the steps beneath. Everything about this castle is light and airy, as if the sky hanging low above the water was personified.

I watch the captain peel away from his guards and head beyond those towering doors. He walks stiffly, seemingly unexcited about the task at hand. But when Kai's rough knuckles brush against mine, the observation and my accompanying curiosity swiftly float away on a salty breeze.

My eyes flick up to find a crease of concern nestling between his brows. 'Are you all right?'

The question is worrying enough to startle one in response. 'Why, do I not look all right?'

'Gray, you always look far more than all right.' He says this with a low chuckle, his voice soft enough to slip past the guards unnoticed. 'But I know this is a lot. I want to make sure you're doing okay.'

'Quite the gentleman you've become,' I croon.

'Only for you.'

His words have my smile melting into something sweeter. 'I'm . . . okay. Just hoping my benevolence doesn't fail me,' I say weakly before continuing to whisper, 'I have no idea who to be or what to say. Better yet, I have no idea how to speak to a queen, let alone be one.'

He shakes his head, gaze unfaltering. 'I think you know exactly who you want to be. Who you are.' His words are like a soft battle cry. 'You're the leader you always wanted for Ilya. You're our Silver Savior.'

I reach for his hand before realizing that I shouldn't. Instead, I settle on a relieved smile and a lingering look in which I'm lost within the storm that is his eyes. It's only when a shadow falls over his face that I rip my gaze from it.

'Now, there's a ship name!' Captain Torri shoves past a guard to invade the little space we have. 'The *Silver Savior*. If we make it back to Ilya, I'll need to find me a new ship, and I may just name her that.'

I glance at Kai. Then back to the captain. 'I'm flattered.'

'Speaking of ships,' Kai adds quickly, 'how is ours looking? I can't help but notice that you seem . . . skeptical about returning to Ilya.'

Torri blows out a breath that I lean away from. 'Well, I'll be honest with you, Highness. She's not looking too pretty right now. But I've got the crew on it, so hopefully she will be patched up before we set sail.'

I'm preparing to ask a few questions I likely won't want to know the answer to when a stern voice echoes behind me. 'The queen is ready for you.'

I spin on my heel, finding the captain of the guard beckoning me forward. The men crowded around us tear away at the silent command, freeing me from the cage of spears. My tired feet carry me towards the mountain of steps, Kai at my side while Torri lingers behind.

I spin the ring on my thumb, seeking comfort from the cool steel. The shimmering doors above swing open as we near, and I watch Izram's captain stroll into the hall beyond. The comforting sunlight is stolen from my skin when I follow him into the castle.

My gaze widens before gliding across the gilded room.

This is certainly not Ilya.

This is the opposite of bold greens and dark details. This is teeming with puddles of light and pops of blue. The long hall stretches into a pair of curved staircases on either end, each of which are wrapped in soft carpet. Everything here is gleaming and simple and crawling with delicacy.

There is no show of strength, no obvious need for attention. And its simplicity is breathtaking.

'She will see you in the throne room,' the captain informs without turning to look at me. Continuing his steady pace, he leads us to another pair of shiny white doors. 'The court also awaits you after hearing of Ilya's unexpected arrival. And that's the only useful information I have for you.' He nods to the pair of guards framing the doors. 'The queen will see you now.'

My heart pounds as the throne room slowly comes into view. A long blue carpet awaits me, leading all the way to the dais. Windows line the room in a wave-like pattern, bordered by spiraling molding.

My eyes flick over the several circular tables littering the gleaming floor that allow the court members to comfortably enjoy the show.

But it is the woman seated elegantly on a throne of bones that thoroughly steals my attention.

The queen lounges in a skeleton of sorts, though I haven't the slightest clue what animal it once belonged to. Thick vertebrae create the center of the seat while long rib bones jut out from it and curl around her. Beneath her tanned shoulders, the bones curve upward to hang slightly over her head of black hair.

I force my feet forward despite the urge to stand and gawk. Even from this distance, the queen's piercing green eyes seem to cut right through me. I've never seen such a bright color dwell within someone's gaze. It's not the light green of Kitt's eyes, crisp and warm. No, this is a vivid, gleaming sort of shade, as if she sees the world through a sheet of emerald.

When we halt before the dais, Zailah's gleaming stare turns to Kai when he speaks. 'Your Majesty—' he bows gracefully, reminding me to attempt a curtsy, '—I apologize for the unexpected visit. I'm Kai Azer, Enforcer to Ilya's king, and I have escorted Paedyn Gray here to welcome trade back into our kingdom.'

The queen's eyes flick back to mine, as striking as they are searching. 'I've heard whispers of you, child. You seem much too young to have caused such trouble in Ilya.' She smiles, and I catch the glint of sharp canines. 'I admire that.'

'Well, my days of causing trouble are behind me. Hopefully,' I add with a small smile of my own. Kai steps aside, ushering Torri with him. 'I'm here now to help create a new and better Ilya.'

'You see,' Zailah says slowly, 'the last time I heard your name, it was followed by a list of treasonous crimes against Ilya. There was even a price on your head if you ever managed to make it across the Shallows.' She raises a sharp nail at Kai. 'Now you're in my kingdom with the Enforcer. And wearing a very shiny engagement ring.' Another smile curls her perfect lips. 'Do tell. You've intrigued me, and that is no simple task.'

I lick my dry lips. 'In short, Ilya is in need of resources. Over the decades, we have exhausted our food supply and overpopulated the land behind our closed borders. With Kitt Azer on the throne, he has become aware that the kingdom must return to its more welcoming roots. Ordinaries and Elites will coexist once again—' I gesture to the queen, '—along with trade between the surrounding cities.

'To encourage this . . . unpopular change, I – an Ordinary and survivor of the Purging Trials – am to marry the king. This will bridge the gap between Ordinaries and Elites.' I take a breath, ready to spew more information—

'And what of your treason?' Zailah asks, seeming amused. 'Has the king so quickly forgotten how you killed his father? At least, that is what I heard.'

'That was a misunderstanding. One the kingdom has become aware of,' I state as convincingly as possible. 'And I am here to not only prove myself to you, but also to Ilya.'

She quirks a dark brow. 'Go on.'

'I competed in the Purging Trials as an Ordinary.' My throat has become absurdly dry. 'And now, to earn the respect and trust of those Elites who despise the idea of an Ordinary on the throne, I have stepped into a series of my own Trials.'

The queen blinks before a laugh transforms her harsh features. The sound is biting against her beautiful face. 'So you crossed the Shallows. Barely.'

I smile politely. 'Yes. Benevolence is the second of the three B's by which Ilya's rulers live.'

'Benevolence, really?' She scoffs. 'I'm not sure I live by that myself.'

'Then accept mine,' I say quickly. 'As a gesture of good faith, I've brought roses for you and your kingdom to use. I hope the many healing properties they possess are enough incentive for you to welcome us.'

Her eyes narrow in a scrutinizing sort of way. 'They are a gift from your king?'

'Yes, Your Majesty.'

Zailah's voice is a soothing sound. 'And you know nothing else of it?'

'No,' I answer evenly.

'Hmm.' She sits back, looking oddly comfortable in her throne of bones. 'All I have heard, Paedyn Gray, is a cry for help. Ilya only opens its borders when in need of something. Only allows us *Ordinaries* – as you say – into the land when there is no other alternative. And you speak on behalf of a king who—'

'I do not speak for Kitt Azer.' My voice rings out over the queen's, drawing a hushed gasp from the court. 'I speak for myself. For the powerless who deserve to live within Ilya. Not a king.'

My echoing voice fades from the throne room, leaving only a stifling silence. I lift my chin and force my gaze to remain on the queen I so blatantly interrupted. But I can't afford to show remorse now. No, I must stand here and exude a strength I don't currently feel.

Zailah lets the tension stew between us. Then, another biting smile. 'Still, I do not welcome Ilya.'

My breath catches, hope sputtering out in my chest—

'But I welcome the fact that you need me. The powerful, arrogant Ilya – brought to its knees.'

My gaze lifts in time to watch the next words fall from her lips. 'Hear this, child. Ilya has done nothing for my kingdom. We have been shut out and cut off from your coveted resources for three decades now. I have no desire to help Ilya out of whatever goodness remains in my heart. But you . . .' Her red lips twitch. 'You remind me of myself. So youthful. So determined. I only hope that drive doesn't darken you.'

Her words hit a nerve, forcing me to fight off my flinch. Because I know what darkness she speaks of, feel it festering in the gaping hole of my heart where Adena once lived. And for the sake of her memory, her goodness, I shove it down.

The navy dress hugging Zailah's curvy form flashes as she shifts in the throne of bones. She lifts a hand, inspecting her sharp nails. 'So, for you, I will attempt benevolence. For Ilya, I will attempt mercy.'

Relief floods through me. 'Thank you, Your Majesty. Your generosity will not go unnoticed.'

'No, I would hope not,' she says airily. 'Now, tell me, how did an Ilyan ship survive my Shallows?'

Her obvious possession of the sea has me pausing long enough for Captain Torri to speak. 'Well, Your Majesty—' he steps onto the blue carpet, snatching the hat off his head before sweeping into a bow, '—I managed to captain the *Reckoning* across the treacherous sea. It was no simple task, but I am also no stranger to the water—'

The queen raises a silencing hand. 'So, I take it that you didn't encounter the beast?'

'Uh . . .' Torri stutters. 'Well, no, but—'

'Then you have survived nothing at all,' she states simply. 'You may gloat only after you meet such a beautiful creature. And live to tell the tale.'

Torri opens his mouth, shuts it, and steps back beside Kai. Zailah smiles at this. 'I'll allow you three days to piece back together what is left of your ship. Rooms will be arranged within the castle for Paedyn alone.' She waves a dismissive hand. 'The rest of you may sleep on your leaking boat. That is the extent of my generosity.'

I offer a bow of my head, if only to hide the grin spreading across my face. 'Again, thank you, Your Majesty.'

'Yes, yes, I'm magnificent.' Her eyes slide hesitantly to the captain of her guard, allowing me to study her fully. She seems to glow with beauty, making it hard to look away. Her features are a contradiction of young and old, sharp and soft. Everything about her is a mystery, right down to the age she embodies.

'Adyn,' she calls, even as those green eyes fall back on me. When her captain appears beside me, I realize that the shouted name belongs to him. He folds stiff arms behind his back, locking his brown gaze on the dais's floor.

'Escort Paedyn to her rooms,' the queen orders. 'And ensure the others make it back to their ship.'

Adyn nods, his eyes flicking up momentarily. 'Happily, Your Majesty.'

CHAPTER 32

Rai

Rough bark tears at my sweating palms.

I cling to the tree trunk, feeling my feet sway atop the thin branch beneath me. Extending my free arm, I rap my knuckles against the window beside me.

She takes her time. Of course she does.

I watch a devious smile curve her lips as she strides slowly towards the bedroom window and into the streaming moonlight. She takes a long moment on the other side of that locked glass, committing the sight of me begging for her attention to memory. So I stand there helplessly, gripping a branch while entirely at her mercy.

Shaking my head at her cruelty, I will myself not to look down at the gaping span of open air beneath me. Izram's rocky soil grows few plants and even less grass, but I discovered a small patchy field behind the castle on my search for a discreet way into Paedyn's room. The few trees that sway back here are clustered close to the white stone, one of which even brushes against Pae's window.

And now I've climbed it for her.

I hear the latch click before she's finally pushing open the swinging glass pane. 'You've already broken one arm climbing a tree. Do you

really wish to tempt fate again?'

I smile, because I can't seem to help it when she plays with me, but also because she remembers what I had told her under that willow so long ago. 'Kitt and I were visiting Ava when that happened, you know.' I watch her eyes widen at the confession she could have only understood now. 'He bet that I could never climb the willow as quickly as Ava once had, and I knew damn well he was right, but . . .'

'But you tried,' she finishes with a small smile. 'And landed face-first in the dirt.'

I chuckle and carefully inch closer to the window. 'It was worth it. I was visiting A, and for a moment, it felt as though she was with me.'

My words have something shifting in her expression. 'And if you fell now? Would it be worth it?'

I reach through the window to grip the sill, my knuckles brushing her hips. 'Well, I'm visiting you, aren't I?' She flashes a worrying smile that has me adding, 'That's not an invitation to push me, Gray.' Her laugh skitters over my skin as I climb through the window, planting my boots beside her bare feet.

My gaze falls to the scar peeking out from beneath the thick strap of her tank. This look doesn't go unnoticed, and she is quick to turn back towards her borrowed bed. 'What are you doing here?'

I clear my throat. 'I didn't see you yesterday. Figured you missed me.'

'That's why you climbed through my window?' She snorts. 'Because I missed yo—?'

I've moved before even realizing. My hands are on her hips, and I'm spinning her around to face me before my mouth crashes into hers.

It's incessant. Fervent. Relief.

She's startled for a heartbeat, but parting her lips for me in the next. I pull her close, feeling her hot skin beneath the thin clothing she wears. Her body melts against mine, and a soft sound slips between her lips that has me gripping that silver hair between my fingers.

I force myself to pull away, smiling at her reluctance to let me go. 'Fine,' she breathes against my lips. 'I might have missed you a little.'

246

I chuckle before planting kisses along her jaw. This has a soft sigh dripping from her parted lips, and I'm not sure she knows how much power the sound has over me. I feel her throat bob beneath my fingers. 'How are . . . how are things at the ship?'

I pull back with an amused smile. 'That is what you want to talk about? The ship?'

'Well, we leave tomorrow afternoon,' she says breathlessly. 'I'd like to know my odds of survival.'

My voice lowers into something more serious. 'And if I say that this could be your final night alive?'

'Darling—' she flicks my nose lightly, wearing a cool smile, '— every night could be my last.'

The use of my name for her has a ridiculous grin lighting my face. But then she's spinning on her heel and plopping down on the plush covers of her bed. I follow slowly, shoving my now-idle hands into the pockets of my dark pants. 'Well, the ship is still floating, if that is what you're asking. Though, I'm not sure for how long.'

'You don't think it will survive the trip back?' she asks slowly.

'Only time will tell.'

She sighs as if I've told her something she has already known. With a beckoning pat of her hand against the comforter, I swiftly obey and sit. That blue gaze drifts over me in the dim moonlight. 'You . . .' Her finger finds the ring on her thumb and begins spinning it swiftly. 'You said "A" earlier. Is that what you used to call Ava?'

I nod slowly. 'Yes. It was.'

'That's what I called Adena.' She blinks rapidly, as if to ward off tears before they form. 'I guess I'm just not used to hearing the nickname for anyone else.'

Something in my chest begins its steady ache. It might just be my blackened heart or stained soul. Or perhaps it's the piece of me that belongs to her, and I'm simply feeling a sliver of the pain she possesses.

'She was my A.' My throat tightens. 'Ava was my Adena. But they don't go far.' I gently lift her arm until she's pressing a palm to her beating heart. 'Your A lives here now.'

Paedyn nods, again and again. Her voice is a choked sound as she blinks back a wave of emotions. 'Don't leave me. Please. Especially not now, but please not ever.'

'Never,' I whisper, tipping my forehead against hers.

Her breath hitches. 'You can't leave me. I don't have enough room in my heart for the both of you.'

I let go of her wrist to cup the face above it instead. 'Death himself couldn't drag me from you.'

The morning light on my face tells me it's time to make my escape.

I blink groggily while attempting to carefully slip my arm from beneath Pae's head. She stirs when the heat of me slides away, though I quickly replace it with a blanket around her bare shoulders. This seems to satisfy, her breath slowing and body relaxing.

A strange sensation tugs on the corners of my consciousness, though I ignore it for the distraction lying beside me. I reach for a stray strand of silver hair and—

Someone clears their throat.

My hand is suddenly beneath the pillow, gripping the hilt of Paedyn's dagger before I've even turned towards the sound. But when my eyes crash into a dazzling green pair, I'm startled enough to stop and stare.

The queen sits stoically in one of the plushy seats beside the stone fireplace, her gaze gleaming with amusement. Focusing on her pristine features, I feel that strange sensation grow beneath my skin, as though something stirs at the mere sight of her. A teacup sits delicately in her palm, its rim stained the deep red of her lips. 'Sorry to interrupt,' she muses evenly.

My eyes dart to the still-sleeping Paedyn beside me before flicking back to the expectant queen. I clear my throat. 'You're not interrupting.'

'No?' She clicks her tongue at me. 'I figured you would be a better liar, Enforcer.'

'May I ask why you're here, Your Majesty?' This is said with as much respect as I can muster.

'You may.' She shrugs an eerily smooth shoulder. 'But I may not give you an answer.'

'Of course,' I murmur between my teeth. 'Well, as you can see, Paedyn is sleeping so—'

'I like her, you know,' she cuts in dryly. 'Perhaps due to the fact that she killed your father. Because, well, let's face it.' Her long nails click against the porcelain teacup. 'He was a dick. Though, I'm a bit jealous I didn't get to finish him off myself.'

I stare at her, uncertain how she expects me to respond to that. Nearly every person outside Ilya would say the same about Edric Azer, though I have a strange sense that her hatred runs deeper than the isolation of her kingdom.

Conscious of my shirtless body and disheveled appearance, I run a hand through my hair. 'I can't say I was too torn up about his death either.'

'Hmm.' She taps a finger to those full lips. I study her for a moment, taking in the near ethereal glow she exudes. It's startling. 'Yes, I figured you might feel the same. Considering the whispers I've heard of what he did to you.'

This has my eyes narrowing in a slight show of surprise. I hadn't expected the tales of my torturous childhood to reach her ears across the Shallows. But her sigh of indifference cuts through my thoughts. 'So, does your brother know?'

I stare at her. 'Know what?'

She takes a slow sip of her tea, flicking a finger between my body and the one sleeping beside it. 'Take a guess.'

Heat flushes my body, but I keep my voice steady. 'I'm her Enforcer.'

'Oh, I know.' She laughs dryly. 'I just didn't think this was part of the job description.'

'This is the best way for me to protect her,' I manage. 'She is the future queen of Ilya, after all.'

She nods in a slow, mocking way. 'Right. Right.' Another sip of tea. 'So you're in love with your brother's betrothed?'

'I . . .'

'Sorry,' she says innocently. 'That's just what I'm gathering from this little interaction.'

I stand from the mattress and pull a shirt over my head. 'I'm just doing my duty.'

'Well—' she sets the teacup down on the small table beside her, '—in my experience, there is love. And there is duty. But there is never both.'

My chest rises and falls quickly. 'I know I can't have her.'

'Do you?' She tilts her head at me, black hair tumbling over a shoulder. 'It seems as though you've convinced yourself otherwise.'

I open my mouth, only to hear her speaking again. 'There is love within duty, and duty within love. You can't have one without the other, and yet—' she takes a deep breath, her gaze distant, '—you can never truly have both. So choose, Kai Azer. The girl. Or power. And whether or not she is worth the destruction of everything you are.'

I say nothing as she waves her dismissal at me in the form of wiggling fingers. 'Now, out. I'll be having breakfast with a fellow queen now.'

Her sharp words follow me out the door. 'You know, you are quite the pretty prince. In a different life of mine, perhaps I would have kept you for myself.'

CHAPTER 33

Paedyn

My teacup lands on its saucer with a wince-worthy clang.

I glance up at the queen, only to find her eerily green eyes already running over my disheveled appearance. She seems content to watch me squirm under her gaze, following each fidgeting movement I make.

I'd awoken with a start, as though commanded from my sleep. But there she was, sitting lazily in a velvet chair and sipping from a porcelain cup. I was forced to stumble from the bed and sit immediately at her impromptu tea party.

My eyes wander over my shoulder quickly, meeting the rumpled bed sheets I rolled from. I only hope Kai did as well – long before the queen slipped into my room.

'Oh, he left,' she says evenly, lifting the teacup to her lips.

I nearly choke on my sip. 'I'm sorry?'

'The Enforcer,' she clarifies. 'Yes, we had a quick chat before I sent him on his way. Didn't want a boy here during our tea time.'

She says this as though we share a secret jest. As though her last sentence was far more important than the one before. 'So . . .' I clear my throat, trying to sound unbothered. 'So, you saw him.'

'I did.' She gives me a slight smile, revealing the sharp glint of her teeth before the emotion vanishes. 'I also saw right through his obvious feelings for you.'

I open my mouth, heart racing and lips forming the beginning fragments of a lie when she speaks right over my attempt to salvage the situation. 'But I'm rather bored of that topic already, so we will move on to another.'

My teacup rattles against the delicate saucer when I set it down with shaky hands. 'And what topic would that be?'

'So formal,' Zailah muses. 'Practicing for when you're queen, yes?'

'Just practicing to survive. Like I always have.'

'Oh, yes.' I seem to have captured her attention enough to have her scooting to the seat's edge. 'Do tell me about the king and that bit of survival. I want to hear every gory detail. Did you really plunge a sword into his chest?' Her expression is giddy. 'And then a dagger through his throat?'

'I did.' My ring taps a steady beat against my leg. 'Though, you make it sound far more . . . exciting.'

'Ugh.' She sits back, her arms draped over the chair. 'That's because I'm jealous. He was a bastard, that king. I wish I was the one to lure him into Death's arms.'

My eyes drag over her perfect form. 'Really?'

Her smile is sharp. 'You should know better than most that looks can be deceiving, Paedyn Gray.'

On that, we agree. And she's slightly less intimidating for it.

'How did you hear about me?' I venture. 'It seems the whole kingdom knows who I am, and yet, there is no longer a way to relay information across the Shallows.'

Her smile is fearsome. 'I have my ways. Perhaps one day I will share them with you. Now—' another sip of her tea, '—what about this new king? Do you plan on killing him as well?'

The queen's words are smooth, thought out, even. Her genuine question has me gawking. Such an innocent sentence has never struck so hard.

'Of course not,' I breathe into the chilled air between us. 'I . . . I would never.'

She clicks her nails against the wooden arm of her chair, shrugging slightly. 'Well, if you say so. I figured he was as much of a dick as his father, so—'

'He's nothing like his father,' I cut in and try not to regret that decision when her eyes narrow. 'He is saving Ilya, even begrudgingly. And I will marry him if it means the kingdom is united.'

She raises a hand, her nails piercing the air. 'Fine. I didn't realize you trusted him so much.'

I manage a nod, though I'm not sure I should be agreeing with her. My relationship with the king is strained. And I fear my actions have forever driven an invisible wedge between us.

'Tell me, Paedyn,' Zailah croons, her voice a sort of lulling melody. 'Are we going to be friends?'

My answer is honest. 'I hope so.'

'Splendid.' She smiles like it's a weapon. 'I do love a good enemy, but I have no need for any more of those.'

'As do I.' A pause. 'Thank you again for your generosity. I hope you find the roses to be a fair trade for it.'

She stands, signaling the end of this conversation. Her gaze is piercing, as though searching for something within mine. 'Yes, our healers are not nearly as advanced as those in Ilya.'

Her words are blunt in a way I admire. 'Of course. But it seems you've already helped this city thrive without our assistance.'

She smiles distantly. 'They didn't want me to rule. And now, here I am, their savior.'

She turns away, leaving me to watch her glide towards the door. 'Oh, and Paedyn?' She turns, her long fingers wrapped around the handle. 'Don't fear power. Wield it. Perhaps even let it control you.' The queen smiles sharply. 'Being an Ordinary is not what makes you weak. It's your heart.'

'I miss land.'

I say this, of course, around the stale bread sticking to the roof of my mouth. Kai picks at the plate of bland food atop his lap, legs spread out on the wooden floor. My own are crossed beneath me while my back rests against the bed.

This has become something of a routine – the two of us sitting on the floor of my humid cabin, talking about nothing in the hopes we will forget to taste the food in our mouths.

Kai's gaze lifts to mine. 'Well, you still have five more days of missing it.'

'Thanks for the reminder,' I grumble before taking a sip of warm water. 'I'm not sure if it will be you or this unbearable heat that has me jumping into the Shallows.'

'You know,' he says genuinely, 'I can't think of a single reason you'd wish to escape me.'

'Your arrogance is astounding as always, Kai.'

'Thank you.'

I cut him a glance. 'That wasn't a compliment.'

'Then don't say my name, and I won't thank you for the sound.'

The corner of his smile is decorated with a dimple. I roll my eyes, if only to distract him from the blush stinging my cheeks. 'The sea has been relatively calm,' I say instead of something I'll likely regret.

'Yes.' He takes a bite of salty beef and twists his lips in the same way he always does. 'It's been eerily quiet. I'm not sure that's a good thing.'

I nod, having worried the same myself. The heat hangs over us thickly, as though weighing down the waves. Compared to the storms we barely survived on the way to Izram, the sea is strangely still beneath us.

'The queen mentioned you spoke yesterday,' I say suddenly, surprising myself.

'Did she?'

I nod. 'Did she talk about Kitt at all?'

He clears his throat, setting aside the half-empty plate. 'She asked if Kitt knew about . . . us.'

I stiffen. 'Us?'

'Yes, us.' Confusion crinkles his brow. 'Everything going on between you and me. She saw me in your bed, Pae.'

'I know, but—' I swallow before hurling the harsh truth at him, '—there is no us. There can never be an us, Kai. Not really.'

Silence.

The words hurt, tearing ribbons of regret up my throat. I can feel the slow shattering of my heart with every day we spend pretending. And speaking the inevitability of our doom only fissures the organ further.

Something shifts behind his gaze. Maybe it's hurt. Perhaps disbelief. In fact, I don't care what emotion lingers behind the mask he's suddenly put up, only that there is one and I'm staring at it.

He seems to dull – something I've never seen happen when his eyes are on mine. We promised to have no masks between us, and yet, I've forced him to wedge one atop the hurt I caused.

His eyes drift from mine. A cold huff leaves his mouth. 'The queen seemed to think as much.'

I take a deep breath before trying to justify the damage I've caused. 'Kai, you know it's true. You've always known it was true. This—' I gesture between the two of us, '—is a fantasy.'

'Right. Pretend.'

'No,' I say sternly. 'Nothing about the way I feel is pretend, but . . .' I lift my hand, letting the diamond there catch the streaky light. 'I'm still marrying your brother.'

And I hate that.

He's shaking his head now, and the bite in his voice makes me wince. 'And I'll watch you two look down at me from the dais, nothing more than a weapon you can wield just like the king you killed had.'

Disgust drenches my voice. 'You think so little of me?'

'I wish I did.' His eyes are icy. 'I wish I could think about anything else.'

My voice settles into something stern. Hurt hardens me, and I spew the damning truth I've avoided for so long. 'What did you think we were going to do? Hide for the rest of our lives beneath the willow tree?'

The words are harsh enough to penetrate his mask. He blinks at me, voice low. 'Well, that's where I will be. Hiding from the royal couple.'

I shake my head. Tears sting my eyes. 'You know why I have to do this.'

He laughs, and it's a biting sound I forgot him capable of. 'Of course I know. But don't you see? That doesn't matter.' He lifts a hand towards my face before thinking better of it. 'I'm selfish, Paedyn. I burned your home to the ground just to have you and now it is all of Ilya standing in my way, tempting me to light a match.'

His words are jarring enough to have me stumbling over my own. 'I'm s-sorry. You know I never wanted any of this—'

'Well, it doesn't matter what either of us wanted, does it?' He leans back, expression cold. 'It was all a fantasy anyway. Kitt is who you, the Silver Savior, were destined for.' I watch him stand to his feet in one swift movement. 'I was nothing more than a distraction.'

I follow quickly after him, my expression hardening at the mocking nickname. The words I hurl at his stony facade are far from the truth, but hurt sharpens them on my tongue all the same. 'Maybe you're right.'

'You'll find that I typically am, Majesty.'

My chest heaves, mere inches from his. It's anger at our cruel fates that has me lashing out. 'Maybe I should distance myself from this distraction.'

A muscle twitches in his jaw. 'Maybe you should.'

'Fine.'

'Fine.'

I give him one last withering look before spinning on my heel and heading for the door. But the harsh words he mutters have my feet halting atop the rocking floor. 'And what exactly did the queen ask you about Kitt?'

I stand there for a moment, hand clutching the door's rough edge. Then I'm whipping around to meet his gaze of indifference with words that are equally so. 'She asked if I was going to kill him.'

There is a long pause wedged between us. 'And are you?'

'Again,' I say between clenched teeth, 'you think so little of me?'

'You know I do not.'

My eyes flick up his rigid body. 'Then you should know the answer to her question.'

He looks away, crossing his arms over the broad chest beneath. 'Good. Because if I have to choose between you or Kitt . . .'

'I know,' I murmur. Tears threaten to wash away the anger I'm cowering behind.

'Do you?' Those gray eyes glide over me in that way I'm certain I'll never get used to. 'Because I sure as hell don't.'

Edric

The king has a knack for deceit.

This isn't something one would typically brag about, but rulers are nothing if not cunning. Spinning such a lie about the death of Queen Iris is not the first Edric has spewed to his kingdom. More than a decade has passed since nearly every Healer in Ilya was generously compensated to spread the lie that Ordinaries bear a disease that dwindles Elite powers. Though, the people needed little convincing to throw out their weak neighbors and friends. Most Elites were eager to support the Purging. Power is a sickness that corrupts all those who get a taste.

Edric spends the eve of his wife's death in silence. He does not speak, or cry, or mourn in the ways a soul should. Instead, his heart only hardens without the softness of Iris's countenance.

He awakens to something like a stone inside his chest, and a knock at the door. Three figures stand in the hall beyond, all varying in size. The first is a trusted adviser, Oliver Rowe, who stands beside a young woman of bold beauty. The third sways at their knees, green eyes like the king's and bright smile like the mother Kitt no longer has.

The prince bursts into the room, all giggles and childlike wonder.

Edric shows him little affection, finding it difficult to look at the boy who is half the dead wife he loved. Instead, the king sets a colorful map before the child — it is never too early to begin studying his future kingdom — and turns all attention to his adviser.

'Your Majesty,' Oliver begins, 'I am terribly sorry for your loss—'

'Iris died two years ago, giving birth to my heir.' Edric gestures vaguely to the boy. 'There is no reason to console me now.'

The adviser bows his head in understanding. 'Of course, Your Majesty. That is what I wished to discuss with you.'

'Make it worth my time, Oliver. You interrupted me in my private quarters.'

Urging the woman forward, her black hair battling in beauty with her gray eyes, the adviser murmurs, 'Apologies, my King, but you will find this to be a delicate matter.'

Edric steps aside, allowing the guests to enter his quarters before shutting the door. 'Will I?'

Oliver clasps his hands together. 'As one of your advisers, it is clear that before we inform the kingdom of the queen's death, we must ensure that every detail is accounted for. Such as the two years since Iris's death.' He gives the king a look, as if the two of them share a similar thread of thought. 'This is why I am presenting my daughter to you. For marriage.'

Edric doesn't so much as blink. 'Explain.'

Oliver's play for power is as unsurprising as it is futile, but greed alone would not have the adviser disturbing him. No, the king silently determines that this awaiting offer must be worth his while. Or else it will cost a good man his head.

'You see,' Oliver continues while his daughter huffs out an irritated breath, 'the kingdom has not heard of Iris for some time now, so it won't be difficult to convince them of a death that occurred two years ago. But the people will want a reason as to why they were not informed sooner. That is where Myla comes in.'

Miss Rowe looks anything but pleased to be a part of this plan, but she says nothing as her father continues. 'You, Your Majesty, would tell the kingdom that you had mourned their late queen for a few months after her passing. Once the appropriate grieving period had ended, you took a wife in order to continue securing your line. As there are no Elite royals for you to marry, a private union to the daughter of a trusted adviser was the obvious choice.'

The king listens, intrigued by this proposal. He admires a cunning plan.

Oliver, after taking a deep breath, adds, 'You did not tell the kingdom of this marriage sooner because your new wife, Myla, was already with child. In order to ensure her safety, your union remained a secret until long after the birth of your spare.'

Edric slides his skeptical gaze to the stiffening woman. 'You already have a child?'

'She does,' the adviser answers on her behalf. 'He is still a babe – barely a year old and could easily be passed off as your own.'

The king considers this for a long, suffocating moment. 'This is a bold suggestion, Oliver.'

'As your adviser, it is my duty to aid you.' He places a stern hand on his daughter's arm. 'And this is the best solution to your predicament.'

Edric turns to Myla, his voice dull. 'Who is the father?'

'No one of any concern,' she answers curtly.

There is a long pause.

The king would laugh if he hadn't forgotten how to. 'And what makes you think I want your bastard?'

Oliver swallows, his breath shallow. Myla narrows those gray eyes.

The king swings open the door with a stipulation sliding from his tongue. 'If I am to call another child mine, he can be nothing less than powerful.'

'He is,' Myla blurts, ever the protective mother. 'No one in Ilya is like him.'

This equally intrigues and amusing the king. 'We will see about that.'

Myla hands her son to the Silencer, hating how empty her arms feel without him in them.

The baby doesn't fuss or fidget, rather, he simply accepts the fate forced upon him. Black hair clings to his small skull, curling around his ears to copy that of his mother. He looks up at the foreign man holding him, and those gray eyes don't stray from the Silencer.

'Well?' Edric's impatience echoes through the room.

Damion's gaze lifts to his king, looking less solemn than usual and more impressed than ever. 'The boy is extremely powerful. I've never felt anything like it.'

The king grins. Marrying Myla Rowe will earn him power. Earn him a son he can mold into a weapon.

This is all it takes for the king to claim the child as his own. All the power. All the glory.

'I accept your proposal,' Edric says to his adviser, eyes still pinned on the strength squirming in his Silencer's arms. 'He will be mine.'

CHAPTER 34

Rai

Dice clatter across the table.

Laughter echoes after my roll, followed by large hands that scoop away my shillings. 'Better luck next time, Highness!' the burly sailor bellows.

This heartfelt sympathy is followed by another from across the table. 'Damn, Azer, you're makin' this too easy.'

I lean back in my chair, shaking my head at the four men. 'It seems my mind is elsewhere this round.'

'Just like the five before!' This shout from the burly man continually stealing my money has the rest of them laughing.

'All right, all right.' I stand to my feet and sway with the rocking ship. 'I think I've lost enough shillings for one night.'

'No, don't go yet!' The man's gold tooth winks at me between his words. 'I'm savin' up to buy me my own barrel of rum.'

'Aye!' They all but yell this in unison as I head up the stairs for the main deck.

'Evening, gentlemen,' I yell over my shoulder, making them laugh harder with my choice of words.

Lifting open the grate, I climb onto the deck and into the night.

I take a deep breath of muggy air and head for the poorly patched railing. The sea is eerily still beneath me, the waves a mere rolling reflection of the moon hanging above. It's been unbearably hot the past few days, though the unbearable part is likely due to my lack of *her*.

I run a hand through my ruffled hair, still angered by our argument days ago. The hours have dragged on without her to brighten them, leaving me with nothing to do but gamble away my shillings and drink enough rum to convince myself it tastes good.

I've seen glimpses of her, shared looks she refuses to hold. I can sense her presence on the other side of my wall, feel the empty space in my bed that once occupied her warmth. It's absurd, really. The fight. The truth.

Because that is the root of it all – truth. Something I am not strong enough to hear.

I lean over the rail to peer into the sparkling water below. It is selfish of me to be angry with her, I know. But it is easier that way, as though I'm looking for a reason to lose her that isn't my brother.

Soft footsteps suddenly echo behind me.

I don't need to turn to know who they belong to. She must have wanted me to hear her coming.

'Hi.'

I spin slowly towards the uncharacteristically timid sound. 'I figured you were too stubborn to come talk to me first.'

Paedyn crosses her arms. 'And I figured you were smart enough to beg for my forgiveness first. But—' she lifts her hands into the air between us, '—here we are.'

I sigh. 'I've missed you, Gray.'

'It's only been a few days of not speaking,' she retorts, moonlight dancing on the ends of her silver hair.

'No.' I shake my head, watching her hesitantly step closer. 'It was the beginning of the rest of our lives.'

'Kai, please don't—'

'I was wrong to be angry with you about the truth,' I say quickly. 'It was something I needed to be reminded of anyway.'

I step back then, a physical representation of the boundary I'm attempting to set. This hurts her. I can see it in the way her face crumples against the lantern light, as though she wasn't the one to remind me of our separate fates.

'I . . .' She's spinning that ring on her thumb, and I hate that I'm the cause of such discomfort. 'I need you to know that—'

Hair rises on the back of my neck.

I stiffen, lifting a hand that cuts off her words. I can only imagine the annoyed look on her face because my eyes are already on the sea beyond her. My head tilts slightly, cocking towards that strange pull in the pit of my stomach.

'Kai?'

Paedyn's voice sounds muffled against my back as I strain to focus on this intoxicating feeling. I've felt power my whole life. Learned the way it moved beneath my skin and ignited in my veins. Even the inkling of it is a slight hum in my blood, a tickle at my fingertips.

But that is not this.

This is no Elite. Not entirely.

'Kai, what is it?'

She's standing beside me now, reaching a tentative hand towards the body I've abandoned in pursuit of this feeling within my very soul. Eyes fluttering shut, I reach towards that foreign power. Tug at the lethal connection in the pit of my stomach.

And it comes racing towards me.

'Everyone, get down!'

The warning has only just escaped my lips when the ship lurches violently.

I lunge for Paedyn, managing to throw an arm across her waist while the other grapples for the railing. My hand hooks around the torn wood as the hull bucks beneath us. Sailors topple across the deck, yelling as they slide towards the opposite dipping rail.

The ship rolls until my feet have nearly lifted from the floor. I strain to hold us there, grunting as my fingers slip on the slick rail. Shaken from her initial shock, Paedyn begins tearing at the wood with her nails, desperate to help hold her weight as we dangle above death.

I'm panting, arms burning while screams and shouts ring through the night air. A series of splashes have me wincing for the crewmen who have found themselves overboard. Torri's booming voice cuts through the chaos, shouting orders to whoever still clings to the deck.

The ship rocks once again, this time falling back towards its intended position atop the waves. With a colossal crash, the starboard side slams down into the waves. Water careens over the rails, pelting us with salt and a biting coldness. Our knees buckle with the force and send the slippery deck flying towards us.

Paedyn coughs, pushing a mop of wet hair from her eyes. Every bit of lantern light is swallowed by the wave, leaving only the moon to illuminate this chaos. She looks over at me, soaked to the bone, just as I am. 'What . . .' she pants, 'was that?'

The sailors all around us seem to be shouting the same question, all drenched and dazed. But when my eyes lift and land on the captain's, I don't need to see the terror within his gaze – I know it mirrors my own.

He can hear it. I can feel it. And we may not live long enough to say we had.

My voice is an awed murmur. 'It's found us.'

Wood splinters beside my head.

I throw myself over Paedyn, shielding her from the showering of jagged pieces. A looming darkness falls over us as the ship bucks with the sudden impact. Ears ringing, I barely hear Paedyn's scream beneath me. Barely register my own when I look up towards the source of this devastation.

Teeth.

Hundreds of them, glinting in the moonlight. Rows upon rows of jagged death.

The long, piercing fangs are currently skewering the wooden railing we were just hanging from. I gawk at the creature, only scrambling away from its maw when Paedyn pulls at my arm.

Its scaly green skin is worn and scarred, dripping with the sea. A noise emanates from deep in the monster's throat as it tries to pull those milky teeth from grainy wood. The low growl is accompanied by an odd clicking sound that sends chills down my spine.

'What the hell . . .' Paedyn whispers, her terror a foreign sound.

I push her back, covering her body with my own. 'Stay behind me!'

My shout is nearly lost in the dozens of others as men spill onto the upper deck, ready to hurl their power at the monster. I watch in horror as a man runs towards the railing, spear in hand. With a grunt, he throws it at the creature's head, only for it to glance off the hard skin like a pathetic toothpick.

This only seems to anger the monster. It hisses, vibrating the deck as a circlet of fleshy skin and scales lifts around its head. Rippling like a gruesome petal, shredded and slimy, it encircles the creature's pointed face. From this angle, I can see part of its long body that disappears into the sea. It resembles an enormous sort of eel with that snakelike form and fleshy fin, along its spine.

And yet, everything about this animal is unnatural.

It is nearly the width of two masts, and we have yet to find out the length of this beast. The sheer size and strength alone are a testament to the Plague's alteration.

This creature could easily be a century old.

A Blazer steps forward from the terrified throng to hurl a ball of fire at the monster's face.

But it never lands.

With a roar that rattles the ship, the beast rips away from the railing. Once again, we are showered with bits of wood before a wave of water follows.

'It's gone,' Paedyn sputters, water dripping from her lashes.

That formidable power lurches in the pit of my stomach, so like the Elites', and yet, not at all. 'No.' I give her a shake of my head that dusts droplets of water at her feet. 'It's only just begun.'

Gusts are urging the wind to propel us across the water while Teles hold spears at the ready with their minds, uselessly armoring the ship. I turn to Paedyn once again, grabbing her by the shoulders. 'I need you in your room.'

'Are you coming with me?' she asks pointedly.

'No, I'm staying out here and—'

'Then so will I,' she insists. 'I won't sit and wait to learn of your fate, Kai.'

266

I cup her face, urging her to understand. 'Please, Pae, don't fight me—'

A screeching roar echoes all around us, drowning out every other sound. I'm suddenly being pushed to the ground, Paedyn's body rolling over mine. We tumble across the deck, narrowly escaping the beast's slamming body.

I hear the ominous sound of cracking wood before turning to see the damage. Its long body lies across the deck, the impact of its arch sending a spiderweb of cracks throughout the wood. The monster slides farther, exposing the alarming length of its body. Sailors jump out of the way, some lost to snapping teeth or a forceful shove of the scaled body.

Elites hurl their powers at it, though they seem to do little damage. Fire, telepathy, strength, and weapons do nothing in the wake of such might. I join in despite the futility, throwing fire or attempting to pull the massive creature away with my mind. But for the first time, I'm witnessing Elites rendered completely powerless. *I* am rendered completely powerless.

Slithering across the deck, the beast breaks through the opposite railing to plunge back into the water. I tug Paedyn against me, trying to keep my unsteady footing atop the violently rocking ship. 'We can't fight it!' I yell at the dazed crewmen.

It's Torri I hear boom back. 'All hands on deck! Every Gust at the ready!'

'We can't outrun it,' Paedyn pants. 'We can't do anything.'

Another lurch of the ship and a massive spiny tail crashes over the deck. The wood beneath our feet cracks again and boards fall into the depths of the ship. Grabbing Paedyn's hand, I run between the growing gaps while the swishing tail knocks men into the sea.

Screams amplify when the monster's face appears on the other side of the ship, its body squeezing the vessel from beneath the sea's surface. On one end, teeth the length of my forearm await, snapping at what is left of the wooden railing. And on the other, a rampaging tail decorated in jagged fins.

I shove Paedyn against the pair of doors leading to our rooms at the same moment one of those pointed spikes skewers a sailor.

He screams, helplessly draped over the monster's tail to display the bloody barb lodged in his chest. Moonlight streams down on the gory scene, shiny against the pool of blood blooming beneath his torn clothing.

Paedyn's gasp is quickly covered by her shaking hands when the man is tossed into the ocean with a flick of the beast's tail. I don't waste another moment before ripping open the door beside her. 'In. Please!' I shout the word into the night, willing her to hear the desperate plea within it.

'I can't leave you!' she yells back, bending to pick up a forgotten spear. 'I won't!'

I'm about to argue further when the ground is suddenly stolen from beneath my feet. I hear Paedyn scream when my body hits the deck. Then again when the bony tail connects with my spine.

Pain explodes down my body.

I'm suddenly being dragged across the wood, wrapped in slimy scales as my trailing body knocks sailors from their feet. Panting, I bite my tongue against the pain and slip a dagger from my boot. Grabbing hold of the massive tail hugging my leg, I plunge my blade into one of the beast's many scars.

A screech tears from its throat before the tail lifts sharply, me in tow. I cling to it, fingers slipping on the slick scales. Then I'm yelling as it flings me into the open air.

The starry sky blurs around me.

I'm falling.

Paedyn screams my name.

Falling.

The churning sea suddenly appears beneath me.

Falling. Falling. Fa—

Desperately, I claw at a nearby Tele's power, urging it into my palms and bending it to my mind's will.

My stomach drops as I plummet towards the water.

Throwing a strand of power towards one of the many ropes wrapped around the mast, I summon it to me. Obeying, it shoots towards my outstretched arm.

Paedyn's silver hair glints over the ship's railing. And that is the last I see before my body collides with the sea.

Biting water swallows me whole, numbing every limb with its frigid fangs. I tumble in the sea, mind sluggish. Salt bombards my senses, filling my mouth and nose. I kick furiously towards what I hope is the surface, though I can see nothing but darkness.

My lungs burn.

I fumble for the Tele's power, reach for that rope.

I'm dizzy, floating in a dark abyss.

I strain for salvation. Beg for life. Beg to live it with her.

The rope plunges into the water.

I grab hold of it, pulling my body upward with weak arms. Moonlight streams above, beckoning me. And when my head breaks through the surface, I'm spewing water.

I cling to the wet rope, choking down air before lifting myself from the sea. A hysterical sigh of relief sounds from above me, and I look up through sea-soaked hair to find Paedyn leaning over the railing above, tears streaming down her cheeks.

For her, I pull myself up that rope. My arms burn, as do my lungs, but I push the pain aside. With raw palms, I set my feet against the ship's belly and scale it.

By the time my arms hook over the railing, Paedyn is practically pulling me over the edge. I let her, unable to muster the strength. My arms are draped over her shoulders, and she grunts beneath my weight.

Pain shoots down my body with every tug. And when my boots hit the deck, I crumple to my knees. Paedyn's body eases my fall, her arms wrapped tightly around me even after we hit the deck.

We stare at each other for a long moment, content to ignore the beast raging behind us. I fear it would take much more than that to pull my gaze from her.

With a choked sob, she presses her face into my neck, wiping tears across my skin. 'I thought I lost you,' she whispers, half laughing.

I lift a numb hand to her soaking hair, running fingers I can't feel through it. With chattering teeth, I manage, 'You c-can't get rid of me that easily, Gray.'

She cups my face, head shaking and smile trembling. 'Damn fate, and duty, and every other word meant to keep us apart.' Tears slip from those blue eyes I would happily drown in. 'I want to hide with you beneath the willow tree. You are the secret I will spend the rest of my life keeping.' Her voice quivers beneath the weight of such a promise. '*Us.*'

That alone is enough to have tears springing to my eyes. So I nod. Her face in my hands, my heart in hers.

The countless screams echoing all around finally manage to capture our attention. Before either of us can spew a comforting lie, the ship is tipping again. We slide across the wood when the creature lifts its head farther onto the deck. Serrated teeth lash out for the captain, and he narrowly avoids being swallowed whole.

The boat is crumbling beneath the weight of this creature, straining to keep us all afloat. 'We need to do something,' Paedyn murmurs.

'Whatever you're thinking, don't,' I order.

She looks over at me then, and I remember just how much I missed her doing something as simple as acknowledging my existence. A small smile pulls at her lips. She's breathtaking in this light, as though her hair is a collection of the moon's rays. 'You forget, Kai.' Her fingers wrap tightly around the spear. 'This is my Trial.'

And then she's running.

CHAPTER 35

Paedyn

The spear grows slick in my hand.

My boots pound against the slippery deck, drowning out the sound of Kai's shout behind me.

But I've watched this beast. Learned its strengths. Discovered its weakness.

And this is not the first monster I have faced.

So when it turns its luminous green eyes on me, baring numerous rows of jagged teeth, I do not back down. I do not fail, or falter, or feel remorse.

Every beast can be defeated.

A creature. A Trial. A king.

I lift the heavy spear, cocking back my arm. Hot breath washes over me when the monster roars. Scaly skin flares around its face as it slithers closer, jaw snapping and teeth glinting.

And I roar right back.

The creature screeches louder, blowing my hair back and watering my eyes. Still, I stand before it. My chest heaves; heart hammers. And then I let the spear fly from my hand to meet the beast racing right for me.

The monster's jaw widens, readying to sink those lethal fangs into my flesh—

I look Death in the eye as my spear sinks into it.

The beast roars in pain, body bucking as blood pours from its once-glowing iris. Screeching, it rattles the ship, shaking its head in an attempt to dislodge the piercing weapon. I stumble when the boat pitches, falling to my knees beneath the creature. Even when staring up into the embodiment of terror, I realize that this is still half the beast I've faced in the past.

With one final roar of anguish, it arcs over the ship, over my crumpled body, and dives into the waves.

I feel numb. I'm shaking as water sprays onto the deck, misting me with salty droplets. What remains of the crew stands stunned and bloody, all staring at the stirring sea where the creature disappeared.

Kai is beside me in an instant, hands frigid atop my skin. His palms have slid around my neck to tangle numb fingers in my soaking hair. 'What were you thinking?' he scolds, wide eyes searching mine. 'Do I need to order you to your room next time?'

I smile weakly. 'That won't work when I'm queen.'

His lips are stained blue with cold, and yet they still twitch into a smile. 'I can be very persuasive.'

'Well I'll be damned, the Silver Savior does it again!'

I turn towards the captain's bellowing voice, his timing impeccable as ever. The limping crew gathers around him, some dripping with water, others blood. Torri holds an arm tightly to his injured chest and pushes the pain from his voice. 'We've conquered the beast!'

A weak chant begins to rise from their collective throats, one I thought I would never hear again.

'Silver Savior!'

'Silver Savior!'

'Silver Savior!'

And I might have liked the sound of it.

I've never been so relieved to step foot in Ilya.

Mostly because I'm looking forward to standing on something solid without the worry of it caving in beneath my feet.

The ship is in ruin, and it has been for the last two days. Only by the strength of Elites has it managed to reach Ilya's dock. With nearly half the crew lost to the sea and the beast dwelling within it, surviving this final stretch of the Shallows was no simple task. Teles worked in shifts to hold the most vital pieces of the ship together with their minds while Gusts blew a constant stream of air into the torn sails. Any excess weight was thrown overboard in an attempt to help keep us afloat, leaving only bread and water to fill our stomachs.

I lean against one of the only remaining chunks of railing, readying to spring out of the way if the boards beneath my feet give way – which they have done on several terrifying occasions. The hull groans in agony against the waves, as though begging for a swift sinking into the sea. Even the *Reckoning* pleads for rest.

I keep my gaze on the approaching dock even as Kai comes to stand beside me. My voice is quiet. 'Do you think he's down there?'

Kai's gray gaze falls to the cluster of bodies awaiting us on the rickety moor, their faces blurry from this distance. 'Kitt?'

I nod coolly.

A shake of his head. 'I hope not. It's dangerous for him to be so exposed without me. But—' his sigh is weary, '—he probably is.'

Thoughts spill from my mouth. 'I don't think he wants to be looked after.'

'He should be grateful that someone cares enough to do so,' Kai retorts stiffly. 'Not all of us had that luxury.'

I turn towards him, taking in the stony expression he now wears. 'Why did your father treat you two so differently?'

The question seems to surprise him. 'We had very different roles in life.'

'I know, but . . .' I grapple for the right words and try again. 'He could have tutored Kitt with the same callousness and hate that he trained you with. I mean, that is why your brother still cares for the king you hated.' My eyes wander back to the approaching dock. 'You knew different versions of the same man.'

'That is exactly why Kitt never fully understood my disdain for Father,' Kai adds quietly. 'Why he lived to please him while I lived to spite him.'

I smile slightly. 'Is that why you chose to spend so much time with me during the Trials? To spite him?'

He seems to weigh his words carefully. 'Among many other reasons.' I roll my eyes before he adds, 'Although, I always thought it was odd how boldly Kitt befriended you. Father hated that I was associated with you, so for Kitt to go against the king's wishes because of you . . .' He shakes his head. 'It was unexpected.'

'And now he's marrying the Ordinary your father hated,' I murmur. 'The same one that killed him.'

Kai takes a deep breath. 'Kitt has always feared failing our father. But I think . . . I think he also fears turning into the one I hated. Along with that letter Kitt found, your fight with the king may have helped him see reason.' He shrugs slightly. 'The king came after you out of hatred for what you are not.'

I glance over at him. 'And you believe me about that?'

'After that battle at the Bowl, the Sight who witnessed your fight met with Kitt and me privately.' He looks over at me, grief in his gaze. 'We watched some of what happened. With the rain, we couldn't make out what was being said, and Kitt couldn't bear to watch more than a minute of it.'

It is then that I see his grief is not for the king I killed. But for me and everything I endured by his hand. I blink, bewildered by this new information. 'Why didn't you tell me?'

'You still killed the king,' Kai answers evenly. 'Kitt was still angry. So was the kingdom. At the end of the day, you were still a murderer.' His eyes flick over me. 'And I wanted to hear your side of the story, because we still didn't know what really happened.'

I've now buried that vicious fight in the darkest depths of my mind. It sits among the bloody pool in which my father lies, right next to an image of too-short curly bangs and the unseeing hazel eyes beneath.

Unanswered questions swirl near that dark corner, drifting in and out of my thoughts. One belongs to the true identity of my parents while another lies within that battle against the king – his motives and confessions equally confusing. Adena's presence in that final Trial never fails to keep me up at night, mocking me in my dreams with ways I might have saved her.

I swallow. 'He all but told me that the Ordinaries' disease was a lie, you know.'

There is a long pause filled only with the sound of a slapping sea. 'And you didn't tell me?'

'Would you have believed me?' I counter.

He says nothing.

'I had no proof but my own word, and that meant little after what I'd done. So, I wanted you to discover the truth yourself.' I glance down at the sparkling ring on my finger. 'But I still am a murderer.'

'And you're still far better than most.'

I shake my head. The stifled darkness within me says otherwise.

I'm quiet until a soft question surprises my lips. 'So, what do you fear?' He looks over at me, subtlety intrigued. 'You told me what Kitt fears. Now I want to know what could possibly frighten Ilya's mighty Enforcer.'

He chuckles darkly. 'I'm afraid of plenty.'

I raise a brow. 'Is it me you're scared of, Prince?'

His answer is quick and earnest. 'I'm scared of what could happen to you. What *I* could do to you.' A muscle twitches in his jaw. 'I fear every swipe of my sword and every command from my mouth. It haunts me.'

Emotion clogs my throat, forcing me to swallow back a sudden wave of grief. My heart aches for this boy who never got to be one. 'It's not fair,' I manage. 'This life you're forced to live.'

His eyes are a storm that sweeps over my face. 'It might just all be worth it if it means I can protect you.'

I shake my head at him as the ship lurches against the dock. Kai steps away at the reminder of who we are supposed to be to each other in this city. Glancing down at the dozens of awaiting faces, he says, 'Why ask? About Kitt and our father?'

I tip my head towards the dock, eyes pinned on a pair I know to be green. 'I guess I'm just trying to understand him better.'

Kitt's blond hair ruffles in the wind beneath the crown he wears, both glinting gold within the circle of Imperials surrounding their king. He looks oddly . . . dulled. Weary. His hands are folded over the fine green tunic he wears, and—

And his eyes are on mine.

For a moment, I feel as though I'm back in the Bowl, meeting his gaze from afar as I stand within a game meant to prove myself.

'Pae?'

The sound of that nickname tears my eyes from the dock below and I fix them on the Enforcer beside me. 'Hmm?'

'I asked if you were ready to get the hell off this thing.'

My smile is tight. 'Yes, very.'

I follow him towards the wooden ramp, feeling it creak beneath my weight as I descend onto the dock. A wall of Imperials on the rocky shore separates the gawking Ilyans from us, though I can feel the countless pairs of eyes raking over me. I bristle beneath the many gazes examining every inch of the girl they likely hoped to never see again.

The captain follows closely behind as we make our way over to the king. Kitt smiles tightly at me, and it's a relief not to be scrutinized by him as well. Perhaps he is happy to see me return in one piece. Perhaps distance, and the likelihood of my imminent death, really does make the heart grow fonder.

When the Imperials part to let us greet him, it's Torri who speaks first. 'Your Majesty—'

'Kai!'

A flurry of limbs pushes through the throng of Imperials to bound towards the Enforcer. Kai barely has enough time to spread his arms before Jax crashes into them. The boy clings to his brother, face buried in his shoulder.

Jax sniffles. 'You're alive.'

'Of course, J,' Kai murmurs. 'I had to make it back home to you.'

My gaze is torn from their heartfelt reunion when Torri clears his throat. 'As I was saying, Your Majesty, it was an honor to sail under Ilya's colors once again. As you can see—' he gestures to the battered boat behind, '—we encountered the beast that lurks within the Shallows, but under my command, we now live to tell the tale.'

Kitt nods his appreciation. 'Thank you, Captain Torri. Your bravery and service to our kingdom will be greatly rewarded.'

Kai clears his throat, arm still slung around Jax. 'I believe praise is due to the one who saved us from that beast.' He lifts a hand towards me, and the gesture alone has every eye back on my disheveled figure.

Heat stains my cheeks as I throw a warning glance Kai's way. This doesn't go unnoticed by the king. His tired eyes flick to me. 'Is that so?'

I take a breath and paste a warm grin on my face. 'I may have helped deliver the final blow. Which wasn't very benevolent—' I clear my throat, '—towards the creature.'

Kai dips his head, hiding a smile. Jax follows after his older brother, though far less discreetly with a choking cough. And Kitt—

Kitt just stares at me.

I can't read this look, and I typically pride myself on being able to do just that. Something like realization lights those green eyes. Or perhaps it's awe I see traced within the lines around his slight grin. But before I can decipher this expression, he's reaching a hand towards me.

His knuckles brush mine before I let him interlace our fingers. This is for the people piled on that rocky shore, their prying gazes pinned on us. 'It seems you'll make a fine queen.' The diamond on my finger grows heavy. 'It's as though you were born for this.'

CHAPTER 36

Kai

Candlelight flickers down the length of the table, dousing every plate of food in a honeylike glow.

The court sits snugly together to crowd around the feast. They talk idly, drowning in their finery while nibbling at their meal. Dragging a hand through my hair, I catch myself wishing this banquet was a ball, if only so I could slip away unnoticed within the swirling bodies.

Instead, I sit stiffly to Kitt's right, on display and at his disposal. He seems distracted, green eyes glazed over. I can't help but notice the slight gauntness of his face or rasping of his voice. He looks worn enough to warrant concern I can't currently give before his court. It seems the king did not rest, as he promised.

Paedyn shimmers across from me, picking politely at the food on her plate. For a moment, it feels as though we are seated back in time at that dinner before the Purging Trials, the one where I all but forced her to eat. The night she became my weakness.

It's familiar, this scene. Simple.

Except that it's not, and the king beside her is not my father.

I've spent most of the evening watching Kitt lean over, conversing

quietly with his betrothed. Paedyn smiles each time, the action tugging at that scar trailing down her throat. The elegant high neck of the dress she wears conceals the far more vicious one below, though my gaze continually falls to where I know the carving to be.

This should not upset me, their closeness with each other. They are engaged, after all, and speaking civilly is the tamest of actions. But I cannot seem to shake the gnawing envy in my gut, the jealousy that flares with every look shared and word exchanged. It's tiresome, this turmoil between love for my brother and love for his betrothed.

'You seem to have quite the appetite – just not for your food.'

With a heavy exhale, my eyes flick towards the source of that accusing tone. Beside me, Andy raises a brow, her nose ring flashing like the challenge in her eyes. I give her a tired look. 'Just spit it out, Andy.'

Using only the corner of her mouth, she fires back, 'Stop staring at what you can't have.'

I lift a piece of turkey to my mouth. 'I wasn't.'

'You were.'

This voice belongs to the girl beside my cousin, her sheet of black hair swaying as she leans over the table to meet my stare. I don't know the Crawler well, but I recognize her as Andy's friend from the ball. Though, with a quick glance beneath the table at their interlaced fingers, it seems safe to assume that their relationship has progressed further.

'See,' Andy says smugly. 'Jasmyn is my witness.'

'Yes—' I take a quick sip of champagne, '—thank you for your astute observations.'

Andy tucks a strand of wine-red hair behind her ear. 'Kai, we talked about this—'

The shrill clinking of glass saves me from my cousin's wrath. I turn towards Kitt, watching him stand at the head of the table. Scanning the room, he offers a small smile to his court. 'To Paedyn Gray, your future queen. Who successfully showed not only her bravery, but also her benevolence.' He peers down the table distantly. 'Onward to her brutality. And long live the Silver Savior.'

When I lift my glass, the entire court is quick to follow. 'Long live the Silver Savior,' they mutter in unison, most begrudgingly.

Champagne bubbles against my tongue, warming my throat. My eyes are back on Paedyn, though her own are pinned on something far down the lengthy table. I watch her gaze grow suddenly cold, lethal in a way I know firsthand she can be. Following that look, I scan the many faces decorating the throne room.

And then my eyes stutter over her.

The lilac hair falling over Blair's shoulders seems to oddly complement Lenny's fiery red waves to the left. She sits comfortably in the seat beside her father, arms crossed and lips teasing the Imperial. They look familiar, at ease with each other in a way that is likely making Paedyn's head spin.

I glance back across the table at her, watching as a sheet of icy anger creeps over her expression. She looks ready to avenge Adena right here and now. Staring at this version of the Silver Savior, I fear for those who make her feel nothing.

No remorse. No compassion. No worry for her stained soul.

I raise a hand, hoping to stop her from doing something reckless, when she stands suddenly. Her chair squeals against the marble floor and turns every head in her direction.

Panic pushes me to the edge of my seat, awaiting her next move. But it is the false smile she plasters on her face that has me truly worried. Lifting a glass, she clears her throat in preparation for a toast.

My fingers curl around the table's edge.

Paedyn's bright smile and cold gaze fall back on Blair.

'To the Ordinaries,' she says cheerily. 'And every unjust death. May they be avenged.'

Then she tips her head at Blair and lifts the glass to her lips.

I glance down the table to find a lilac head of hair bowing right back.

'To the Ordinaries.'

I barely register the grumbled words that only half the court bother repeating. And it is only when Paedyn takes her seat that I'm able to draw a deep breath. Uncurling my hand from the table, I wait for another wave of dull chatter to sweep over the room.

When all eyes have fallen from Paedyn, and every mouth has moved on to another topic, I lean forward to murmur, 'Well, that was suspiciously civil.'

Those blue eyes flick up to meet mine. 'I wouldn't call a threat civil.'

'For you,' I amend plainly, 'that is.'

Taking an interest in our hushed conversation, Kitt chimes in with a discreet, 'Once again, you know why I can't let you hurt her, Paedyn.'

Gripping her fork, she rolls a piece of potato around her plate innocently. 'And you know why I can't let her live.'

'Pae.' Kitt's gaze snaps to me at the familiarity in the word. Shit. I carry on quickly before any of us can ponder what I've just said. 'You can banish her when you're queen if you like, but don't do anything rash before you wear that crown.'

'I don't need to hide behind a crown,' she grits out.

'Yes, you do,' Kitt murmurs evenly. He brings a napkin to his mouth before coughing into it. I narrow my eyes at the hoarse sound he cuts off quickly. 'Ruling is all about hiding. The truth, motive, yourself – all of it. And the earlier you learn that, the easier it will be for you in this castle.'

Paedyn blinks at him, and I can't help but do the same. There is that piece of Father he possesses. Swallowing, she places her palms firmly on the table. 'It seems like we could all blow off some steam.' Then a sudden, wicked tug of her lips. 'Now, where is this wine cellar you always used to sneak off to?'

🌺

Wine dribbles down the fingers I have tightly curled around the bottle's neck.

Paedyn's dress is an emerald pool atop the floor of the cellar, flickering in a beam of candlelight. She tips her head against the cool stone wall and laughs loud enough to have my face splitting into a smile.

Turning her bewildered gaze on me, she manages, 'You did not!'

'He did,' Kitt blurts on my behalf. 'I'm the one who broke his fall.'

281

Pae's mouth falls open as I attempt to defend myself. 'I was five, all right. I could barely use my power, let alone know which ones even exist.'

'So he climbs up onto the roof of the stables,' Kitt explains, a drunken smile turning his lips. 'Now, Kai Pie here was convinced there was an Elite who could fly—'

Paedyn snorts, quickly muffling the sound with a palm to the mouth.

'—so he decides to jump from the roof and test the theory,' Kitt finishes with a laugh aimed at me.

'Why,' Paedyn huffs towards me, 'would you think that was a good idea?'

I take a swig of wine before answering. 'In my defense, I could barely sense powers at that age, so I thought a . . . flying Elite might be possible. Now, that didn't mean there was one nearby, but . . .'

Kitt slaps a hand against the stone floor, laughter morphing him into the boy I grew up with. Giddiness bubbles from Pae in a way I rarely get to witness, evidence of the wine loosening her tongue and lifting my spirits. I grin brightly and wonder just how much of it is due to being with my brother in this cellar again.

'So you crashed right into me,' Kitt declares, slapping a hand on my shoulder, 'and broke my leg.'

'Well, your body broke one of my ribs,' I counter. 'Besides, it was your idea to test my theory.'

'That doesn't mean you should do it.'

I catch Paedyn's eye, aware of what it is she sees. We are so very free in this moment – laughing together like old times and living like life never got in the way. Cheeks flushed and duties forgotten, we sit here as brothers who bear no titles.

'I like you two like this,' she says softly.

I bring the bottle to my lips, swallowing the dark wine. 'Like what? Drunk bastards off our asses?'

Kitt laughs, clinking his flagon against mine. 'I'll drink to that.'

Paedyn shakes her head at us. 'No – well, maybe – but I just like the two of you being so . . . carefree. Together.'

That has Kitt looking suddenly serious despite the ruffled hair and unbuttoned shirt. His gaze is earnest as it slides to mine. 'Just like old times.'

'Just like old times,' I echo.

'I missed you, Brother.' Kitt sighs. 'I miss us.'

'I'm right here, Kitty.' My smile is soft. 'I haven't gone anywhere.'

'Haven't you?' The words are a startling snap. And then the king is laughing, smothering that accusatory tone with a smile. It's an odd flickering of emotions I doubt he intended to show us. But when he turns to Paedyn, bottle lifted sloppily into the air, his tired eyes are bright. 'To old times.'

CHAPTER 37
Paedyn

I stare blankly at the dozens of fabric squares surrounding me atop the bed.

'These all look the same,' I blurt in Ellie's direction. 'They are all . . . white.'

She pulls the thick curtains together, blocking out the starry night beyond. 'Well, wedding dresses typically are.'

My mouth goes dry at the reminder of what one of these little squares will soon become. I shake my head, admitting defeat. 'Here. You just pick for me.'

'Paedyn.' Ellie's tone is surprisingly scolding, enough so to have me smiling with pride. 'This is your big day. I refuse to pick out the fabric of *your* wedding dress.'

I run a finger across the strip of samples, feeling each texture and pattern alongside the growing pit in my stomach. 'What if I don't even live to wear it, hmm? I mean, there is still the final Trial and—'

'And you'll be just fine,' Ellie reassures gently.

'Why, because I have no problem being brutal?'

The words come out in a rush, like an uprooted fear typically does. She walks over to me, sitting on the edge of the bed only after I pat

the quilt insistently. 'There is no shame in that when justified,' Ellie states. 'It's not knowing an end to your brutality that's the problem.'

My eyes fall to the surrounding fabrics and each finger gliding over them. It feels wrong to touch something so blindingly pure with such bloody hands. My soul is stained with death and drenched in the regret of it.

I never asked for this brutality, this darkness. It was asked of me.

Clearing my constricting throat, I lift one of the squares into the lamplight. 'How about this one?'

Ellie leans in, her brown eyes tracing the faint pattern of twining vines etched in white thread. 'It's beautiful.' With a sad smile, she adds, 'Adena would have loved it.'

'She would have been jealous of the needlework,' I agree with a light laugh. 'She always did hate doing that herself.'

Ellie watches me run my thumb over the fabric a few dozen times before saying, 'I'll let the seamstress know what you picked.'

I nod and numbly collect the fabric into a pile that Ellie tucks beneath her arm. 'Tomorrow,' she insists sweetly, 'we will pick the flowers for the ceremony.'

Groaning, I tip my head back against the wall. 'If I pick now, will I be free of these decisions?'

'I suppose, but—'

'Perfect,' I say cheerily. 'Roses.'

Ellie gives me a knowing look. 'Is that just the first flower that came to mind?'

'Maybe, but it seems fitting,' I defend. 'I admire the rose and its thorns. Even the prettiest things can bite.'

Slowly, Ellie nods in agreement. 'Then roses it is.' I watch her bustle around the room once again, ensuring everything is in order for the night. 'And they will certainly be easy to find. There is a private rose garden here on the grounds. Pretty pink ones, I believe.' I bat her away when she tries to fluff the pillow behind my back. 'Now—' she straightens my boots beside the wardrobe, '—I will see you in the morning, miss.'

I shake my head at her, even as a smile turns my lips. 'Good night, Ellie.'

Tipping her head timidly, she offers a quiet 'Good night, Paedyn.'

I watch her slip out the door before spreading my tired limbs out on the bed. Even after I did little more than waste away the day and take full advantage of sleeping on solid ground again, my eyelids still manage to droop. The dagger beneath my pillow is a comfort I clutch as I drift into sleep.

I dream of Adena, as I always do. It is unpleasant, as it always is.

The memory of her death resurfaces, swirling in and out of focus. A collage of every way in which I should have saved her plays behind my heavy eyelids. This nightmare is as torturous as every one before, and I claw uselessly at my subconscious to free me from it.

When I finally wake, it is to a sweaty brow and still-darkened sky. Though, most alarming of all, is the plan I've determined. With my mind set and heart aching, I stand to my feet. I don't bother changing my large shirt and the thin pants beneath, though I quickly add Adena's torn vest to the ensemble. It is only right to visit our home with her hugging me closely.

I step out into the shadowed hallway, looking like the resident of Loot I once was, ready to rob an unsuspecting prince. It's fitting that I look like my old self, feel like the girl just trying to survive one sunrise at a time.

Before I was the Silver Savior, the king killer, the queen-to-be, I was Paedyn Gray.

And she is going home.

Soft light slips between the cracked cobblestones and crawls up the sooty walls. I breathe in the familiar stench of Loot, nearly choking on the thick air. My senses are bombarded with the past and every memory that accompanies it.

Dawn dares to creep over the horizon, painting the alley in a warm glow. While walking that graveled path from the Bowl Arena, I watched the night slowly flee from a rising sun. Those quiet hours were spent reliving the last time I stumbled down that road, bloody and broken. I passed the tree whose roots are decorated with that bundle of forget-me-nots, passed the rocks and plants that were once stained with my blood. Everywhere I looked, my past stared back.

It follows me still, here on Loot. I walk the same uneven cobblestones, dodge the same sneering Imperials. Though, I have never been so aware of the stubborn stench that ceaselessly wafts from the slums, not since staying in the castle.

This realization stings slightly, a reminder of everything I no longer am. So much of myself lives within these streets, both the broken and the resilient. Adena lives here, on every warm breeze and colorful banner. Her name is written across the stones I step on, and I let her soft presence lead me back home.

Merchants roll their carts right across my path, cutting me off with an unbothered yawn. Some start the day early in the hopes of claiming the most populated parts of Loot. I scan the rickety stalls as I pass, finding the shortage of resources on display. Food was something I rarely paid for, let alone observed for long before shoving it into my mouth. Still, I saw it dwindle over the years, slowly enough that only the merchants knew for a long while.

I was so busy surviving the streets of Loot that I didn't know the extent of what was happening on them. Homeless huddle against crumbling buildings, no bed to sleep in or money to live with. A stack of sticky buns glisten on a merchant's cart, each one an outlandish five shillings. I realize now that I've never actually paid for one, and thus, have no idea how expensive *living* has become. More than ever, I see Ilya for what it is – shambles.

But that is going to change.

I tug the fraying vest around me and quicken my pace. A small crowd spills out onto the alley, snatching what food they can afford. I weave between the bodies, and it feels like falling back into a familiar rhythm. The tranquility of blending in is a beauty that even the castle cannot offer me. I have not felt peace like this since . . .

Since I left Adena for the Purging Trials.

The thought falls away when the Fort comes into view.

My heart stutters in reminder of its missing piece. I stumble towards the alley's end, my eyes pinned on the barricade. A ray of sunlight brushes the worn rug and reaches for me to rejoin it.

The Fort looms closer, and my pulse quickens. Squinting through the shadows, I falter at the unfamiliarity before me.

This is not the home I left.

No, this fort now bears a colorful banner above it. The fabric squares have been sown onto the yarn, painstaking proof that this was Adena's doing.

I can't seem to breathe.

Behind the barrier, our belongings have been rearranged. The usual pile of cloth is sorted neatly beside a new blanket and pillow I never got the chance to share with her.

Even in the dull light, her vibrance exudes from the space.

And I tremble in the presence of it.

My knees hit the cobblestone, and I welcome the shock of pain.

It's as if I'd expected her to be sitting there, waiting for me to return from a day of thieving. As if she would phase through our fort and come bounding towards me in search of a sticky bun. As if I didn't hold Adena's dying body in my lap or see her blood gushing between my fingers with every glance at my incapable hands.

A tear slips down my cheek, splattering the ground with a drop of my anguish.

She was waiting for me to come home.

Muffled footsteps sound behind me.

But she she never made it home.

My stare remains distant, even as a deep voice rings out behind me.

'This alley is taken. You'll have to find another place to—'

I turn to let my teary gaze fall on this stranger.

His brown eyes widen with a recognition I don't share. Strands of black hair fall around strong cheekbones while the rest is pulled back with a loose strap. I blink at the lonely silver streak threading among such darkness, as though a lock of my own hair lives on his head.

'It's you,' he breathes.

The scar slicing his lips curls with the words. I tense. 'And who are you?'

'After all this time, you're finally back to visit her,' he mutters.

Understanding dawns, so blindingly clear I have to blink. 'You're the boy. The one Adena was seeing during the Trials.'

He sinks to the cobblestone beside me, and in the morning light, I can just make out the dark splotches under his eyes. It's more than a lack of sleep around his gaze; it is a smattering of bruises. 'She talked about you all the time. And then she died for simply knowing you.'

His words are a blunt knife to my chest. 'I know.' I choke on the emotion in my throat. 'It should have been me. Not her.'

Those brown eyes bore into mine. 'She was coming to see you, long before being summoned as your seamstress. We had it all planned.'

'I don't understand.' My back hits the grimy wall. 'How did you two . . . ?'

'Hera was my cousin,' the man says dully. 'When I discovered how close you and Adena were, I knew she would help me get into the castle, just to see you.'

'Then Hera died in the first Trial,' I recall numbly at the memory of Braxton driving a blade through her invisible chest.

'And Dena in the last.'

I feel the moment my heart shatters, feel the shards of it pierce my lungs until I'm gasping for air.

Dena.

She was my A. But she was his Dena.

'I'm so sorry,' I choke out. 'I'm so, so sorry. About Hera. About . . .' A tear slips down my cheek. 'About Dena. I couldn't save her. Why didn't I save her?'

Something shifts behind his dark stare. Perhaps it's pity or another entirely demeaning emotion. But I watch it begin to smother that stony expression, erode the anger etched into the corners of his eyes. I doubt this is the monster he expected to face. Instead, a crumpled, crying girl is falling apart before him.

'This is all my fault.' I turn my blurry gaze back to the Fort, every bright color a mockery without her here. 'She redecorated for me. To surprise me when I got back from the Trials.' Tears are falling in front of this stranger, but I can't seem to find the will to care. 'But it was her who never made it back. And it's all my fault. This is all my fault—'

'I couldn't save her either.' The stranger sounds choked. It takes that thought for me to realize how much more he is than that. This man is one of the last pieces of Adena. 'I . . . I couldn't do anything but watch her die.'

'You were there for her when I couldn't be,' I say firmly. 'And that was enough.'

He shakes his head of dark hair at the cobblestones beneath us. 'I have spent weeks being so angry with you. With the girl who killed her.'

'Me too.' I almost laugh, even as tears refuse to shy from my gaze. 'You can't blame me – or Blair – more than I already have.'

The silence that stretches between us only reminds me of Adena. She is not here to fill it.

The man shifts, slipping from the shadow that once draped over him. I let my gaze fall from his face for the first time, as if the dull light has tempted me to investigate further. My stare scours over his broad shoulders, then the fabric hanging over them. The black vest is cut close to his body with pockets and pockets and—

I know those pockets.

My chin dips. I stare down at my own torn pockets.

'She made you a vest.'

The stranger now stares at the olive fabric wrapped around me, his dark eyes glassy. 'She did.'

All the air has left my lungs. Hurt curls around my body, choking until it's crushing my will, my hope, my heart. I grieve Adena all over again, because I was not the only one she lost. Two great loves were left behind, and both hug what remains of her close to their heart.

Tears fall, but I don't care that my vulnerability is on display. I kneel at the foot of our fort and cry for the girl who once brightened it. The stranger swipes at his cheek but is quick to aim the sharp planes of his face at the ground.

'What is your name?' I finally manage to whisper.

It takes him a long moment to find an answer. 'Mak.'

I nod quickly, the action shaking tears from my eyelashes. 'Can I . . .' My voice cracks. 'Can I give you a hug, Mak?'

He doesn't do it for me. I can tell by the tensing of his shoulders. No, he does it for his Dena – my A. We fall into each other, bodies shaking with grief and anger. In his embrace, I understand how someone so rigid and stoic could only be molded by the gentlest of hands. He was drawn in by Adena's warmth, forever imprinted on by her now-broken sewing fingers.

We hold each other, strangers connected by a mutual love. And when Mak finally pulls away, his eyes rimmed with red, a streak of sunshine falls heavily over our kneeling bodies. The beam of light coats us thoroughly enough to dry the tears staining my cheeks.

The scar cutting through Mak's lips curves with a sad smile. 'What?' I ask weakly. This man does not look like the type to smile easily, though that may have only been the case before Adena gave him a reason to.

He shuts his eyes to bask in the warm light. 'Just admiring the sun.'

CHAPTER 38

Kai

The sun wakes before I've even gone to sleep.

It peers down at me from behind the string of orange clouds smothering the horizon. It wasn't until soft light scared away the shadows, and a warm breeze grazed my sweaty skin, that I realized my night was spent in the training ring.

I swing a sword at my side, repeating the same movements I have since stepping into this circle of packed dirt. The dull edge of my blade meets the chipped practice dummy opposite me with a thud. With a series of swift movements, I would have thoroughly disemboweled a figure not carved from wood.

'You need something more challenging to beat down on.'

I smile at the sound of Kitt's voice as I yank my lodged sword free. 'What, are you offering?'

I watch him step into the ring with a slight cough. 'I could use the exercise. Plague knows I haven't sparred with you in weeks.'

'Miss getting your ass kicked, do you?'

He catches the dull sword I toss at him. 'Maybe I missed spending time with you, Brother. Even if it means getting my ass kicked.'

I begin treading a slow circle around the ring, Kitt following my

lead with his weapon raised. 'Don't go getting all soft on me.' My grin is crooked. 'I'd rather not feel bad about throwing you around.'

I catch the slash of his blade with my own.

He wears a wild smile as he pulls away and attempts a jab at my ribs. I dodge swiftly before swiping my blade towards him. Kitt ducks, leaving behind the swoosh of torn air when dull steel sweeps over his blond head. 'It seems I'm not too out of practice after a—'

The pommel of my sword meets his unguarded stomach. His words turn into a cough, my smile into a laugh. 'Spoke too soon, Kitty.'

He sucks in a shaky breath. 'Well, that . . . certainly woke me up.'

Straightening, he advances on me with a speed I hadn't expected. I'm pushed towards the edge of the ring as our blades clash against each other. This allows me a moment to evaluate my opponent, study the dark circles beneath Kitt's eyes and the slight hollow in his cheeks. Even the force behind his blade feels weakened. 'Are . . .' Scrutiny stalls my words. 'Are you all right?'

Kitt pushes away. 'Why do you ask?'

I shake my head, unsure what it is I'm sensing. His power coils beneath my skin and slips between my attempts to grab hold of it. 'Something . . . feels different.'

'I've been a bit under the weather recently. It will pass, I'm sure. Now,' Kitt pants, 'have you been out here all night?'

My laugh is huffed. He evades my lunge. 'After all these years, that shouldn't surprise you.'

His blade arcs through the air before slamming into mine. 'I figured you were with Paedyn.'

My movements stutter long enough for him to land a solid smack of steel to my ribs. I grunt against the pain before knocking his sword aside. 'I haven't . . .' Now I'm panting. 'I haven't seen her since the cellar.'

Kitt manages a shrug among the swiping of our weapons. 'I'm surprised.'

I block his blow and stare between the crossed blades at my brother's chilled features. 'And why would that surprise you?'

He pushes away. 'You know why.'

'Enlighten me,' I challenge.

'Because you love her!' The rough admittance seems to startle even him. I stare at Kitt, chest heaving and sword hanging at my side. He clears his throat. 'Perhaps more than anything.'

My heart pounds – a reminder that each beat belongs to her.

'Don't be ridiculous, Kitty,' I deflect. 'She is your bride.'

'And I am your brother,' he says quickly. 'Always. No matter what.'

His tone suggests this is a question I'm meant to answer. This isn't the first time Kitt has tiptoed around the subject that is our intertwined futures. He wishes to hear that his marriage to Paedyn won't change anything between us. And for our sake, I will pretend that it hasn't already.

'You and me.' My throat is dry. 'Always.'

We share a warm smile before swords are clashing between us.

A familiar dance tugs at our feet. We slip into a graceful sort of chaos, one that has been practiced since childhood. This very ring of dirt beneath us has broken many a fall over the years. I'm reminded of the days I would beg Father to let Kitt train with me until, suddenly, I no longer needed to ask for permission. Two princelings grew into men here, yet we always return to that same string of practiced movements.

Kitt smiles slightly behind the flurry of steel, his gaze distant with reminiscence. We follow a pattern, a structure, a memorized sequence of steps. This vicious dance is one we created as boys – and it feels like tranquility.

Our movements are precise. Each swipe of the sword sure.

I jab my blade towards his chest and wince when the blow lands. Kitt groans at the prodding of a dull sword. He backs away, breaking the trance we once shared.

'You're supposed to dodge that, Kitt,' I say sympathetically.

He rubs at what will soon be a blossoming bruise beneath his tunic. 'Yeah, well, I forgot. That's why I'm the king, and you're my Enforcer. I'm not good at fighting my own battles.'

I chuckle. 'Come on, you know these steps.' My palm pats his cheek gently. 'Let's run it again.'

'Plagues, do you ever sleep?'

I give him a skeptical look. 'Do you?'

His smile is sad. 'Fair enough, Enforcer.'

CHAPTER 39

Paedyn

A piece of parchment slides under my door.

The rustling sound has me looking up from my book begrudgingly. Unfolding stiff limbs, I stand from the bed and pad over to this folded mystery. My whole being is tired, drained mentally and physically after my trek to Loot. So, when I bend to pick up the paper, I can hardly find the energy to be intrigued.

That is, until I hear his voice accompanying each sprawling word.

You said to be on my best behavior, and I can't possibly do that if I'm in the same room as you. Besides, all I do is spend my days in the training yard, attempting to teach a bunch of lazy bastards how to punch. Reminds me of when I had to do the same for you. And don't roll your eyes; I know you loved it.

For now, this will have to be our pretend. Kitt spent most of the morning with me, and he seemed good. Great, even. But I know my brother. I think he's trying to keep me away from you, slowly distance us. Maybe he wants you as badly as I do, but not at the price of losing me. He wants

us both. I know the feeling.

Now, please entertain me, darling. I'm bored. What am I to do if not count your freckles?

Your Cocky Bastard

It's only when I've finished reading that I feel the stupid grin on my lips, even despite the worrying notion he voiced. Shaking my head at his words, I determine to make him smile at my own. The large desk adorning the far side of my chamber has gone untouched since my return. Taking a seat in the stiff chair, I rummage through the many drawers in search of paper and a writing utensil.

I stare at the assortment of scavenged items before finally letting ink stain the parchment.

I see you finally signed your name correctly. It's about time. Now, I'm not sure anything I have to say is entertaining, so I'll just ramble until something interesting falls onto the page. Don't forget that you asked for this, cocky bastard.

I had to pick out fabric for my wedding dress. Of course, that only reminded me that Adena isn't the one making it. So, when I saw the Fort this morning with all that fabric that smelled like her, and the scissors I used to cut her bangs with—

Did I mention I went to Loot? Maybe I should have started with that. I just needed to see the Fort and run away from my future for a short while. But I met a new friend there, one that loved Adena just as much. It was nice, not being alone in my grief.

Anyway, I doubt you want to hear about wedding plans or what flower I chose for my bouquet. I'm trying not to focus on Kitt and my inability to read him. Just know that if I could do it all over again, I would have run from that poppy field with you when we had the chance.

Now, go hit an Imperial for me today, would you? Or I could remind you just how well I can throw a punch — you seem to have forgotten. And, yes, I did roll my eyes.

(We need to find you a hobby that does not include counting my

freckles. How many are there again? Twenty-three?)
    Your Pae

I slip the note beneath his door, though I know he is not on the other side. Several hours pass before the Enforcer retires to his room for a short break in training, and soon after, a response is slipped into my room.

I'm glad you were able to visit the Fort after everything that happened. You deserve to have that time with Adena. I only wish I had known. We both know that you can handle yourself, but that doesn't stop me from worrying about you.

As for these wedding plans, it sounds to me like you're getting cold feet, Gray. We could still make a run for it, you know. Head back out onto the Shallows. Find Astrum and keep sailing. Just say the word.

(Twenty-eight, darling. But I could do a recount if you like.)
    Your Cocky Bastard

My next note is handed off in person. I pass the Enforcer on my way to dine with his brother. Dirt mars his brow, mingling with a sheen of sweat that was coaxed from the beaming sun outside. His tousled black hair ripples when he looks up, gray eyes piercing straight through me. My heart stalls at the sight of him. It's been days since we have spoken in private, and I'm tempted to shove him towards that broom closet he once carried me into.

But there are so many eyes in this castle, so many reasons to pretend with the Enforcer. I hold his gaze because that is all I'm allowed. He holds mine because it is the only piece of me he can have. I cling to this moment in which we have evaded the future.

Kai strides past. Our hands touch. My heart stutters. The note is slipped between his fingers.

You know firsthand that my feet are always cold. But you are all bark and no bite, Azer. Your loyalties are here with Kitt, so don't pretend you would go running off with me. The king is your duty and marrying him is mine. But we will always have the willow tree.

(You'll have to get close enough to count them, Prince.)
Your Pae

'Good evening, Paedyn.'

I stride into the throne room, my hopes high. 'Good evening, Kitt.'

We eat. Talk idly. Attempt to repair the bond we once had.

'Any plans for the night?'

I smile at his question. 'Just the usual.'

In truth, I have a very exciting evening ahead of me, one that the king would never allow if he knew.

I nearly step on Kai's reply when I return to my room.

You think I would not beg to run away with you? My duty may be to the king, but my heart, Pae, is wherever you are. It is in the palm of your hands, the pad of your thumb. So if you leave, I will follow. If you stay, I will bow. Because there has never been a moment when you did not own the only piece of me that mattered – loving you made me matter. And I ache to be full again.

I sit there, stunned and still and staring at the very meaning of devotion. I've never witnessed beauty look so content in its brokenness. Unabashedly, he pleads for me. Unflinchingly, he lays every mask at my feet.

My gaze falls to the final line, and the corner of my mouth twitches upward.

(Oh, I can bite. You only need to ask, darling.)

I slip his note into the drawer of my bedside table, reuniting it with the others before taking a seat at the desk. My father's ring raps against the wood as I fight to write those three little words that clog my throat. They are seemingly harmless until those who earn them are ripped away from me. I shake my head, writing instead a short string of letters.

On paper, you really do sound like a poet. Or a fool. I won't let you ruin yourself for me.

His response arrives quickly.

I want you to be my ruin, remember?

Edric

The princes are inseparable.

Kitt balances a book on his lap, though it's difficult to focus on anything with his younger brother waving a wooden sword in his face. Myla stands to comb back Kai's unruly hair, all while ignoring the boy's huff of irritation. With the turning of a page, Edric's heir grows suddenly studious in the presence of a mother who is not his.

Both boys have been continually told the very same lie as the kingdom beyond their castle walls. Kitt's mother died giving birth to him before the king remarried and had Kai, making the princes half brothers. That is what they know to be true. Anyone who knows differently is part of the staff, sworn to secrecy, and stowed away within the palace.

In the many years of Edric's marriage to Myla Rowe, a unique kind of love had blossomed between them. She was bold and stubborn in a way that Iris never had been, managing to rile the king more than he cared to admit. It was a rocky road that led them to each other, one that neither imagined treading. But Edric's stony heart had started beating again, still only for his Myla.

The family clutters the king's study, though two members are

missing. One a weak child who remains in the west tower, and the other a forgotten princess who is just that. Edric thinks no more of the daughter he doomed to death. Rather, Iris's end by something as weak as an Ordinary only enflames his hatred for them. And he will stop at nothing until his kingdom is rid of every last one. They were a mistake he is determined to remedy.

Myla looks up at her husband, watching him pore over the puddle of parchment on his desk. She offers him that bright smile, the one Edric had spent their first year of marriage coaxing out of her. For his wife, the king smiles back.

Catching the odd show of emotion, Kitt straightens before beaming at his father.

Edric only nods to the book in his heir's hand and does not smile back.

CHAPTER 40

Paedyn

The halls are quiet at this hour.

Shadows paint the ornate molding in an ominous light as I pass by. I've spent the entire day confined to my room or slipping notes beneath Kai's door. It was a pleasant distraction until nightfall. But now I'm off to restore balance to the world, peace to my mind. I have been aching to do this since that final Trial, since returning from the Fort with rekindled vengeance.

I turn a corner and—

A flash of lilac in the moonlight.

There she stands, casually leaning against the wall. A dull look rests on the face she turns towards me, boredom creasing her brow. 'So, apparently, you think you can kill me.'

My dagger is already gripped between trembling fingers. The image of Adena's limp body in my lap is all I see when I meet Blair's unfeeling gaze. I think of Mak and his hurt that magnifies my own. Anger explodes behind my vision, rage momentarily blinding me as I stride towards her. 'I will do so much worse,' I pant. 'I'll make you beg.'

Blair's laugh is breathy. 'You know, I like you much more like

this. It's a shame you're trying to kill me when we could be such good friends.'

I don't think before flipping the dagger in my hand and launching it at her face. It flips through the air in a feeble attempt I know she will simply halt with her mind. But I don't care. I'm content to let her cower behind an ability, if only so I can watch the life flicker out in her eyes.

They're vicious, these thoughts. Cruel. So unlike Adena—

Adena isn't here to save me from myself anymore.

Blair lets out a low whistle as she stares down the length of my blade. Its tip is mere inches from burying between her eyes. 'I didn't think you had it in you, Gray.' She lets the dagger clatter to the ground. 'You're different.'

I bare my teeth. 'You made me this way.'

She backs away, clicking her tongue. 'No, this has always been inside of you.' Candlelight pools into the hallway when she opens the door to her room and steps inside. 'You just wanted someone to blame for it.'

Snatching my dagger from the floor, I follow her into the room. The blade shakes in my raised hand. 'You don't know me. You don't know what I've been through.'

'Plagues, Paedyn!' Blair leans against a bedpost with a roll of her eyes. 'Don't act like you're the only one who's been through some shit. Yes, I killed your friend, and you know what?' Her throat bobs in the flickering light. 'It haunts me. But that was the Trial. And I won.'

A crash behind us has me whirling towards the door.

An Imperial pants in the doorway, his red hair rippling in the firelight. 'What the hell?' Lenny's eyes dart between us. 'Paedyn, you need to go right—'

'Quiet, gingersnap,' Blair huffs. Her eyes never leave mine as she throws his body against the wall, pinning him there with her mind. 'The girls are talking.'

'Paedyn!' Lenny wriggles against Blair's hold on his body. 'Please, you can't do this!'

'Personally, I agree.' Blair gives me a dull look. 'I don't think you can either.'

I charge.

303

My feet pound against the wooden floor, dodging the dozens of candles littered across it. Dagger in hand, I—

I stop.

My body is suddenly stuck.

I rage against Blair's power, roaring when her mind tightens its hold around me. 'I do marvel,' she says quietly, 'at how incredibly Ordinary you are.'

I still within her invisible grip.

Because for the first time in my life, I don't hear weakness in those words.

No, I hear a little girl crying over her father's dead body and surviving despite it. I hear the roar of an Elite crowd, chanting for the Ordinary beneath their noses who crafted her own power. I hear strength where shame once was, fearlessness where I would once cower.

A slow smile spreads across my lips. Blair blinks at the expression, a flash of fear flitting over her features.

'Of course you marvel at it,' I say slowly. 'Because you will never know real power. Yours was given. But mine . . .' I shake my head. 'Mine was found.'

She gawks. 'I could crush your heart with a single thought.'

'Maybe your ability could.' My gaze is lethal. 'But *you* couldn't.'

I watch her take a deep breath. Watch the words fall from her mouth and still don't believe she's saying them. 'I am sorry about your friend.'

Then her eyes flick to Lenny.

And the room goes up in flames.

A wave of heat slams into me, and with Blair's hold on my body now broken, I nearly fall over. Fire flares around my ankles, crawling up bedposts to swallow us whole. I don't know how it happened, but I'm suddenly choking on the thick smoke.

Blair stumbles away, arms lifted to shield her face from the heat. I leap over a wall of flame before it can lap at my legs. But I don't head for the door, for my escape from this sweltering heat. The only freedom I seek resides in ending the girl who took away my light.

I lunge for her.

My body crashes into Blair's, and we tumble to the ground atop a trail of flame. We both cry out as the fire sears our skin, singes hair. But I am not finished.

That dark, terrifying side of me stamps out all fear and pain and sane thought as I pin Blair Archer to the scorched floorboards. A numbness spreads through me, like every nerve has decided to turn a blind eye to my violence. Fire burns its way through my pants, rippling along my thigh as I lean over her pale face. Thick smoke wafts from my own clothing, my own flesh, but still, I feel nothing.

Flame curls to the right of Blair's head, licking that lilac hair. She whimpers, out of fear or pain, I'm not sure. I no longer feel either. The sleeve of her tunic is thoroughly singed to display angry, red skin beneath. I memorize this moment, right down to the terror flickering in her gaze.

The palm of my hand meets her cheek.

I cough through the smoke crawling down my throat.

I push against her face, turning it slowly towards the eager flame.

Lenny's shout is lost behind the wall of fire encircling us.

Blair's head swivels slowly beneath my palm. 'You don't know pain,' I whisper. She fights against me with her own strength, too weakened to use her power. I smile. 'Not until it skewers you through the chest.'

'Please,' Blair blurts.

I shove her closer to the flame.

'Please . . .'

My voice is even and rough with smoke. 'I told you I would make you beg.'

She screams when I force her face into the hungry wall of fire.

The side of Blair's pretty face bubbles and burns within the heat. My hand, still shoved against her unharmed cheek, is scorched by the mere proximity to flame. The stench of fried flesh fills the air, accompanied only by the screams of Adena's killer.

I cough again, my lungs constricting.

That comforting numbness bleeds from my body until all I feel is pain.

And then I feel nothing at all as everything goes dark.

CHAPTER 41

'**W**here is she?'

I shove Imperials aside, quickening my pace down the cramped hallway. Smoke hangs thickly in the air, wafting from a charred room that Hydros huddle around. They do their best to tame what is left of the flames with waves of water.

Lenny is raising his hands in surrender before I've even reached him. 'She's fine—'

'Take me to her,' I order.

The Imperial takes a breath. 'She's with a Healer, but there is no need to worry.'

'No need to worry?' I almost laugh. 'I woke to an Imperial beside my bed and smoke in the air. So I'll ask again. Where the hell is she?'

Looking utterly defeated, Lenny reluctantly leads me through the throng. We turn down a quiet corridor to stop before an unsuspecting door. Opening it, Lenny gestures me inside where I'm greeted by several gazes.

But it is only hers I search for.

Paedyn sits on a stool, clothing charred and hair blackened. Burns run down the length of her body, pink and blistered. A bloody gash

sits right above her brow, making her flinch when a smile reaches the eyes beneath.

I rush over to her, not caring who bears witness to my worry. 'Are you all right?'

She nods. Winces. Curses the burn climbing up her neck. 'I'm fine,' she eventually grits out, voice like gravel. 'Everything happened so fast.'

I take a breath, fighting to keep my voice steady. 'Why were you even in Blair's room?'

'She . . .' Her eyes flick behind my back, and I turn to find Kitt leaning against a wall. He gives me a slow nod – or perhaps it is for Paedyn. 'She practically invited me in. I was angry and . . .'

Paedyn's eyes dart to Lenny, and the pleading look within them has him sighing. 'Blair had me pinned. There were candles lit, and one must have gotten knocked over because, suddenly, the room went up in flames.' He shakes his head. 'This wall of fire separated me from P, and by the time I finally got her out . . . Blair was . . .' Lenny swallows, his brown eyes shining. 'I took care of the body.'

I whirl on my Imperial. 'You should have prevented this!'

Lenny's gaze drops. 'Sir, I—'

'It wasn't his fault.' Paedyn's voice is weak. 'He couldn't have stopped it. I . . . I wouldn't let him stop it.'

I give her a knowing look. 'You still went after her, didn't you?'

The anger on her face doesn't mask the guilt beneath. I know what it looks like to get lost in the rage, the power of controlling another's fate. And I see it reflected on her features. My voice is a consoling murmur. 'Oh, Pae.'

A Healer steps forward then, his voice grim. 'Well, it's a good thing Miss Gray got out when she did. A little while longer and—'

'I know,' I hear myself bite out.

'She needs to rest.' It's Calum who says this, though I don't bother to look at him. 'Heal.'

'I'm fine,' Paedyn mouths to me in a way that's only slightly reassuring.

A hand on my shoulder has me turning. Kitt's expression is stern. 'It was a terrible accident. That is what her father, and the rest of the court, will know. I'll . . . find a way to cover this up.'

I nod, because it's the agreement he wishes for.

I stand, because the look in Paedyn's eyes say she will find me later.

And I leave, because she is not mine to worry about.

I'm not even surprised when she bursts into my room.

I've been up for hours, pacing in the darkness and hoping she will stride in to brighten it.

'Where's your sword? I need to hit something.'

A ray of sunshine, this one.

I lean against a bedpost. 'I take it you're feeling better?'

Paedyn huffs damp hair from her eyes. 'That Healer made me sit in there for hours. Even after taking care of the burns.' She waves a hand. 'Something about smoke in my lungs.'

I nod slowly. 'What happened to keeping our distance?'

'I'm making an exception.'

'Because you wish to hit something?'

'Yes.' A smug smile. 'And for once, it's not you.'

'I'm a bit offended, actually.'

She shakes her head distractedly. 'I need to blow off some steam.' I'm skewered with a pointed look. 'Sword?'

Fighting my smile, I retrieve a battered sword from beside my desk. 'And the reasoning behind this sudden urge for violence?'

'Sudden?' She snorts. 'I've been kicking your ass for a long time now, Prince.'

I push the sword into her palm, our bodies close. 'Maybe I miss it.'

Her smile is wicked. 'Maybe you'll have another opportunity to lose soon.'

My answer is lost in the sound of steel slicing wood. She rains down blows upon the already mutilated bedpost. Again and again, the sword sinks into the shredded wood, spraying splinters in its wake.

I grab her arm, stilling the strained muscles there before she can swing again. Silver hair flicks me in the face when she whirls, cheeks pink with anger. 'What?'

Her tone is biting, meant to ward me off with a single word. But she doesn't scare me away – I almost wish she could. Life would be so much easier if I didn't want to spend it with her. But nothing so stunningly formidable could go unwanted.

'Pae.' I let her see the concern on my face. Let her see the devotion it derives from. Let her see everything I am not and the little that I am. 'What is really going on?'

Her lashes flutter. I watch that blue gaze sink to my chest and stare blankly. 'I killed her. I . . . I was a monster. Her skin was melting beneath my palm and still I—' She sucks in a breath. 'I have never been so vicious. It was terrifying, this person I became. This darkness swelling within me. And worst of all,' she chokes, 'it didn't help.'

My heart aches in a way it only ever will for her. 'I know.'

'I thought it would help this hurt,' she whispers. 'This hole in my heart where Adena used to be. But it's still there.' Her eyes lift, brimming with tears. 'Just as gaping as it was the day she died in my arms.'

'I know,' I say again, hating the hurt on her face.

'It didn't bring her back.' The sword clatters to the floor, her tears falling with it. 'I'll never get her back.'

I wrap my arms around her trembling body, pressing my mouth to the top of her head. 'I know, love.'

Tears soak through my shirt, and yet she barely makes a sound. I hold her tightly, running a hand down her damp hair and the back stretching beneath. She melts against me, soothed by the touch and many murmurs against her hair.

But when my body goes rigid, she lifts her tear-streaked face towards mine. 'What is it?'

Power bubbles beneath my skin, one so familiar I almost don't notice it. 'Kitt's coming.'

'What?' She blinks before peeling herself away from me. 'Here? Now?'

I lower my voice. 'Yes, and quickly.'

His Duel ability is one I've memorized since I was a boy, could pick out from a crowd. But dwelling on it now, something feels indescribably *off*.

'Well,' she sputters. 'What do we do?'

My eyes flick to the wardrobe.

She gives me a dull look. 'You can't be serious.'

'Would you like your betrothed to find you in here with me?'

Her frustrated groan is followed by an exiling into the wardrobe. Paedyn glares as I shove her among my clothes, tears momentarily forgotten. She picks up a particularly bright shirt and raises a brow. 'I've never seen you wear this.'

'That would be because it belongs to Jax,' I say quickly. 'I'm winning a bet. Don't worry about it.'

With a slight scoff and shake of her head, I begin shutting the doors on her face. 'Oh,' I add quietly. 'Try not to step on my shoes. I just got them shined.'

I can practically feel the roll of her eyes even after a thick layer of wood separates us. But I've barely managed to pick up the strewn sword before my door creaks open.

Kitt steps hesitantly into the room. 'Oh, good. You're awake.'

I lift the sword in answer. 'Just blowing off some steam.'

'Right.' The king seems distracted. 'Well, I just wanted to stop in and let you know that the third Trial will be taking place tomorrow.'

My eyes widen in surprise, just as I know Paedyn's are behind me. 'Tomorrow? You're not announcing it to the court?'

Kitt rubs a hand down the back of his neck. His gaze is distant, clouded. 'It's meant to be . . . unexpected. For Paedyn, at least.' Quickly, he adds, 'It will take place in the Bowl.'

'I see.' A beat of silence stretches between us before I ask, 'Kitt, are you all right?'

That unsettling feeling washes over me again when his power slithers beneath my skin. I hold my brother's gaze, but he doesn't seem to be looking at me. It is as though he has retreated into his mind.

'Hmm?' His unfocused gaze falls just over my shoulder. 'No. No, not yet,' he mutters distantly. 'It's not time . . . I need the right time . . .'

I glance behind, finding nothing but open air. His mumbled words have me taking a worried step forward. 'What? Kitt, is everything okay?'

Those green eyes flick back to mine. He blinks. Then plasters a smile onto his features. 'Yes, no need to worry. It seems I need some more sleep. Just . . . just trust me. I have everything under control.'

I nod, despite my concern. 'Of course. I trust you with my life.'

He coughs. The grin that follows is genuine. 'I've never doubted that about you.'

Then his hand is on the door, mind somewhere else entirely.

'You and me, Brother.'

'You and me,' I echo softly.

CHAPTER 42

Paedyn

I'm awake long before the knock at my door.

In fact, I'm already dressed and well into overthinking by the time my escort to brutality arrives. I barely slept after slipping from Kai's room last night, wide-eyed with the worry of what I'll have to do today to prove myself.

With a deep breath, I swing open the door. Lenny's eyes drift down the length of me from behind his mask, narrowing slightly at my lack of disarray. 'I'm here to escort you to the third Trial?' He says this like a question, as though unsure if he's the first to inform me of this.

I smile tightly. 'I had a hunch.' Slipping my dagger into the sheath at my side, I add casually, 'Ready?'

'Not as ready as you,' he mocks. 'Did you go to sleep in these clothes?'

'I'm just ready to get this over with,' I bite back.

'Well, it seems you're already in the brutal mood,' he mutters as we head down the long hallway.

'I'm . . . sorry. About yesterday.' I glance hesitantly over at him. 'You were never meant to be involved.'

'And it's a damn good thing I was,' he scolds. 'You nearly died, P. And I would have never been able to live with myself if you had.'

His words crumble something inside me, maybe the stony indifference I've built around my heart as of late. I touch his arm, hoping to say something my lips can't form.

Lenny's brown eyes fall to that gesture, smiling grimly at my splayed fingers atop his uniform. 'And you might be sorry for me, but you're certainly not sorry about Blair.'

I swallow and spur my mouth into motion. 'No, I'm not. I mean, I'm not happy about what I did, either. But . . .' I pull away, hugging my arms around a beating chest. 'But I don't regret it.'

'You were . . . merciless.' When he finally lands on the cruel word, I flinch. 'I've never seen you like that before.'

'Neither have I. Not like that.' I avoid his gaze. 'But I've seen glimpses of it ever since fleeing Ilya. I'm . . . I'm not proud of it.'

He nods distantly, red hair rippling. 'Well, now you're free of her.'

'So are you,' I remind.

'Eh.' He turns a corner, pulling me along with him. 'She wasn't too bad. You only knew the part of her she had to be.'

I glance sidelong at him. 'Well, you don't seem too upset about her . . . passing.'

He shrugs stiffly. 'I'll see her again. One day.'

I debate scoffing at his words, because I doubt Lenny will end up wherever Blair has. But he's suddenly spewing another sentence, this one lighter than the last. 'Don't be nervous today. You're going to kill it.'

I groan slightly. 'I'd rather not do any more killing, thank you.'

I step out into the streaming sunlight, now made all the more blinding by the dozens of crisp white uniforms reflecting it. Imperials swarm to create a cocoon of bodies around me as we head for the Bowl. The long path to the arena stretches before me as if to join the past with this bleak present.

The first time I walked between this row of drooping trees, it was for survival.

The second, a promise.

And now, a title.

The pink blossoms that once fell from these trees are long dead – not unlike so many other things since then. They crunch beneath my boots, a mere decaying memory. I tug my promise to Adena more tightly around me, feeling the frayed edge of what is left of her. I see the flowers beneath my feet that once littered a prince's head, crowning him long before my brutality made him king.

My eyes wander over this tunnel of trees, each end leading me into the unknown.

Once, I risked my life for a piece of Adena.

Now, I stride towards a kingdom who doesn't want me.

Soon, I may sacrifice myself in the hopes I mean something more in death than I did in life.

We walk in silence down the path, nothing but the sound of crunching petals passing between us. I spin the ring on my thumb incessantly, pleading with the band of steel to calm me. Lenny lingers at my side, occasionally offering a sidelong glance at my fidgeting.

But silence flees at the sight of the Bowl.

A distant rumbling grows with every step. The stomping of feet swells, followed by an orchestra of shouts and cheers. My heart beats in time, drumming in my ears as we stride into the Bowl's menacing shadow.

My gaze lingers beside one of the many tunnels leading into that stony structure. The king's lifeless body is long gone, the blood washed away, but the scar above my heart still sears with the memory of a mud-streaked girl at the mercy of a monster. Until she became one herself.

Everywhere I look, the past lingers.

There, an Enforcer was born. Hovering over his father's body, he threw a blade with the aim of a warrior, but the damning heart of a fool. I can still feel that knife cut through the air beside me, intention alone steering it from my flesh.

Here, he told me to run. And I did.

Right back into his arms.

Our footsteps echo off the stone tunnel now, the expanse of gray leading us into an explosion of chaos and color. This arena was once filled with Resistance members, covered in the blood of those brave enough to fight for themselves but too weak to win.

The muffled cheers of thousands grow into a gentle roar as I emerge from the surrounding stone. The sun peers down at me, forcing my hand to lift above watering eyes. Bodies pack every inch of the Bowl, and I tip my head towards the sky, following the slope of this crowded arena.

Fear seizes my heart in this familiar place. I haven't been back in the Bowl since Adena died within it, since a piece of myself died beyond these walls. The roaring of thousands hungry for a show makes my stomach flip violently. Every fiber of my being recoils at the thought of stepping foot in that arena once again.

Imperials usher me along the path as a deafening shout washes over us. The audience is craving a bloody act of brutality, and with the sudden crescendo of spirited shouts in my direction, they are likely hoping I will be the casualty.

My gaze drifts to the railing beside me, then farther still to the stretch of sand below. The last time I saw this Pit, it was streaked with Adena's blood. My stomach lurches once again as I scan the sea of white sand for any sign of a scarlet stain.

Nothing.

All trace of her death is gone, having abandoned this place to dwell inside me. Every drop of blood, every cry for help, every moment that passes without her is etched onto my soul.

Our lap around the raised ring leads us to the glass box beside it. Kitt sits cozily within, filling the seat his father once had. And just like the king before him, those green eyes pin me to the path.

It's like looking into the face of a ghost.

Past and present collide to create the confusing concoction that is him. Not quite his father, but not quite the boy I once knew. He tips his head, a near reflection of the man who made me a murderer. And I nod back, a mere mosaic of each jagged piece of strength and cutting recklessness it took to have me standing here once again.

Hands are suddenly at my back, shoving me towards the railing.

Kitt stands abruptly, watching me behind that spotless glass before his Imperials can push me into the Pit. Calum appears beside him, smiling grimly even as I'm escorted to what will likely be my doom.

Still, I hold my breath, watching the king's mouth open and eyes flash with regret.

And then – nothing.

Kitt straightens. Lowers himself into that plush seat. Fixes a slight smile onto his features.

I blink at the sudden change, bewildered by his—

'Hey, Princess.'

I startle at the fingers Lenny is snapping in front of my face. 'Hmm?'

'Listen up, all right?' He's forced to yell over the restless crowd engulfing us. 'Take this and use it.' The hilt of a sword is suddenly shoved into my palm. 'Just get it over with, and you're free from these Trials. I know how terrifying you can be, so just . . . be that.'

I nod numbly, my gaze clinging to the sharp blade I now hold. Lenny reaches a gloved hand towards my face and pats it gently. 'I need you to win this, okay? Don't stop being a cockroach now, Princess.'

I have no idea what it is I'm winning. No idea if it will be worth it in the end. But a weak laugh surprises me, the sound buried in chaos before reaching my ears. 'I'll try my best.'

'After this,' he shouts, 'I won't get to call you Princess anymore.' His smile is bittersweet. 'I'll have to call you Queen.'

And then I'm forced down into the Pit.

I trip over the steep steps until my boots finally sink into the sand beneath. Staggering back, I lift my head towards the crazed crowd. I'm panting, blood pounding, as I take in the arena with one slow spin.

The Bowl is gaping, and I stand there, swallowed within the sheer size and sound all around. The sword's hilt grows sweaty in my palm, its sharp point dragging in the sand. Chants and shouts are muffled by the continuous pounding of feet, like a death march long anticipated. The sun weighs heavy on my arms, warming my bare skin with its close presence. It seems that even the sky leans in to witness my brutality or the brutal end I'll meet.

I squint up at that box high above the Pit's floor, watching the king stride out onto the path. A familiar shock of teal hair shines beside him, and when the Amplifier rests her hand on Kitt's shoulder, the arena falls silent.

'Welcome, Ilyans, to Paedyn Gray's final Trial. Here,' he says evenly, 'we will test her brutality.'

The crowd erupts at his words, bloodthirsty and rabid for a riveting show. Kitt calms them with a palm to the air before continuing. 'If Paedyn can complete this Trial, she will have proven herself to be brave, benevolent, and brutal. These are the three characteristics my father believed made a good ruler. If she manages to succeed today—' Kitt's gaze pins me to the Pit's floor, '—Ilya will have its queen.'

A roar rips through the arena, and I'm quite certain it's not intended to cheer me on. Men and women stand on their benches, pumping fists and spouting curses into the air. My gaze sweeps over the rowdy crowd until I'm startlingly staring back at myself.

The scrutinizing expression I wear is projected onto a large screen above the Pit for even those in the highest stands to see clearly. My eyes dart across the sand, landing on the Sights currently projecting what they see. Four of them stand at the other side of the Pit, though only three stare at me with glassy eyes and arms raised upward. With white cloaks rippling in the soft breeze, their heavy stares have a chill skittering down my spine, dread pooling in my gut.

'As a ruler,' Kitt continues over the chaos, his voice echoing, 'brutality is often needed. So for this Trial, it will be a fight to the death.'

My breath catches. Throat dries.

To the death.

I have to kill someone.

The crowd's responding cheer is lost to the sudden ringing in my ears. I turn slowly towards that glass box, finding a king peering back.

Not my friend. Not my betrothed. Just a king who ordered me to be his killer.

And suddenly, I know how Kai must feel.

My knees go weak at the thought.

Kai.

Frantically, I scan that glass box for any sign of his familiar figure. A lock of tousled black hair. A glimpse of those damn dimples. A flash of that cocky smile.

'Bring out the opponent!'

My whole body numbs at the king's words.

Gasps ripple through the crowd, shock slipping between the fingers that press to gaping mouths.

I won't turn around. I *can't* turn around.

The crowd errupts with a sudden, sickening wave of excitement when the king's voice booms over the arena. 'An Ordinary versus every Elite. The ultimate test.'

My head is shaking. I shut my eyes, squeezing out the cruel world beyond.

This is a nightmare. This is pretend.

Footsteps behind me grow louder atop the shifting sand.

I press a hand to my pounding heart, feeling the rapid rise and fall of my chest.

This is pretend. This is—

'Paedyn.'

I can feel the exact moment my heart shatters.

It's when I turn, my eyes crashing into ones well memorized.

When mist meets the deepest sea.

When a Shadow faces its Flame.

When inevitability meets its end.

When I stare into the face of what it is I love most.

CHAPTER 43

Paedyn

The sword trembles in my hand.

I'm meant to drive it through his chest.

'No.'

The word is a choked whisper, not the scream I intended. It's disbelief, denial in its most docile form. I'm shaking my head at him, feet stumbling back.

This is not an opponent. This is the boy who braids back my hair and dances for the both of us. The boy who would chase me to the ends of the earth if it meant he could hold me one more time. This is a man who would bury another for me – would bury *himself*, if only I asked.

He is a fool for me. He is *my* fool.

This can't be happening. Why would Kitt allow this?

Kai raises a calming hand. 'Paedyn—'

'No!' The scream rips from my throat, springing tears to my eyes. I turn then, lifting my rage to the railing above. And when my gaze crashes into that cool green one, I suddenly cannot remember which king I am looking at. 'No! I won't do it!'

The arena roars right alongside me, only they look forward to

watching their mighty Enforcer cut me down. I stumble in the sand, seemingly unable to suck air into my lungs. Tears burn my eyes; anger clogs my throat.

This is a nightmare. This is pretend.

We were never supposed to fight each other again.

A rough hand tugs at my shoulder, whipping me around to face the stern expression Kai wears. 'I need you to focus, okay?' I nod furiously at his quick words. 'We have to make this fight look good if they are going to believe it. So that means you're on your own to stay alive against whatever power I throw at you.' He nods to the arena surrounding us. 'The Mute is gone. They want to see you fight Elites.'

I swallow a shuddering breath. 'They want to see me die.'

His eyes flick over my face, as though seeing it for the first time. Or perhaps the last. 'So don't.'

I watch his skin turn to stone – then watch his fist fly towards my face.

I've barely ducked in time, the gust of air above my head making me gasp. I leap away from a hard hook to the stomach, dropping my sword and narrowly avoiding several cracked ribs. Borrowing a Shell's power, he cycles through a combination of punches, pushing me on defense. I can do nothing but dodge, his rocklike skin making it impossible to land a hit of my own.

And the Enforcer is relentless. He throws countless stony fists at me until one clips my shoulder. I cry out in pain as bone crunches beneath his knuckles. The crowd roars in my ears as I clutch my arm, forced to duck beneath another flying fist.

I stagger away from each of his attacks, conscious only of the throbbing shoulder beneath my fingers. When my back hits the towering wall of the Pit, panic swells inside me.

I'm trapped.

'Kai—!'

I choke on my shout, forced to duck beneath another blow with words hanging from the tip of my tongue. His fist sinks into the stone behind, crumbling the rock there. Panting, I watch him struggle to rip free from the wall, sending chunks of stone flying.

Kai turns to me then, gray eyes flicking to my injured arm.

320

His words are nearly devoured by the ravenous crowd. 'Come on, Paedyn. We have to make this a good fight.'

I let my hand slowly slide from my aching shoulder and nod ever so slightly.

We are enemies here. We are pretend.

And if I am going to die, it will be one hell of a show.

Kai nods back. Then his hands ignite with fire.

I let myself sink into a familiar fighting stance, fingers wiggling at my side. When he launches that first ball of fire, I duck and roll behind him. Sand clings to every inch of me, but I don't bother standing to my feet quite yet. I sweep a leg out, catching Kai's ankles with enough force to send him toppling down beside me.

The packed sand he slams into has the air rushing from his lungs and a collective groan echoing from the crowd. I throw myself over him, pulling back my uninjured arm to let a fist fly towards his face. Knuckles connect with his jaw, followed by a stinging pain that shoots down my hand.

It's odd to hit him like this, hard and intentional. Even as enemies, a piece of me always held back. Because that piece always belonged to the Enforcer, and perhaps I did not want to break it. But now, in this arena, I've never been more aware of the death that lurks within his veins. Power bends to his will, aches to obey.

I have never seen him without a soft spot for me. It seems today is that day. His desire for me to survive him seems to have erased all other sentiment he has for me. He is lost to this game, this power he has continually stopped himself from using against me. But the Enforcer knows he can't throw the fight, otherwise I'll likely be killed anyway, leaving us both dead for nothing.

I cock my arm again, ready to strike when his fingers wrap around my wrist. Searing, hot pain ignites beneath his palm as the Blazer ability scorches my skin. I barely bite back my scream, barely think through the dizzying pain.

The smell of burning flesh floods my senses before a wave of nausea crashes into me. Only yesterday, this stench followed my fury as I held Blair's face into an open flame. Now it is I who's burning.

I gasp before driving my knee into the elbow of his raised arm.

His scalding hold on me breaks at the same moment I hear his bone do the same. The sickening snapping sound is accompanied by a hissing grunt of pain through Kai's clenched teeth.

I wince, hating that I hurt him. Hating that we are in this position in the first place. But I force my stinging arm back, readying to—

His uninjured arm flies into my stomach, lifting my knees from the ground. The hit has me panting for air as I dangle off the ground. Only the strength of a Brawny could allow him to throw my body off his with such ease.

I'm flipping over his head, the sand flying towards my face. Kai's hand is still pressed to my stomach, guiding my body over his when I grab hold of his wrist. Tucking my chin, I collide with the ground, rolling onto my back at the same moment I tug his broken arm flat against my shoulder.

He cries out in pain as the snapped bone pokes through bloody skin. I hold his arm at that awkward angle, shutting my eyes against the damage I've done. Our heads are nearly touching, bodies sprawled in opposite directions, both of us panting atop the sand.

Until I no longer can.

Thorny vines spring from the earth to clamp around my throat. A choked scream escapes my gaping mouth before the air is squeezed from it. The barbed branches tear at my neck as Kai breaks from my hold. He staggers to his feet, commanding the Bloom's ability with a weak flick of his hand.

My fingers fumble for the dagger at my side when the vines tighten around my throat. Blood seeps between the leaves, thorns tearing at my flesh hungrily. A heavy blackness creeps into the corners of my vision as I lift the blade towards my own throat.

With one shaky slice, I cleave through the choking vines. The dagger's tip sloppily grazes the side of my neck, likely leaving the beginnings of another scar there. The ravenous plants fall limply from my bloody skin to sink back beneath the sandy earth they sprung from.

I lie there, panting in pain as blood drips from my shredded throat. My blurry gaze is on the cloudless sky above until the ringing in my ears ceases, and the crowd's dull roar reminds me where I am. With

322

a grunt, I lift myself up onto my palms, eyes falling to Kai's looming figure.

He runs a hand over the severed bone beneath his elbow, wincing slightly. My eyes widen when that dangling arm snaps back into place with a satisfying click. Kai sighs in relief before abandoning the Healer's power for—

The Enforcer multiplies, creating a wall of muscle and a dozen stormy gazes staring back at me.

Cloner.

I scramble back, palms digging into the hot sand. My frantic gaze runs over the arena, searching for a plan before landing instead on the glinting something a few feet away. I'm suddenly on unsteady feet, blood dripping from the tears at my throat to trail a scarlet path between my breasts. I swipe a hand over it, accomplishing little more than adding sand to my sticky skin.

The Kais begin closing in on me, their powerful strides spurring me into a sprint. I lunge for the sword, my fingers curling around the hilt and—

A worn boot slams atop the blade.

A frustrated cry tears from my throat as I drive my foot into the clone's knee. Bone crunches with the impact, but before he can tumble into the sand, another Kai is yanking me back. A calloused hand is on my shoulder, but when I throw an elbow at the jaw behind, his grip loosens. Taking advantage of his shock, I grab that arm, step into his chest, and muster enough momentum to throw him over my uninjured shoulder.

I barely hear the crowd's responding hollers with the blood pounding in my ears. Turning, I snatch up the sword and raise it between my bloody form and the several other surrounding Kais.

Stay calm. Find the real Enforcer.

My eyes skim over them, studying every familiar figure. The 'Psychic ability' I've so narrowly survived by has been rather buried these past few weeks. But I let it rush to the surface now, a flood of observations and comparisons.

So when my gaze locks with a particular gray one, I know I've found him.

His hand lingers just above the arm I'd broken, as though the bone hasn't quite healed correctly. And that hurt belongs to him alone.

I'm dropping the sword once again and flipping my bloody dagger in an equally stained hand. A clone charges at me the same moment I let that blade fly.

Time slows. Kai reaches for me, fingers grazing my throat. The cool steel of my dagger sinks into its target. The clones vanish when Kai staggers back, a blade embedded in his shoulder.

I loose a shuddering breath before reaching up to graze shaking fingers over my throbbing neck, as if to ensure my head is still attached. Swallowing, I watch Kai pull the blade from his flesh with a pained grunt. He tosses it aside, blood gushing from the open wound.

Even knowing a Healer's ability rests beneath his fingertips, I couldn't bring myself to aim for the heart. Everything about this fight already feels too real, and if I were to bury my blade in his chest, I fear a piece of me would die instead.

Our eyes lock across the stretch of sand, blood dripping from the damage we've caused each other. The angry cut through Kai's lip is evident even at this distance, as is the deep dagger wound above his collarbone. I sway on my feet beneath the beating sun, shoulder aching and throat throbbing.

Through the pain, I muster a small smile, one that is only for him. One to reassure that our pretending is just that. This audience alone keeps me fighting the Enforcer when I wish for nothing more than to collapse against Kai.

My soul is hopelessly tethered to his.

So when he suddenly Blinks into nothingness before my eyes, teleports behind, and drives a knee into my back, I wonder for the first time if perhaps I am the fool.

My body slams into the sand, nearly swallowing a mouthful as my face scrapes against the rough grains. A kick to the ribs has me rolling onto my back, coughing blood. Through a blurry haze, I see Kai standing over me, his expression unreadable.

He's not himself. It's as though every emotion has been muted. As though something other than pretend is guiding each blow.

Maybe he really does want me dead.

Another kick to the stomach.

Maybe he's hated me this whole time. For what I did to his father—

I curl in on myself when the toe of his boot sinks into my stomach again.

For what I did to his brother—

Something cracks inside me, and I'm not sure if it is my heart or a rib.

For what I did to him.

A strangled cry claws up my throat, the product of pain and panic. I lash out with the last of my strength, aiming a foot for his knee. My boot collides with the glowing force field of a Shield, the purple hue warding off my attack.

With wide eyes, I slowly lift my head, scared of what I will see on his face. And yet, even more terrified that I will see nothing there when he looks down at me. The sun is blotted out behind his threatening figure, though its rays comb through that wavy hair like a halo. As though I'm staring at the angel of death.

Since stealing those silvers from him on Loot to fleeing his pursuit across the Scorches, I have never feared him more than I do in this moment. It's the Enforcer who stares down at me, not the Kai who counts my freckles. It's the Deliverer of Death in this Pit, not the man who would hunt down anyone who dared hurt me.

Is this an order? Did Kitt command him to kill me?

Terror courses through me, an emotion I'm unaccustomed to when in Kai's presence. Rolling onto my stomach, I dig my fingers into the hot sand and abandon all dignity. Panting, I crawl away from him, tears stinging my eyes.

A sudden sob slips past my lips, jolting my bloody body as I scramble away aimlessly. My shoulder aches as it strains to hold my weight. Blood drips from my neck to speckle the sand beneath.

His shadow falls over me, and terror grips the heart that once felt nothing but love for him. He is devastation dressed with the shell of devotion.

So this is it. In the end, an Azer will always choose duty. And my death has just become that.

Laughter echoes all around, drowned out only by my racing thoughts. The Elites holler at my cowering form. They chant for their Enforcer to finish me. And for the first time in my life, I don't fear Death.

I fear him.

Dragging my fingers through the sand, I grasp enough to throw into the stoic face looming above. His shadow staggers back before my feet are suddenly under me, sand flying from my heels as I stumble away. Pain pounds through my body, nearly pulling me back to the ground. But I run, tears doing the same down my bloody cheeks. My lungs burn as I try to gulp down the thick air—

The sand erupts beside me.

I'm thrown backward with the impact, part of the Pit flying up with me. I feel myself scream but can hear nothing through the ringing in my ears. Colliding with the ground, my body rolls, only to nearly be hit by another explosion.

Kai has taken the form of an Ignite. And he's going to blow me to pieces.

Everything is hazy. I try to stand, but my balance is fleeting, like trying to grasp wind between my fumbling fingers. The world is muffled. Blood trickles from my ringing ears as I stagger into a run. The ground tilts beneath me with every step, but I force my feet forward as I try to outrun the inevitable.

Another blast has the sand beneath my feet caving in. I scream, ankle twisting before I'm suddenly falling into the sinking chasm. Hot sand envelopes me, rapidly climbing up my body as I slip farther into the Pit.

I'm gasping for air, flailing for the surface. This only pulls me down faster. Sand rises to sting my raw neck and trap me beneath. Another scream pours out of me, this time a desperate plea for him. For the boy I love, not the man ordered to make me his next mission to complete.

'Kai!'

My voice cracks as sand slips over my chin.

I'm going to be buried alive.

CHAPTER 44

Kai

Fight back, Pae.
I need you to fight back.

CHAPTER 45

Paedyn

The Pit is swallowing me whole, and yet, my eyes never leave his face.

I suck in a breath, readying to sink six feet under this arena into a sandy grave.

I close my eyes and see for a moment Adena's hazel ones staring back at me. She feels like home. I see my father, smile on his lips and book in hand. He feels like safety. The moment of peace is fleeting.

An invisible hand is dragging me out of Death's clutches.

I burst from the sand, Kai's Tele grip on me tight. The tips of my boots hover above the sand as I sputter, trying to catch my breath. Rough sand coats every inch of me. It fills my mouth, clings to my lashes, sticks to my bloody skin.

I'm yanked forward, my stiff body shooting towards him. The roaring crowd manages to cut through the ringing in my ears as air rushes around me, sand flying from my skin. I force my blurry gaze into focus long enough to watch Kai unsheathe the sword at his side.

My heart stutters, aching right alongside the rest of my body.

He raises that long blade, aiming it at the chest racing right towards him.

It's fitting, actually, this end to my struggled survival.

I shut my eyes again, letting him carry me into my demise. Hoping Adena and my father will be there on the other side of this blade.

Then a hand slams into my shoulder, halting my fate.

Shouts grow muffled. The world quiets. And we are at the center of it.

I see three things after mustering the strength to open my eyes.

The first is the tip of a sword, hovering a mere breath from my chest.

The second is more of an out-of-body glimpse at the scene we have set. My body still hovers above the ground, suspended there by nothing more than Kai's mind and a borrowed ability. Despite this, he has a hand braced against my uninjured shoulder, as if to stop me from being skewered before he could look me in the eyes.

And the third . . .

The third thing I see is the look on his face. It's conflicting, like a combination of determination and compassion contorting his features. He seems to be battling with his own mind. His hand trembles, and the blade does the same, nicking my skin. But I never take my eyes off the storm brewing in his own, terrified he won't be the last thing I see.

'It's okay,' I whisper, my voice as broken as the body still hanging before him. The toes of my boots whisper above the sand I'm dripping blood onto. 'Adena died here. I want to die here too.' Blood trickles from my ears, mingling with the tears racing down my face. 'I couldn't save her then. But I can save you now.'

He stills, tears gathering in his eyes. I reach slowly towards him, cutting off the curt shake of his head. My bloody hand rests gently atop his pounding chest. 'Through the chest, remember?' A tear rolls down my cheek, carving a path through the sand sticking there. 'That is how I want to die. Just like the ones I've loved.'

The Enforcer breaks.

Tears stream down his face as emotion finally cracks through the thick mask he had shoved on. The Tele's hold on my body snaps, allowing my feet to hit the sand – only, I fall to my knees. Kai does the same, letting the sword slip from his fingers.

We stare at each other, knees touching and tears streaming.

Kai's whisper is choked. 'I'm sorry.'

'You're the Enforcer,' I manage weakly. 'An Ordinary was never going to win this.'

He shakes his head at me. 'But you are not quite ordinary, are you?' Then, with a steadying breath, he orders, 'Now follow my lead.'

Kai stands to his feet with an ease I envy. My body begs for rest, and yet, I order it to rise. With shaking limbs, I straighten before him.

The crowd's approval is jarring against my bloody ears, enough to have me lifting my gaze to the stands. Rows of crazed Ilyans rise into the sky, all awaiting my imminent end. Even the sun peers over them, curious enough to stall its trek across the sky.

When my tired eyes fall back to Kai, he gives me a single nod and a curt 'Right hook.'

This is followed by a flying fist towards my face.

I dodge, bobbing left after the warning of his punch. Stunned, I almost don't hear his murmured 'Jab.'

Again, I'm heeding his words and jumping back before he can land a blow to my stomach. 'Good,' he pants. 'Now hit me – cross, right hook.'

I duck under his cross before blocking the hook with my forearm. This leaves his chest open enough for me to land a hard kick that has him stumbling. I take advantage of this, throwing another boot at his side. He catches my leg against him, gripping it tightly as he spins and throws me into the sand.

His heel is suddenly flying down towards my chest, but I manage to roll out of its path. I'm on my feet before he throws another punch that I step into, catching it over a shoulder to then drive my knee towards his stomach.

I hear the air rush out of him when my blow lands. My free hand is behind his neck as I sink my knee into him again and again. Grunting with the effort, I push his head down and throw my leg over it, clamping tightly behind his neck while the other lifts to hook beneath his jaw.

The momentum has us careening towards the ground, and I tuck my chin before the sand hits my back. Trapped in the tight hold between my legs, Kai is thrown onto the ground while I roll to my feet.

The Enforcer has barely lifted himself onto his knees before I'm driving a kick towards his jaw. Panting, he blocks it swiftly, but I'm already throwing a hook towards his temple. This he ducks beneath, catching my wrist with a hand before plowing a shoulder into my stomach.

My feet have suddenly left the sand. Within a single heartbeat, he's hooked a hand around my thigh and thrown me across his back. Standing, he tips backward, pushing my legs into the air in a crude sort of somersault that has me hurtling to the ground.

The little air in my lungs leaves in a rush. I'm left sputtering at the sky, every inch of me throbbing. I barely notice Kai scoop up my forgotten dagger, hardly care when he points it down at me.

'Come on, Paedyn,' he murmurs. 'Don't give up yet.'

My eyes drift towards that screen above the arena, finding my bloody face staring back. I look tired – so, so tired of surviving. For the first time, I want to be free of my fight.

But for Kai, I give myself a demise worth remembering. My leg lifts suddenly, connecting with the hand holding my dagger. The impact has the weapon flipping from his fingers. Silver glints in the shining sun as my blade sinks into the sand beside me.

I don't waste this sudden sliver of strength. My other foot hooks behind one of his shifting feet and tugs with every bit of might I can muster.

Just as I had done with the king, I now do with his son.

Kai crashes into the sand as I fumble for the dagger. I'm throwing a leg over him, straddling his body like I have so many times before. Weapon in hand, I loom over him, my victory a plunging blade away.

Instead, I watch those gray eyes widen when I push the dagger's hilt into his palm.

My fingers wrap around his, wanting to hold them one last time. The blade is aimed at my chest, inches from my pounding heart. 'It's

331

okay,' I whisper. 'I'm ready. I've been ready my whole life.'

He shakes his head, lifting it slightly from the sand. 'What if I want to save you today?' The dagger turns, his hand guiding its tip towards his own chest. 'Maybe that will help make up for every time I haven't been able to save another.'

'No,' I choke out. The blade's point grows dangerously close to his chest, even as I uselessly fight against his strength. 'No, stop it.'

His eyes remain locked on mine. 'It's okay.'

'No!' I croak, now grabbing his hand with both of mine. Tears blur my view of this sickening scene. 'Kai, stop!'

The dagger's tip meets his chest.

I'm begging now. 'Please! Kai, I need you!'

'It's okay,' he repeats softly. 'It'll be okay. Just help me now.'

Tears stream down my face. Am I breathing? 'No, I won't!' I try to pull my hands from the blade, but he lifts his free one, clamping it around mine.

Steel pierces his skin.

'No!' I struggle against him, trying to pry the dagger from where it's begun sliding into his chest with a sickening sound. 'No, please!' I fight the slow fatality with all my strength. It's no use.

The blade sinks farther, springing bright blood from the deepening wound. My tears splatter into the pool of crimson, sobs tearing free from my raw throat.

One last time, he whispers, 'It's okay. It was a good fight.'

And then the blade is buried to its hilt.

I scream.

It's the sound of my heart shattering. I can feel the drifting shards in my chest, piercing lungs that can no longer draw breath. I'm choking on disbelief, clawing at the slipping strands of a life I wanted with him.

The finality of this moment is chilling enough to quiet the voices of thousands around us.

'No, no, no . . .' My trembling hands press against the wound, blood staining my palms and stinging my nose.

Kai's eyes are on the sky, his gaze growing distant. 'Pull it out for me?' His shuddering gasp is accompanied by a trickle of blood at the corner of his mouth. 'I want you to have it.'

I climb off him, my body shaking as I shift on the sand. Gently, I lift his head onto my lap. 'No, I – I need you to heal yourself,' I beg, voice cracking. 'Kai, you have to heal yourself for me.'

He manages a subtle shake of his head. 'I'm not very good at healing.' His smirk is subtle. 'Not enough . . . practice.' A rasped cough has blood sputtering from his mouth. 'Besides . . . there is no way to heal this . . . hurt.'

'No.' The word sounds so useless falling from my quivering lips. 'Help!' I lift my frantic gaze towards the silent crowd. 'Somebody help me! I – I need a Healer!' My screams echo through the arena, useless in the faces of those unwilling to help. 'You're Elites!' The broken shout is met with silence. 'Fucking do something!'

I bite back a frustrated scream. At the Plague. At Elites. At my powerlessness.

Looking down, I brace a hand against Kai's cheek. 'You're going to be fine, okay?'

It's the same lie I told Adena in this very Pit.

'You're my cocky bastard—' I force a trembling smile, '—you can't let me win.'

His gray eyes blink blearily at me. 'Just . . . just this once.'

He laces sticky fingers between mine, his grip weak. I shake my head, chest heaving. 'But I need you.' A sob racks my body. 'You're all I h-have left. You know I need you!'

It's as though Adena is dying all over again. I'm spouting the same broken words atop the very sand that was once speckled with her blood. The same crowd is leaning in, once again watching the spectacle that is my heart splitting at the seams – a tear that Adena isn't around to stitch back together.

Here I am, facing déjà vu and Death himself. History repeats itself in the center of this Pit as love begins its slow death in my arms. Kai's blood coats my palms, mirroring the moment I felt Adena's life leak into my incapable hands. The Enforcer wears a wound in his chest, just as the seamstress before him.

And if I weren't already on my knees, I would fall to them now and beg him to stay with me. I press my forehead to his, swallowing back a sob. 'I can't lose you, too. Please . . . please don't leave me.'

Kai's body shudders beneath mine, as though shaking off Death's cold hand to hold mine for a few moments longer. 'I'm sorry. I . . . I wish it didn't h–have to be this way.'

'Shh.' My tears splatter his face. 'You're okay, Kai. I'm here. I'm not going anywhere.' I squeeze his hand, hiding my sobs between each whispered syllable. 'It's just you and me. Under the willow.'

A smile lifts his stained lips, displaying a row of bloody teeth. And when those damn dimples come into view, I choke on the cry crawling up my throat. Regret washes over me for every moment spent pretending I hated them – every moment spent pretending I hated *him*.

His eyes stray from mine. 'See . . .'

I lean in, hanging on words I'll never get to hear.

Because the light leaves those gray eyes.

'No.' The word is defiant.

'No.' This one is pleading.

'No!'

Anguish. That is what courses through me before pouring from my mouth.

I shake his unmoving chest. Again and again. 'Kai. Kai, come back to me.'

I can barely breathe through my gasping sobs. His gray eyes are glassily trained on the blue sky above, but I fight to force them back on me. 'No, you can't go! You promised you wouldn't leave me, remember?'

My forehead meets his, and I murmur the words I thought would take him away from me. It's a confession I was too cowardly to voice – and now it will become my biggest regret.

But I whisper it now, over and over. 'I love you, Kai. I love you. I love you. I love you.'

Agony.

That is this feeling. The one wrenching me in half, tearing apart my soul. But I don't bother smothering it any longer.

Leaning back on my heels, I unleash my anguish.

It's a chilling scream, one that can be heard even in the highest stands. I want the arena to feel my pain, taste it on the wind that carries away the soul Kai stained for me. Hot tears spill over my skin to drip atop the lifeless body of the boy I love.

Hazy and hysterical, I notice the shifting figures surrounding me for the first time. Blinking through the blur of tears, my burning eyes focus on the forgotten Sights. My head whips towards the screen, finding Kai's empty gaze displayed there.

Whatever composure was left within me suddenly snaps.

'Get away from him!' I shout, waving a weak arm in their direction. Disregarding me with continued vacant stares, they reach for his body, each of them grabbing a limb. I snatch the discarded sword from the sand and swivel it between the four of them. My voice is lethal, crazed. 'Get. Away.'

This has them blinking, the action breaking their broadcast onto the screen. My arm shakes beneath the weight of the sword, but I don't dare drop it. Still, the Sights begin to drag him away, leaving a streak of blood behind.

'*No!*'

I toss aside the sword, all my fight gone, to reach for his still body. He is being tugged across the sand and all I can do is stumble after him. 'No, get away from him!' I trip in the trail of his blood, falling to my knees. Sobs shake my shoulders as I watch the Sights so carelessly yank him away.

'Please,' I whisper into the wind. It smells of death. Of ruin.

I could almost laugh.

That is what I was in the end. His ruin.

I stand on shaking limbs, coated in Kai's blood. It's still warm on my palms as I turn to—

Rage surges through me.

'*You.*'

I know he hears the accusing word from where he sits comfortably in that glass box. I'm not even sure who I am looking at anymore. All I see are the green eyes of a murderer.

My arm rises, and I point a quivering finger at the king. Anger rips from my throat, fueled by pain and the pillaging of my one love left in this world. 'How could you?! He was your brother!'

Blood pounds in my ears, loud enough to drown out the sudden spark of murmurs spreading through the crowd. I bend, wrapping bloody fingers around the hilt of that discarded blade once again. The sword drags through the sand behind me, its hilt pressed into my sticky palm. My steps are steadier than they should be as I march towards him, leaving a trail of blood in my wake.

'How could you?!' I scream again, my throat raw.

Kitt lowers his gaze, his head shaking slightly.

'Look at me!'

The demand rings through the arena, shutting the mouths of every gossiping Elite. I stand there, a lowly Ordinary, panting in the Pit beneath him.

And yet, when I command, he obeys.

Kitt's eyes flick to mine, filled with a mixture of disbelief and despair. He takes me in, every grain of sand and drop of blood.

'How could—!'

An arm wraps around my torn neck, pressing a damp cloth over my nose.

My knees buckle beneath me.

My blazing eyes roll back.

And for a short time, I know nothing.

Not even the agony.

CHAPTER 46

Rai

I am grief. I am sorrow. I am anguish alike.

CHAPTER 47

Paedyn

Morning light has my heavy eyelids lifting.

I sit up swiftly, my head and heart pounding.

Gulping down air, I force my frantic thoughts to calm.

It was just a nightmare.

I blow out a breath, letting the foreign rush of relief wash over me. My gaze slides to the window and the bright sky beyond.

Today is my third Trial.

Last night was a nightmare.

I let out a shaky laugh before reaching to rip the many blankets from my sweaty skin.

Something slams into me at the sight of my hand. I can't quite identify it at first – not until my fingers begin to shake.

It's that familiar agony, I realize.

That shaking begins to spread across my body, leaving me shuddering with a sudden sense of horror.

I'm covered in blood.

It's staining my palms, crawling up trembling arms to wrap around my neck. Sand coats my body, covering me in a layer of grit and memory. Petrified, I peer down at my hands, knowing it is not my

blood that clings to them.

This is my living nightmare.

I scream.

The choked sound has Ellie scurrying into the room as I leap from the bed. My bloody fingernails tear at my skin, trying to claw away the proof of this Trial.

'Paedyn!' Ellie's shout sounds muffled. 'It's okay! Paedyn, you're okay!'

I whip towards her, tears streaming down my face. 'Where is he?! Tell me it wasn't real, Ellie.' My fingers dig into her shoulders, as if trying to shake the answer from her lips. 'Tell me he's not dead. Please,' I whimper. 'Please tell me it's not real.'

Her mouth opens. Then it closes.

I back away slowly. 'No.'

Tears pool in her eyes. 'You've been sleeping for nearly a day.'

'No,' I whisper, my lip quivering. 'No, it was just a nightmare. Today is my Trial.'

Ellie shakes her head. 'I'm sorry, Paedyn.'

My knees hit the floor.

I held the dagger as it sunk into his chest.

She holds me as I cry.

I know what it feels like to kill him.

CHAPTER 48

Paedyn

I sit in a pool of red.

I'm surrounded by scarlet swirls, the tub stained with the remnants of my final Trial. My gaze is red-rimmed and unseeing, fixed blearily on the wall opposite me.

A soft hand wraps around my wrist. I don't fight the gentle touch even as it lifts my limp arm from the tub's porcelain edge. A rough bar of soap then scrubs against my skin, back and forth until the hardened blood loses its grip on my flesh.

Back and forth. Back and forth.

I watch what is left of Kai drip into the water. And for the first time in weeks, I'm not repulsed by blood – in fact, I wish to cling to his.

'How . . . how are you feeling?'

It's the first shy string of words Ellie has attempted since I woke from my drugged haze. I can't say I blame her for the prolonged silence. It's a rather tame response to my reaction this morning.

My tone is flat. 'I don't feel anything.'

It's not a lie. Though, I doubt I could muster the energy to tell one at the moment. My entire body is numb – mind, soul, and shattered

heart. I am utterly hollow without his love to fill me.

My scar is exposed, the bloody water lapping a soothing rhythm against it. I don't need to look at Ellie – I can feel her wide gaze trailing over it. Even more concerning is the fact that I can't find it within me to care.

She lifts a cloth to my ear, swiping tenderly over the dried blood that poured from it. I'm reminded then of how eerily quiet the world was when I awoke from the dizzying drug. Gone was the incessant ringing from the explosions, leaving me with nothing to drown out my screaming thoughts.

The assortment of wounds I'd collected from the Trial had vanished. Broken ribs were restored, sliced skin sewn back together, the burn on my wrist healed – but I would give anything now to have that handprint branded back onto my skin.

Nothing but the mingling of my and his blood remained.

'I'm . . .' I clear my throat before trying again. 'I'm sorry about this morning.'

Sympathy pulls at Ellie's delicate features.

I hate that look. It's the same one I would see thrown around the slums, mothers saddened by the sight of a forgotten child. The fortunate disheartened by those of us sleeping on the streets. Only the weak earn this expression, the foolishly brokenhearted. And I have been that my whole life.

'You weren't yourself,' she reassures. 'I knew you would be scared when you woke up.'

I let out a bitter scoff that has her stilling. 'I wasn't scared, Ellie. I was broken.'

Because I let myself hope.

She swallows. 'And now?'

My empty gaze meets her concerned one. 'I'm angry.'

The king's green eyes flash before my mind. My hands curl into fists, fingernails biting each palm. The question I shouted at him in that arena still echoes in my skull.

How could you?

With a steadying breath, I stand abruptly, suddenly unable to sit in Kai's blood any longer. Wrapping a robe around my scrubbed skin,

I turn demandingly towards Ellie. 'I need to speak with the king.'

The words are far more docile than I intend to be when I see him.

Ellie straightens with a bashful turn of her lips. 'You can't leave.'

My tone is dull, expression unflinching. 'Oh, I can't?'

'The door is locked.' Another flash of sympathy. 'The king has ordered that you stay here until he says otherwise.'

That smothered sorrow threatens to seep back over my numb body. The anger and betrayal I've buried it with will only fend off my suffering for so long. No, I need my rage, my distraction, my king to answer for what he's done. Because without that, I am forced to face a life *he* is no longer in.

'Ellie,' I say slowly. 'I need to get out of here.'

'Paedyn, I . . .' She chews on her lip uneasily. 'I can't. I'm sorry.'

I clear my throat, attempting to ignore the lump growing within it. 'Do I at least get to eat while I'm locked in here?'

'Oh, yes, of course.' Ellie scurries to the door I desperately wish to walk through. 'I'll go get you some food from the kitchens.'

With a knock and verbal verification to the Imperials outside that she is not their prisoner, a series of locks click open. Ellie then slips from the room, allowing a sliver of the world beyond to spill inside this cozy cage. I've barely glimpsed the guards decorating my door before a gloved hand is slamming it shut, the thud followed by a turning of locks that makes me wince.

I stand there, shivering as water drips from the ends of my short hair to splatter the bare collarbones beneath. Swallowing, I stare at the empty room. An unsettling coldness sweeps through me, as though despair itself drags a finger along my bones.

I am utterly alone.

There is nothing left. Not within myself or the world beyond.

Trapped in this room, I am forced to face reality. Forced to face the gaping loneliness within me. My very being is decaying, and love is the culprit. Love has killed every person I care about.

The walls begin to close in all around me.

'No,' I whisper to my betraying mind. 'Please, no.'

The plea is promptly ignored.

My lungs constrict, squeezing my shattered heart until it aches.

I'm suddenly panting at the feel of claustrophobia clutching my body. I shut my eyes, trying to block out the world that wishes to smother me.

It's no use. I need to get out of here.

Stumbling to the door, I slam my shaking fist against it. 'Let me out. Please.'

Silence.

'I can't be in here any longer.' My voice cracks beneath the weight of a mind trying to crush me. 'Please!'

I pound against the door as the walls continue their steady suffocation.

I'm struggling to breathe. My forehead tips against the door's smooth wood as I choke, 'Let me out! I can't do this!'

The walls crawl closer.

My fist hits the door with one final thud. I turn slowly, letting my back slide against the wood until my body hits the floor harshly. 'I can't do this,' I whisper. Tears well, stinging my sore eyes as I pull trembling knees into an aching chest.

I'm little more than the shell of a girl, sitting among ghosts.

My father sits beside my shaking form with a comforting hand on my knee, the exact color of his eyes fading from my memory. Adena rests her head against my shoulder, crooked bangs falling into a soft, honeyed gaze.

But Kai . . .

Kai stands before me, so strong and stunning. I can almost hear his voice, the sound distantly ringing from the depths of my mind . . .

'Where is she?!'

It's so familiar, so real—

'Where the hell is she?!'

I straighten at that growing voice, scared of my own deceiving mind.

It's not real. He's gone.

Heavy footsteps echo beyond the wooden door I'm slumped against.

I shake my head angrily, tears spilling down my face.

He's gone. Just like everyone else. I killed him—

'Move aside. Or I'll make you.'

My hollow, broken heart stutters at that command.

It can't be true. I can't let myself believe this, and yet, I scramble to my feet. Palms pressed to the door that separates me from hope, I mutter, 'Kai?'

The muffled shout that returns has me laughing through a disbelieving sob.

'Pae!'

I shove away from the door, my heart pounding at the presence of its other half.

'Your Highness, we have strict orders from the king to—'

The door flies from its hinges.

As it falls to the floor with a thud, there is nothing left to separate me from the ghost behind. Not even Death himself.

Our gazes meet.

Smoke meeting fire; life meeting the walking dead.

He stands there, so perfectly intact. His chest heaves, free of my dagger and the bloody handprints I left beside it. A storm brews in his gray eyes, so unlike the last time I saw them glassily pinned on the sky above. Everything about the Enforcer is impossibly exactly how I'd left him the night before that final Trial.

I can't seem to move, afraid this is some cruel dream, some phantom that will slip between my fingers. But then his eyes are welling with tears. Familiar lips are pulling into a relieved smile, those dangerous dimples framing it.

Kai's words are choked. 'I heard you killed me?'

That is all it takes to have my feet tripping over themselves.

I am more than his shadow. I am a moth to his flame.

A sob swells in my throat, springing hot tears to my eyes. I can hardly see through the blur of disbelief, but still, I race towards him. He doesn't hesitate before striding across the room, heading right for the hand that helped kill him.

I trip into his arms before my knees can buckle beneath me. My hysterical laugh is muffled against his tunic, face buried above a heart that beats wildly.

Alive. He's alive.

344

The feel of his arms tightening around me is so familiar, so seemingly *right*, that I cry harder at the thought of truly losing him. *Alive.*

He is so stunningly alive, and strong, and standing for the both of us. Kai's chest shudders against me as tears leak from his eyes, same as mine. I pull away slowly, scared that I might startle back to reality and find him to be nothing more than a figment of my grief.

But nothing this exquisite could ever be imagined.

My trembling fingers brush his face, and the whispered touch has Kai's eyes fluttering closed. A tear slips down the sharp planes of his face, colliding with my fingers. I shake my head while struggling to speak past the lump in my throat. 'How are you here?' My voice is a cracked whisper. 'I watched . . . I watched you *die*.'

His hands slide down my body, as if to ensure I'm real as well. 'I'm sorry. I'm sorry for everything you were put through—'

'I don't care.' I cup his face, my own earnest. 'I don't care so long as this is real, and you are alive.'

'This is real,' he almost laughs. 'Not pretend. Not ever.'

I nod and press my palms to his neck as a smile pulls at my quivering lips. 'I just don't understand. My dagger . . . I felt it slide into your chest.'

My fingers trail down to his chest, finding no trace of the blade that was once buried there.

'I know.' His voice is suddenly as icy as the eyes flicking between mine. 'I wouldn't have let it happen, but I was drugged that night before the Trial.'

My mouth falls open. 'What?'

'I was supposed to sleep through the Trial. The Healers locked me in my room.' A muscle flexes in his cheek. 'The cheering from the Bowl woke me up, and I . . . I knew it was you. So I fought off the drug and stumbled to the arena. Imperials held me back before I could get in, but I saw, Paedyn. I saw you fighting *myself*. And it . . .' His voice breaks. 'It destroyed me. I tried to push my way to you, but the drugs weakened me, and I just . . . stood there while you fought for your life. Fought *me*.'

His rough hands cup my tear-streaked face. 'You almost died

thinking it was me who killed you. Thinking that I would ever lay a hand on you again for any reason other than a caress. I told you I would never fight you again, but there I was, hurting you like I promised not to.'

'Shh.' It's difficult to talk through the emotion clogging my throat. 'It's not your fault. You didn't do this.'

He nods. I melt against him. Memorize this moment, because I thought we wouldn't have it again. He runs a soothing hand down my back, chin resting against my hair. 'It looked too real. Like I was watching myself lose control,' he finally whispers.

His voice breaks. Pulling back, he cups my face with trembling hands. Gone is the Enforcer and every mask that accompanies him. This is Kai alone – my fool and my love.

'I couldn't save you. Not even from myself.' He nearly chokes on the words. 'Forgive me. Please.'

I shake my head at him. 'There is nothing to forgive. Because I . . .'

I'm crying again. It seems that I haven't stopped in days, but possibly for the first time in my life, it doesn't make me feel weak. This is relief that pours from me, a mingling of happiness in his presence and fear at the admittance in my throat. 'Kai, I—'

My feet leave the ground for a moment before landing atop his. I laugh through the tears, propped on his boots just like I had when it was a chain tethering us together, not something far more unbreakable. His arms twine around my waist tightly. 'Tell me, Pae.'

Swallowing, I force out the string of words. 'I watched you die in that arena. I watched my own dagger sink into your chest with my hands wrapped around the hilt. And then, you were slipping away.' I blink, gaze blurry. 'And I hadn't even said those three words I was so sure would take you away from me. It took your death to find my courage, and by then, you were . . . you were gone.'

My voice trembles. Cracks. Crumbles with my composure. 'But I can't wait for another tragedy. So I'll tell you now, because fate likely won't allow us a future. Kai, I—'

'I love you.'

Kai steals the words from my mouth with a spreading smile. And, distantly, I realize this isn't the first time he's uttered such a declaration. He lifts a hand to my tear-stained face, stroking a thumb over the flushed skin there. 'Paedyn, I love you. Like nothing else before, *I love you*. And I've been waiting to tell you since I realized your eyes are my favorite color and your freckles the only constellation worth looking at. I could lie – say that you've stolen my every thought and heartbeat like the thief you are, but all of me was already yours. Pae, you are my inevitable.'

Tears stream down my face, dampening Kai's fingers. He's crying just the same, and yet, his eyes never leave mine. He utters the words again, as if they have consumed his every thought and begged to be loosed. 'You are my inevitable. In death, and in love.'

'And you are mine.' I smother my sobs long enough to whisper, 'I love you, Malakai. I love you.' I can't seem to stop spewing the words now that I've said them. It's freeing, letting go of the fear that accompanied that phrase. 'I love you. I love you. I love y—'

His mouth is on mine, tasting the words from my lips. I breathe him in greedily as tears mingle with the kiss. His hands run down my body, gently memorizing every curve beneath the robe. Sighing into his mouth, I twine my arms around his neck. I feel delicate in his embrace, as though he is holding something priceless.

Love.

That is what this feeling is. And it is all-consuming.

He pulls back slightly, lips still lingering above mine, and lands a light flick to the tip of my nose. 'My pretty Pae. Look what you have done to me.'

I smile up at him, returning the favor with a flick of my own fingers. 'I could ask you the same, pretty Prince.' My gaze shifts to a pair of heels sitting innocently beside my wardrobe. 'You already told me you loved me, didn't you?'

A smile tugs at the corner of his mouth. 'You seemed more interested in the shoes I'd found discarded on the dance floor.'

I nod at the vague memory. 'You carried me to my room.'

'Well, you were becoming quite the tripping hazard on the dance floor.'

My throat is dry. I swallow thickly. 'You love me.'

'Then.' His hands cup my face. 'Now.' My lips brush his. 'Always. And I'll find your shoes for you in every lifetime if you'll allow it.'

We stand there, held in each other's arms for several silent moments. But that is all it takes for the questions to creep back towards the forefront of my mind. So when a shadow of confusion crosses my face, Kai asks, 'What is it?'

'Kitt knew it wasn't you in that arena,' I murmur.

My eyes fall to his unscathed chest.

'So who did I kill?'

CHAPTER 49

Kai

'I see you two found each other.'

That is the first thing Kitt says when we walk into his study. The second is a sighed apology. 'I'm sorry for what I put you both through. Truly.'

Paedyn draws a deep breath beside me. 'I want answers.'

Kitt stands from his seat. 'Oh, I know. You looked ready to rip my throat out in the Bowl. It was chilling, that look you gave me.' Stepping in front of the cluttered desk, he leans against the stained wood. 'I think the kingdom finally saw you for what you are – fearsome.'

'Glad to see something good came out of my pain, then,' Pae bites out.

'A lot of good,' Kitt corrects, 'came from very short-lived pain. That is why I did it.'

I step forward, crossing my arms. 'And what exactly did you do, Brother?'

Kitt coughs into a handkerchief. This worries me, but his gaze looks clearer than it had that night before the Trial. 'I'm sorry about the drugging. But, Kai, it was the only way to keep you locked

away and out of sight – which didn't seem to work, as it was. And, Paedyn—' he gestures to her weakly, '—the only way Ilya would accept you as queen was if you proved yourself to be stronger than the strongest among us. And a Wielder is that.'

'Fine. But it wasn't Kai I fought.' She glances over at me. 'Clearly.'

'No,' Kitt sighs, 'it wasn't. But I wanted you and the kingdom to think it was the Enforcer. Conquering him would be a huge feat – not just because he is a Wielder, but because he is just as dangerous without an ability.'

He says this plainly, despite how startling I find his words. Kitt has never spoken much of my power, always conscious of the differences between us. But I've known how much he despises not being able to prove himself physically like I have my whole life. As the heir, power is controlled, not wielded.

'And maybe,' Kitt continues, 'I wanted to test your loyalty to me. See if you would actually . . .'

Paedyn stiffens, and before she can say anything damning, I hurry to ask, 'How did you do it? What Elite could pose as me?'

Kitt's eyes climb slowly to mine. 'We found a Wielder that needed to be taken care of.'

A growing numbness spreads through me at his words.

'It's true?' Paedyn breathes, whipping her head towards me. 'There are other Wielders in Ilya that are being killed because of it?'

'There are very few,' Kitt answers on my behalf, his worried gaze on my growingly distant one. 'Father discovered three during his reign, but he would—' a clearing of his throat, '—take care of them to ensure that Kai was the strongest Elite in Ilya's history.'

My voice is icy. 'I never wanted that. I thought we agreed to stop—'

'We did,' Kitt cuts in sternly. 'But this Wielder came to us. He knew the risks and decided to fight anyway.'

Paedyn is shaking her head, muttering, 'Why would he do that? And how did he look exactly like Kai—' Her eyes light up, indicating a realization like they always do. 'Illusionist. There was an Illusionist disguised as a Sight, wasn't there?'

Kitt nods solemnly. 'He was casting Kai's image over the Wielder.'

'She could have died!' I shout, throwing out a hand towards Paedyn. 'At least if it were me in that Pit, I would have ensured my own death instead of hers.'

'Don't you think I know that?' Kitt counters. 'That is precisely why I couldn't let you in that arena. You would have sacrificed your life for her. And I refuse to lose you.'

I stare at him, at this sliver of a brother I have never seen. This Trial was perfectly calculated, devised to ensure the outcome he wished. I see now that this was precisely what Father trained him to be – one step ahead.

'But you were willing to risk losing her,' I say evenly.

Kitt's gaze flicks to Paedyn. 'She had to prove herself. It seems I have more faith in her than you, Brother. I knew she could do it, and she did. Neither of you had to die.'

'He's right.' Paedyn crosses her arms, agreeing begrudgingly. 'It had to look real. And now the kingdom is one step closer to bending the knee.'

I shake my head, hurt seeping across my features. 'You drugged me, Kitt. Locked me in a room.' My throat tightens. 'That is the type of shit our father – my king – would put me through.'

Paedyn's head dips towards the floor, but the anger on her face is not so easily concealed. I watch Kitt step before me, blocking my view of her. His face crumples with regret. 'I never wanted to hurt you, Kai. I'm . . . I'm so sorry. Please forgive me.' The expression he wears grows stern. 'I never want to remind you of Father. I am better than that.'

I nod slowly. 'I've always known you were better than Father.' Kitt seems partially pleased by this first step towards forgiveness, allowing me to move on with a bland, 'So, I'm just dead, then.'

Kitt doesn't so much as bat an eye before stating, 'Actually, I was going to make you even more powerful. Tell the kingdom you survived.'

I blink. 'You really think they will believe that?'

'They don't need to believe you. They need only to fear you. You will be the Deliverer of Death who has met him and lived. And you—' Kitt's gaze slides to Paedyn, '—have now earned the respect of your kingdom and will be their queen.'

I tilt my head at the powerful lie he's spun. 'So much for never reminding me of Father.'

The study grows stiffly quiet as we all stare at one another. Several seconds pass before Paedyn is clearing her throat and directing our attention to the look of resolve she wears. 'I want to see this Wielder.'

Kitt hardly looks surprised by this request. 'Paedyn, I'm not sure you will want to see that. His body is in the dungeons and—'

'I want,' she says slowly, 'to see. And don't think I've forgiven you yet for what you put me through. What you made me do – whether or not it was truly Kai.'

The king shoves away from his desk, eyes clouded with something close to remorse. Or perhaps that inkling of hysteria I've witnessed. 'Do you think that was easy for me? Do you think I wanted to watch my brother die, even knowing it wasn't truly him?' Kitt's gaze slides to mine, timid as it takes me in. 'I hated it. I didn't want to do it – any of it. And, again, I'm . . . I'm sorry, Brother.'

I watch his kingly facade crumble beneath the weight of my stare. For the first time, I see just how incredibly lost he is. Where a kind and charming brother once stood, now resides the corpse of duty and power.

A lump forms in my throat as I nod. And then I'm pulling him into a crushing hug. Kitt clings to me, his hold weaker than I remember. For a moment, we are boys again, seeking comfort during Ava's death or congratulations after a brawl. His breath quivers, as if he is trying to compose himself before murmuring, 'I need you with me, Kai.'

I pull away, clapping my hand on his shoulder. 'And I hope to never find out what I'd be like without you.'

Simultaneously, our gazes shift to where Paedyn stands beside us. She's fighting a smile at the sight of such a heartfelt moment before straightening her features. Swiftly, she steps aside with a gesture to the door. 'Lead the way, Majesty.'

So, with a sigh, the king obeys. We head out into the hall, setting a quick pace towards the dungeons. Imperials line the occasional wall, looking unsurprised by my very much alive presence. Even the passing servants hardly glance in our direction, and the utterly unperturbed response has me stating, 'The castle already knows it wasn't me in the arena, yes?'

'They were informed a few hours ago,' Kitt replies, rounding a corner. 'And they won't speak a word of the other Wielder. You know how good the staff are at keeping secrets. They've been doing it for decades.'

I nod absentmindedly, knowing this to be true. I'm beginning to think Ilya itself was built on secrets – and I doubt I know the half of them.

The dungeons' thick door looms before us suddenly, its frame decorated on either side by two Imperials. They nod stoically to their king before swinging open the heavy metal entrance they guard. Stone steps await us beyond, descending into darkness and the dungeons below.

The thick air and accompanied coldness greet us at the bottom of the stairs. It's as though I've been welcomed back to my forgotten den of torture. I haven't been down here since the Resistance's Silencer, Micah, occupied one of these cells.

I haven't been down here since I killed him.

Smothering the memory, I stray behind Kitt and Paedyn. The cells are empty of the few Resistance members who once filled them after the battle in the Bowl. They now occupy the several training rings beyond the castle, sprinkled among the numerous Imperial rotations.

'You know,' Kitt reminisces, his voice echoing off the grimy stones, 'the last time I was down here was when I led you straight into the tunnels you were looking for, Paedyn.'

She takes a breath, looking pained. 'Not a particularly fond memory, I assume.'

'I understand, truly. There is always a reason for the hurt we cause.'

Paedyn opens her mouth before abruptly shutting it at the sight of an occupied cell. Her feet slow; mine do the same.

A body lies on the stone floor with a familiar silver dagger buried in his chest.

It's odd, seeing a man with my same power be reduced to such a simple death. I have never met another Wielder, never got the chance before Father's hunger for power ensured I was the only one of my kind. But looking at this Elite, a part of me wishes I had someone to bear the burden of this ability with.

Still, Paedyn stands there, rooted to the spot outside that cell. Her voice is alarmingly small. 'It's him.'

Kitt steps forward. 'What?'

'It's Adena's boy from Loot.' She chokes on his name. 'Mak.'

My head whips back towards the body, eyes tracing the identical pattern of his vest. Every pocket and every seam – exactly the same.

This is the friend she met at the Fort.

Paedyn staggers into the cell, her gaze gliding over the man. I follow her, taking in his shaggy hair, long enough to tickle the sides of his neck. A silver streak peeks out among the black strands while a scar slices through the corner of his mouth. Brown eyes stare blankly at the ceiling above, though a vague sort of relief seems to fill them.

Slowly, Pae drops to her knees beside him. His skin is leached of all color, contrasting starkly with the dark vest hugging him tightly. Blood stains his clothing, surrounding that silver dagger in a pool of crimson. With shaking fingers, Paedyn traces the soiled seam of his vest. She sucks in a breath before following the rise and fall of every pocket stitched onto it.

Her fingers stumble over a string of stitched words. The blue thread is splotched with blood, dulled beneath one of the many pockets. I hear Paedyn's breath catch before the murmured words that follow. 'See you in the sky.'

Eyes wide and rimmed with tears, she lifts her gaze to mine. 'He was trying to say that in the arena. He was dying, and that was the last thing he wanted to say.'

'Paedyn . . .' I crouch beside her and place a gentle hand on her back at the same moment Kitt rests one on her shoulder. Our eyes meet for a single, uncomfortable moment, in which we glimpse the rest of our lives. Paedyn will always be between us. Soon, she will no longer be mine to comfort, mine to have.

And pathetically I will still love her. She is forever lodged within me, the only pure spot on my stained soul. But for now, I do not pull away. Not until vows are wedged between us, and that ring on her finger holds a greater weight. Until then, I will have her in whatever way she lets me.

'Even after our time on Loot together, he still blamed me for Adena's death,' Paedyn breathes. Her fingers curl around the vest's perfect hem. 'The way he was fighting . . . he really did want to hurt me.'

My stomach twists, hating that she ever believed it to be me in that ring with her. But tensions were high, and this Wielder was there to play a part – me.

'He wanted to avenge her.' She shakes her head. 'I can't blame him for that. I only blame myself.'

My eyes meet Kitt's over the worried girl between us. She leans back slowly on her heels, a silent stream of tears decorating her skin. 'But he decided not to kill me,' she murmurs. 'He could have killed me. If we hadn't met, I wonder if things would have been different.'

Paedyn's head falls onto my shoulder, and for a moment, I forget my brother's presence. Kitt looks away, his throat bobbing with emotion. Perhaps it's envy, irritation, even, and I hate it. This is all wrong, seeing him like this. Being like this with him—

Paedyn slips an arm through Kitt's, tugging him close.

I stiffen slightly, Kitt doing the same at the sudden inclusion. But Paedyn doesn't so much as flinch. She simply stares at the body before us, her own pressed between two brothers.

The sheer vastness of Pae's grief pulls my attention back to her. She clings to Kitt's arm with her head tipped against my shoulder. I also know this girl better than she lets most. I can read each tremble and unspoken word.

She wants silence. She wants to sit in this grief. And when she is ready to be pulled out, her betrothed and his brother are right here to do so.

'We never got to say goodbye to her.' Paedyn's whispered words are not meant for our ears. 'But at least we could share how much we both loved her.'

It's a long while before she breaks away from the press of our bodies and lifts a hesitant hand towards the Wielder's glassy gaze. She shuts his eyes gently, offering him the peaceful end she couldn't give in the arena. Numbly, Paedyn straightens his vest before brushing stray strands of hair from his cool forehead.

'Take care of her for me,' she whispers atop his pale skin. 'Take care of her, Mak.'

I almost don't hear her final, broken whisper.

'See you in the sky.'

CHAPTER 50

Paedyn

I hardly remember leaving the dungeons.
Even less is recalled after returning to my room.
It was harder knowing him.
The corpse had a name.
Mak.
Mak.
MAK.
Dead bodies have no use for names.
The last piece of Adena died in my arms, just as she had.
He wore her vest. And now it keeps his dead body warm.
Mak.
Ellie says she only learned this morning that it wasn't Kai in the arena.
I tell her that I know.
I think I'm selfish for the relief I feel at Kai's resurrection.
Why does my love deserve to live and Adena's does not?
But they are together now, decorating the sky.
That is what he wanted, I'm beginning to realize.
He only wished to see her in the sky.

A waterfall of white cascades down my body.

'Are you almost done back there?' I ask with a shade of concern.

Popping her head over my shoulder, Ellie sighs at me in the mirror before us. 'There has to be a hundred buttons.'

I shake my head before she ducks and returns to the meticulous task. My gaze wanders over the dress, tracing the delicate curve of its cut against my body. Soft white fabric hugs me closely while a layer of delicate lace falls over it. Clusters of small flowers decorate the dress, climbing up the thick straps around my shoulders to hang down the back in long ribbons.

It's the perfect picture of purity.

And I'm not sure I should be the one wearing it.

'There,' Ellie declares before straightening. 'Oh, you are going to make such a beautiful bride.'

I swallow. Force a tight smile.

'Now,' she continues gently, unaware of my discomfort, 'it's not finished yet. And, um, I can ask the seamstress to widen these straps a bit further, if you like?'

A sliver of my scar still peeks out from beneath the fabric. I brush my fingers over the mangled skin, staring at the odd contrast between such delicacy and animosity. 'Maybe,' I say distantly. 'I'm not sure if—'

A light knock at the door interrupts my hesitant answer. I whip towards the sound before smiling at the source of it. Calum stands in the doorway, smiling slightly. 'Is this a bad time to offer well-wishes to the future queen?'

I wave him over as Ellie steps away, giving us some privacy. 'No, not at all. I'm happy you're here, actually.'

'Oh?' He steps beside me, blond hair bright in the setting sun streaming through my window. 'All good reasons, I hope.'

My smile is small. 'Well, see . . .' I'm fidgeting with the ring on my thumb. 'You're the closest thing I have to a father now. And I was wondering if . . .'

'I'd be honored to walk you down the aisle, Paedyn,' Calum says with a solemn nod.

'Really?' I breathe. For the first time in a very long time, I feel like a little girl again. I feel like *someone's* little girl again.

'Of course.' His scrutinizing gaze drifts over the elegant dress before returning to my face. I catch the slight bob of his throat. 'You really do look like your mother.'

I'm flattered until reminded of the truth. 'That's right,' I sigh. 'I never got the chance to tell you about my father's journals.'

Calum's eyes bore into mine, uncovering the buried thoughts behind them. He blinks then, voice soft. 'Adam wasn't your father.'

'Apparently not.' I shake my head, gaze falling to the ring on my thumb. 'His wife died in childbirth, and a week later, I showed up on his doorstep. Just another unwanted Ordinary. So . . . who knows if I look like my real mother.'

'Adam never told me.' There is a long pause before Calum adds, 'Did he write about anything else in this journal?'

I shake my head. 'He mostly documented his patients and the Resistance's growth. But if anything else was mentioned, it would have been on the pages I used to feed a fire in the Sanctuary of Souls.' I glance up at him, slightly skeptical. 'Why?'

Calum manages a slight smile. 'Just curiosity for an old friend.'

'Hmm.' I fiddle with the ring on my thumb. 'But you think I look like my father's wife, Alice?'

'From the few pictures I saw of her, yes,' he answers softly. 'Now, I must rush off to a meeting with Kitt, but I will be sure to tell him how beautiful you look in this wedding dress. The roses from my garden will look lovely with it.'

This makes me pause. 'Your garden? How did you manage to grow anything in the short amount of time you've been here?'

He backs away. 'Well, the Blooms have been very helpful. They are to thank for persuading my flowers to grow.'

'Right.' The mutter is followed by a hurried 'Thank you. For everything.'

He dips his head, offering one final glance. 'I hope you're not covering up that scar. You should be flaunting it.'

The Mind Reader is gone before the smile has turned my lips. Ellie hurries back to my side, staring at my figure in the mirror while straightening the dress's several seams. 'What do you think?'

I run a hand down the fabric. 'I'm just thinking about what Adena would say.'

'Probably a lot of things,' Ellie says earnestly.

The truth of that prediction makes me laugh. And then my fingers are straying to the thick straps slipping over my shoulders. Calum's words ring in my mind, but it's a sweeter voice that echoes in my heart. That is where Adena lives, and she is telling me to display my survival. Showcase the power I was forced to find within myself.

This fabric has never felt Adena's soft touch, and I never will again. If I am to be married, I want to be wearing a piece of her. So, the least I can do is display my strength in her honor.

'Actually, I've decided against the straps.' I fight to subdue my triumphant grin. 'I'd like them gone.'

Ellie nods. 'I'll go fetch the seamstress, then.'

I watch her slip from the room before returning my gaze to the mirror. The face that stares back is foreign in a freeing way. There is a certain boldness within it that I look forward to familiarizing myself with. It is not quite the image of a queen, but perhaps something just as powerful.

There is strength in sacrifice. And that is what this marriage is.

So I smile at my reflection, unable to recall the last time I have.

Faint footsteps echo from the hallway beyond, to which I absentmindedly call, 'Ellie, am I wearing a veil?'

'I would happily beg you not to.'

My heart stutters at the sudden sound of his voice. I turn towards it slowly, fabric swishing around my ankles. Kai stands in the doorway, his eyes roaming over the length of me with a look that distantly resembles devastation.

'Oh?' I challenge breathlessly.

'Don't deprive me of seeing your face one last time.'

I falter. 'It wouldn't be the last time.'

'It wouldn't be the same,' he answers quickly.

The ache in his voice makes me flinch. 'Kai . . .' I step quickly towards him, once again walking that dangerous line between duty and desire. I may be wearing a wedding dress meant for the king, but it's his brother I continually run back to.

'Don't,' Kai practically chokes. 'Don't walk towards me wearing that dress.' I've never heard the Enforcer sound so shaken. 'It only reminds me that I won't be the one awaiting you at the end of that aisle.'

My feet stutter to a stop. I nod slowly, hating the hurt on his face. My throat burns. 'I don't want this either.'

He stares at me for a long moment before closing the distance between us. 'I only came to slide a note beneath your door.' My breath catches when he presses a folded piece of parchment into my palm. 'But now that I'm here . . .' He takes a step back to thoroughly look me over. 'I can tell you that your outfit is missing something.'

This blatant statement makes me blink. 'Oh?'

Kai's mouth twitches. 'You have nothing sharp to threaten me with.'

'That is a problem, isn't it?' I agree.

With a growing grin that showcases those dimples I love to hate, he reaches into his boot to retrieve—

'My dagger,' I breathe.

Its swirling, silver hilt winks at me in the dying light. I take it gently from his hands, smiling as I'm reunited with this piece of my father. Until I'm reminded why I didn't have it in the first place.

I stare down at the clean blade. 'You . . . pulled it from his chest.'

'He had no need for it.'

My gaze falls to the calloused palms at his sides. His nails are rimmed with dirt, though his hands are scrubbed clean of the mud that once coated them. That sight alone sends me back to the Whispers, where a cocky prince once buried a girl for the sake of another. And again, in the slums of Ilya, another littered body of mine was put to rest by the man meant to drag me to my doom.

'You buried him.'

It's not a question. But it's not a surprise, either. Not anymore.

'Nothing gets past you, Little Psychic.' Kai sighs out the words before adding, 'Out in the poppy field. I figured that was a good place for him to rest.'

'Thank you.' I choke on the words. 'I only wish Adena was there with him.'

His fingers find my chin. 'I know, Pae. I wish I knew what happened to her after that Trial.'

I nod quickly, not wanting to dwell on that thought more than I already do. 'Thank you,' I say again. 'You really are becoming quite the gentleman.'

'Only for you, darling.' He flicks my nose gently before backing away with a wry smile.

I blink at his retreating form. 'Where are you going?'

His palms rise as if accepting defeat. 'Somewhere you cannot torture me, Gray.'

An exasperated sound tumbles out of my mouth. 'Torture? I haven't even raised my dagger to you yet.'

'Are you completely unaware of how devastating you are?' Kai chuckles darkly. 'You don't need a blade. I would bleed if only you asked.'

'Then I wouldn't ask,' I retort sternly.

'No, you wouldn't.' He steps out into the hall, tossing his next damning sentence over a shoulder. 'As my queen, you would command it.'

CHAPTER 51

Kai

The sound of muffled voices slips beneath the throne room's looming doors.

Kitt stands beside me, straightening the golden crown that bleeds into the hair beneath. 'She should be here by now.'

I get the strangest sense he wasn't speaking to me. My gaze sweeps down the hallway, searching for any flash of silver hair. 'She will be here soon. Probably.'

The king runs a hand over his face, eyes blurry. 'Well, the court is growing restless. We should head in there.'

Sighing, I turn towards the door.

'What?' Kitt asks skeptically. 'Spit it out.'

'I've just never been dead before.' I shrug a shoulder. 'It was kind of nice.'

Kitt's laugh bounces all around us. His stare seems to clear suddenly. 'Peaceful, I'm sure.'

'I should die more often.'

His smile is so equally familiar and earnest. 'No chance, Kai Pie. I need you with me.'

The doors begin to slowly uncurl, revealing a sliver of the court

within. We face them, the kingdom, the life we have been thrown into, just as we have everything else – together.

Kitt glances sidelong at me. He smiles wider.

I grin back.

'Ready for your resurrection?' he murmurs.

I take a breath. 'So long as you're here to help me survive this time.'

The doors fly open, and gasps echo through the room.

Every gaze is pinned to the walking corpse among them. I learned many years ago not to grow flustered beneath scrutiny, so I slip a mask over my features, smothering any emotion that isn't indifference. Shocked whispers follow my every step, disbelief nipping at my heels.

Reaching the dais, Kitt turns to greet the stunned court. 'Good afternoon. I trust you are all thoroughly surprised at the sight of your Enforcer after witnessing Paedyn's final Trial in the Bowl.' The king rests a firm hand on my shoulder. 'It seems you all needed to be reminded that Kai Azer is the strongest Elite among us. His death will not come so easily.'

The crowd erupts, cheers rippling throughout the throne room. It's likely out of fear that they celebrate, concerned by what I might do to them.

'They don't need to believe you. They need only to fear you.'

Kitt's words ring true, but it's Father's voice I hear saying them.

I stand there, pretending as though I am a man whom Death himself fears. And all it cost me was the torture of watching myself nearly kill Paedyn. Witnessing my deepest fear come to life while I tried uselessly to claw my way to her.

The court claps for me, shouting praises deserving of a hero. And they know better than most that I am anything but. Even so, I offer a slight nod of my head and—

The doors swing open.

Every head turns towards the rumbling sound. Gazes widen when they land on her face, gawk when they glance below it. I can hardly help but do the same, though, for very different reasons.

She stands there, draped in emerald green. It spills down her body in dozens of layers before billowing around her feet and draping behind her heels. The gown hugs her waist tightly, climbing up her body in a strapless corset.

And there, on display above her beating heart, is the king's carving.

Paedyn's spine is straight beneath the crushing weight of eyes against her chest. The mangled O sits crudely atop her smooth skin, the scar flowing grimly into the slice down her neck.

Boldly, she casts her own scrutiny over the crowd. Vulnerably, she shows those who hate her the one thing she hates most about herself. And unashamedly, they stare.

Hushed whispers drift through the crowd, forcing the king to cut through their gossip loudly. 'Your future queen, Paedyn Gray.'

Kitt has always worn his emotions blatantly – a quality I equally admire and envy. So when I look over at him, finding an unsurprised expression on his face, I realize that this isn't the first time he's witnessed the cruelty our father engraved on Paedyn.

A prick of jealousy, hurt, even, slips beneath my unbothered mask. I'm not entirely sure why, perhaps because I know that scar to be incredibly intimate to her. Something that she fought to keep me from finding, only to willingly bare herself to my brother.

But of course she would. They are betrothed. This is only the beginning.

Paedyn strides across the marble floor, splitting the now silent court. Emerald fabric flows behind her with every step towards the dais. She holds her head high, silver hair brushing tanned shoulders while that scar tugs at the skin below.

Her foot reaches the first step, and those blue eyes crash into mine. The look she gives me is sharp – same as it always has been and likely always will be. Because no matter how much our feelings grow or confessions spew, we will always remain precisely as we are. I will tease her until my dying breath, spar until I'm buried six feet beneath her feet.

I am forever her rival, and I revel in it.

She turns to face the court, every bit the queen they made her become. Her gaze falls to Kitt, just as it will for the rest of our lives. He offers her a slight dip of his head, encouraging her mouth to open and—

'So, the Ordinary couldn't kill him.'

My eyes snap to the crowd, landing on a man who must long to meet Death. 'That means—' he raises a hand towards the dais, '—she didn't even complete the Trial. It was to the death, was it not?'

Paedyn is speaking before I have the chance to choose a more violent method. 'Would you like me to complete the Trial here? If you wish to be satisfied, it is your blood I can spill instead.'

Her voice is lethal in a way I've yet to be graced with. The man's face slackens at the words, growing paler with each one spoken after. 'It wouldn't be difficult,' she says smoothly. 'You recently lost your dominant hand, and as a Crawler, that would severely put you at a disadvantage. Any punch you try to throw would be weak, and your defense even more so.'

She says all of this as if stating the weather. I reach out with my power, twining it around the stunned man.

Crawler.

My lips twitch into a smile I can't help.

Not quite a Psychic. Not quite an Ordinary, either.

'And your wife.' Paedyn's cold gaze flicks to the woman beside him, now inching closer to her husband. 'Even being a Healer, she couldn't save your hand. And deep down, you despise her for it.'

The court stares up at their future queen, their eyes wide with disbelief while her own remains on that man's face. 'Am I wrong?'

His mouth opens and closes.

She doesn't hesitate. 'Am. I. Wrong?'

He dips his head, shaking it solemnly as the crowd explodes into a flurry of whispers.

Psychic, indeed. Something else, entirely.

Paedyn's voice cuts through them all, a soft sort of demanding. 'I am no Elite. And that is all you see when looking at me – everything I am not. So let me tell you what I am.' She takes a deep breath, the scar above her heart rising and falling. 'I am power earned, not gifted. I became one of you. Observant enough to pose as a Psychic, strong enough to survive your Trials. Over and over, I have proved myself worthy of your loyalty.

'But I have faced far worse things than my own powerlessness.' She

366

lifts an arm, running fingers over the scar beneath her collarbone. 'I once wore this carving with shame, but now it is proof of my survival. No ability could have withstood what I alone have.' A smile touches her lips. 'A king left his mark upon my heart, and now, I will leave mine across his kingdom.'

I've never seen something so beautiful, so bold, so blatantly right for me, this kingdom, this hope of a united Ilya. And I fear I may forever be in awe of her. Looking at Paedyn Gray, I see a reckless sort of fearlessness, a power that swells from her vibrant soul.

'The Plague runs through my blood, same as yours.' Paedyn's voice is clear, carrying over the silent throne room. 'But it did not bless me with strength. I took it.'

Stepping to the edge of the dais, she lets her gaze wander over the crowd. 'I am Ordinary. Elite. A power of my choosing. And I will be your queen – all that I am and fiercely what I am not.'

Silence.

The court stares at her in shock, in a confusing concoction of fear and respect. And Paedyn Gray stares right back.

'Silver Savior . . .'

The hushed whisper meets my ears, spurring me to step forward. 'Bend the knee to your future queen of Ilya.'

Pae's eyes snap to mine, and for a moment, it's as though we are the only two souls occupying this room. There is that electrifying tether between us, tugging at my heart with every second I'm beheld by her. But the sound of shifting feet has my gaze tearing away and—

And every knee has met marble, every head bowed towards it.

Paedyn swallows at the sight of the court kneeling before her.

I smile.

Kitt grabs his queen's hand.

'To the Silver Savior,' he calls over the crowd. 'In three days' time, she will be your queen of Ilya.'

CHAPTER 52

Paedyn

The rough wall is cool against my bare back.

My dress spills onto the floor, layers of emerald coating the cellar stones beneath. The bottle's neck is strangled between my fingers while sweet wine stains my lips.

'To the Silver Savior.' The liquor has loosened Kitt's lips, allowing a rare moment of praise directed at me.

My head is dizzy, and yet, I still shake it at him. The king resembles nothing of the sort as he sloppily raises his own bottle into the air. His Enforcer grins beside him, happily following his brother's lead while I simply laugh at them.

Frowning, Kitt slides a hand beneath my elbow, pushing it upward. My bottle rises in turn, earning a satisfied look from the king. 'Now,' he tries again, 'to the Silver Savior. The most fearsome Ordinary. And—' Stopping suddenly, he offers a contemplative glance at Kai. 'Is there anything you'd like to add, Brother?'

In response, the Enforcer clinks his bottle against ours. 'And to many more terrifying speeches like that one.'

Kitt hums his approval before fixing his gaze on mine. I clear my throat, feeling the wine cloud my thoughts. 'To a united Ilya.'

I take a swig from my bottle, spurring the brothers to do the same. The cellar is damp, illuminated only by dull, flickering lights. Long shadows fall over the king and his Enforcer, but huddled this close together, I can see them clearly – and can't help but smile.

'How did you know those things?' Kitt inquires. 'About . . . who was it? Commander Orson?'

Kai nods. 'He's a pain in my ass, so I quite enjoyed the show. But, yes,' he continues slyly, 'I would also love to hear how the Little Psychic pulled that off.'

My look is smug. 'And to think you ever doubted my Elite ability.'

'Rightfully so.'

'Less bickering,' Kitt demands with a cough. 'More explaining.'

'Fine.' I sigh, thinking back to the moment I saw the commander a handful of hours ago. 'When he raised his hand towards me, I immediately noticed how red and raw his palm was. There were scrapes and bruises where calluses would form, telling me that he had been using that left hand far more strenuously than normal. And what Elite uses their hands more than any other? Obviously, a Crawler.'

'Yes, *obviously*,' Kitt muses. He seems like his old self with me tonight. Perhaps that is thanks to the alcohol.

'I then realized that his hand was so wounded because he no longer had the use of another,' I continue evenly. 'So, when I glimpsed the stiff glove on his right hand, everything started to click. He was concealing a wooden limb in place of the one he'd lost.'

'And his wife?' It's Kai's skeptical voice that asks this. 'How did you know about her?'

I blow out a breath. 'Honestly, that was even more of a gamble. I glimpsed a tan line on the Crawler's wedding finger, and yet, he wore the ring on the one beside it. The wife wore her own ring proudly while glowing with that sort of health that most Healers do.' I twist the steel ring on my thumb. 'Father taught me how to point out a Healer from nothing but the glow of their skin. He would tell me how most use their abilities on themselves to stay looking as young as possible.'

Clearing my throat, I glance up at the stunned brothers. 'Anyway, I could see how she reached for him, only to be ignored. I figured then that she must have tried to save his hand and was unable to.'

'And he despised her for it,' Kai finishes softly.

'I'm sorry,' Kitt cuts in. 'But how the hell did you know that was all true?'

I shrug, swallowing another mouthful of wine. 'I didn't?'

'It's all a gamble.' Kai shakes his head at me. 'That is a dangerous game, Gray.'

'Oh, I am well aware,' I admit. 'But so much of observing is taking risks. Coming to a logical conclusion. And I have been wrong before, sure, but I've spent a lifetime mastering this Psychic ability.' Frowning, I add, 'Though, I haven't had much need for it over the past few weeks.'

'You could always practice on us, if you like,' the king offers.

Kai laughs, and the sound has my gaze snapping to his as goose bumps tickle my bare arms. 'Yes, why don't you read us, Gray?'

I laugh. 'You think I didn't do that the moment I met you both?'

'Well,' Kitt urges. 'What did you learn?'

'That, you—' I gesture to Kai, '—were a cocky bastard. And, you—' a nod at Kitt, '—were a charming prince.'

The Enforcer smirks wryly. 'And now?'

'You're even more so,' I answer sweetly.

'What about me?'

I force my gaze towards Kitt. 'I'm . . . I'm not sure anymore. You are far more difficult to read.'

The king watches me for a long moment. 'Well, you will have plenty of time to figure me out.'

'Right.' I swallow. 'The wedding is in three days.'

This was as much a surprise to the kingdom as it was to me. I froze on that dais, hand in the king's and heart in my throat.

Three days.

So soon I would lose my freedom, my heart, my love. Kai's eyes flick to mine, and the hurt in his gaze only amplifies the grief in my own. I will be tethered to him for the rest of our lives, but not in the way either of us had hoped.

'Easel insists that we perform a second ceremony on Loot,' Kitt says curtly. 'He thinks it will help unite the people further if the slums are included in our celebrations. It's unusual, for sure, but—'

'I think that's a great idea,' I add quickly.

Kai's nod is distant, but I don't miss the bite in his voice. 'Two weddings. Even better.'

And then he is on his feet.

'Kai—'

He cuts through my plea with curt words of his own. 'There is much for me to do before the ceremony.' Those stormy eyes meet mine. 'I'll give you two some time to figure one another out.'

Before I can argue, he's disappeared up the shadowy stairs.

I loose a sigh into the damp air. 'He has a lot on his mind, I'm sure.'

'You, mostly.'

I whip towards him. 'I'm sorry?'

'There is no need to feign surprise, Paedyn.' Kitt's words are clipped. His face dulls without his brother to brighten it, gaunt cheeks stark in the flickering light. Ruling has already taken its toll on him. 'We both know that Kai's heart belongs to you.'

'And you,' I add sternly. 'He loves you enough to not interfere with your plans.'

Kitt stares down at his bottle, swirling what remains within it. 'Time will tell.'

I clear my throat, unsure what should come out of it. Kai is typically a topic we avoid poking at. So I let us sit in silence for several tense moments before finally scrounging up enough words to fill the gaping space between us. 'I picked roses.' I should clarify. 'For the wedding. I hope that's okay?'

He almost smiles, though I can't decipher what emotion lies beneath it. 'Yes, I would have chosen those myself.'

'Really?'

'My mother seemed to like them,' he says distantly.

I straighten against the stone wall. 'You don't talk about her much.'

'I don't know enough about her,' he counters. 'Only the little that Father deigned to tell me and, now that I am king, what I've found out on my own.'

Disgust coats my tongue. 'He should have never kept you from knowing her.'

'I am the one that killed her, after all.' The king sounds as though a shrug is stuck in his throat. 'Perhaps that was why I was never good enough for him.'

I fight to keep my voice even. 'That wasn't your fault, Kitt. Didn't she die in childbirth?'

He nods. It's a distracted movement. 'She died. I lived. Father hid her memory from me.' His gaze grows distant after the devastating words, fixed intently on the wall behind me.

'Kitt, you—'

'It's getting late.' He runs a hand down his face, thoroughly wiping it of the sadness once settled there. A cough rattles in his chest. 'We should get some rest.'

The king stands. I follow his lead.

'I won't be my father.' He walks stiffly towards the steps while I hang on every word. 'I – *we* – are changing Ilya. And long live the queen who has helped make that happen.'

CHAPTER 53

Kai

I take a seat in the rigid chair, forcing an equally uncomfortable smile.

'Hello, Mother.'

Her tired eyes give me that knowing look. 'Kitt told me. In fact, you just missed him.'

'Oh?' I take in the cot she hasn't left in nearly two months. 'He still comes to see you?'

A sharp cough rings through the empty wing before she manages, 'We've . . . bonded since the passing of his father.' Her hand reaches weakly for mine. 'But don't go changing the subject, Kai. I know.'

Sighing, I run fingers through my disheveled hair. 'Two days.'

'How does the throne room look?'

I almost laugh. 'Like a garden. Blooms have woven dozens of those pink roses along the aisle and around pillars.'

'It is a royal wedding,' she says, voice hoarse. 'They typically are extravagant.' Hurriedly, she adds, 'Well, not mine and the king's, of course.'

'Because Father had to remarry quickly after the death of Kitt's mother,' I nearly recite.

It's like looking into a mirror, her eyes. They study me for a long moment, seemingly in search of something within them. 'I forget that you are so young. Still so much for you to learn.'

The words sound vaguely like a warning I'm meant to heed. But when the queen succumbs to a fit of coughs, all thoughts are overshadowed with concern for her. I raise a glass of water to her lips, tipping her reddened face back until the cool liquid has cleared her throat.

'I'm . . .' She swallows before trying again. 'I'm sorry you have to see me like this.'

'Shh.' It's a stern hushing for a queen. 'I won't be seeing you like this for long, because you'll be healthy before we know it.'

Her smile, once so vibrant, has dulled. 'You can lie to yourself all you like. But don't do it to your dying mother.'

I shake my head, refusing to believe her words and wishing to speak of different ones. 'You're okay with Kitt marrying Paedyn?'

'Kitt has his reasons,' she says simply.

I'm not entirely convinced by this answer.

She coughs. I wince. 'Rest, Mother.'

'So . . .' A ragged heave of her chest interrupts the words. 'So much to learn.'

Heat envelops the kitchen, wafting the scent of freshly seasoned potatoes into the air.

'Jax is practically salivating beside me,' Andy points out with a snort. 'Gail, how much longer? He's scaring me.'

The cook turns, her round face wearing a bright grin. 'Almost there, hun. The turkey needs a bit longer yet.'

Perched on my usual counter, Kitt sits beside me as though we are boys again. Andy and Jax occupy the far ledge while Paedyn leans against an open wall, observing the lot of us.

'Hang in there, J,' Kitt comforts, albeit teasingly. He seems better with our company, his mind clearer of whatever haunts it.

Jax puffs out his chest, long legs dangling over the counter. 'I'm a hungry, growing boy.'

I laugh. 'Oh, you better be done growing.'

'Yeah—' Kitt gives him a sympathetic look, '—we can't have our little brother looking down on us.'

Andy's burgundy eyebrows fly up her forehead. 'If he has to look down on me, he has to look down on you two.'

'I simply won't allow it,' Kitt states.

'Great idea.' Andy dips a finger into the bowl of mashed potatoes beside her, sneaking a taste. 'Let's make that your next decree, yes?'

Gail doesn't bother turning around. 'I saw that, Andrea.'

With wide honey eyes, Andy hisses in our direction, 'How the hell does she do that?!'

Paedyn laughs, drawing my attention to the opposite side of the stove. Every eye rests on her and the stunning smile she wears. 'The pot. Gail can see your reflection in the pot, *Andrea*.'

The cook whirls on Paedyn, though her grin never falters. 'Don't go givin' away my secrets!'

'Why, thank you, Miss Gray,' Andy says sweetly. 'Next, I'll need you to figure out how Jasmyn keeps cheating in cards.'

Paedyn nods. 'Anytime.'

'Oh!' Jax nearly jumps from the counter. 'Can you figure out where all my left socks are going?'

'Yes, quite the conundrum.' My cousin throws an arm around Jax's shoulders. 'But the future queen owes me a favor or two after fixing her door. Twice.'

Her gaze then slides accusingly towards me. I lean casually back on my palms, meeting her stare with a slight smirk. 'I was dead for a day, and it's the door you care about?'

'Oh, please,' she mutters. 'We knew you weren't dead. But, don't worry, I still mourned the presence of my dear cousin.'

'What decree did you have in mind?' Kitt cuts in, addressing Andy. 'Jax must stop growing, was it?'

It's clear he wishes for a change of subject, and thankfully, our cousin is more than happy to oblige. 'I think that is a very kingly declaration.'

'It is not!' Jax protests.

I let them bicker among themselves, if only to relive a piece of our past. Everything is so much simpler in this kitchen, as though the world beyond stops when we step behind these stone walls. A relief of sorts resides on Paedyn's face. Perhaps even she has found a semblance of solace here. With us. This family she never had.

'All right,' Gail bellows. 'Grab a plate now and set the table.'

We do as we are told, filling the rickety table on the far side of the kitchen. Bowls of food promptly descend upon the wood, covering every scratch and stain. After shooing us all into a seat, Gail sits at the head, scooping her feast onto our plates.

As children, this was our sanctuary – sitting around this table, hiding from the pressures of a court we didn't understand. Now, it is even more so.

Jax and Andy argue over which piece of turkey they deserve while Kitt laughs, doing little to mediate between them and their appetites. I rarely see him this happy outside the kitchen or company of family.

Paedyn sits across from me, piling beans onto her plate. She lifts her eyes, giving me a knowing glance that has me grinning.

'So you do like green beans,' I say slyly.

'Well, since you forced me to eat them when I arrived at this castle,' she reminds, 'they have grown on me.'

'Among many other things since you've gotten here.'

'Don't push it, Azer.' She smiles, and I wish for nothing more than to kiss it from her lips. 'I have plenty of knives at my disposal to press to your pretty neck.'

'See—' I point my fork at her, '—if you call me pretty, I hear only the compliment. Not the threat.'

She rolls her eyes, but I'm robbed of whatever lovely response she was ready to give me when a familiar voice cuts through the chaos. 'The king informed me that dinner would be served in the kitchen tonight.' Calum stands in the doorway, his daughter occupying the shadow he casts. 'I hope we are not interrupting.'

'Not at all.' Kitt waves at them to join. 'There is plenty of food. Please help us eat it.'

My gaze flicks to Paedyn, now patting the empty seat beside her. 'Mira. Come sit.'

She does, despite the disinterested look she wears. Calum then takes a seat at the table's end before lifting his glass into the air. 'Let us thank the Plague for this royal union to come.'

Kitt's eyes are fixed on the Mind Reader as he raises his own drink. 'Thank the Plague.'

The mumbled phrase carries its way around the table until every glass is raised. But it is Paedyn alone who does not thank the Plague. Instead, she tips her head, turning back to Calum expectantly.

A smile touches my lips.

She will not thank what has stolen everything from her.

I'm still staring at my queen when Calum declares, 'To saving Ilya.'

CHAPTER 54

Paedyn

It is my last day of freedom.

Though, I haven't had much of that as of late.

I wake. Dress. Ellie helps, because of course I am incapable of doing that alone. Eat. But I must not fill my own plate. Walk the halls – Lenny is at my side. Seek counsel from Calum about helping rule a kingdom. Eat again, but do not touch the serving spoons. Walk the gardens. Silently dread my wedding. Search for Kai wherever I go but force myself to turn away when I find him. Soak in a bath. Eat in bed – I am to be queen, after all.

I am to be queen.

Ellie cleans up my dishes – I tell her not to.

I am to be queen.

Further dread my wedding.

I am to be queen.

'Would you like to wear a dress tonight?'

I blink, startled from my thoughts. Ellie stands at the end of my bed, staring expectantly. 'Hmm?'

'To meet the king.' Her smile is only slightly concerned. 'Do you want to wear a dress?'

'Oh. Right.' I slip out from beneath the covers to plant my feet on the cushioned floor. 'Yes, that's fine.'

With a nod, Ellie hurries over to the armoire in search of a gown. 'Sorry,' I direct distantly at her back. 'Today has been such a blur. I feel like I'm sleepwalking.'

'It's likely just all of the excitement,' she reassures me. 'Tomorrow is a very big day.'

'It certainly is,' I murmur.

'The castle is buzzing.' Ellie pulls a navy dress from the depths of my armoire. 'We rarely get to plan such fun events. They want everything to be perfect for the royal wedding.'

'At least the castle is happy about it.' I sigh, stretching my stiff limbs. 'I doubt the rest of the kingdom is.'

As she ushers me behind the dressing screen, Ellie's soft voice spews comforting words. 'You don't know that. After your third Trial, and the speech at court, the people may be thinking differently.'

'Time will tell, I suppose.' I step into the flowing blue dress before pulling the thick straps over my shoulders. It's not quite formal attire with its linen fabric, but the striking cut of it ensures I won't be overlooked.

I duck my head, offering a sad smile to the floor. Perhaps I did learn a thing or two about fabrics over the years. I only know what it is I'm wearing because Adena trained me to steal exactly what cloth she needed. She would make me sit behind our fort, memorizing the feel of each fabric until I could differentiate them by touch alone.

My breath catches when Ellie pulls at the laces above my waist. Panting, I manage a mutter between my teeth. 'You didn't tell me I'd be wearing a corset.'

Another yank of the laces. 'I'm afraid you will have to get used to it, My Queen.'

I gasp before Ellie finally ties off the torture device and guides me towards the mirror. Navy fabric spills to the middle of my shins, flaring out beneath the cinching corset. Matching tulle peeks out along the square neckline to tickle my lifted breasts. My hair shines above my shoulders, contrasting the dark blue like a full moon against the night sky.

The scar is there, ever on display. So, I stand a little straighter, showcasing it in a way I hope would make the king roll over in his grave.

'You like it, don't you?' Ellie smiles, and it's a sweet sort of savagery. 'Corset and all.'

'Fine,' I drawl. 'I like it.' Tilting my head towards the ceiling, I proclaim, 'You hear that, A? I like the corset. You win.'

Ellie giggles, and I allow myself to do the same. Heading for the door, I'm presented with a pair of flat dark shoes that I happily slip on. 'I'll meet Lenny in the hall,' I say over my shoulder. 'Thank you for your help, El. You can have the rest of the night to yourself.'

'But it's your wedding ni—'

'And you will have much to do tomorrow.' I swing open the door. 'Rest. I insist.'

I catch her begrudging nod before striding into the hallway. It only takes a few steps before Lenny has found his way to my side. 'Evening, Princess.' He winces. 'Queen. Whatever it is I'm supposed to call you.'

'You could try my name?' I offer.

'Hmm.' He considers this mockingly. 'I don't think our relationship is quite there yet.'

After elbowing him in the stomach, I allow myself a smile. We turn down another hall, and right as I think I've escaped the question, he asks, 'You ready for tomorrow?'

That pinch of panic I have been feeling all day grabs hold of my heart once again. 'Not even a little bit.'

'Everything will be fine.' This is slightly reassuring until he adds, 'Hopefully.'

'You really are such a comfort to me.'

'Hey,' he practically laughs. 'You'll be fine, all right? You always are.'

'Right.' I glance over at him. 'Like the cockroach I am.'

Those red curls fall over his brow with a shake of his head. 'That does sound less and less like a compliment, I'm beginning to realize.'

I surprise myself with a weak laugh. 'You don't say?'

As we turn a corner, the throne room's large doors come into sight. I take a deep breath, worrying once again what it is I might see behind them. My determined avoidance of wedding decorations will now come to an end.

We are nearly at the doors when Lenny grabs my arm, pulling me aside. 'Hey, uh, I wanted to ask you something.' He fidgets with the mask on his face, running fingers along the freckles peeking out beneath.

'What is it?' I say, slightly concerned.

'Well, when you're queen—' he gestures to the looming doors, '—which will be very soon, I was, uh, wondering if you would do something for me.'

'Of course.' The answer is quick. 'Anything.'

He takes a deep breath. 'Release me from my post. I'd like to be free of my Imperial duties. See what Dor or Tando has to offer me.'

I blink, stunned. 'What? Is that what you want?'

He scratches the back of his neck. 'I think? Maybe?'

My hand finds his arm, and I'm forced to swallow before saying, 'Well, if that is what you wish. But—' I point a finger in his face, '—we are going to talk about this later. Okay?'

His relief is palpable. 'Of course.'

I smile at him before turning towards the doors. They are open a handful of heartbeats later, and as I step into the throne room, Lenny's voice follows. 'Thank you, P.'

Nodding over my shoulder at him, I nearly stumble into my own wedding.

A plethora of light pink roses twine together to create a path down the center of the room. They climb up the dais, bursting into a bed of petals to pad our feet. Awe parts my lips at the twisted arch of foliage hanging above it all, a lacing of vines, roses, and drooping white flowers.

The pillars are covered in more of the same, their marble lost in the beauty choking them. Thick white ribbons string between the windows and dance alongside the intricate molding. The room itself glows in the setting sunlight, kissing every flower with a drop of warmth.

'It's beautiful, isn't it?'

Thoroughly entranced by the ethereal expanse before me, I startle at Kitt's words. 'Yes, it's . . . it's unlike anything I've ever seen.'

His smile is faint. 'You are happy with it?'

I had nearly forgotten what all this was meant for. At the reminder that he – the king – will be forever tethered to my soul at the end of this flowery path, I feel a bit faint.

'Mm-hmm.' The uncertain sound is all I can manage at the moment.

'Good.'

He steps closer. I fight to keep my feet from running out the doors.

Is he paler than usual? His lips are chapped, gaze bleary above them.

'I know this is a lot. But it will all be over soon.'

His words grow distant. And just like that, the walls are closing in.

I swallow, corset suddenly suffocating. 'I'm okay. Just . . . have a lot on my mind.'

'I know the feeling,' he agrees. 'This is not an easy . . .'

I don't hear the rest of his words. No, my focus is wholly on those doors and the freedom beyond.

'I'm sorry,' I suddenly rasp, cutting off his muffled voice. 'I think I just need some time alone.'

The twinge of confusion on his face has me attempting to soften my demand with a quick 'I will see you tomorrow, though. And everything looks gorgeous.' Running sweaty hands down the front of my dress, I set an impressive pace towards the doors. 'Thank you,' I call over my shoulder. 'Truly.'

And when the king has disappeared from sight, I run towards that yawning, open air beyond the castle. I trip down the stairs after bursting through the doors. Wind claws at my hair as I step into the courtyard, dress rippling all around me.

Legs pumping, I run for the gardens, feeling freer than I likely ever will again. A rolling of dark clouds begins to smother the setting sun, covering it with the promise of rain.

Still, I run. From my fear. From my future. From my now.

The slippers on my feet beat steadily across the garden's spiraling path. Petals brush playfully at my legs while thorns bite at the fabric encasing them.

Thunder rumbles in the distance.

Still, I run.

Past every crumbling statue, every soft flower bed, and every drop of water the fountain spits at me.

My feet meet the plush field of grass beyond and, still, I run – right to that willow tree. Rain splatters my face as I part the curtain of drooping leaves and duck beneath its refuge.

My heart stops at the same moment my feet do.

There he is, stunningly sprawled atop a large blanket.

I'm panting, heart pounding at the sight of its other half. Kai looks up at me, hands resting behind a head of black waves – I nearly fall to my knees before him. He has always been a prince, always a puppet for power or instrument of Death. But just as constant and formidably fierce, he has been my home.

In my search for comfort, it is him I crawl back to. Peace is the place he resides, and passion is a word I only understand when I look into his eyes. He is the freedom I cannot grasp.

We are inevitable. We are tragedy.

'Pae.'

I follow the plea in his voice and stride slowly towards that alluring sound. Rain pelts the canopy of leaves, slipping between the occasional branch to sprinkle my skin. It grows steadily darker beneath the willow's solace, but the shadows refuse to hide his face from me as I lower myself down onto the blanket.

Kai sits up. Reaches for my face. Thinks better of it. 'It's the eve of your wedding. I've hardly seen you in days, so I certainly wasn't expecting your company tonight.'

It's a blatant statement, one he's wrung all emotion from. I swallow, letting my eyes trace up the strong column of his neck. 'I know.' There is a pause. It is filled with a flurry of thoughts and fluttering of my heart. With the intensity of conviction and impulsiveness of longing. But I made my choice the day I stole those coins from him so long ago – passion. Thrill. Something all-consuming.

'Tomorrow is my wedding day,' I finally murmur. 'I think that is why I'm here.'

'Paedyn, I won't watch you marry him.' His voice is little more than a growl. 'I can't bear to lose you.'

'So have me.' The tips of my fingers trace his knuckles. 'One last time.'

He stills beneath my touch, eyes flicking up to meet mine. They are searching, surprised by the boldness of those words. 'I don't want a last time,' he breathes. 'I want a first and forever.'

My hand is steady as it reaches for his face. Kai leans into the touch, pressing his cheek against my palm with an eagerness that makes my heart pound. 'Just pretend with me tonight.' I touch my forehead to his, brush his nose with my own. 'Pretend we have a forever after this.'

The deep breath he draws in is the very sound of restraint. 'But Kitt—'

'Is not my husband yet,' I finish instead of his protest. 'And starting tomorrow, I will give him the rest of my life. But to you, I give my heart. Myself.'

A deep sound hums in the back of his throat. It makes me shiver. Rain splatters his hair, sticking dark waves to his forehead as he greedily wraps an arm around my waist, tugging me closer. I can't help but gasp when his head dips, lips grazing the side of my neck.

My head falls back as he kisses a dizzyingly slow path down the sensitive column of my throat. His lips drag across my flushed skin, mouth mingling with the cool rain that drips from my jaw. My hands wrap around his neck and claw at his hair in a futile attempt to tug him closer.

I need him closer.

Kai's breath is warm against my throat, his voice quivering with restraint. It's a murmur of his lips against my skin. A plea. A demand. 'Tell me what it is you want, Pae.'

My whole body ignites beneath his touch, something unleashing within me at the sound of his desperation. I lean back to cup his face in my hands and whisper a promise onto his lips. 'You,' I breathe. 'You, always.'

His mouth crashes into mine.

I melt against him, letting this wave of wanting consume me. He kisses me deeply, and I have never tasted something so intoxicating.

I'm quickly pulled onto his lap, one hand in my hair and the other gripping my hip like this is a dream he's terrified to wake from.

His lips claim me, more than they ever have before and ever will again. My mouth parts for him, our tongues meeting greedily. Thunder rattles the sky; rain pelts the canopy of leaves. But I am lost beneath this willow, knowing nothing but him and this moment.

My lips move against his, even as I grab the hand he has wrapped around my waist and guide it towards the laces at my back. He pulls away, chest heaving against mine. The corset is gripped tightly in his fist, as though to hold himself back from tearing it off me.

'I promised that if I had you—' his thumb traces the curve of my lips, '—it would only be because you let me.'

'So have me.' It's a desperate demand from lips that already miss his.

'You don't want me to beg for you first?' he drawls.

My fingers catch his chin. 'Is that not what you've done since the moment we met?'

He chuckles, and the sound snakes its way down my spine. The tie at my back grows loose as Kai toys with the knot. 'And it is what I will do until the moment I meet my end.'

A response is ready to roll off my tongue when air suddenly floods into my lungs. With one precise tug, Kai has freed me from the corset's confines. I gasp, staring at him in shock while a breathy laugh surprises me.

He tilts his head, wearing a dimple-framed grin. 'I'm quite good with corsets.'

I laugh again, the sound cut off by the press of my lips against his. My teeth nip at his lip playfully, so unlike that night atop the roof in Dor. He breathes me in, kissing me like I've commanded it of him. I sigh into his mouth, and the sound has something snapping within him.

Swiftly, he flips me from his lap to the blanket beneath us. I lie there, panting up at him. My back is bare beneath the arm he has wrapped around it, the blanket cold and wet.

And nothing has ever felt so perfect.

His hold grows suddenly gentle, and I catch a slight trembling of his fingers when he tucks a strand of hair behind my ear. I am delicate in his arms, devoted in his gaze. 'Are you sure, Pae?'

I smile up at him, having never been so sure of anything in my life. 'Yes,' I answer softly. 'Tonight will be our forever.'

The loosened corset has a strap falling from my shoulder. Holding his gaze, I slip the other off my arm — an invitation. His chest heaves as I reach for his tunic and the trail of buttons down its center. One by one, I pull them free, revealing a sliver of skin beneath.

Kai's gaze glides over my collarbones, the lifting of my chest, the falling of my fingers from his shirt. He holds my stare and shrugs the fabric from his shoulders before casting it aside. Beads of water roll down his bare chest and the swirling tattoo there. Raindrops trail the length of his stomach, following the path of ridged muscle.

I've never found breathing to be such a chore.

My fingers skim over the rough leather belt hanging low on his hips. Slowly, I trace the hilt of a thin dagger, clinging to the side of his pants. My eyes never stray from his as I pull the weapon free and toss it aside.

His smile is dangerous. 'I've never seen you pass up an opportunity to threaten me.'

'Don't sound so disappointed,' I whisper slyly.

That grin grows greedy, but when he lowers himself over me, the movement is gentle. I run my hands across his bare back, feeling every muscle that ripples down the length of it. Then his mouth is on my skin again, kissing the length of my collarbone. The hollow of my throat. Above the heart that aches for him, and the scar his father gave me.

Kai's eyes flick up to mine then, after he's skimmed his mouth over the mangled skin. His lips form a murmured promise. 'No part of you will go unloved.'

I nod, rain splattering my face and rolling down my cheeks like the tears I refuse to shed. I nod, because I believe him. I nod, because there is not an inch of myself that I will not give him.

My confession is breathy, nearly lost on the wind. 'I love you.'

Then I shiver, because I want him so recklessly that it shakes me to my very core.

And tonight, he is mine.

Lighting strikes, illuminating the fierce cut of his body above mine, muscles tense and gray eyes molten with heat.

'I love you,' I say again, and pull his face up towards mine.

He kisses me, and the world falls quiet. 'I love you.'

And when the dress slips from my skin, leaving only the rain to clothe me, he seems to whisper into my very soul. 'You are my forever.'

Shadow and Flame.

Formidably inevitable.

'Forever my undoing.'

CHAPTER 55

Kai

Dawn streams through the willow's branches, slipping between the gaps in her embrace.

I roll groggily onto my side, skin slick with morning dew. My hand reaches for her warmth but finds only cold air. Blinking awake, I sit up rigidly atop the damp blanket, my bare chest exposed to the morning chill.

My frantic gaze lands on her. Then it calms. Evolves into something akin to awe.

Pae sits at the end of the blanket, light dappling her smooth skin. Shadows of willow leaves paint her body, ever shifting in the slight breeze. She is a vision, something so ethereal in this moment that I may just believe there is a God. She is the closest thing to a deity.

Her smile is soft, lingering at the corners with a slight shyness she rarely lets me see. 'Good morning, Prince.'

My pants are damp with dew, but I bend my knees, propping elbows on them loosely. 'Good morning, darling.'

I watch her pull each strap of that damp and dirtied dress over her shoulders. She can feel the gaze I drag over her and kindly lets me continue. Inching closer, Pae turns her bare back to me. 'I know

you're better at unlacing corsets, but I can't walk through the castle with my dress falling off.'

I smile, letting my fingers glide down her spine. This makes her shiver, skin pebbling in a way that has me swallowing. I memorize the feel of her, slow and deliberate, before tying a loose knot at the base of the corset.

'Thank you,' she murmurs, turning to face me.

I shrug. 'I could use the practice when it comes to lacing corsets.'

Paedyn rolls her eyes, even as I pull her against me. 'If it is more practice you need, then how would you like to be the queen's maid?'

My fingers find the tip of her nose and flick it lightly. 'I'm afraid I would be a terrible distraction. Your clothes would rarely make it on.'

'Is that so?'

'Only one way to find out.'

She shakes her head at me before growing suddenly solemn. 'Thank you for last night.'

'I love you, Pae.' I say this sternly, unforgivingly. 'And I am honored to get the chance to.'

She presses her forehead to mine, lips quivering as she whispers, 'There is nothing I regret more than not having the time with you.'

Her hands are cupping my face. Mine are buried in that tousled silver hair I cut for her. And when she kisses me, it's as though she is taking one final breath. Her mouth clings to mine, memorizing a moment we pretend will be our forever. I taste her lament on my lips, a lingering goodbye I'll relive long after she's gone.

Pulling apart before I can feel her trembling hands, she gets to her feet and steps away. 'I need to go.' Another step backward. 'Ellie will want to get me ready soon.'

Now I'm standing, chest tight. 'I can't watch you marry him, Pae.'

'Kai, don't make this harder than it already is. Please.' She swipes angrily at the tears slicking her face. 'You know I have to do this.'

I shake my head. 'You don't.'

'You have your duties,' she breathes. 'And I have mine. We don't choose our fate, remember?'

I stare at her, and the feeling of my heart wrenching in two nearly brings me to my knees. Her feet fumble backward until the willow's branches are tangled around her shoulders. 'But I would choose you every time, if only I could,' she whispers. 'Know that.'

The sun streams through her hair, crowning it with a halo of light. I swallow, throat burning. 'I'll see you after the wedding, My Queen.'

A tear rolls down her cheek at my words.

'As your Enforcer,' I finish weakly.

With one last regretful look, she parts the curtain of leaves and steps into her future.

Without me.

CHAPTER 56

Paedyn

A queen stares back at me in the mirror.

Her gaze is sharp, bright like the Shallows she survived and lined with kohl as dark as the cave she crawled out of. A slight shimmer coats her eyelids, right above the darkened lashes that fan atop powdered cheeks. Her lips are stained a deep red, masking the flush of a stolen kiss. Gone are the tear streaks, buried instead by makeup and facades.

She looks lethal. Formidable.

And, oddly, she doesn't look like a stranger.

Ellie fusses with my hair, tying two braided strands at the back of my head. It's elegant, yet simple, allowing for most of the silver waves to tickle my shoulders. Maids I've never met rush around the room, prepping my dress and every detail. I sit stiffly before the vanity mirror, forcing my thoughts from my imminent future.

Ellie takes a step back to examine her handiwork. 'I think I'm all done.' Her dark eyes shine with pride. 'You look so beautiful.'

I force a smile. 'Thanks to you.'

She presses her lips together in a soft smile before shooing me behind the dressing screen. 'Time to get you in your dress.'

Stripping among several strangers is the least of my concerns at the moment, so I don't hesitate like a different version of myself would have. The cluster of maids crowd around me, helping each leg into the skirt and every inch of fabric to lie precisely as it should.

Stepping out before the mirror, I assess this altered dress. Its sleeveless bodice hugs me closely, draped in a flowery lace. Both delicate and bold, it sprawls over my skin while long lacy ties fall down the low back. Only a few buttons remain at the base of my spine, not so unlike the laces of my corset last night.

Laces that he loosened, replaced with lingering fingers. His skin was on mine, hot and cold and dripping with rain. Dress forgotten, fears abandoned, sins laid bare—

I shake my head, trying to shove thoughts of him away. Ellie's concerned gaze stares back at me in the mirror. 'Are you unhappy with the dress?'

'No,' I say quickly. Then again, to ease her mind. 'No. It's beautiful. I love it.'

One moment, she's sighing in relief, and within the next, she's dismissing each maid. They file out the door, allowing me to take my first deep breath all morning. I turn towards Ellie, pulling her hand into mine. 'Thank you for everything. You've made me look like a queen.'

'I did nothing of the sort.' She shakes her head at me. 'You have always been more powerful than you believe.'

I swallow. Nod slowly. 'Calum will be here soon. He'll walk me to the throne room when it is time.' I toss my head towards the door. 'Now, go enjoy the wedding celebrations.'

Her brows furrow. 'Are you sure?'

'Yes.' I sigh wearily. 'I think I'd like a moment to myself.'

She offers me a dip of her head. 'My Queen.'

As soon as she slips out the door, I eagerly shut it behind her. My forehead falls against the cool wood, eyelids fluttering shut. I stand there for a long while and try to enjoy every last moment before meeting my fate.

It's quiet now. This room. My thoughts. Even the inside of my mind sounds like acceptance.

I am getting married today.

No denial. No frantic urge to flee.

Blowing out a deep breath, I push away from the door at the same moment a knock sounds from the other side. My fingers are wrapped around the handle within the next second, turning it until—

A hand shoots out, halting the door before it can swing open. 'Wait, it's me.'

The king's voice is slightly muffled, separated by the slab of wood. I lean forward, voicing my confusion to the thin crack between us. 'Kitt? What are you doing here?'

'Look,' he mutters quickly, 'I know we are not supposed to see each other. But . . . I wanted to bring you something.'

There is a soft thud when he places said something onto the floor. 'My mother loved her jewelry, or so I've been told. And it's all been collecting dust in this box for years.'

He pauses long enough to have me pressing an ear to the door, waiting for whatever words he's struggling to say. 'So, I was hoping you would wear something of hers.' Rushing on, he adds, 'I obviously don't know what your dress looks like, so I just brought the whole jewelry box for you to look through. I'm not even sure what is in here, really.'

I smile sadly. Nod even when he cannot see it. 'I would be honored, Kitt.'

The relief in his voice is endearing. 'Thank you. I just want a piece of her with me today, you know?'

My gaze falls to the steel ring on my thumb. 'Oh, I know.'

A comfortable silence lingers between us. 'I'll leave this out here, then,' Kitt finally says. 'Just give me about ten seconds to sprint out of sight.'

I laugh. 'Brilliant plan.'

He stands to his feet, the sound of rustling clothes reaching my ears. 'I'll see you soon, Paedyn.'

And then the king is gone.

I stare at the door, my gaze tracing the grooved wood impatiently.

Two, three, four . . .

My fingers fiddle with the lacy flowers cascading down my body.

Seven, eight, nine . . .

I swing the door open.

Kitt is gone, leaving the hall empty, with the exception of several stationed Imperials. At my slippered feet sits a wooden box, embellished with intricate carvings. Its lid is covered in deep swirls that vaguely resemble Ilya's crest, while small drawers line the long length.

Picking it up swiftly, I slip back into my room. Decades of dust dulls the beautiful box, seemingly frozen in time with the exception of several fingerprints. I set it carefully on the bed and am about to follow when I notice that forgotten piece of parchment on my bedside table.

The note has sat there since Kai's unexpected visit and was quickly forgotten at the sight of my dagger in his hands. Now, I abandon every thought for what is etched into that paper. My heart races as I reach for it, unfurling each edge beneath my fingertips.

His handwriting is neat with consideration. These are words he has ached to say. And time slows painfully as I wallow within them.

I know how you refuse to thank the Plague. It is understandable, admirable, even, how valiantly you despise the thing that made your survival so difficult. But I do thank the Plague. I whisper my gratitude for it when you are sound asleep in my arms, when your fingers flick the tip of my nose. In the quiet moments, I thank the Plague for you. If it weren't for the dividing of Ordinaries and Elites so many years ago, I would have never found my way to you. My coins are always at risk in your presence, but no saving of my life would have been necessary that day. No Silencers. No Purging Trials. No stolen moments under the willow. When I thank the Plague, it is not for the power it has gifted me, but for the privilege of you. Nothing makes me stronger than the weakness that is you, Paedyn Gray. And if, in the next lifetime, you choose to steal from me again, I would happily give you my soul if it meant a place beside yours. But until then, I will watch you become another's reason to thank the Plague. You, Pae, are my inevitable.

(I love you.)

I'm paralyzed by every bittersweet sentence. Grief and acceptance mingle between each syllable to leave me staring numbly at the blur of ink. The words flow from a place he rarely lets another into – his heart.

He is a poet. A fool. A man writing his final goodbye.

I shake my head at the note, unable to let him go so easily—

A knock at the door shatters my silent mourning for the boy I cannot have.

'Come in.' The books atop my bedside table tremble as I shove the note into the drawer beneath with the others. Calum slips into the room, blond hair combed back and suit pressed neatly. I manage a weak smile. 'Is it time?'

'It is.' He approaches me slowly. 'Just get through this first ceremony.'

I can't seem to decide if I want to laugh or cry. 'Yes, and then I'll have to endure the second one on Loot.'

Calum's smile is solemn, and it's a familiar sight on his face. 'One thing at a time, Paedyn.'

'Right.' I nod, gather my courage, and stride towards the door. With one last sweeping gaze over my chamber, I say goodbye to the girl who inhabited it. Because today, she becomes a queen. A *wife*.

My eyes land on that bedside table where my heart remains, shoved aside for the future of this kingdom. Then they stutter over that jewelry box atop my bed. I waver in the doorway, reminded how I hadn't picked out a piece of jewelry like Kitt asked.

'Paedyn, we have to go.'

I turn towards Calum and the slight urgency in his voice. With a distant nod, I stride from the room.

There is always the next ceremony.

We walk in silence down the halls. Calum must sense my unease and graciously gives me a moment to myself. Or maybe it's just my panicked thoughts that tell him I am in no mood for conversation. I hide shaking fingers in the many folds of my dress, curling my nails into the lace.

My heart pounds as we near the throne room. Sunlight streams through the many windows surrounding us to decorate this dark day with light. I blow out a breath as we round a corner, as if that alone could calm the swelling terror within me.

Surely, we will not go through with this wedding. Something will happen to stop this insanity. Kai will steal me away, or perhaps his brother will simply come to his senses. But there cannot possibly be a union at the end of that aisle.

I realize, as we halt before the throne room doors, that I never intended to make it to this day. Even when I let Kitt slip that ring on my finger, I hadn't imagined we would ever get the chance to solidify that symbol with vows. I did not even expect to survive the Trials, let alone live to see my wedding day.

And after everything I have faced, this may be the most terrifying of them all.

I don't get the chance to run from my future before the doors are swinging open.

Horrified, I stand there, watching my wedding slowly sprawl before me. My view of the throne room grows wider, displaying dozens of flowers with every inch. The mass of people only grows, all standing on either side of that rose-framed aisle. And when the doors groan to a halt, every eye turns to me.

Feet shuffle; heads turn. My body trembles; heart thrashes against my chest.

The look I'm wearing is alarming enough to have hushed whispers wafting over the crowd. I don't hear them – I don't hear anything past the blood pounding in my ears. My gaze lifts from the flowered aisle, dragging up slowly to meet the king's.

He stands atop the dais, a Scholar behind him. A crown is perched atop a pedestal, its silver points elegantly lethal. Long emerald gems are fastened around it, only emphasizing the delicacy that deadly things often have.

I blink at it vaguely before recognition dawns on me. This is Queen Mareena's crown – the trophy of my first Trial. It has been restored, impressively, to the ethereal state it likely once was. A lump forms in my throat at the thought of placing it on my head after robbing the first queen's body of it.

The king's own golden crown sits among his hair, paired with the deep green suit he wears beneath. Kitt's eyes gleam, bright beneath the canopy of drooping flowers. Though the dark smudges surrounding them have been expertly concealed, the ashen color of his skin is stark within the swarm of color.

He looks as lost as I feel.

His hands fidget with the cuffs of his sleeves, twisting the buttons there incessantly.

He doesn't want this either.

In another life, I might have offered him a comforting smile. Might have walked down this aisle on my father's arm. But this life is harsh, and cruel, and has barely allowed me to live it.

And worst of all, I do not love him.

The thought is jolting, not because it shocks me, but because I have finally allowed myself not to want this. So many weeks have been spent justifying this union – for the kingdom, the Ordinaries, the hope of a better future. But what of my own? I do not love this man. No, it is his brother I have given my heart to.

Calum urges me forward with his arm twined around mine. I take my first step. Lips move around me – I don't hear what they say. Kitt is staring at me with a distant look that smothers the handsome features of his face.

I walk stiffly to that altar, every step more damning than the last. Calum is an anchor at my side, helping to guide me to this fate. This is duty, I remind myself. This is hope for the future and forgiveness of the past. This is sacrifice.

One foot in front of the other.

My chest heaves.

I do not want this.

Kitt reaches for my hand.

I do not love him.

I hesitate. My heart stutters, begging me to damn sacrifice and choose selfishness. Choose Kai. Choose love.

But I'm not sure I know how to choose myself anymore. Or perhaps I never have. So I take the king's arm, letting him guide me onto the dais. His skin is worryingly warm.

Roses surround us — a large crown of them above our heads and petals beneath our feet. I turn to face the king before allowing him to pull my slick palms into his own. We stare at each other, unsurety shrouding each of our faces. My heart pounds beneath the displayed scar etched into flushed skin, the sound echoing in my ears. I feel suddenly hollow, as though I have no control over my limbs, my life.

The Scholar begins speaking between us. I don't want to hear his damning words, but they pelt me just the same.

'. . . gather here today to join Kitt Azer, king and savior of Ilya, and the lady Paedyn Gray in holy matrimony. Bear witness to their union and . . .'

My ears begin to ring, blotting out the bellowed decree. I stare pointedly at Kitt for any sign of regret or change of heart. But, terrifyingly, he looks rather content to stitch his soul to mine. That only has my gaze flicking frantically over the crowd in the hopes of finding some way out of this.

We can't possibly go through with this.

The Scholar slips a ring onto Kitt's left hand.

Right?

'Do you, Kitt Azer, take Paedyn Gray to be your wife and queen?'

My eyes crash into the green ones before me. I think I've stopped breathing. Kitt stares at me long enough to have hope sparking in my tightening chest. But the words that fall from his lips do not mirror that hesitance. 'I do.'

I feel dizzy. The Scholar turns his attention to me.

'Do you, Paedyn Gray, take Kitt Azer to be your husband and king?'

My stomach flips, heart hanging on to the thread of freedom I have left. I am a single 'I do' away from signing my soul with another's name. One that is not Kai Azer, Enforcer, my cocky bastard.

The throne room is smothered in silence as I scan the expectant crowd. I look for him in every face, every gap between finely dressed bodies. Jax, Andy, Calum, Mira, Gail – strangers. Kai is nowhere to be found, just as he promised.

'Paedyn?' The Scholar raises his bushy brows at me.

Still, I wait for something to save me from this moment. I teeter before the rest of my life and beg for someone to catch me before I fall. My dress grows too tight as hope flees from my chest, stealing all the air with it.

It takes me a long moment to realize that nothing and no one will ever save me. Those who have in the past are dead. The one who would in this present is likely under a willow tree, already mourning me. So I face my fate alone and look it in the eyes.

Kitt shifts slightly, his gaze urging me to speak what I must.

Stronger than I feel and more damning than I let on, I utter, 'I do.'

'Then I pronounce you husband and wife.'

The king nods slightly. I nod back as his queen.

'You may kiss the bride and seal this union.'

My mouth dries. I had forgotten about that bit.

Kitt, ever kingly and calm, leans in to press his lips to mine. It is soft, a bearing of his soul despite never doing so with words. This kiss tastes like the sweet end of an apology, or the lingering of a farewell. And when he pulls away, I'm left staring into the face of my husband.

I expel the panic from my being and swallow the realization of what I've done.

We turn towards the court, hand in hand. The Scholar lifts that lethal crown from its pedestal and lifts it high above my head. Bending my knees, I force the constant tremble from my limbs.

'People of Ilya, I present unto you, Paedyn Azer, your undoubted queen consort.' The Scholar's decree rings through the throne room. 'And your king, Kitt Azer, savior of Ilya. May their union bring prosperity to our kingdom and greatness to our histories.'

The court claps, forcing smiles onto begrudging faces. We step from the dais a married couple and walk down the aisle as royals. I focus only on making it beyond those open doors as we parade through the center of this court.

My gaze is fixed distantly on the sliver of freedom ahead when I see him.

Time slows. My heart splinters.

Kai stands in the doorway, his chest heaving as though he has sprinted past his best judgment and found himself here. A broken sort of acknowledgment of my fate fills his face. I see the exact moment he realizes he is too late.

His gray eyes flick between the two of us in disbelief. Even the Enforcer did not believe I would go through with it, and his hurt cuts me deep.

I failed him. I failed us.

Still, he musters a small smile.

It is the look of letting someone go.

And it tears me to pieces.

He was going to save me.

CHAPTER 57

Kai

Shadows skitter over my skin, as if summoned by the darkness brewing within me.

Rough bark digs into my spine, kneading my back with gnarled fingers. I lean my head against the willow's sturdy trunk, watching warmth filter through the veil of branches. The long, drooping leaves cast shifting shadows across my skin as they sway in the breeze, dappling me in both light and dark.

I haven't left the willow's comforting embrace since Paedyn left mine. My gaze lifts to the sun above, winking at me through the shifting umbrella of leaves. The wedding has likely started already, but I'm rooted to the spot like this tree beside me.

Tears sting my tired eyes. I can't remember the last time I truly cried.

Aside from my reunion with Paedyn after her third Trial, there was the day Ava died.

I look down at the patch of soft grass beside me.

Father carried out our training as if nothing had happened, continuing to carve open my skin and push perfected power from my body. I could do nothing but numb every inch of myself, force

a mask atop my grief. Every tear was hidden until I returned to my room, bloody and shaking.

Then there was the night I took my first life.

At the time, I hadn't even known the extent of what the king made me do. But I wept for Paedyn's father all the same. I wept for the piece of me that died alongside him.

That was the first night I drove a sword into the posts of my bed. Over and over again.

Wood splintered beneath my blade, chunks of it flying in every direction. Grief drove me to find something more potent within myself, something to smother the hurt – fear. I would become a monster, a puppet of death, if it meant I felt nothing else.

Then I met her.

Paedyn rivaled me, the stars, the very sea with her gaze. She had me in the palm of her hand the moment she grabbed mine in that alley. And for the first time since I was a boy, fear gripped my heart. Right then and there, I knew she would be my undoing.

We are inevitable, the Silver Savior and me. Our pasts are as irrevocably intertwined as our futures now will be. But it is not love that has tied our souls together. It is duty.

My vision grows blurry behind the foreign feel of tears. I lay a hand on that soft grass, shutting my eyes against this wave of emotion. 'I don't know what to do, A,' I whisper.

She says nothing. She never does.

A tear rolls down my cheek. 'I'm tired.'

Tired of the loyalty that has taken everything I care about. Tired of standing by while happiness finds its home elsewhere. But most of all, I am tired of losing her.

Then there is now – when I cry for the future I so badly wish to live with her. It's a silent stream of tears that I try my best not to acknowledge. I take a shuddering breath before swiping at them roughly.

'*Don't let her be your weakness.*'

Mother's warning came far too late. She is not only my weakness – she is my everything.

My voice is weak. 'I can't lose her too, A.'

I comb a hand through my unruly hair, raking fallen leaves from the strands. The shadows wave their goodbye as I stand to my feet and stretch stiff limbs. 'I have to do something.'

My gaze falls to the rumpled blanket beneath me, a mere remnant of last night. The cool breeze in her hair, gasp in her throat, warmth in her touch. Now it is a memory that will haunt me.

I stride from beneath the drooping branches, evading the willow's reaching fingers.

My skin smells of her. My heart aches for her. The Enforcer bows to her.

I'm off to find my queen.

CHAPTER 58

Paedyn

The crown is just as heavy as I remember it being.

Only now, it carries far more weight with a queen under it.

Kitt walks beside me, the sound of a dismissing court echoing in the distance. We head for my room in a rather dull silence, soaking in this sliver of peace before our second ceremony. The feasts and dancing in celebration of our union won't begin until tomorrow, and I wish for nothing more than to sleep this day away.

The thought makes my ears burn. I doubt I'm intended to sleep alone tonight.

'You did well,' Kitt finally offers into the silence.

My heels continue hitting the ground with a rhythmic click. 'Thank you.'

'Now, as soon as you're changed and ready, we will head out to the coaches.'

The elephant in the room stomps beside us as we continue to pretend as though we are not bound together for life. I whirl on him suddenly. 'Did you want this? Despite our marriage being for Ilya, did you want this?'

My question makes him pause. 'I know how Kai feels about you.

So, no, I didn't want to do this.'

'But you married me anyway.'

'And I would do so much worse for him,' he says quickly.

I swallow. Despite everything, I understand. Our marriage is for Kai as much as it is for Ilya. The Enforcer will never have to take the life of another Ordinary. He will no longer be controlled by guilt or shame. And above all, this kingdom will remain standing.

I can manage little more than a nod.

Reaching my door, I place a hand on the knob. 'I lost track of time earlier, but I'll pick something out from your mother's jewelry box now.'

'Thank you—' A raspy cough cuts the sentiment short.

'Are you—' I spot something that looks suspiciously like blood splatter his handkerchief, '—all right?'

He wipes his mouth. 'I'm fine.'

'Kitt, I think you're sick—'

'I said I'm fine, Paedyn,' he snaps, eyes suddenly wild.

I take a bewildered step back and watch the king compose himself. He clears his raw throat. Shifts into something deceivingly docile. 'Thank you for your concern.'

I nod. My voice is weak. 'I'll meet you in the courtyard.'

The king is striding down the hall before I slip into my room.

I lean against the door and shut my eyes, shoving aside the tears I desperately wish to cry. My heart aches at the vivid memory of Kai standing behind those doors with a look of betrayal seeping onto his features. Then he slipped into the crowd before my trembling lips could form an apology.

I pull the crown from my head, hardly noticing when the jagged points bite into my palm. The sharp emeralds reflect my weary face back at me like a glimpse into my future. I see a life of torture beside the man I love. My husband sits on the throne, but he is not who holds my heart. No, that man stands to my left, never looking in my direction. The mask he wears has choked all emotion from his face, and without me to pull it free, he becomes a shell of the man he once was.

A gnawing numbness has begun its slow trickle over me. Ellie helps pull the extravagant wedding dress from my body, each word a congratulations, each turn of her lips a smile. I'm quickly swaddled in more white fabric, this dress lighter and softer than the last. The swishing skirt billows out from my waist and flows to just above my bare ankles. Its bodice is relatively simple, though embroidered with a tangle of beaded vines. Thin straps hug my shoulders, and white heels clutch my feet.

'You don't want to look *too* dressed up on Loot,' Ellie reassures while toying with my hair. She says this like I didn't already know. Showing up to the poverty-stricken slums in a gown expensive enough to feed several of them for weeks would hardly make the best impression.

She steps away to examine me. 'But you still look like a very elegant bride.'

'Thank you, Ellie.' I clear my tightening throat. 'That will be all. I'd like a moment alone.'

Nodding her understanding, Ellie slips from the room. I sigh into the silence and wish I could hide behind these four walls indefinitely. More out of comfort than necessity, I strap my dagger to a thigh beneath the dress. This makes me feel better, having a piece of my father with me on my wedding day.

The jewelry box taunts me until I finally pad over to it. Sitting carefully atop the bed, I adjust the dress around me and tip open the lid. I stare into its velvet-encased depths, swallowing my gasp at the sight of so many glimmering jewels. They sit against the green fabric, so perfectly intact. Diamonds, sapphires, and an impressive number of emeralds wink up at me. I reach for a particularly blinding necklace before thinking better of it.

Queen Iris certainly had a taste for finery.

I have never seen such wealth. I'm not even sure how to hold it.

These jewels alone could feed all of Loot.

I'm suddenly snapping the lid shut, nauseated by the mere sight of something so fine. There was once a time when I would have done unspeakable things to steal even a single gem. Now, I get to wear them around my neck like a trophy.

Or a pretty noose.

I shove the thought away and pull open one of the small drawers. It is stuffed with shiny rings, all bands of shimmering gold and silver. Beside it is a drawer littered with bracelets. But it's the one beneath that has me pausing.

No jewelry. No gems. Only the brittle head of a rose.

I run a gentle finger over the dried petals, watching them crumble beneath my touch. My breath catches in surprise. This flower is older than I am.

A folded piece of parchment lies beneath its severed stem. Carefully, I slip it from the drawer's clutches, though the wood clings fiercely to it. Time has aged the note, creasing the edges and yellowing the paper. I unfold it slowly to reveal a hastily written message in looping handwriting.

Meet me in the garden at midnight. Wear a cloak – you are too beautiful to be seen with me. My heart is yours, always.

I stare blankly at the note.

This was not meant for my eyes. I feel as though I've intruded on an intimate moment that was supposed to remain forever preserved within this box. And yet, I can't seem to tear my gaze from it.

This was not the king she was meeting. No, the queen would not sneak about the castle with her own husband.

She had a lover.

I set the paper down with a sigh. It feels odd to pluck a piece of one's life from belongings of the dead. To accuse the late queen of being unfaithful feels stranger still. And yet, staring down at the note, something nags at me distantly.

I dismiss the feeling, deciding instead to explore the other drawers. Hair clips in one, more rings in the other. My fingers tug at the last compartment, fighting to free the shallow drawer. With a groan, it gives up, sliding out to unveil a stack of crumpled notes.

It's that same smudged handwriting that stains each piece of parchment. I skim through the short letters, each one more cryptic than the last.

Time. Place. *I love you, always.*

My fingers fumble blindly around the drawer, searching for any forgotten pieces of the past. A creased sheet of parchment lives in the corner of the compartment, contorted against the wood for what has likely been years. I pry it out before forcing deep ridges from the yellowing paper, flattening it against my dress-draped knee. Inspecting further, I flip it over and—

I've never looked into the face of a ghost, but I imagine this is what it would feel like.

My whole body goes numb as the photograph slips from between my fingers. Something grips my very soul, certain and crushing. It's familiarity, I realize. It's recognition of yourself within another.

I stare at the woman. She stares up at me.

Her bright blue eyes are nearly as vibrant as the smile she wears. There's a certain warmth in her gaze, in the rosiness of her cheeks. Light blonde hair cascades over her shoulders, falling in loose waves. And her nose . . .

I take a shuddering breath before lifting the photograph in front of my face.

Her nose is dusted with freckles.

I stare at the queen. She stares up at one.

Blood claims blood. And when I look at Iris Moyra, the late and beloved queen of Ilya, I see a shade of her coursing through my veins. And blood never forgets.

The parchment flutters to the bed as I press a steadying hand to my thumping heart.

This is absurdity.

That is what I tell myself, over and over again. This is a coincidence, a picture that shares a slight resemblance.

I am no royal. I am no daughter of a queen.

The door creaks open, and I hardly hear the footsteps that follow. I'm still studying the photo when a figure strides into view, stopping before my bed. My gaze lifts begrudgingly from Iris's face to land on Calum.

He stands there, stoic as always. But I watch the color drain from his face.

Time seems to stall – Calum's gaze on the pile of notes, mine on the bouquet of flowers he holds.

Pink roses.

It's my bouquet. I realize now that it had been forgotten after rushing to the throne room. He must have been bringing it to me. Blinking, I lower my gaze to the crumbling flower beside me, plucked years before this moment.

There is that something tugging incessantly at the corner of my subconscious once again. Like the intuition that senses a fight before the first punch is thrown. Or the moment before I've fit every observation together, molding the story into place with my mind. Or how a memory resurfaces at the exact moment I need to pick it apart. Because nothing goes unnoticed.

'I must rush off to a meeting with Kitt, but I will be sure to tell him how beautiful you look in this wedding dress.'

Calum was standing mere steps away from where he is now when the compliment slid from his tongue. But it's the following string of words that I focus on. The damning ones that echo through my mind.

'The roses from my garden will look lovely with it.'

I had felt that distant nagging then, that prick of intuition, and chose to ignore it. My trust in Calum had built a wall around my heart, yet all it took was a rose to have it crumbling.

Everything is happening so fast, like the inevitable trip before a fall. My thoughts blur, all bleeding into one another. The past comes racing towards my current present, overlapping to create one clear conclusion.

I glance down at the decaying flower.

Ellie's words suddenly surface from the depths of my mind.

'There is a private rose garden here on the grounds. Pretty pink ones, I believe.'

My head swims.

That rose garden has been here for decades.

Each breath grows shallower.

A Fatal. A Resistance leader. A man who is always in the right place at the right time.

A flood of unanswered questions pours into my reeling mind, making me dizzy. Confusion creeps into every thought, every moment spent with Calum. From his Resistance speech at the Bowl to the very ring on my finger.

I claw at my mind, prying apart strands of my past. A wave of realizations crashes over me in a series of disconnected thoughts.

The notes.

The handwriting.

The Purging Trials.

My mind is a muddled melody of rhymes, all scrolled in that loopy penmanship. One from a scroll in the Whispers. One at the base of Plummet, and one read at its peak.

My heart pounds as pieces of this puzzle begin falling into place.

When I fought the king, his words meant nothing. Until now.

'. . . *a friend told me of his intentions and this* Resistance *he was a part of.*'

A friend.

Someone close to my father, and the king.

Someone loyal to the latter.

Blooms did not spring flowers from the earth for Calum overnight. No, he has been tending to them for years.

Because he is the king's Mind Reader.

It's as though the world has tilted beneath me.

But that is not all. That is only the beginning.

I don't look up at him. It's the queen who holds my gaze now.

That is when everything clicks.

Father – my *real* father – taught me to trust my instincts. Never falter. Never leave anything unnoticed. It's as though I'm back on Loot, facing an Imperial who has ordered me to demonstrate my Psychic ability. So when I speak, the words are sure, unshadowed by doubt.

Even a Mind Reader can be read.

'You know—' I stand slowly, the dress swishing around my ankles, '—I meant to thank you again for giving me those books. They kept me occupied on the boat.'

I pick up one of the faded spines on my bedside table, flipping open the front cover. 'For Paedyn,' I read aloud. The rose sketched above the words makes me smile faintly.

Calum's gaze has yet to meet mine.

I set the book among the littered notes, lining up the identical handwriting. 'I would add the scroll from my Purging Trials, but I didn't get the chance to keep one as a souvenir.'

I pick up the photograph next, flapping it between my fingers. 'Do you still think I look like my mother?'

Silence.

'I thought it was odd when you mentioned that I looked like her from the pictures you had seen,' I say slowly. 'See, we didn't have any photos of my father's wife, Alice.' My feet tread a path across the carpet, the dress's hem lapping at my ankles. 'I mean, a Transfer is needed to impress a Sight's memory onto the page, and it all becomes far more expensive than it's worth.'

I wave my hands, dismissing the explanation. Then my feet falter, changing course until I'm standing right before him. I lift the photograph between us, forcing those blue eyes onto Iris's.

'. . . *that is not the only royal you have killed.*'

Calum's words ring in my mind, another piece of the puzzle that is my past.

'But Alice was not the mother you were talking about,' I breathe. 'It was the queen you loved. The one who died giving birth to me.'

I'm shaking, every inch of my body. The adrenaline coursing through my veins has my heart hammering against a tightening chest, blood pounding in my ears. The gravity of this truth I have uncovered threatens to bring me to my knees.

'You were Iris's lover,' I pant, my eyes wild. 'And the king's Mind Reader, feeding him information about the Resistance the entire time. That is why he was always one step ahead.'

Knees trembling, I stand my ground as Calum's gaze lifts to mine. It's agonizingly slow, this moment in which I stand between the past and the present.

'So I'll ask you again,' I say, deceptively calm. 'Do I look like my mother?'

When his blue eyes finally meet mine – the *queen's* – I watch him pluck every thought from my head. He reads the mistrust, mulling it over carefully. I stare up at the Fatal, unsurprised when he finally says, 'And who else do you resemble?'

This is not the first game I have been forced to play.

And it will not be the first I lose.

So when I send the words to the forefront of my mind, I mirror the shadow of a smile that lifts his lips.

Hello, Father.

CHAPTER 59

Paedun

Father.

The title tastes bitter for any man other than the one who raised me. I stare up at Calum, letting him read every bit of mistrust in my mind. This man was once like a father to me, and now that I've discovered he has been precisely that all along, hurt rams into me.

'This is more upsetting to you than I thought it would be,' he observes simply.

'So I'm right,' I breathe. Then a wave of anger rolls over me, smothering the fleeting triumph that accompanies unraveling a lifetime of lies. 'You left me on a doorstep!' I throw my hands into the air. 'I was a baby! And all so the king wouldn't find out I wasn't his child?'

Calum's eyes grow wild. It is as though something has snapped within him. Like every solemn expression and kind word was an act he despised. And now that I know who he truly is, there is no use for deceit. 'The king did think you were his child – and he didn't want you.'

I stumble back a step, my lips parting slightly.

'After you *killed* Queen Iris,' he bites, 'the king handed you off to a Silencer. That is when he discovered that an Ordinary – an *Ordinary* – killed one of the rarest Elites known to Ilya.'

The room spins around me as I comb through my memory. Recalling every book of history Father set before me, I finally find her power hiding in the corner of my mind. She was—

'A Soul.' Calum utters the words he'd read from my mind. 'That's right. The ability to sense another's emotions and alter them, take them upon herself. And her power paired with mine – a Fatal's?' He laughs, and it is a crazed sound. 'You were supposed to be formidable. But you are nothing.'

He spits out the words, each one coated with years of rage. 'You were an embarrassment to the king, one he told me to take care of. And he spent his life covering up the Ordinary he thought was his. But you were mine, and Iris died—' he runs a hand over his hair, '—all for you to be nothing! A worthless Ordinary!'

The scar burns above my heart.

O.

The king thought I was his daughter.

Two Elites have never made an Ordinary. Yet, here I stand, powerless. The product of strength with none to show for it. And maybe, for the first time, that makes me extraordinary.

Tears blur my vision, anger stinging my eyes. I flex my fingers in the soft skirt of my dress, feeling the comforting outline of my dagger beneath the layers of fabric.

'So that is why you hate me?' I choke out. 'Because the woman you loved died giving birth to me?'

'Because it should have been you,' he growls. 'It should have been you that died that day, not the queen who bled out for an Ordinary.' His head shakes, and the wild look in his eyes has me stepping back. 'Before you showed up at the castle and sat beside Edric during that first dinner, I thought you were dead. I may not have been able to kill you like the king had wished eighteen years ago, but I hoped you met your end in the slums.'

'But I didn't,' I breathe. 'And he still kept me alive.'

After that third Trial, standing in the pouring rain outside the

Bowl, I asked the king why he hadn't killed me sooner. That was right before his sword sliced open my forearm.

'*Because I needed you alive.*'

'He did,' Calum says in response to my memory. 'I convinced him that the Resistance needed you to find the tunnel into the Bowl, and if the Trials didn't kill you, then he could after.' He lifts a shaking finger at me. 'But you have her eyes. He recognized you the moment you sat down at that table.'

I fight to keep my voice steady. 'How did you know I would find the tunnel?'

His smile is cruelly sympathetic. I bare my teeth right back.

He is not going to tell me.

Every unanswered question begins to resurface until they are practically bubbling out of me. I spit one out, hoping he will deign to answer it. 'I thought the queen died giving birth to Kitt?'

'The whole kingdom thought so.' His eyes gleam, boring into mine. 'The king kept Iris locked away — safe from any threats. So much so that when she became pregnant with you, the kingdom knew nothing of the queen or her child. And after the shame you brought him upon your birth, he sealed the true records away and told the kingdom she had passed when Kitt was born.'

There is a long pause in which I try to swallow the sudden realization.

'And my father . . .' I choke on the words. 'You told the king about him. You are the reason he is dead. Because you found out about the Resistance.'

'He was helping in the castle during fever season,' he says simply. 'We passed in the hall, and I read his mind. Learned of his plans for a Resistance. But that was not what killed Adam in the end.'

I blink at him. 'What are you talking about?'

That moment in the basement of my childhood home, surrounded by Resistance members, comes racing back. Calum had shown a shred of confusion when I assumed my father's death was due to his association with the Resistance.

'No, Edric kept him alive to grow his Resistance,' Calum was saying. 'He was content to use him until Adam discovered something he shouldn't have. Something for the kings alone.'

'What are you talking about?' I urge again through gritted teeth.

Calum's responding silence has a frustrated sound crawling up my throat.

'That is why you were asking about my father's journals,' I pant. 'You wanted to know if he wrote that secret something down.'

My head spins. I shove this new piece of confusing information beside the dozens still sprawled across my mind. But the truth of my father's death didn't seem to interfere with Edric Azer's obsession with the Resistance.

I'm suddenly flung into another memory, one where I am bloody and broken and barely surviving against the king. His boot is crushing my chest as I stare up at him, rain pelting my stinging face. Mud squelches beneath my back. He watches me struggle to wriggle free.

'I've planned for this day a long time, waiting until I could rid myself of this Resistance.'

'He had,' Calum murmurs, seeing the vivid picture I've painted in my mind.

My gaze is distant, clouded with realization. 'The king didn't want to wipe out the Resistance when he first found out,' I mutter. 'He wanted it to grow, wanted to gather all the Ordinaries in one place.' My gaze flicks to Calum's while my mind wanders to that battle at the Bowl. 'And you were his spy.'

Calum confirms with a pitiless nod of his head. 'But your *father* needed to be taken care of before we had collected enough Ordinaries for the slaughter. So I took his place as the Resistance's leader.'

Slaughter.

My stomach heaves.

The Pit was littered with bodies, and the memory of that bloody stretch of sand has my mouth drying. 'It was all a ploy.' My chest heaves, anger swelling within it. 'Everything. You don't care about the Ordinaries. You never have. Not after one killed your lover.' I take another step back, bumping into the bedside table behind. 'From that very first night in my home, you were playing me.'

'Your father would be proud.'

That is what Calum had said to me after I pledged myself to the

Resistance's cause. And proud he was, having finally caught me. A ghost of the woman he loved in the body of a worthless Ordinary he hated.

'And I am.' Calum laces those long fingers behind his back. 'Very proud of the puppet you became for me.'

Get out of my head.

Disgust coats my voice. 'What game are you playing now?'

I let him hold my gaze for a long moment. 'We need to get you to your next wedding ceremony.'

'Why?' I retort. 'Why would you want an Ordinary on the throne?'

'I have great plans for you, Paedyn.' He's suddenly striding towards me. 'I will ensure the Scholars write your name into every history book.'

That intuition begins a slow tug within me once again, and this time, I do not ignore it. These past several weeks play out in my mind, like a constant stream of memory. I think of the moments spent with Calum, yes, but more importantly, the ones without. He was always in the background, always whispering into someone's ear.

I blink at the floor before beginning to spew my thoughts. 'You told King Edric not to kill me when I showed up at the castle, and he didn't. You told Kitt to marry me, and he did.' The veiled accusations fall from my lips in a rushed murmur. 'He trusted you so easily. You convinced him to let me compete in these Trials, advised him to start training his troops. And he does it all.'

Calum's eyes narrow, but he says nothing.

I almost laugh. 'You say the Blooms grew your rose garden, and in that moment, I believed you. What you demand, others do. You had the entire Resistance eating out of your palm – my *father* included. You're not just a Mind Reader, are you?' I take a slow step towards him. 'You are a Dual. That is why you hate me so much. I still managed to be Ordinary, even when you aren't just one Fatal – you're two.'

Still, Calum says nothing.

Having figured it all out, I smile. 'You're a Mind Reader, and a Controller.'

When he lunges for me, I send an elbow arcing towards his temple.

I'm surprised when he jumps back, swiftly avoiding the hit. My dress ripples around me as I dart forward to throw a right hook at his jaw.

Again, he evades me.

I sink onto the balls of my feet, blood pounding in my ears.

Jab.

Right hook.

Cross.

Nothing.

Nothing is hitting him.

I let out a frustrated cry that he finds humorous. 'Don't hurt yourself, Paedyn. I know your every move.'

Of course he does.

Get. Out. Of. My. Head.

Calum chuckles again while dodging the next fist I send flying towards his face. My blood boils, staining my cheeks with heat. But my mind is clear, and I know he reads the thought that pounds through it.

There is no way in hell I am leaving this room with him.

He reads my only plan, blue eyes locked on mine and lips twitching into a smile.

I pause.

Maybe inside my head is exactly where he should be.

I take a slow step towards him.

You're the failure. Not me.

Calum feigns boredom.

'Not only were you unable to kill an Ordinary baby, but you left me on Adam Gray's doorstep so you could keep an eye on your daughter.' His eyes narrow as I advance slowly. 'I'm right, aren't I? A part of you wanted to watch me grow up. Every meeting, every conversation with my father, you were learning about *me*.'

I jab a finger towards the pile of books beside the bed. 'You brought those to the house when I was a child, didn't you? Even wrote my name in the covers. Because you cared for *me*—'

'Enough,' Calum drawls.

All your power, and you couldn't even make an Elite.

'Pathetic.' I spit the word aloud, watching it hit him like a blow.

418

You blame me for Iris's death, because you couldn't do anything to save her.

One foot in front of the other.

I bet you couldn't even hold her hand, couldn't even say goodbye, with the king there.

My thoughts are sharp, cutting through the cool facade he wears with ease.

'Stop it,' he mumbles.

She was never yours, Calum.

Rage has his body trembling. 'Stop.'

But I am. I will forever be your greatest failure.

I'm close enough now to see the tears glossing his gaze.

Do I look like her, Father? Do I haunt you?

Calum's hands clamp atop his ears. 'Enough!'

Look. At. Me.

His eyes squeeze shut, and that is when I strike.

My palms meet plush carpet as I drop to the floor, sweeping my leg out. I hear the sound of tearing fabric before Calum topples to the floor, having lost his balance. Fumbling with the dress's draping layers, I find my dagger beneath and pull it from the sheath.

My chest heaves. Hovering over him, I bring the tip of my blade to his neck. He stares up at me – betrayer, liar, killer of Ordinaries.

Father.

That is the most damning title of them all. And I don't even know the half of what he's done.

A thin line of blood stains the dagger's point.

Do it. Kill him.

'That's right,' he whispers beneath me. 'Do it.'

I bare my teeth.

He has used every person I care about.

'Are you going to kill me or not, Daughter?'

A low growl spills from my throat, driven by hurt and hate. My body trembles.

And then I yank the blade away.

His smile is cold. 'You're so weak—'

The swirling handle of my dagger – my real father's dagger – connects with Calum's temple, cutting off his words.

He lies there, unconscious beside a kneeling bride.

Sweat sticks to my brow, and I swipe at it numbly. The weapon slips from my hand to thud softly against the carpet. My legs shake as I pull them beneath me and force myself off the floor. Fabric flows down my legs, unfurling to my feet in a waterfall of white. I look down to find a large tear slithering up the side of my leg, splitting the lace and exposing a sliver of my skin.

Dazed, I stumble towards the door, head spinning.

I need to tell Kitt.

Throwing the door open, I glance one last time at the scene I'm fleeing.

Notes litter the bed, an open book beside them. The smell of roses grows bitter, life and death, past and present, all mingling in the air. A decaying flower atop a jewelry box, a fresh bouquet decorating the floor. A photograph of a stranger who is suddenly so much more. Calum is sprawled beside the evidence of his treachery – a man who was once my friend, turned Father who is now dead to me.

I step out into the hall and don't look back again.

Edric

Eighteen years after Iris's death, Edric sees her again.

Not in body or soul, but rather, a reuniting of something long stolen.

Kitt, obsessively loyal as he was, told the king in passing of his meeting with the Slummer who had saved his Enforcer from a Resistance Silencer. The heir spoke vaguely of her alluring appearance – the dripping silver hair she greeted him at the door with, but more intriguing, her burning blue eyes.

The king, upon hearing each unnecessary detail, thought nothing of the girl who would likely die in his first Trial. Having no clear memory of his mother, Kitt saw little more than a pretty face before him. Any portraits of the late queen were locked away or in the possession of the king, who rarely displayed his lost love. But for the few times Edric allowed his son to admire them, he remembered nothing of note to connect the queen and this contestant.

But Kitt had never memorized the eyes of Iris Moyra quite like his father had.

The first time Edric sees his daughter since she was an embarrassment

in his arms is when she confidently takes a seat at his table.

Each contestant has filed into the throne room before His and Her Majesty make their grand entrance. The sight of Paedyn's eyes – Iris's eyes – nearly brings the king to his knees. But with a knack for deceit comes the gift of composure. Edric forces a stoic strength into his voice, addresses his contestants, and sits mere feet from the forgotten princess.

The king has not given thought to her, or the disgrace she had temporarily brought to his name, in eighteen years. But with her blue eyes locked on his, that flood of hatred carves a destructive path to his heart once again. She is more than everything Edric despises – she is his weakness.

Paedyn Gray.

An Ordinary, sitting at his table and pretending that she is not. His Ordinary, sitting here as though she is not meant to be dead.

'So, *this* is the girl who saved you in the alley?'

The king says this to his Enforcer, disguising every bit of bite in his voice with feigned intrigue. But when the Ordinary looks up at her father, he finds a loathing there to rival his own.

'I must say, I've never met a Psychic before. Your powers are . . . intriguing.'

A sham. A lie. A disgrace to his name.

These are all things Edric could have said in that moment, but he knows how to play his cards. He will not show his hand any more than she will. Instead, the king will watch her squirm until the moment he finally puts an end to her pathetic, Ordinary life.

A rehearsed explanation leaves Paedyn's lips at a calculated pace. Not too fast – this would make it seem like the lie it is – but not entirely slow, because why would she need such time to think on her own ability? It's admirable, really, her commitment to passing as an Elite. Even becoming the lowliest of them is a challenge.

Every word, every reasoning, is so deliberate that the king might have believed her if those eyes weren't so incriminating. Kai seems unworried by his inability to sense her power, or perhaps, the Enforcer is simply too distracted to question her reasonings further. But Edric says nothing of the truth he knows, because this Ordinary will die in his Trials, and he need not raise a finger to do it.

This time, he will not make the same mistake. This time, he will watch her die.

What a shame, to have survived this whole time for nothing.

Nothing. Just like the daughter before him. Like the powerless child who killed his wife, the waste of Elite power.

Paedyn mentions the man who raised her, forcing the king to further fortify his unbothered expression. Edric believed the surname Gray died with the man whose growing uprise became a pawn to satiate the king's appetite for power. Adam Gray was meant to help eradicate the remaining Ordinaries, albeit unknowingly. But the Healer's life was swiftly ended after he stumbled upon a secret meant solely for kings.

Only, the forgotten princess having been raised by the former Resistance leader was not a detail Edric was informed of.

Still, it feels good to blame another man for the weakness she is. For that reason, Edric happily confirms what she already believes to be true.

'Ah, yes, your father. Adam Gray was a great Healer. A very educated man.'

To her credit, the girl feigns surprise at the king's memory.

'You . . . you knew my father?'

The king answers her question, though the both of them already know the answer.

'Yes, I did. He would come to the palace during fever season to help our own court physicians when there were too many patients to attend to.'

That is how Edric became aware of Adam's plan to raise up a Resistance. His Mind Reader gathered the information while briefly passing in the halls. It was hardly shocking to discover the Healer's agenda, considering his continual refusal of the bribe offered to him. The king could not buy Adam's silence about the legitimacy of this Ordinary disease, but as a resident of the slums, he seemingly posed little threat.

Only, he raised the king's daughter into something that mockingly resembled an Elite.

Edric rises from the table, his eyes on those that once belonged to his wife.

I will watch her die, just as I have my wife. I will mar her heart, just as she has mine.

Calum does not need the king to vocalize the rage that roars within his head. He can read it easily enough, like a scribbled scroll rolled out before him. Edric's anger is an all-consuming ailment, one the Mind Reader has grown to understand better than most. And he knows now the reasoning behind this wrath.

'She was a baby. I could not bring myself to kill her.'

The king's eyes flash. 'And now an Ordinary sleeps in my castle. Competes in my Trials as if she is worthy.'

'Forgive me, Majesty.' Calum hangs his head solemnly, folding sweaty palms behind his back. 'I should have disposed of her like you asked. But I've kept an eye on her for years, ever since working with Adam and the Resistance. She was never meant to find her way back to the castle—'

'But she saved my son,' Edric spits, angered still by the Enforcer's inability to defend himself against a Silencer. 'And now Paedyn Gray is here to taunt me with her mother's eyes.'

The Mind Reader's throat bobs. 'I know.'

'I want her dead.'

'She will be,' Calum reassures. 'The Trials will likely kill her, but before they do, we can use her.'

This intrigues the king. 'I'm listening.'

'The Resistance is ready. This is what you have been waiting for all these years.' The Mind Reader tips his blond head. 'We only need someone to help us find a way into the Bowl after the third Trial. Finally, you will have a sea of Ordinaries in one place.'

'The tunnels,' Edric muses. 'You want her to lead the Resistance through the tunnels.'

Calum allows a rare smile. 'She only needs someone to show them to her.'

The king knows to whom he refers.

With a plan in place, Edric leaves his Mind Reader with a twisted sort of glee at Paedyn Gray's arrival. He would get to use her, get his revenge, before eventually watching her die. The king could think of little more that would bring him such enjoyment.

CHAPTER 60

Kai

I'm swallowed by a wave of bodies.

People pour from the throne room, all pushing their way down the hall. I shove against the human current, my movements sluggish beneath the weight of so many powers.

The court parades towards the gardens to enjoy refreshments and swap gossip while the second ceremony on Loot commences. Most Elites here despise the idea of the royals setting foot in the slums, let alone conducting another wedding there.

Another wedding. Because I couldn't stop the first.

I lean against a wall in the emptying throne room. Petals float from the canopy of flowers above to fall gracefully towards the dais beneath. That is where they stood, exchanging vows, while I was foolish enough to think I could stop it.

I was too late.

She is a wife. She is a queen.

I sink to the floor, letting my back slide down the smooth wall. What would I have done? Stolen my brother's bride away? I was so plagued by the decision between duty and desire that I became stuck somewhere in the middle as a begrudging bystander.

And now I've lost her.

I was too late.

Her life will pass by mine, and yet, we will never stop to live within each other's. She is a tragedy I will be forced to relive every waking moment. I am her Enforcer, and she, my queen. Anything more is now in our past, and anything less is likely to come.

I mourn her on the floor of the throne room.

I am lost without the purpose she planted in me. For her, I was better. I was a mere shadow of the beast my father made me. Now, I fear what I will become when bowing at her feet. I would have kneeled for her a hundred times over, not for duty but devotion.

She has become my mission once again, this time a queen I'm meant to protect. But it is my brother who will have her. In his life, in his heart, in his bed.

My fist meets the wall beside me.

A shock of pain shoots up my arm as the smooth surface crumbles beneath my knuckles. I curse under my breath, then again, loud enough to offer some relief to my sudden rage. White dust drifts to the marble floor when I pull my aching hand from the wall. Chunks of debris fall from the fist-sized hole I've made. It seems that my anger may have latched on to a nearby Brawny without my permission.

I am dangerous this way. Lethal when stripped so bare. Devastation lives just beneath my skin, and I am aching to unleash it.

She is gone. I have lost her. I am lost without her.

My head hangs in hands that will soon forget the shape of her.

Beasts don't get the beauty.

CHAPTER 61
Paedyn

The dress ripples around my pumping legs.

I cling to fistfuls of fabric, trying to free my restricted steps. The hall passes in a blur, sunlight streaming from the many windows I race past. None of the Imperials lining the wall so much as twist their heads at my mad dash and disheveled appearance.

I'm panting by the time I skid to a stop before the front doors. They are sealed shut, framed on either side by a dozen Imperials. Several eyes dip behind those white masks, scrutinizing their queen. I bite back the vicious retort on my tongue at the sudden realization of my bare legs. Dropping the hem of my skirt, I let it flutter to my feet before declaring, 'Open the doors.'

The Imperials obey my command, and I try not to look overly shocked by this. I bound down the stone steps that descend into the courtyard, sparing only a glance at the decorated coaches awaiting me. Kitt stands beside a particularly gilded one, where he converses quietly with Easel while surrounded by a swarm of Imperials. He, too, has changed into something less extravagant, though a ceremonial sword swings at his side.

'Kitt!'

His head whips in my direction to find the queen rushing towards him. My leg slips in and out of the tear that climbs up my dress, only amplifying my disheveled appearance. Kitt even allows concern to crinkle his brow at the sight of me. 'What happened?'

'I figured it out,' I pant. 'Calum was your father's Mind Reader, and I know his Fatals were hidden from you, so when the Resistance leader showed up after that third Purging Trial, you didn't know who he was—'

'Slow down, Paedyn,' Kitt urges, his body tense. 'What are you trying to say?'

I blow out a breath. 'Calum worked for your father. The whole Resistance was a sham and . . .' My mouth grows worryingly dry. 'And he is my father.'

Uttering the words aloud sounds like a death sentence. I watch them land on Kitt, watch every emotion ripple over his face. Confusion, disbelief, worry. We stand there, staring blankly at each other until Kitt finally sputters, 'What?'

My eyes drift closed so I don't have to watch his world shatter beneath my words. 'Your mother, Iris, she . . . she had an affair with Calum but passed the child off as your father's. When I was born an Ordinary, the king wanted me killed, but his Mind Reader placed me on Adam Gray's doorstep instead. The whole thing was covered up and—'

'My mother died over twenty years ago,' Kitt counters.

'The records were forged.' The words tumble out in a rush. 'The kingdom hadn't seen Queen Iris since your birth – the king kept her hidden away, paranoid of her safety. So when she became pregnant with me, Ilya never knew.'

Kitt's gaze grows vacant. 'And then she died.'

'Yes,' I murmur. 'And the king was able to cover up my existence by telling the kingdom that Iris died giving birth to you – not an Ordinary. *That* is what you and Ilya have believed for decades.'

'And the staff . . .'

'You said so yourself.' I shake my head. 'They have been keeping secrets for decades.'

A stifling silence smothers us.

'I know it sounds crazy, but Calum admitted it—'

'We are half siblings,' Kitt finally blurts.

I blink at my husband, then down at the ring on my finger. The thought had somehow never crossed my mind until this very moment, and now I feel as though I may be sick.

'Holy shit,' I breathe, because there is little more to say. We were just bound in holy matrimony less than a single hour ago, only to find out that our lives have been knit together long before then.

Kitt's hands are suddenly gripping my arms tightly. That glimpse of paranoia is back in his gaze. 'Did he say anything about me?'

'Wha—' I shake my head. 'Kitt, he has been controlling you. Calum is a Dual, just like you are. Everything he asks, you do.'

Kitt only stares at me, processing this information before my eyes. 'Think about it,' I urge. 'You never wanted to marry me, and yet, you did. Calum wanted you to, and I'm afraid to find out why. Don't you see? He is using you—'

The doors swing open with a thud.

My dagger is clenched in Calum's fist as he slowly descends those stone steps. I stiffen, feeling fear course through me at the sight of a man meant to be my father. My head is still spinning, my chest still hollow, after what I learned. Only a handful of minutes separates me from the life that was and the one I've now been thrown into. Everything I thought I knew is a lie, and everything I didn't know is even more hurtful.

Kitt drops his hands from my arms before taking a step forward. Imperials dash to their king's side at the scene unfolding, but Kitt waves them off. I watch Calum slowly descend the stairs with a calming smile spreading across his face. 'Kitt, let's not do anything rash. Paedyn is clearly confused.'

My skin flushes with anger.

Kitt meets my father at the bottom of the steps, and for a long moment, they do nothing but hold each other's gaze. There is a single, terrifying moment in which I fear they may smile, perhaps take a bow. It dawns on me then that I could have misjudged everything – that is, until Calum's body goes rigid. It's eerie, watching one's face drain of all color.

'Don't do this, Kitt—'

A sword sings as it's pulled from a sheath.

Kitt's responding growl echoes through the courtyard. 'Get out of my head.'

His blade sinks into my father's chest.

I blink and the world spins to a sudden, jolting stop. Blood gushes from the wound in Calum's chest as his king callously yanks the blade from his body. I watch those blue eyes widen on Kitt, then flicker with fleeting life.

My hand lifts towards the jaw I've dropped above. This is not the first time I've lost a father. This is not even the first time I've lost one to a sword through his chest, or an Azer brother at the other end of that blade. But this death is different. Watching this man die feels like a relief.

Calum is the reason for my true father's death, and this is the retribution I have searched for since Adam Gray died in my arms. The blood of every Resistance member is on this Fatal's hands, and he deserves to meet this brutal end.

Kitt staggers back, letting Calum slump to the stone steps. Blood drips from the king's sword in a way that makes him suddenly resemble his Enforcer. I step carefully beside Calum's crumpled body, ensuring the growing puddle of blood oozing down the stairs does not stain my pure attire. His blue gaze falls sluggishly to mine as I pry my dagger from his fingertips. Then I lean in, letting his dwindling power pluck words from my mind.

This isn't a goodbye, Father. Only a good way to say bye until we meet again. Because I will haunt you in every lifetime. A shadow of the woman you loved, trapped in the body of an Ordinary you hate.

I smile. His eyes widen as though the torture has already begun.

Until then, Father.

His blood drips from the blade of my dagger, and I wipe it off on his tunic before standing. As soon as I have slipped the knife into its sheath on my thigh, Kitt is turning me towards him with a heavy hand on my shoulder. 'Paedyn, did he say anything about me? About my father?'

I open my mouth—

'What the hell happened?'

431

My gaze lifts to the top of the stone steps where the Enforcer scrutinizes the scene below him.

King. Queen. Dead body.

Kitt's grip on my arm slips away beneath his brother's stare. 'The better question is where the hell have you been?'

Kai joins us beside the cascade of blood. His raw knuckles don't go unnoticed. 'Sorry I missed the ceremony.' His eyes flick to me. 'Congratulations. Now, what the hell is going on?'

The king turns to me, urging a quick explanation from my mouth. I recount my interaction with Calum, all that I discovered and all he told me. A dark shadow crosses Kai's face when I speak of what the prior king had done, but it's a shade of recognition I see when mentioning Calum's true identity.

'He always looked so familiar,' Kai mutters. 'I must have seen him pass me in the halls growing up. And at that battle in the Bowl, I knew I recognized him. I should have known—'

'It's not your fault,' Kitt reassures. 'He was manipulating all of us. Paedyn thinks he was a Dual, and it makes perfect sense.'

Kai's attention falls to me. 'A Dual?'

'I think he was a Controller *and* a Mind Reader. Look,' I say in a rush, 'I know it's rare, but whatever he says always goes. Kitt had no intention of marrying me until Calum said so.'

'She's right.' Kitt shakes his head. 'He always had this . . . pull. Like, I couldn't help but do what he wished. Either way,' he sighs, 'Calum was a danger. A liability. So, I did what I had to do.'

Kai blinks. 'You killed him?'

I stiffen.

He thought it was me.

'I did,' Kitt says simply. 'Like I said, he was a danger.'

Kai stares at his brother, even as Easel approaches timidly. I had nearly forgotten our wide-eyed audience. 'Your Majesty, I must insist that we head to Loot for the second ceremony.'

My stomach churns at the sudden reminder of what we have learned. 'No, we can't possibly—'

'Holy shit.'

I glance over at Kai to find his features arranged in equal parts shock and repulsion. 'Took you long enough,' I sigh.

'You're fucking related,' Kai spews. There is something like awe in his voice. Because this is hope. This is a way out of a marriage neither of us wants. 'You can't possibly go through with this ceremony.'

'Majesties, if I may,' Easel cuts in, 'this wedding must go on.'

Kai almost laughs. 'Like hell it will.'

'Easel,' I begin sensibly, 'we are half siblings and—'

'And you are already married.' Firmly, he stands his ground. 'If the kingdom so much as catches a whiff of annulment rumors, they will dash every bit of progress that has been made towards this united Ilya. Your marriage is a symbol, and if you rip that away, the people will never accept these new rules – even if they are meant to save them.' He takes a deep breath. 'This kingdom, and your relationship with every surrounding one, rides on this marriage. An Ilya who welcomes Ordinaries is who Dor, Tando, and Izram will trade with. And for now, Paedyn is our greatest asset. We need more time.'

Kai doesn't even take a moment to consider this. 'No. We will find another way.'

'He's right.' Kitt's murmur has the Enforcer shaking his head at the sky. 'The kingdom needs to see a united front for them to follow.' His gaze meets mine. 'What do you think?'

'I don't know what to think,' I blurt. 'I just found out my mother was a queen, and then watched another father bleed out in front of me.' I let out a quivering breath. 'I need time to think about this. On my own.'

Kitt nods. 'That is only fair.'

'All this time,' Kai mutters. 'You had a claim to the throne.'

Easel tilts his head, that shock of mint hair slipping over a shoulder. 'It is weak as a bastard, but yes, I suppose Paedyn does have a claim.'

Kitt shifts on his feet. 'We will need to find the true records. Discover what really happened.'

'Calum said they had been sealed away somewhere,' I say dully.

I feel nothing. All my life, I have *been* nothing.

I barely survived to discover my true heritage. It's steeped in secrets and buried further in disloyalty, but it was always there, pumping in my veins. The blood of a queen flows through me, an Ordinary from the slums. The juxtaposition is jarring enough to almost make me laugh.

So much of my life was ascertained in a collection of short-lived moments. I didn't even have the time to process one before another revelation rolled in. So, in this slow moment, I allow myself a single breath.

One crisis at a time.

'Let's get to Loot, then figure the rest of our lives out.'

CHAPTER 62

Kai

Their knees are touching again.

Except, this time, there are wedding vows wedged between them.

The gold band on Kitt's finger catches the light with every jostle of the coach. Just like our last parade onto Loot, we ride over the uneven cobblestones with the sun weighing heavy on our shoulders. No roof resides above our heads, allowing us full view of the awaiting crowd gathered on the long market street.

Collectively, all of four words have passed between us, consisting of 'Are we there yet?' An impatient Jax sits beside me, clearly tired of our bumpy crawl through the slums and likely regretting not riding with Andy. Pathetically, I am thankful he is here, if only to ensure my anger cools before my mouth opens.

I can do little else but seethe in the absurdity of this all. Within the last conversation shared between us, I discovered that Paedyn is the daughter of the late Queen Iris and my father's Mind Reader – whose blood is currently being scrubbed from the castle's front steps. She is an Ordinary born from the rawest of power. And Kitt is her half brother.

For the first time since I was a boy, I fight to keep my mask of

indifference from slipping off. As nauseating as this news is, it may just be Paedyn's way out. My hope is selfish, tainted by the desire to be hers alone. But Kitt is not the only one committed to protecting this kingdom. Ilya is our home, and if the only way to save it means Paedyn plays wife in name alone, then . . .

Then let's hope it doesn't come to that.

The coach rumbles to a stop in the center of this crowded street. Emerald banners hang between crumbling buildings, secured there by Crawlers offered a shilling for their labor. They display both Ilya's swirling crest and the Azers' shield high above hundreds of starving Mundanes beneath.

We step into a makeshift circle, decorated by multiple pedestals connected with thick ribbon – a pretty barrier the people know better than to cross. My Imperials, now far more attentive with their resumed training, place themselves around the perimeter as an extra precaution. It all seems rather pointless when looking at it from this angle. All I see before me are hungry, hopeless Elites who behave themselves for the promise of stale bread, coin, or shelter.

How did such a mighty kingdom fall?

It was not like this at the beginning of Father's reign. I have read what histories date before the Purging, even those immediately after. No, this deterioration of Ilya began when King Edric's hatred for Ordinaries became an obsession. Right before his eyes, the kingdom began to crumble, and still, he cared only for the ratification of weakness. That desire is what brought Ilya to its knees.

Kitt reaches for Paedyn's hand. She hesitates. I turn away.

I melt into the circle of Imperials and begin a slow pace behind them. By the time I look back at the royal couple, they stand on a large platform before the people, arms interlocked at the elbows. The wooden riser beneath their feet is draped in emerald carpet and adorned with a Scholar. This makeshift ceremony so starkly contrasts with the one held before the court. Dripping with roses and gilded finery, the castle perfectly put into perspective the slums' poverty. And also, its priorities.

'People of Ilya, we gather here today to join Kitt Azer, king and savior of Ilya, and the lady Paedyn Gray in holy matrimony. Bear witness to their union and abide by the power granted unto them.'

The rickety man drones on, reminding me of a simpler time when I despised my studies with the Scholars. But this is no long-winded lecture – these are the words that bind their souls together. Paedyn's hands now rest within my brother's, lifted between them to display the shining rings they share. Both the king and queen look distantly detached from the ceremony they are standing within.

I pull my arms behind a stiff back, widening my stance and planting my feet so they don't carry me away from this unbearable display. No, I am the Enforcer. I am now an Enforcer to the both of them. It is duty that roots me to the spot, forcing my gaze to grow vacant as vows are exchanged and fates are bound.

Kitt stands at Paedyn's side, holding the hand of his bride. I roll my neck. It is harder to hate this situation when my brother is half of it. I loved him more than anyone, and until a clumsy thief ran into me all those months ago, I never believed I could love anyone as much. There is little more I want than to see Kitt happy, and that little more happens to now be his wife.

'People of Ilya, I present unto you, Paedyn Azer, your undoubted queen consort.'

The crown Paedyn retrieved from the Sanctuary of Souls is placed onto her gleaming hair. She is the very portrait of a queen, somehow more formidable now than the day we met. The Silver Savior has morphed into a fearsome creature, dressed in finery and armed with a future of her making.

A sudden shift in the crowd has me stepping forward, poised to strike if a threat presents itself. I squint, watching this ripple of movement flow through the hundreds of cramped bodies. My gaze flicks between each side of the packed street as I assess every wrinkle in the sea of people. Even the Scholar has stopped his babbling, leaving Paedyn and Kitt to swivel their heads in confusion.

'Silver Savior!'

The shout has my Imperials beginning to close in around the platform, but I raise a staying hand.

That title was said with reverence.

And when the tremble of bodies grows close enough, I watch

knees bend before their queen. Hundreds of Ilyans kneel atop the cobblestone they once shared with Paedyn Gray. I stare as the people of these slums show their devotion for the girl who escaped – and has now returned to save them.

I glance up at Paedyn and the shock she fights to suppress. Her chest heaves as she takes in the respect they so readily give her. It is as though the people can smell that royal blood within her veins, are unable to help but bow before those destined to rule. But they know not of her heritage, only that she was – and forever will be – one of them. This is Paedyn's home, and they welcome her back a queen.

Kitt stands stoically beside Paedyn as she lifts her chin, crown piercing the air. Echoed murmurs of the Silver Savior lap around the edge of the ceremony's circle. A queen now stands where a thief once had – brave, benevolent, and brutal. She stands victorious.

The Scholar's final decree is a startled afterthought. 'And your king, Kitt Azer, savior of Ilya. May their union bring prosperity to our kingdom and greatness to our histories.'

Paedyn Gray—

No.

Azer.

And just like that, I am jolted from this remarkable moment and tossed right back into my bleak reality.

The king and queen step from the platform.

Their Enforcer follows.

438

CHAPTER 63

Paedyn

My first evening as queen is spent watching the sun sink towards the garden below my balcony.

I blow gently on my steaming cup of tea, legs curled snugly beneath me in the plush chair. I've hardly been past those stunning glass doors since gawking at my chamber for the first time. Now, with nothing to do but sit within my thoughts, I decided it best to weather the storm inside my mind with a calming view.

Rows of color fan out beneath me, framing each cobblestone path and stretching towards that fading sun. Birds chirp softly at the approaching dusk as shadows begin their slow crawl across the earth. I take a sip of tea and shut my eyes as the warmth of it spills into my stomach. This has the potential to be the most peaceful moment I've had since being sent to the Purging Trials. Until the flash of my wedding ring reminds me of the wreckage that is my life.

I'm still reeling, hours later, from every revelation ripping my past apart. Royal blood flows through my veins, and yet it has coated Imperials' whips and drenched the late king's sword. Edric Azer's blatant hatred for me was a fire that sparked the day I was born an Ordinary. And I have been fighting to survive since.

I stare down into my rippling teacup. A forgotten princess stares back, abandoned for power and hated for surviving despite it.

I blow out a breath while my mind struggles to connect all the pieces of my fragmented life.

Iris Moyra lived within this very castle, smothering her love for a man she could not have. They hid their affections like a thorny wall of roses, both beautiful but dangerous. Today, I watched the man my mother loved in secret bleed out before me. I hadn't felt grief at his death. No, I felt a shiver of ghostly similarities between my mother and father's doomed love. Their notes, their stolen love – it is Kai's and my life mirrored. And if the Enforcer will someday meet the fate Calum has—

I cut the thought off before it has time to fester.

Perhaps Iris loved them both – the king and his Mind Reader. Perhaps in very different ways.

I think of Kitt and the blood we share. I think desperately of a way to undo this binding of our souls, one that does not rip the growth we have made for this kingdom out at the root. My chest tightens, the teacup rattling in my hand atop its saucer.

How am I going to find a way out of this?

A shifting shadow below catches my eye. I set my cup aside and squint into the growing darkness. The figure walks smoothly to a stop beneath my balcony and calls, 'Guess who, Little Psychic?'

My heart stutters, yet I somehow manage to keep my voice steady. 'Someone who has already forgotten my new title?'

Kai's dry chuckle drifts into the breeze as I stand to lean over the railing. 'Majesty, I have many titles for you. Not all are appropriate to shout.'

I roll my eyes. I can't help but leap at the distraction he offers from my spiraling thoughts. 'What do you want, cocky bastard?'

'You forgot the "my" in front of that endearing nickname.'

'You shouldn't be here,' I challenge. 'As *my* Enforcer.'

His tone echoes my own. 'Then command me to go.'

'Don't tempt me.'

'That would only be fair.'

I stare down at his shadowed form. 'You're deflecting.'

'Maybe I'm stalling.'

My eyes narrow. 'And why is that?'

'Call it a desperate attempt to steal more time with you.'

I hide my smile with a duck of my head. 'Do you intend to stand beneath my balcony all night, then?'

'No.' His gray gaze has faded away in the darkness, but I can feel it on me all the same. 'We are going to visit your mother's chamber.'

CHAPTER 64

Kai

Gail places the plate of sticky buns between us, warm as the smile on her face.

'Look at you boys, back in my kitchen and begging for food.' Gail says this with so much endearment that she nearly chokes. She presses a hand to her heart. 'Oh, how I missed this.'

Kitt nudges my shoulder with his own, looking happier than I thought possible after a day like this one. 'Just like old times.'

My teeth sink into the honeyed dough. I nod. Swallow. 'It would be more like old times if I threw you over this table.'

'Absolutely not,' Gail warns. 'The both of you are much too big for that now – my kitchen can't take it.' We smile at her scolding before she adds, 'Where is Paedyn?'

Kitt takes a breath. Then he clutches his chest and coughs. 'Is our company not enough for you anymore, Gail?'

'Don't be smart with me, Kitt.' She plops her hands on full hips. 'Forgive me for asking where your wife is on your wedding night.'

I stiffen.

'I just didn't expect you to be spending the evening in my kitchen. Although—' the cook smiles sweetly at Kitt, having already forgotten

he is now her king, '—Kitty, sweetie, if you wanted to use that nifty Dual ability of yours to wash my floors like you used to, I would not be opposed.'

I am grateful for the swift change of subject. It seems Kitt is as well, because he chuckles, sounding relieved. 'Don't forget that Kai Pie here can do that for you too.'

I drop the sticky bun onto my plate. 'You hate when I borrow your power.'

The words fall from my honeyed lips, though they still manage to taste bitter. I would like to blame the accusation in my voice on the very upsetting day I've had, but in truth, I would simply like to know where the brother went who so desperately wished to fight his own battles. The one who ached to enter the Purging Trials if only to prove the strength Father never let him use. He was tutored; I was trained. And Kitt had always dreamed of being a victor.

His earnest gaze slides to mine. 'That was before I truly realized what a great team we make.' He smiles softly. 'You are my strength. I am your control. We are matchless.'

I brace my arms against the rickety table. 'And when did you finally figure that?'

'When I discovered my need for you was greater than my wish to be you.'

This shouldn't startle me, but somehow, it does. 'Why would you ever want that, Kitt? Father ensured that the worst parts of himself live within me.'

'So we will be so much better than him.' He holds my stare fiercely. 'You and I, we will create our own legacy – a greatness that Father could have never dreamed of.'

I smile for him, because I feel as though I should. He looks happy, relieved, even, as though uttering the words has lifted a weight from his chest. Though, this tender moment only reminds me of the drastically different one I had witnessed hours ago. I've managed to bite my tongue until now, seeing through Kitt's eager attempts to avoid the topic. But unfortunately, I love my brother too much to let his evasion of the subject and its accompanying awkwardness still my tongue.

'Kitt . . .' I start slow. 'We should talk about what happened in the courtyard with Calum and—'

'Gail—' Kitt's eyes flash a warning, '—these sticky buns are delicious. Did you do something different?'

I stare back at my brother, not caring that Gail is in the room for a conversation long overdue. But I understand his secrecy on the matter, having watched him inform the Imperials that word of Calum's death was to be contained. Few of the staff know of the brutality their king committed mere hours ago, and Gail is certainly not one of them. She does not even know what we have now learned.

'Well, I added an extra spice in this batch.' She wipes her hands on the stained apron around her waist. 'This is how your mother always liked her sticky buns, Kai. She ate her fill that first year of marriage to the king. I was planning to bring one up to the tower for her.'

'A pregnancy craving?' Kitt asks, in the hope of remaining on this topic.

Gail's face falters. 'I . . . perhaps.'

I stare at the woman who raised me when the queen could not. The paling of her face is odd. She would have taken care of my mother when she was pregnant with me—

My heart sinks, heavy with a sudden realization.

Paedyn was born eighteen years ago, the daughter of Queen Iris and my father's Mind Reader.

And yet, I am a year older than she.

My throat goes dry.

This is the first quiet moment I have stolen all day. Until now, I have hardly spared a thought to fit the pieces of Paedyn's birth together. And there are still several missing – *I* am missing.

Gail is talking idly with Kitt. I can't seem to make out what she is saying through the ringing in my ears.

'When were you going to tell us the truth of Queen Iris's death?'

The cook gapes at my words. 'Kai . . .'

'I mean—' my sudden laugh sounds crazed, '—Kitt just married a lost princess, and he didn't even know it until Father's Mind Reader filled us in on the details.'

'What? You know . . . ?' Gail chokes.

Kitt stands from the table at the same moment I do. 'Kai, what the hell are you—'

'I'm going to find answers,' I breathe. 'We are drowning in secrets, Kitt. Your wife isn't the only one who was lied to.'

Gail's hand is pressed to her heart, the look of regret on her face the last thing I see before striding out the doors. Kitt follows in a flurry of confusion. His steps echo behind me. 'Brother, just tell me what is going on. Please.'

I turn only slightly. 'I will. But only after I've ensured I'm right.'

Then I'm off to steal away my queen.

CHAPTER 65

Kai

The sun is long set before I'm finally rapping my knuckles against Kitt's study door.

'This night is never-ending,' Paedyn huffs.

She spins the ring on her thumb incessantly, gaze far from the grooved door before us. Her mind is likely where mine has drifted off to after everything we discovered. But I've forced myself to wander back to my brother, as promised. Just as I always have over the years.

I swallow. 'I'm taking a page out of your book, Little Psychic.'

Paedyn's mouth opens, but before she can answer—

'Come in.'

Kitt's voice is muffled behind the slab of wood I now push open. He sits at his desk, lamplight flooding the room in a flickering glow. Parchment sprawls the span of chipped wood in front of him, and I am consistently astonished how every sheet is marred with hasty handwriting. But what captures my attention is the ceremonial sword leaning against the fireplace. Gone is the blood of Paedyn's father, replaced with a silver shine.

The king ushers me in with a wave of his inky hand. His skin is pale, stark against the indigo veins that crawl from his temple. My

eyes narrow at the striking sickness crowding his features. Bloodshot eyes and gaunt cheeks meet my scrutiny. I've never seen him like this, never noticed how unwell he truly looked.

The maids.

They have been concealing his illness as best they could.

I stride into the glowing room, and comfortingly, Kitt smiles at my company. But the shadow stepping behind me makes Kitt falter slightly. 'Paedyn. I didn't expect to see you tonight.'

I force a deep breath into my lungs.

It is their wedding night.

If it weren't for recent discoveries, together is precisely what they would have been. The thought has something sinister awakening within me, but I stamp it down, right alongside the jealousy that festers there.

'I didn't either,' Paedyn states truthfully. 'But Kai . . .'

'Wanted your wife here when we finally discuss what happened today.'

The words surprise even me, mostly because they weren't meant to be biting. I can feel Paedyn's gaze crash into me as Kitt's does the same. Slowly, the king gathers his stack of scribbled parchment and shoves it into the drawer beside him. 'I'd rather not speak of it. You of all people should understand that, Brother.'

The words are honed masterfully. They cut deep enough to make me momentarily rethink this approaching conversation. I stare at my brother, seeing once again that sliver of cunningness he holds so close. There was once a time when I would have considered myself to be the calculated brother and he the caring one. But it feels as though a lifetime has been wedged between those characteristics, and I'm no longer sure who is deserving of them.

'Kitt,' I say slowly. 'You killed someone today.'

He leans back in his chair. 'I did what I needed to.'

'That was your first kill.'

'It was?' Paedyn steps forward, shaking her head. 'Of course it was.'

'I'm fine, Kai,' the king murmurs. 'It was a necessity. Now, can we please stop—'

I brace my palms on his desk. 'The brother I know would be in shambles after driving a sword through a man's chest.'

'Well, he grew up,' Kitt fires back. He shoves the bite in his voice aside. 'I am a king now, and everything I do is for the greatness of this kingdom.'

I study the tight paleness of his features. 'Tell me what is going on, Kitt. There is something you're not telling me.'

Paedyn clears her throat. 'I should let you two work this out—'

'No,' I order. My eyes don't stray from the king. 'You're an Azer now. This is exactly where you should be.'

Kitt rubs a hand behind his neck, just as he has always done since we were boys. It tells of his anxiety. 'Brother, you know what happened. Paedyn discovered the truth of Calum's role and how he has been manipulating me to do his bidding. He was a threat that I put an end to.'

I shake my head, a twinge of disappointment trickling through me. I think back to that panicked moment I walked into – Calum dead on the steps and Paedyn spewing her theories. 'Don't you think I would have known if he was a Dual?'

Kitt is quick to nod towards Paedyn. 'You've been wrong before about one's abilities. Besides, how do you know he wasn't controlling you to ignore the true extent of his power?'

It's a well-rehearsed rebuttal. And if I didn't know my brother better, I might have believed him. 'So Calum's death had nothing to do with those letters in Iris's jewelry box?'

Kitt says nothing.

Paedyn pounces on the familiar speculation. 'You'd already read those notes, hadn't you? You recognized Calum's handwriting and were worried that you might be a bastard.' She takes a breath, realization crashing over her like a wave. 'That is why you asked if he said anything about you.'

My brother tenses. 'I meant to dispose of those before giving you the jewelry box, but I got . . . distracted.'

A sad sort of understanding seeps onto my features. 'If he was a loose end that needed to be taken care of, I would have done that for you. That is why I am here – to save you from brutality.'

'And what if I don't want to be saved?' Kitt counters. There is a certain intensity in his eyes that startles me. 'What if I want to save you for once? Save us.'

My head tilts. 'Kitt, I—'

'If you were there,' he begins slowly, 'and Calum stepped between me and your beloved Paedyn with that dagger, who would you have protected?'

Something shifts between us at those words. The tension grows taut. I glance over at Paedyn. She scrutinizes the situation. I fight against the understanding that begins to dawn.

'You would choose her,' Kitt whispers. 'You've already chosen her, over and over again.'

'This is ridiculous, Kitt—'

The king stands, nearly toppling the chair in such haste. 'It should only ever be us. You and me, always.' His gaze grows wild. 'You remember that, don't you? Before she came into our lives and left it in shambles.'

Paedyn's voice is small. 'What are you talking about, Kitt?'

But he doesn't speak to her. No, his words are directed only at me. 'She ruined us, Kai! Everything went wrong in our lives the second she stepped into it. Hell—' his laugh is ragged, '—even the second she was born, Paedyn managed to begin destroying this family.'

My chest tightens painfully. The crazed look Kitt wears is one I recognize. Father – the king – would wear the same one when speaking of Ordinaries. It was what he wished to destroy more than anything. I know now that his hatred stemmed from the death of his wife, and the birth of an Ordinary girl.

But Kitt's aversion for Paedyn does not resemble his father's. Edric sought out power – Kitt aches for companionship. Brotherhood. Me alone.

'Don't you see, Brother?' His exasperation hangs in the air between us. 'She killed our father – my mother. She is the wedge that will drive us apart.'

I can see the shadow of jealousy on his face, the same darkness that falls over him when Paedyn is near. But I realize now that it is not envy for the Silver Savior on display, but envy *of* her. She has me, and Kitt hates it.

I step away from his desk, my head shaking. 'She killed your father, not mine.' Kitt's face falls before I even land the final blow. 'Paedyn is more your family than I am.'

CHAPTER 66

Paedyn

Kai escorts me through the halls, ignoring every wandering eye. After he walked from the gardens to meet me outside my chamber door, we set a quick pace between the Imperial-lined walls. The urgency in his steps has me biting back every question pelting my weary mind. But the Enforcer is on another one of his missions, and I am simply relieved to not be on the other side of it again. So, I let him lead me past each tall window and the fading sun beyond.

We turn down a corridor I don't recognize before stopping at the threshold of a seemingly unsuspecting door.

I glance skeptically at my guide. 'This is it?'

He turns the handle, stepping almost cautiously into the space. 'Odd, how it's just a regular room after all those years of wondering what was inside.'

My feet falter. It feels as though I've disturbed a piece of the past, intruded on a stranger I now call 'mother' in title alone. I scan Queen Iris's chamber slowly, taking in the four-poster bed hiding beneath a layer of neglect. Dust blankets every piece of furniture – the desk, vanity, and bookshelves all warmed with white grime.

'Father never let anyone in here.' Kai's words only emphasize the

clear signs of isolation. 'Always claimed that he wanted to preserve it for her.'

My gaze drifts to the shelves once again, noting the toppled books and wedged papers between them. On her nightstand, dust collects around the shape of a rectangle at its center. 'This is where Kitt got her jewelry box from,' I murmur.

Kai nods. 'During your first Trial, I found him in here holding it. He must have been looking through some of her old things.'

I halt my slow pacing at the end of an untouched bed. 'If he looked through that jewelry box, he would have seen those notes from Calum.' Thoroughly distracted, Kai only manages an absentminded 'Hmm.'

With a sigh, I drop the subject. His mind is far from my speculations. 'So, what are we doing here, exactly?'

'You don't want to see your mother's chamber?'

I shrug. 'Maybe if she actually felt like my mother. But . . .' I run a hand across that dusty quilt hugging the bed. 'This woman feels like a stranger.'

Kai nods slowly, sympathetically, before he spews the real reason he dragged me here. 'You mentioned Calum saying something about the true records being sealed away.'

I glance around the abandoned room. 'And you figured they might be in here where no one was permitted to enter.'

'Nothing gets past you, Little Psychic.' His following huff is laced with humor. 'Actually, if I am right, then something did get past you.'

This offends me. Greatly. 'Just spit it out, Azer.'

Kai pokes around the desk, pulling at stubborn drawers. 'I am a year older than you, Pae. If my father married Myla after you were born—'

'You would have been a year old already,' I breathe.

His smirk is infuriating.

'Don't be an ass.' I join him at the desk with a lethal look. 'My mind has been a little occupied today.'

'And mine hasn't?'

I almost laugh. 'I got married!'

'And I have been mourning you since the day we left that poppy field!'

My lips part slightly. I stare at him, watching every ripple of emotion cross his unmasked face. He sighs out a steadying breath. 'The slow death of us started the day my brother slid that ring onto your finger,' Kai murmurs. 'And I have had nothing but you on my mind for weeks.' He reaches for me before thinking better of it. 'We will always be inevitable, Pae. But in this lifetime, we are doomed. Today was evidence of that. It's . . .' He swallows. 'It's best we move on.'

A long moment passes between us before he turns back towards the desk, as though he hasn't just crushed my heart in his calloused palm. The ache in my chest is only amplified by the truth in his words. We are ruin.

Kai clears his throat. I blink away the emotion stinging my eyes.

Attempting to let the tension fall from between us, I ask, 'You think the records are in this desk?'

I peek over his shoulder at the fingerprints he's scattered across the dusty wood. Kai tugs at a rattling handle to no avail. 'It's locked,' he mutters. That hardly deters him from yanking it open with ease and stating, 'Brawny.' He tosses his head towards the door. 'Down the hall.'

Within a matter of moments, he is pulling three weathered scrolls from the depths of that locked door and laying them on the desk.

One speaks of birth, the other of death, the final of marriage. Each is a decree with secrets.

We lean in, skimming the swirling dark ink. My eyes flick between the three pages, head spinning. Frustrated, I try to fit Calum's admittances between the scrawled words.

Eighteen years ago, a daughter was born to the king.

Eighteen years ago, Queen Iris died in childbirth.

I was the daughter – an Ordinary the king disposed of. Embarrassed and angry, he hid the truth of his wife's death, claiming to the kingdom that she passed during the birth of his heir. Queens were isolated for safety, so it was a believable lie . . .

I drag a finger across the marriage license. 'This says nothing of a child. Only that Edric Azer and Myla Rowe were wed.'

Kai runs a hand through his tousled hair. 'There is no record of my birth.'

453

'We must be missing something,' I offer distantly. 'Maybe there is another scroll—'

'Maybe,' Kai cuts in. I blink, and he is pushing away from the desk to stride across the room. 'Or maybe we should go right to the source.'

The dowager queen stares blankly at the scrolls.

'I want answers, Mother,' Kai urges.

Myla's long black hair is streaked with silver. Her once beautiful gray eyes are sunken and red. The cot she lies on is stiff, the room around us stuffy. She looks frail in the west wing's sickly hue, as though the rickety tower itself seeps life from her veins.

I fidget in my seat. The queen hardly knows me and now I've come to sit beside her deathbed, disrupting the little peace she had.

'I know the truth about Iris's death,' Kai says slowly, pointing to one of the scrolls. 'How the king married you to help cover it up. But what I don't understand is where I fit into it.' His gaze is piercing. 'If Iris truly died two years after Kitt's birth, then how was I born only a year younger than him?'

The queen's gaze shifts to her son, nearly as hollow as the words she finally coughs out. 'The king didn't tell me the whole story until he decided he loved me. At the beginning, it was my duty to marry Edric — at least, that is what my father told me. As an adviser to the king, he handed me over, a solution to a problem I didn't know.'

She lifts a hand to her son's cheek. 'Despite my father's persuasion, I didn't think the king would want to marry me so suddenly. Because I . . . I already had a son with another.' Her voice grows hushed. 'But I was wrong. It was you he wanted.'

I watch the words hit Kai hard enough to nearly crack his stony facade.

'He had a Silencer sense your power,' she whispers. The queen grips Kai's hand, a cough rattling her chest before continuing. 'The king wanted a strong spare, and my baby boy was extraordinary. Edric wanted him as his own.'

Nothing. Kai says nothing.

I drop my gaze to the fidgeting fingers in my lap. After believing an Ordinary child was his, it is no wonder the king wanted only the strongest of Elites for himself. I was an embarrassment. A mistake. And Kai – the most powerful Elite – would replace me.

'Edric told the kingdom he had mourned his late wife for three months and married me in the next.' The queen chokes on her words. 'He was very convincing, your father – told the people that he didn't have the heart to announce Iris's death until he knew his new queen and son were safe.'

'So he wanted a solution to his problem,' Kai says evenly. His voice is dangerously calm. 'The king was embarrassed by an Ordinary that wasn't even his, so he claimed the strongest Elite he could find as his own.'

'Forgive me, Kai,' his mother whimpers. 'The castle was sworn to secrecy, and I was never to tell a soul the truth. So you were raised believing what everyone else in the kingdom did.'

Kai scoffs. 'But I was never his. My power was not Edric's doing.' His eyes lift to the woman who resembles him so closely. 'So whose doing is it?'

Her throat bobs. 'A man I loved dearly. Many years ago.'

Kai looks away, letting her words hang in the air. I can see the hurt he so desperately tries to hide beneath that mask of anger. 'The king rewrote history,' he seethes, 'and made me his puppet.'

Myla lets out a ragged cough that might have been the start of an apology. When she catches her breath, face splotchy and red, she rasps, 'He was always too harsh on you. And I am so . . . so sorry for that.'

'I was his in name, and still, he hated that I wasn't his in blood,' Kai mutters. 'That is why he never loved me, isn't it? Why he pushed me until I broke? All because my power was never truly his.'

Rage simmers deep in my gut for the boy who was forced into this fate by chance alone. Everything he has suffered, every mask forced upon his face and weapon pushed into his hand, was never intended for him. Kai Azer is not an Azer at all. He was a powerful solution.

'I'm sorry you were thrown into this mess,' the queen attempts. 'At first, we were only meant to cover up how an Ordinary killed the late queen.'

Her gray eyes slide to mine.

Kai scoffs before biting out, 'All this time, you knew?'

'I had my suspicions.' The queen coughs. 'Edric was not himself after seeing her for the first time.'

My cheeks heat. 'I was not the king's Ordinary.' At her skeptical look, I let the truth tumble out. 'I was his Mind Reader's daughter.'

A heavy silence bears down on us, one that Kai graciously lifts from our shoulders. 'The king always kept his Fatals hidden. We never saw them. The Silencer was the only one I ever met while trying to glean information about the Resistance – which I know now was a sham.' His laugh is humorless. 'Though, it sounds like Damion met me long before then, when he told the king of my power.'

The queen's eyes widen on me. 'If that is true, then the king died thinking that you . . .'

'That I was his greatest failure?'

His Ordinary. His weakness. His death.

Even powerless, I killed him.

A slight smile tugs at my lips.

I hope he saw his daughter's face – the Ordinary he despised – as I drove that sword into his chest.

'I'll live with it.'

Edric

A seamstress will soon find her way into the final Trial.

This signals the beginning of the end, or so the king thinks. Adena is little more than a pawn in his game, plucked from the castle and thrown into the Pit for something as fragile as his ego. Edric hates the daughter he believes to be his, and as punishment for killing the woman he loves, the king will take Paedyn's only piece of comfort in this world.

From high above in his glass box, Edric enjoys watching the weakness emanate from Paedyn Gray. She screams, and cries, and begs for a God who is wholly uninterested in such a plight. It is, oddly enough, a gift that the Trials did not end the Ordinary's life – for the king himself wants such a privilege.

But, in the end, it is that rose atop Iris's jewelry box that foretells his doom. Hatred begins to fester in Edric's heart the moment he believes an Ordinary to be born of him. Yet, they share no strength, no morals, no ounce of blood. Paedyn Gray belongs to the queen and her love for a Fatal. But that does not make her any less a princess. Nor does it lend her any more strength as an Ordinary.

King Edric's last moments are spent spilling blood and spitting

enmity at a girl he has spent eighteen years loathing. Even so, he mentions nothing of her lineage, because she is not worthy of knowing the truth. The king wishes her to die having never known of the royal blood in her veins. He will not allow Paedyn Gray the satisfaction of understanding how much she has haunted him.

So he carves a circle upon her heart, just as his wife has done countless times atop his own. Though, this is no gesture of love like Iris intended, but the marking of what was lost, all for the Ordinary squirming beneath his boot. The king ensures Paedyn Gray will wear that mark until her final breath, because it hurts to bear the weight of Iris's touch alone. It is in the Ordinary's skin that Edric writes the truth of her birth, of the great love that died, and the spark of hatred that was born. Atop that muddy ground, mangled flesh spells out his love for Iris Moyra as the king lays her to rest with this final act of justice.

Though, in the end, it is he who is buried beneath the weight of secrets and betrayal. For he never learns the truth of those he loved — and how they loved one another.

CHAPTER 67

Paedyn

'What are you talking about?'

Kitt's words are a hiss, making me flinch. His red-rimmed eyes grow unfocused. My heart pounds beside Kai in this study that seems to be closing in on me. I almost try to convince myself that I've misheard the malice in my husband's voice.

But it is no use. The crazed look he wears only confirms the words he spit so readily. It's as though they have been smothered beneath his tongue for weeks before finally unleashing them.

This is not the Kitt I knew, nor is it the one I was beginning to befriend. This is the embodiment of a fraying mind.

'Edric wasn't my father,' Kai answers, his shoulders stiff. 'Myla already had a child when they were secretly wed – a powerful one that your father only wanted as his spare and weapon. So really—' the Enforcer takes a step forward, so stoic and sure, '—Paedyn is your blood, not me.'

After all that time of calling Kai Azer a cocky bastard, that was precisely what he was. I had uttered the truth on a dozen occasions.

I watch the steely words hit Kitt, and yet, he hardly flinches. 'That may be so, but you are my brother. You are more family than I have ever had. More . . .' He searches Kai's gaze desperately. 'More love

than I have ever had. Father was obsession, Mother a ghost, but you . . . you showed me what love was.'

The reminder of my naivety nips at the corner of my consciousness. I've spent weeks trying to repair a bond I thought was only severed due to the killing of a king. But I realize now that Edric Azer was merely a variable in Kitt's contempt for me. It is Kai he wants at his side – his brother and friend. And I alone stand between them.

'Why did you marry me?' I prod. 'If I am a wedge between you two, then why not kill me?'

Kitt finally deigns to meet my stare. 'My plans for Ilya require you.' I gape at his curt response before he's turning once again towards Kai, features suddenly beseeching. 'Together we will build the greatest nation – stretching far beyond the Scorches and Shallows. We will create a legacy that Father never dreamed of.'

Kai stares at the boy he's called 'brother' his whole life. 'I thought you wanted to be exactly like Father – *your* father. Whatever happened to following in his footsteps, doing anything to make him proud?'

'Again,' Kitt says with a cough, 'I grew up. Father told me of his plan for the Resistance, how his entire life was wasted trying to rid the kingdom of Ordinaries.' He shakes his head. 'I spent so many years believing he was a god among men, that his plans for Ilya were beyond anything I could hope to achieve. But it was all so . . . *mediocre*. Obsessive.'

Kitt wags a finger in the air. 'Yet, he had the gall to make me feel inferior my whole life. All I wanted was his pride, his approval, his love. So now—' his gaze widens with that wild look, '—I will be so much greater than him. His name will be overlooked in the histories beside my own. Beside *ours*.'

Kai's expression grows worried. 'And how will you do that?'

Kitt rounds the desk slowly. His features morph into something so terrifyingly calm, I nearly flinch. 'We have already begun, Brother.'

The look in his eyes worries me more than his words. I swallow thickly. My voice is quiet. 'What did you do, Kitt?'

'No.' He clicks his tongue. 'What did *you* do, Paedyn? You became queen and made the surrounding kingdoms open their borders to us. *You*, a relatable Ordinary, had them lowering their guards against us.'

'And why,' Kai breathes, 'would that be a problem, *Brother*?'

'You know, I'm used to being overlooked.' The king mutters distantly before beginning to pace. 'Kind, caring Kitt, after all. But I really thought that you—' his piercing gaze cuts through me, '—would suspect more from me. You thought *saving* Ilya was the best I could do?' He grins sharply. 'No, I'm liberating every kingdom.'

'Kitt . . .' I begin slowly.

'See, I don't care whether the Ordinaries live or die – obsessing over their existence is what ruined Father,' Kitt explains eagerly. And for the first time, I see a trail of dark veins creeping from his hairline. 'But Elites should not be confined to this city; they should populate every kingdom. And when I rule over every realm on our maps—' Kitt smiles, and it is chilling, '—I'll have earned Father's favor.'

Kai steps hesitantly towards his brother. 'What are you saying, Kitt? Was uniting Ilya just some . . . ploy?'

'Not at all,' Kitt says, sounding almost offended. He coughs into that handkerchief again, splattering it with something ominously dark. 'It was needed for the kingdoms to open their borders and begin trade with us.'

My heart pounds. Each rapid beat of it brings me closer to discovering yet another truth to tear at the fraying seams of my life. 'You're not opening trade to exchange resources, are you?'

The question is hushed, and I fear the answer.

'Of course I am.' Kitt's voice is even. 'So I can exchange resources laced with the Plague.'

Air flees my lungs.

I'm still struggling to breathe when Kai shakes his head. 'You're not thinking straight, Kitt. What are you—?'

'I was waiting to tell you, Brother,' the king admits. 'I wanted all the *distractions* out of the way, but now will have to do. Ilya needs food and land, yes, but that is not what is important here.' He hurries on before Kai can object. 'What I found in Father's letter was so much more than his pathetic plan for an Elite kingdom. I found the truth.'

I stand there, paralyzed by his words.

'The Plague didn't just happen to Ilya.' Kitt grins. 'It was made *for* Ilya.'

The sudden ringing in my ears nearly blots out the king's hurried explanation. 'A century ago, when Ilya was weak and on the verge of being conquered, Scholars thought they concocted a substance meant to strengthen our troops against attack. Favian Azer – funny how I could never remember his name during my tutoring – was at the end of his rule when the Plague began. Perhaps the spread of this virus was accidental, or more likely, Favian unleashed it on the kingdom.' Kitt rasps out another cough. 'You know us Azers and our hunger for power. Either way, what started as something meant to offer our armies a defense turned into a kingdom-wide Plague.' The king's gaze sweeps to mine. 'But it failed to strengthen us all.'

'That can't be right,' I sputter, skin prickling beneath his stare. 'How could we not know the Plague was man-made?'

'You're the Psychic, Paedyn,' Kitt muses. 'Take a look around and observe. Why do you think we even have a fever season? Why Elites, the strongest among us, exhaust ourselves when using too much power? Why there is a dying queen in the west tower, unable to be saved from the grief slowly stealing away her life? Why the Healers couldn't save my mother from dying because of *your* birth.' His words sting, but he doesn't stop. 'The signs were always right in front of us. Because the Plague wasn't right. Wasn't ready. There were never meant to be Ordinaries left on the other side of it. And my father spent his life trying to right that wrong.'

'They should have died with the Plague but instead they plague us. I've planned for this day a long time, waiting until I could rid myself of this Resistance.'

My head spins as Edric Azer's voice rings through it. His spewed admissions beside the Bowl come flooding back, now suddenly clear.

'Don't worry, Paedyn, I didn't just kill your father simply due to some gossip . . .'

I'm panting beneath the crushing weight of realization.

'I killed him to ensure my Elite society remained.'

This was my father's doom – the truth of our Plague.

Calum was right. It wasn't Adam Gray's involvement with the Resistance that cost him his life. It was the secret he was smart enough to figure out.

Images flash before my mind; evidence in plain sight. My father frustrated with his own power and its inability to save a sick child. Scribbled notes in his journal documenting a fever patient he couldn't cure. Elites slowly weakening over time. The death he could not spare Alice from.

I'm a damn Healer and I couldn't even save her . . .

I feel faint, my mind unable to handle any more illuminating discoveries. I'd watched my father trek to the castle every year during fever season, watch him struggle to heal a sick child despite his ability, and never once did I wonder why those named Elites bear such weakness. Perhaps some part of me reveled in the fact that the almighty were not gods, that sickness still stalked them, and exhaustion accompanied the use of too much power. Perhaps I should have listened more closely when father muttered about the Ordinary disease being bullshit. Perhaps he knew that the king was only attempting to right the wrongs of a defective Plague.

Adam Gray died because the king couldn't risk his people knowing the truth of their flaws.

'When the Plague began, Favian swore all of his Scholars to secrecy,' Kitt was telling his Enforcer when I blink back to the present. 'No one was meant to die. But, then again, the Plague was never meant to spread across the kingdom in the first place. So, not wanting to be blamed for the multitude of deaths, Favian instead spun a story for those strong enough to survive, saying they had been chosen by God to become Elites. Now, the truth of this Plague is passed down to the kings alone.'

I press a hand to my tight chest. 'All those meetings with the Scholars,' I mutter under my shallow breath. 'You wanted them to create another dose of the Plague.'

'And they were stubborn,' Kitt admits. 'The kings before me wished to hoard our power just as the Scholars do. But do you not see how many Mundanes crowd the kingdom?' His voice crescendoes into something crazed. 'Our abilities are dwindling, Kai. The Plague has been so diluted in our blood over the decades that Offensive and Defensive Elites are becoming scarce. Soon, we will become nothing more than Ordinary. And now, the Scholars have perfected their dose.'

I bite back my scoff when the king adds, 'Father was too simpleminded to see that every kingdom could be Elite.' His lips curve. 'But I will save us from becoming extinct. And when every city is brimming with powerful Elites, I will be so much greater than Father.'

'Have you lost your mind?' I hiss.

'Think about what you are saying,' Kai utters slowly. 'You might save our power, but tens of thousands would die, Kitt. Half the population from each kingdom – dead. Not to mention how many people you would need to break before they bowed to you.'

'You said so yourself, Brother. That is why you're here. To save me from brutality.' Kitt takes a step closer. 'We make a great team.'

A dark shadow crosses the Enforcer's face. 'So, just like your father, you will use me as a weapon.'

'I am not using you, Kai,' he says earnestly. 'We are working together. Using our strengths.'

The Enforcer's response is biting. 'And mine is death.'

'It is a gift. Brother—' Kitt lifts his arms as though awaiting an embrace, '—together, we will rule the greatest nation this world has ever seen. The kingdoms will be loyal to me, to us, for strengthening them.' He smiles, and it is unnervingly genuine. 'Father has trained me my whole life to rule over Elites. I will make them fall into place, and your troops will help. The surrounding cities will *want* to follow me.'

Silence stifles the room. I step into it, facing the man I've married. 'This is madness. The Kitt I knew once would know that this—'

His biting laugh makes me wince. 'The Kitt you knew?' A fit of coughs steals his breath, but still, he attempts to laugh. 'The Kitt you knew was naive enough to tell his father that you wouldn't dare betray me.'

My voice is choked. 'You knew about Edric's plan for the Resistance?'

'Calum sent you to go find the tunnels beneath this castle, and Father used me to ensure you did.' He shakes his head. 'I was stupid enough to think you wouldn't use me like that.'

'Calum wasn't controlling you,' Kai states. 'You were working together.'

'No, he wasn't controlling me' The king nearly laughs. 'But I was happy to go along with that theory. I already knew of Calum and his role to the king when Father died. So when the Mind Reader found me, hoping to continue Father's plan of exterminating Ilya's remaining Ordinaries, I was hardly surprised.' Kitt takes a step closer, and Kai shifts towards me slightly. 'At first, I mourned my father deeply, as you know. So when Calum advised I marry Paedyn to draw out the remaining Ordinaries, I agreed. But that was before I found his letter. I was reminded then how inferior his goals were, how little he cared for me. So with the knowledge of a man-made Plague that could be replicated, I suddenly knew how to bury Father's legacy with my own.'

My body begins to tremble. 'And Calum agreed to this?'

'He recognized that my plan was far superior.' Kitt waves an inky hand. 'But he did become a liability once I discovered those letters in the jewelry box. If I was a bastard, I couldn't have him telling the kingdom that.' Slowly, his eyes find mine. 'But he was not the only loose end.'

Blood rushes to my cheeks when reminded of its royal qualities. 'I'm not a threat to your throne, Kitt.'

'I saw the way all of Loot kneeled before you,' Kitt hisses. 'If the slums discover the truth of your lineage, they might rise against me to see you on the throne.'

'This is absurdity, Kitt.' A look of concern crosses Kai's face. 'You're not thinking straight.'

The king's laugh is hysterical. 'What, because this isn't your caring Kitt? Because I'm clever enough to devise a plan you've both played into?' Another step forward. He looks like a shell of the boy I once knew, his mind frayed and body frail. 'I must not be thinking straight because no one is used to me thinking at all.'

'What about the Trials?' I blurt. 'Kai training your troops?'

Kitt's sigh is exasperated. 'For Kai, a distraction and safeguard against stubborn Elite kingdoms. For you, a death sentence.'

My face pales.

'But you just wouldn't die,' he says softly. 'The bandits, the crew, the Wielder in that Pit – none of them could rid you from our lives. And that was fine, because I was going to let this next dose of Plague take you on its own terms.' His gaze softens. 'I'm not a monster. I didn't want to kill you, Paedyn. But now you have a claim to my throne.'

My stomach churns, threatening to spill its contents on the worn carpet below.

This cannot be happening.

I must be dreaming, desperately trying to claw myself awake from this nightmare. Because I refuse to believe my life is yet again crumbling around me, all within the span of a single day.

But this is real, and I am standing – shaking – before my husband who used the Trials as a way to kill me. Trials that are typically meant to showcase the Elite powers that were not gifted but created. Elite powers that do not make you a god – they make you a successful experiment.

I don't know whether to laugh, or cry, or rage.

'Just . . . calm down, Kitt.' The Enforcer's arm brushes mine when he takes another step to shield me. 'This is insanity. I won't let you go through with any of it. You cannot ruin yourself for the promise of legacy.'

But the king is hardly listening.

His gaze has fallen to the stretch of skin Kai has pressed to mine. 'Even now,' he whispers. 'Even now.' This proclamation is louder. 'Look at you, protecting her. She has taken everything from us, including each other. We are so much better off without her, Brother.' Kitt reaches out an arm, his fingers curling around the hilt of that ceremonial sword. 'Just like old times.'

There is a wildness to his features, his movements. I watch it unfurl down the length of his body, spreading from that crazed gaze. Something sinister seems to have snapped within the king. I see now that those stoic moments with me were simply a repression of everything he felt, a biding of time.

'Kitt,' Kai utters slowly. 'Put the sword down.'

'It's never going to stop.' He waves the blade's tip in the air as though completely oblivious to the picture of severity he paints. 'You are going to keep choosing her over me. Again, and again. But I need you, Kai!' He laughs out the words humorlessly. 'I need you with me – your focus, your loyalty, your heart. All of it.'

'Kitt, think about what you are saying,' Kai warns.

'She was only ever a means to an end!' The king's sword swings dangerously at his side. Those dark veins bulge against his pale skin. 'I needed her as queen to draw out the kingdoms, open their borders. But her usefulness is short-lived for us, Kai!'

My stomach lurches beneath a clenching heart. I can't help the pang of hurt that vibrates through me. I once considered this boy a friend, a confidant I accepted spending the rest of my life beside. But the hysteria in his voice, the sword in his hand, makes me flinch.

A means to an end.

Kitt is not the only Azer I've been used by before inevitably meeting the end of their sword. This king is a reflection of the last, whether he sees it or not.

'Enough, Kitt!' Kai's chest lifts with quick breaths. 'This is mad. I won't help you spread another Plague through the kingdoms. You told me I wouldn't have to kill Ordinaries while you are king.' He swallows. 'And that is exactly what you would be doing.'

'Kai . . .' The king's gaze grows eerily sympathetic. 'It's already begun.'

My blood chills. 'What are you talking about?'

Kitt swings the sword sloppily at his side. 'Fine. The Trials were more than a death sentence. They were useful to me.'

My mind reels as I drift back to each of the Trials.

Mareena's crown. Mak's death in the Pit. And—

'The roses,' I sputter. 'What did you do to those roses?'

'They were laced, and you delivered them for me.' The damning words slide easily off Kitt's tongue. Then a rattling cough spews from his mouth. 'Izram will be the first infected kingdom.'

Kai's chest heaves. His words are drowned in disbelief. 'What have you done?'

'You will come to understand, Brother,' the king urges. Blood trickles from the corner of his lips. 'Just as you will understand why I must rid our lives of her.'

I take a slow step back. 'Kitt . . .'

Kai stretches out his arm in front of me like a shield. 'You're . . .

sick, Kitt. You know this isn't right.' His stern tone slips into something more pleading. 'And you know I won't stand here and let you hurt your . . . *wife*.'

The king's eyes flash. 'Still, you hate that she is mine. Even married to me she holds so much power over you. Look at yourself, Kai! You are wound so tightly around her finger that *you* can no longer think straight.' He tugs at his hair in frustration, tangling the blond strands. 'Things will go back to the way they were without her. You and me, always.'

I glance nervously at his swinging sword. 'Why would you want to do this? I . . . I thought we cared for one another.'

'Oh, don't take this too personally, Paedyn.' Another step. 'I even began to enjoy your company over these past few weeks, despite how desperately I wanted you out of our lives. But you have to understand – I just want my brother back.'

'Kitt, calm down,' Kai orders. 'You're not yourself right now.'

The blade flashes in this flickering light. 'I didn't want it to be like this. Really.' His eyes are on me, but I'm not entirely sure he *sees* me. Delirium curls his lips into something that makes me shiver. 'But you've forced my hand. I can't have a lost princess stealing my throne from under me.'

'Kitt, stop—'

'I'm not after your throne!' I hurl the words at him, cutting off Kai's and hoping to break through this haze of hysteria Kitt wears. 'I never wanted it. This is all in your head!'

He looks down at his sword. The king seems to be somewhere else entirely. 'Of course you want the throne. All you've ever wished for was power.'

Kai steps forward, and I'm unsurprised to see him pause at an equal distance from myself and the king. That is where he has always stood, torn in two different directions.

Duty. Desire. Loyalty. Love.

Like always, he strains to hold on to both. But his grip is slipping, and a cruel reality is setting in.

One cannot have both.

Kitt lifts the sword, angered that his brother stands in its lethal path.

'I'm doing this for us, Kai. For Ilya. She is all that stands in the way.'

'Let's just talk about this.' Kai lifts his hands slowly, just as one does when attempting to calm a spooked animal. 'You and me, Brother. We will work through this. You're not yourself—'

'This is what I was made to be!' Kitt's voice cracks. 'If this is not myself, then I don't know what is. I was created to be king, and that is what I am. That includes making the hard decisions. The brave, the benevolent, *and* the brutal.'

The sword flashes as Kitt surges towards me.

Kai would never hurt his brother – I know this as much as he does. So when the king lunges towards me, I expect this breath in my lungs to be my last.

Death allows me a single moment to accept my fate. He reaches for my hand like an old friend, our reunion at long last. And I am content. The father who would never dare hurt me is waiting beyond, Adena at his side, and Mak next to her.

The sound of singing steel rings through the room when Kai blocks his brother's blade with a fire stoker. He'd only just snatched it from the hook when Kitt swung, forcing him to step beneath the arching blow and halt it with trembling arms. Kitt drags his sword across the length of the stoker before stepping back. 'Get out of my way, Kai. That's an order.'

'Not until you calm down.' The Enforcer flips the stoker in his palm. 'I will fight you all night if I need to.'

Hurt flashes across Kitt's face. 'You'll never stop choosing her until she's gone.'

The king attempts to shove past his Enforcer again, but Kai steps into the blade's path. That iron rod counters the swinging sword once again, though its pointed tip expertly avoids Kitt's chest. I watch Kai, noting how deliberately he remains on defense. This is not a fight he intends to win – only one he wishes to put an end to.

I can do little more than shake my head at them. 'Stop this, both of you!'

The stoker Kai holds clashes against his brother's sword. 'I'm not choosing between either of you!'

'You already have!' Kitt pants. He shoves a shaky finger towards the empty space beside Kai. 'She told me!'

Staring grimly at the indicated nothingness, Kai murmurs, 'You're sick, Kitt. Let me help you.'

'Sick?' The king's tone is terrifyingly calm. Then he's laughing, the sound somehow more frightening. 'Greatness is not a sickness, Brother. And once she is gone, you will see that.'

A clashing of metal ensues. Jagged shadows are painted across the walls, scrawling an ever-changing story of this battle between brothers. It's hypnotic, the way they flow in and out of each other's ferocity. This is a dance well practiced, one they have been partners within for years.

I blink at their forms, at the fluidity they find within each other. This is hardly a fight – this is reminiscence. It is as though they are back in the training yard, sparring with a routine that is second nature.

Kai steps in, arcing his weapon. Kitt falls back to catch the attack with the blade of his sword. A cross of metal hangs between them as both brothers strain against the other's strength. They push away. Resume the routine they created as boys.

This is the Enforcer's distraction.

I watch them anticipate each movement.

Calm Kitt down without hurting him in the process.

There is something so intoxicating about the way they move. I stand there, stunned at the sight of two people knowing each other so deeply. It is entrancing, like a prophecy foretold finally unfurling before my eyes. Kitt's hostility towards me means nothing in this moment, because there is nothing but peace here.

Steel flashes; metal sings. Kitt advances; Kai evades. The Enforcer feints; the king anticipates.

It is a beautiful sequence of controlled chaos. When their weapons meet again, and they stand face-to-face, a slight smile is shared between them. This is how they know each other – this is how they remember themselves. Before me are the brothers who taught each other to love with a sword in hand and a muddy ring beneath their feet. They found companionship in what they could control, and in this moment, that is each other.

Panted breaths fill the study, shadows stalled on the wall before the brothers break apart. Still sharing that small smile, they fall back into that familiar flurry of movement.

Kitt lunges. Kai parries.

The Enforcer thrusts that stoker towards the king, his broad back blocking my view.

I wait for the answering sound of steel.

I wait longer.

Time grows sluggish.

Something shifts in the air, like a stuttering of the song they were sparring to. Their feet halt awkwardly between beats of this rehearsed dance. The peace that once filled this room flees from it.

A solid back collides with my chest, making me stagger.

That is when a haunting sound fills the room.

A strangled shout cuts through the silence.

My own shuddering breath fills the tight air as I step around Kai.

There is that slight smile on Kitt's face – the one he used to give so freely. Charming and warm. Now it's found his lips again, as if to make up for all the times he had forgotten how to wear happiness.

My eyes drift downward.

The iron stoker protrudes from his chest.

That golden hair lies tousled on his head, glinting like a halo around his pale face.

The king's blood stains the same as his father's had.

Kai rushes to his brother, voice choked. 'No! You were supposed to dodge, Kitt!'

Dazed, the king looks down at the stoker buried in his chest. Touches shaking fingers to the gushing wound. His palm leans heavy on the desk beside him, leaving a bloody print atop his pile of parchment. My whole body trembles as I watch blood seep from Kitt's touch, bathing scribbled words in scarlet beneath his fingertips. His wide green eyes lift. 'I . . . forgot.'

Kai catches his brother when he stumbles.

Stained sheets of paper tumble from the desk.

The king watches them flutter delicately towards the ground.

And then he follows.

CHAPTER 68

Kai

itt's knees hit the floor right beside my own.

I can't think. I can't feel. I can't hear anything but the sickening sound of my brother's flesh tearing, over and over again in my mind.

Rage consumes me, swallowing all sanity. I feel myself wavering on the edge of some irreversible darkness, like a gaping hole my soul is slowly slipping into. But I cling to that flickering light within me, that piece of Kitt he's planted there, and beg it not to burn out.

He sways on trembling knees before beginning an agonizing topple towards the floor. I catch him, my arm curling around his back as I lay him down gently.

This cannot be happening.

None of this is right, not the crazed break in my brother's character or the ashy stoker skewering him.

A puddle of blood crawls slowly across the rug beneath his shuddering body, and I can hardly feel its sticky warmth lapping around my knees. 'You were supposed to dodge,' I say again, my words heavy with guilt. 'I thought you were going to dodge.'

The delirium that was clutching Kitt so tightly begins to slip away.

'I forgot. I . . . I can't even remember myself.'

I try to ignore the tears welling in my eyes as I press trembling hands to his wound. Blood oozes between my fingers. 'I'm gonna fix this, okay?' Now it is I who sounds hysterical. 'You're going to be just fine.'

Paedyn sits stiffly at my side, her eyes wide and glassy. Kitt's eyes drift distantly to his queen. 'I did care for you. I – I don't want to be a monster.'

My hands cup Kitt's face, turning it towards my stern one. 'Hey, I am the monster. Not you, all right?'

His voice is thick with pain, with something cold I don't dare identify as Death's arrival. 'You're a pawn. But I'm . . . I'm the king who plays you. Though I don't remember most of my moves.'

I force a shaky laugh because the alternative is far too damning. 'Always the dramatics with you, Kitty.' My throat tightens as I grab his bloody hand. 'I'm going to make this right.'

A tear rolls down my cheek as I shut my eyes in search of a Healer's power.

Dual bleeding out before me. Hydro down the hall.

I dig further, reaching out into the corridors beyond.

Gust. Shield. Veil.

Every Imperial outside the door is utterly useless to me. I fight against my ability, urging it towards the other end of this sprawling castle where I know the Healers reside – where every one of them is uselessly out of my reach. A wall slams into my power, and terror grips my heart.

No. *No.*

I rail against it, my head pounding with the force. Father used to push my ability to the point of failure, and this is what it felt like. A wave of exhaustion crashes over me, evidence of my weakness. Evidence of a fabricated Plague and its flaws.

Kitt's salvation lies just beyond my reach.

'There are no Healers,' I gasp. 'I need a Healer!'

The shout bounces around the study, replaying my helplessness over and over. Desperation tears from my throat again. 'Paedyn, go find me a Healer.'

She nods, face pale. 'Keep him awake until I get back.'

And then she is tearing out of the room.

I look down at Kitt and his loosening grip on my fingers. 'You're going to be just fine, you hear me?' It's all the comfort I can muster for him as I will the words to be true.

Green eyes grow blurry. His head shakes, a violent rock of his skull against the bloody floor. A whisper leaves me in ruins. 'I haven't felt right for . . . a while. I don't . . . remember. But I'm scared, Kai.'

A sob spills out of me.

I duck my head, shoulders shaking in time to the beat of my shattering heart. 'I'm right here.' My voice breaks. 'You're going to be fine.'

'It was all for us. I remember that,' he murmurs weakly. 'I j–just wanted my brother back.'

'You never lost me.' My words are a plea I desperately need him to understand. 'I have always been right at your side – your brother, no matter our blood.'

'No.' Kitt's soft smile displays the blood seeping onto his lips. That crazed haze seems to have cracked, leaving only the shell of my brother behind. 'You were somewhere between us. N–never able to decide who you loved more.'

I shake my head. Tears spatter his bloody chest. 'I can love more than one person, Kitt.'

'But I cannot,' he whispers. 'You were the only person that loved me, Kai. And I – I was . . . losing you to her.'

I hang my head in hands slicked with my brother's blood. 'This is all my fault. It should have been me!' I choke on the emotion clogging my throat. 'This is my fate. I'm supposed to protect you.'

Kitt sucks in a rattling breath. 'I think . . .' His eyes flutter shut. 'My fate was to save you from me.'

'Don't say that,' I choke. 'You are the king. You are my *brother*.' A sob weaves between each word to follow. 'And we promised to always stay together. Grow old enough that the only thing we remember is each other, and that would be okay, because you are worth every one of my memories. You promised me that, Kitt.' I pull at my hair with a bloody hand. 'Dammit, you promised!'

Kitt lifts his head from the ground, golden hair matted with blood. My knees soak in the pool of it as I reach to cradle his neck. He looks up at me, eyes warm when they land on mine – just as they have always been. 'I don't want . . . to be a monster,' he whispers. 'I – I just wanted to be great.'

Tears stream down my face. 'You don't need to be great, Kitt. You are *good*. You've always been good.'

He shakes his head, and the movement has a rasping cough falling from bloodied lips. 'I don't want to be alone.'

'You won't be,' I say roughly. 'Because you're going to be fine. Me and you, Kitt. Always. You . . . you promised me that.' I lift my head to let another futile cry rip from my throat. 'Help! I need a Healer!'

'Kai.'

It's weak, my name from his lips. But the quiet contentment in which he says it is enough to make me weep.

He has accepted this fate. Broken a promise. Doomed me to a life without him.

'Bury me . . .' Kitt takes several shallow breaths. Then he smiles. 'Under the willow tree. I . . . I won't be lonely there.'

My very soul feels as though it is splitting in two. 'I can't do this without you, Kitt. Please. *Please.*'

He says nothing. His eyes drift shut.

'Stay with me, Kitt!' I pat his cheek, though I can hardly see him through my steady stream of tears. 'I need you to stay awake.'

His bleary gaze finds mine again. Then he's lifting shaking hands to fumble with the wedding ring on his finger. My voice quivers. 'What are you—?'

Kitt slips that steel band free. And with the last of his dwindling strength, whispers, 'Love each other for me.'

Then the ring is pressed into my palm.

'No.' The word is defiant. 'No!' This one drips with anguish. 'I need you with me, Kitt!'

His gaze trails upward. Rests on the silver shadows that cling to the ceiling, staring down on us. 'I wrote you l-letters.' The words are nearly lost on Death's chill. 'So you can see why I'm . . . a monster.'

There is a sudden widening of the green eyes that so easily crinkled

475

with laughter. They grow distant, pinned on a phantom beside me. Breath rattles in his chest. 'I'm scared, Kai.'

I squeeze his hand, pressing it to my forehead with a whimper. 'I'm right here.' I think I might be dying right beside him. 'You're okay.'

A ripple of relief washes over him. His mind seems clear for the first time in weeks, but his words fade away. 'I just want to be great.'

'You are,' I breathe. The tears are falling faster now. 'You will be remembered as Ilya's greatest king. I promise you that, Brother.'

Blood blossoms from beneath his body, like a peaceful pool surrounding a gruesome scene. It stains his hair, turning the tips of each blond strand into a delicate crown, as though Death himself has placed it upon his brow.

'Forgive me, Kitt,' I beg.

The quiet words he aims over my shoulder aren't meant for me. 'I'll go gently. For you.'

Then his gaze is fixed on the world beyond.

Mine goes quiet without him in it.

'You and me,' I whisper against his bloody chest.

Peace is forever pressed into his features.

Anguish rips me raw from the inside out.

'Please . . . don't leave me . . .'

I am numb.

I am dead beside him but cursed to keep living.

Grief is my equal. Misery a mirror.

I call sorrow by its name and speak my own.

My head falls back with a roar of agony.

My brother.

My brother.

My brother.

And when Paedyn throws open the door, a Healer at her side, I am lifeless on the floor beside my brother.

Edric

Before meeting his fate at the hands of Paedyn Gray, the king warns his son of the threat she poses.

Scrutinizing him thoroughly, as he often does, Edric Azer sees the man who fell in love with Iris Moyra all those years ago. The similarities between the king and his heir are eerie, like looking into a warped mirror to see pieces of oneself fossilized on another's face. Kitt stares warily at his father from his assigned seat before the fireplace while Edric reclines casually in his worn leather one, as if he hasn't just metaphorically ripped the floor out from beneath his son's feet.

'So, really,' Kitt ventures slowly, 'you are the leader of the Resistance?'

Edric drums his fingers against the faded armrest. 'Technically. Though, it is Calum who is the face of it.'

'And he is one of the Fatals you've hidden away?' Kitt confirms.

'Yes. Over the years, I've tried to keep their identities as hidden as possible. My Fatals are my most powerful weapons and spies. They are of no use to me if everyone knows who and what they are.' The king meets his son's eyes, and again, that eerie feeling washes over

him. It is as though he's looking into his own gaze. 'Kai still does not know the truth. But you, Kitt, are my heir. It is time you know these things. Know my plans so you may continue to fulfill them when I no longer can.'

Kitt straightens in his seat, a foreign sense of importance washing over him. He has, for better or worse, waited his entire life to prove himself to his king – his father. The boy has wanted for little more than to be needed by the man who has always withheld his affection. Though Edric's relationship with Kai is strained, Kitt finds himself envious of even the begrudging approval his father feels for the Enforcer. It is pride – praise, even – that the heir finds himself craving. But his role is not one that displays tangible achievements, and this forces him to work even harder to prove himself.

Failure is the word Kitt most fears, and it will plague him still, even after the death of his father. He is not quite sure where the overwhelming need to please stems from, only that it seems to fester with each day the king shoves a book beneath his nose. Disappointment Kitt can bear, but indifference from the man meant to love him drives the boy mad. Nothing is ever good enough – not his studies, or etiquette, or practiced charisma. At least with Kai's field of physicality, there is some measure of accomplishment. Some death to be doled out or command to fulfill.

A dark thought has always dwelled in the back of Kitt's mind. Perhaps the death of his mother has tainted his relationship with the king. Even the prince hates himself for her death. When, in truth – one Kitt will never come to know – Edric cannot love something that is impotent. And unlike Kai, the heir is nearly useless until the king's demise, and that does not sit particularly well with him. Though, if Edric were being honest with himself – he rarely is – he would admit how similar Kitt's temperance is to Iris's. This only makes things harder for the king and is perhaps what pushes him to mold the prince into something harsher.

But here, in this moment, the king needs something from his son. And even after all this time, Kitt will do anything to make him proud.

'You want me to show Paedyn the tunnels?'

Kitt says this with a skeptical kind of thrill. Stern, though equally bland, the king elaborates. 'She will try to convince you to take her through them, like I said. You will do so, but not obviously. It should not be difficult for you to reminisce on how you have never strayed far from the castle walls.'

This is a sad truth, one that the heir will have no quandary speaking of. There will be no need to put on a facade for this intriguing girl, but rather, lower his walls and let the feelings spew from behind them. Though, that may prove to be more difficult.

'She wouldn't,' Kitt urges. 'You don't know her like I do, Father. She won't betray me to—'

'She is nothing!' The king's hiss has his son wincing. 'And those that are nothing will take everything from you. Remember that, Son.' He lifts a stiff finger between them. 'Do not make the mistake of feeling for her.'

In this moment, Kitt does not believe his father to be right. He holds hope close to his heart, believing in the goodness he knows his mother would have wished him to.

Later still will he discover the naivety of hope.

Slowly, Kitt nods, ever obedient to his father's wishes. 'And why, exactly, am I doing this?'

The king smiles, and it's joyous enough to tell the heir it isn't meant for him. 'Because I am finally able to put an end to the Resistance.'

The prince thinks on this. His face slackens with surprise. For the first time since he was a boy, the man before him suddenly becomes just that. Behind the facade of a grand king, a god of Elites, there lies a single-minded man. Kitt has always thought his father strived for more than just the eradication of Ordinaries, more than a single kingdom of Elites.

That perfect, powerful image of Edric Azer begins to melt away, leaving a child who is oddly disappointed by the mediocre sins of his father. He has always expected more from the man who so flippantly raised him. If Kitt and Kai had endured their loveless lives for something truly great, it might have been worth it all.

Because that is the truth of it. Kitt has never learned how to love, and yet, he somehow stumbled into it with his brother. But everything else, every hopeless attempt for his father's favor, is born of obsession. That alone is what the king has taught him.

'That is all you want, Father?' The heir clears his throat, intensity building behind that green gaze. 'A truly Elite society within Ilya alone?'

'What more could I ask for?' the king snaps. 'And if I meet my end before it is finished, you shall continue my legacy. Wipe out the Ordinaries for good. As it was always meant to be.'

Kitt blinks sluggishly. That is all his father wants of him? All that is expected of him after everything he has endured?

'Did you hear me, boy?' The king's booming voice does not make Kitt wince. 'I have plans for you.'

The heir nods. He has plans as well.

Kitt will become so much greater than his father. Then, he will have earned his approval. Become worthy of a love he never understood.

Later, Edric will speak with his daughter again, spinning each word to seem as though she is influencing his sons. Each jab is intended to spur her towards spending more time with Kitt — the heir discreetly doing his father's bidding. Soon that boy would become a king, and with the crown comes a discovery of the truth. The letter Edric leaves his son is a reflection of the one Landan Azer left him. And so the secret of the great Plague is passed on.

As for Kai, well, the king does not care for the budding relationship between his Enforcer and forgotten daughter. Nor does he care for the spare who is not truly his. The king revels in Kai's power as much as he despises it. Because, in truth, it was not born of him, making Edric hate how something so strong is not his to claim. This is why he pushes the boy so hard, spills his blood in training and hardens the heart that pumps it. He equally loves and loathes his Enforcer's power, and it drives an immense darkness between them.

Kai does not understand the extent of his father's indifference towards him or why he suffers so heavily at the hand of his king.

Paedyn does not understand the extent of her birth and how it is connected to the king's loathing of her.

Kitt does not understand the extent of his father's hatred towards Ordinaries, but he does not need to. No matter the reasonings, it is inferior to everything the king has put him through. The heir will no longer tolerate being unremarkable in his father's eyes – he will overwhelm every hope and dream Edric has for Ilya. Kitt Azer determines to be the greatness his father never was.

In time, they will come to see what was hidden from them. Every lie brought to light, every secret unraveled.

But the king, dear Edric, will never know the truth behind that rose on Iris's jewelry box.

CHAPTER 69

Paedyn

It is six days after Kitt's death when we gain the courage to gather the stack of bloody letters.

Most are unmaimed by the king's death, having shied into a dark corner of his desk drawer. Ink smears across the pages of some while blood stains the others, leaving words to gasp beneath the large splotches. Each letter plucks apart a different piece of Kitt. Some anger and grief, others calculating or lonely.

Not all are addressed to someone. Most are just a scribble of consciousness or spillage of emotion.

But there is no shortage of tears.

Kai weeps for his brother. I weep briefly for the boy I used to know. Kitt Azer was at war with himself, the pen his weapon and the parchment his foe. The battle that raged behind his eyes was one he fought alone until the very end.

The brothers are lost without each other. Kitt, because his Enforcer is no longer his. And Kai, because his king has died in his arms.

So he weeps.

Kitt is gone, and a piece of Kai with him.

Father is still dead. She killed him.

I'm not sure what else to say, or write, or do.

I can still see his severed neck when I shut my eyes, so I don't sleep.

Paedyn is gone. The girl I trusted is now a traitor to the crown. A killer.

And I am angry. Why am I so angry? He never loved me.

~~But he died before I got the chance to make him.~~

I'm sending my Enforcer after her – I don't think he likes when I call him that. We haven't spoken much since the moment I kneeled in the mud at Father's side.

I feel something fraying inside me. Maybe it's my sanity.

Paedyn,

Did you watch the light leave his eyes?

Those are my eyes. But you knew that.

I am angry. But you knew that.

~~And yet, part of me is still trying to hate you. But you knew that.~~

My Enforcer is coming for you.

Run.

They buried the king. Made me the next one.

I haven't left the study in days. I'm not sure I've spoken to anything but paper in days.

Servants gossip beneath my window.

~~I dump my food there to give them something else to talk about.~~

Everyone thinks I've gone mad, and maybe I have.

Maybe

I

always

was.

Kai does not mourn. I see the concern on his face whenever our eyes meet, like he's trying to understand why it is I grieve.

He will never know what it means to be a failure. Father loved power, and that is what he saw in my brother. But me? I was meek. Kind. Nothing like the heir he'd hoped for.

A disappointment.

I am tired of grieving.

What did he ever do to earn my love?

Was it commanded of me? I only know what to do when he's asked it of me. And he did not tell me to feel. No, I did too much of that. Too kind. Too weak. Too soft. Too unlike Kai.

I am sick of mourning.

I've been mourning the lack of his love all my life.

Everything was for him. All that I am and all I am becoming.

Father. King. You.

YOU.

All of this is for you. Can you see that from beneath the six feet of dirt that separates us? Is this need for your love too weak for you? ~~If you are shouting up at me, you'll have to speak up, Father.~~

Power is what you have always wanted from me.

So I'll become it.

Calum found me, just as I figured he would.

Brave. Benevolent. Brutal.

He told me of his plan to continue my father's work. I was reminded once again of when the king told me of his hope for a truly Elite Ilya. It all seemed so simple-minded, so lowly for a man who expected perfection from his sons.

For so many years, I hoped that something great was to come from his lack of love. But Father's obsession with Ordinaries has brought him to his knees.

Calum tells me to marry Paedyn Gray. My father's killer.

She will draw the remaining Ordinaries out of hiding. Her reign will be a ploy to discreetly rid Ilya of the weak.

But I want to do so much more.

I found Father's letter to me. He wishes for me to fulfill his plans, carry on ridding the kingdom of Ordinaries. And I might have done just that, might have followed in his footsteps, hoping to please him in death.

But then I learned the truth.

Elites could be made, and I could rule over all of them.

With an Ordinary as queen, the kingdoms will open their borders to us. It won't be difficult to smuggle the Plague into each city with laced resources. And when a new wave of Elites is born, I will be their king.

I will be great.

~~I will prove myself to Father.~~

I will be so much greater than him.

Brother,

When was the last time I called you that? It's strange, not sparring with you in the mornings, or visiting Gail to see who can get away with snatching the most food from behind her back.

I miss us. No titles. No duties.

You left for your mission two days ago, and I can't help but wonder if you will return. Do you love this version of me enough? Is that even fair to ask?

~~You are supposed to be loyal to me.~~

I am going to be better for you. For us. No one has ever loved me like you. I need you to make me whole again. You, Kai. I was harsh when you left – I know. But just come home and punish me for it in the training ring. Come home and give me another chance at being your brother.

~~Or perhaps she is where your loyalties lie.~~

We are going to change Ilya, Brother.

You and me. Always.

Calum has agreed to my plan.

The surrounding kingdoms must open their borders at the

welcoming of Ordinaries and the engagement to Paedyn Gray. As much as I wish to rip her from our lives, Calum pointed out the sway she holds within the slums. I only need her on the throne as a symbol to the cities so they will lower their guards against us.

That is, until the Plague rids us of her. Everything fell apart when she stumbled into our lives. She killed my father. Stole my brother. Even now, the traitor is likely tugging Kai back into her arms.

But I need her for a little while longer.

And then I'll have my brother back.

I took a dose of the Plague.

Maybe it was a mistake. I read in Father's letter how he gave a dose to Ava when she was born. He was so terrified of having a weak child that he did everything he could to prevent it. But Ava was only a child - she could not survive the sickness.

When I told the Scholars of my plans for Ilya, they adamantly informed me that there was not enough research done on what would happen to an Elite who took another portion of the Plague. So I became their test subject before they could object. Now they are forced to do everything they can to keep me alive.

I haven't told Kai about the truth of Ava's death - about anything, really. But I will survive this Plague. I have to. I have to be great. Father always thought I was too soft, too weak. Now I will be far more powerful than he ever was. I only need to live.

Kai,

You should be back by now.

Did you run away with her? Did you abandon our forever for a chance at one with our father's murderer?

~~You still love her, don't you?~~

Don't you see how she drove us apart? She ruined us.

Come home. Please.
All will be as it once was.

The Scholars are fighting me.

They want to hoard our abilities like the kings before had. The Healers monitor me closely, waiting for the first signs of sickness - and whether or not I will survive it.

I force them all to fall in line with my plan.

I am not the kings before.

My Enforcer is back with my betrothed.

He brought her home to me.

Perhaps his loyalty still resides with me. Perhaps I've misjudged his feelings for Paedyn. Ridding her from our lives may be easier than I thought.

The court was shocked by my decree. The people must welcome Ordinaries into Ilya so the surrounding cities will welcome us. They have yet to discover how great I will make this kingdom - how far I will stretch our borders.

Paedyn let me slip that ring onto her finger because she hopes for a united Ilya. But I will unite far more than Ilya.

Every city inked onto our maps, from the Shallows to the Scorches, will be ours.

For my own legacy. For my brother. For us.

The bombing at the parade was unpleasant, but effective.

Easel pushed for Paedyn to prove herself to the kingdom by entering another set of Trials - just like I'd planned. I want her gone, and the people want a distraction. But she will be of use to me if she lives to see her second Trial.

I will have Paedyn sail to Izram and leave behind a crate of roses laced with the Plague. If my bandits kill her before then, I will start with Dor.

I'm coughing now, but I do my best to hide it. I don't want Kai to worry. Several Healers and Scholars document my progress daily. Foul-tasting herbs are forced down my throat in the hopes that they will aid my chances of survival.

Nothing is stronger than a woman who is told she's weak.

Something has changed in Paedyn. These Trials have only empowered her. Part of me almost wants to admire her resilience.

We have spent several civil moments together, all while I bite my tongue and smother my feelings. I was wrong to think Kai abandoned his love for her. The two are closer than ever, and I am the one who drove them together. I see the way my brother looks at her, devotion slipping beneath the mask of stoicism Father taught him to wear.

I think Kai worries that I still have feelings for Paedyn, that I push her away in consideration of him. Let him think what he must. But anything I felt for Paedyn Gray died when my father did. When she betrayed me like I believed she never would.

I want her gone. I can feel Kai slipping away from me by the day. He will choose her — I know he will. And I will not lose my brother.

I found my mother's jewelry box.

It was the first time I went into her chamber. For years, I wondered what was behind that door. Now I know that it is only memory. The room is dusty, forgotten, stagnant. There were hardly any remnants of the woman I would have called 'Mother' — only that wooden box of her most prized possessions.

But it was the notes I found inside that were most intriguing. And then they were worrying. It took me several minutes to recognize whose handwriting decorated them. The anger followed quickly after.

If Calum was intimate with my mother, I have no way of knowing if I am the rightful heir. That knowledge belongs to the Mind Reader alone. Even the mere possibility of him being my father makes him a liability. He may have to be dealt with.

Paedyn,

In truth, you're not an easy individual to hate. I wouldn't even say my feelings towards you are so strong. They are, rather, indifferent. There was once a time when Paedyn Gray had both the princes wrapped around her finger, but that was before she betrayed me and killed my father. I don't take it personally, really. Not anymore. In fact, you freed me from the man who was only ever holding me back.

I found something else to chase, obsess over, as I often do. And you are helping me. For that, I am thankful. But please do not take offense to the inevitable demise I will let you meet. This legacy, this life, was only ever meant for my brother and me to share. And I will not share him with you.

When the time comes, I will ensure the kingdom mourns you. You have my word. I don't wish to be your monster, Paedyn. Part of me still cares for you. But I only know how to love my brother.

I steal moments with Kai whenever I am able. He keeps me stable. I feel like myself when I am with him, even as the Plague begins eating away at my sanity.

I only wish to return things to the way they were - before her. His feelings for my betrothed are not ideal, but he will come to see her as the threat she is to us.

I just want my brother back. I want greatness.

Is that too much to ask for?

The Plague has made me weak, dulled my mind. Anger is an emotion that now belongs to the Plague. I feel it wash over me like a wave I cannot control. Kai soothes that fraying part of myself. But Paedyn unleashes it.

It feels good, getting drunk with my brother again. Paedyn is there. Paedyn is always there. But it is bearable when Kai is around. I can be myself, be with him. The Plague allows me that.

I enjoy the time with my brother. And deep down, I enjoy the little time I have left with Paedyn.

They set sail for Izram today.

I may never see my brother again. Doesn't he realize this is all for him? For us? He was never meant to sail over the treacherous waters. But he is in love with her. ~~He will do anything for her because he loves her more than he loves me.~~ I just need him to come home.

Sending Paedyn to Izram was partially with the hope that she wouldn't return. I discreetly informed the captain that dumping her from the ship was an option, if his men so desired. But with Kai on board, he will ensure that Paedyn makes it home in one piece - or neither of them will.

Though, the true purpose of her journey is to gift Izram a crate of laced roses. They will be the first to endure the Plague, but in time, they will thank me for it.

If the sea allows Paedyn to meet Queen Zailah, her Trial still stands. I need her to convince the stubborn woman to accept our peace offering. And I need Kai to come home. I don't know what I will be when he returns.

The royal physicians are worried. My mind is drifting. My body is weak. But I am going to live. ~~I cannot die before I am better than him.~~ I am going to live.

Unlike my father, I do not need Calum to help carry out my plans. Fear festers when I am around him, all rooted in my unknown legitimacy. I should simply dispose of him. It is as though paranoia has planted a seed in my mind that grows by the day.

I don't feel right.

My mind is slipping, and it is not just the Plague at fault. ~~I have piled so much pressure on my shoulders that~~ - No, Father has done this to me. It is because of him that I am this way. Obsessive. Controlling. In constant need of approval. My mind is not my own – maybe it never was.

I don't want to be a monster. I don't want Kai to see me as one.

My ship arrived at the dock in shambles. It's a miracle they survived the sea and its creatures. But my gift was accepted. My brother is back. And what is left of me is here to greet him.

I am coughing up blood now. Another fun side effect of the Plague. I've lost weight rapidly, and I can't remember the last time I slept through the night.

Kai is worried about me. He knows I am not myself.

I watched my brother die yesterday.

Beneath the illusion, his name was Makoto Khitan.

Calum told me how he found a Wielder outside the Bowl after that third Purging Trial. How his mind screamed of grief and rage for the seamstress who was killed. But it was Paedyn he blamed for her being there in the first place.

So I offered him a chance at revenge. Ironically, I used the tunnels to sneak out into the Bowl, then down the path towards Loot. I needed one final push for Ilya to fall into line, accept my changes to the kingdom. But I would not risk throwing Kai into that Bowl. Because I knew he would let Paedyn kill him. ~~Because my brother would die to save her, not kill her to live with me.~~

Makoto agreed to fight Paedyn. But the hefty sum I paid him to put on a good show was futile. He didn't leave the arena alive.

Paedyn Gray has a way of making people care about her.

There are holes in my memory. I ignored it at first, but now I think the Healers are right. The Plague is eating away at me – my mind.

Paedyn Gray is the daughter of Iris Moyra. She is an

illegitimate child. And I could not risk being found out as the same. So when she told me what she learned from Calum, how she believed him to be a Dual, I went along with her theory.

Calum could read the apology in my mind before I shoved my sword through his chest. It was nothing personal. Truly. But I refuse to be reduced to a bastard. Not after everything I have endured, everything I have planned for Ilya.

They bowed before her. All of the slums.

She has a claim to the throne. And I won't let her overthrow me. I need this. Doesn't she know I need this? She has already achieved greatness in my Trials. This is mine. I need this legacy. I need her gone. I need to be great—

CHAPTER 70
Paedyn

Kai didn't move from Kitt's side until his body grew cold.

Even then, it took three Imperials to pull him from the pool of blood. He let them, of course, unlike the dozens prior who dared drag the Enforcer from his grief before the sun rose timidly through the study's window. Rays of light stroked over Kitt's still body, memorializing the sickening scene as though it were a painting – Kitt, a canvas of scarlet streaks.

For as long as Kai kept Kitt company, so did I.

By the time our aching knees rose from the worn rug, blood was crusted atop our skin and caked into our hair. I followed Kai numbly to his rooms and filled the tub with steaming water. He didn't fight me when I peeled off his soiled clothes or urged him into the bath.

His eyes were distant, hollow. But they were on me, and that was something. I lathered a bar of soap across his skin, smelling so distinctly of pine and the man I fell in love with. With a soft sponge, I scrubbed at every patch of hardened blood. His eyes never strayed from mine, shutting only when I softly asked it of him while wiping the stained face of sorrow itself.

He didn't stand from the tub when I finally lowered the sponge.

Instead, he moved with an intent I hadn't seen in half a day. Water dripped from his arms as he unbuttoned the back of my dress. As soon as it had slipped down my body and into a puddle of fabric on the floor, he pulled me into the tub.

He wouldn't let me touch the sponge. The fearsome Enforcer of Ilya swiped every speck of his brother's blood from my skin. It was the gentleness with which he loved, even when he grieved, that made me break. We held each other, weeping for a brother, a broken boy, a loss to the world. Our bodies shook, tears rolling down the shoulders we clung to.

Though, Kitt was not mine to grieve. In the end, he was a shell of the boy I once knew, one who saw me as an obstacle to overcome. But I did not resent him. Rather, I ached for the brother who Kai had lost, not the king with a broken mind. I ached for Kai, as though his grief were my own.

So when the water had gone cold and each breath began to slow, Kai spoke his first words since Kitt uttered his last.

'Thank you.'

The second day after the king's death was arguably the hardest. All of Ilya had learned of the kind ruler's cruel death. It was advertised as a tragic accident, though the people searched for a more exciting tale to tell. Rumors rippled through the kingdom, every mouth speculating how Kitt had met his end in order to fill the void of withheld truth.

They would likely wonder for years to come, and still, we would not tell them. Kitt, even in death, was to remain the kind king he was always meant to be.

Kai pulled his grief back like a tide, hauling it in long enough to panic over the gift we had left in Izram. The crate of roses was likely opened weeks ago to loose a Plague on the entire city. But before we were given the chance to spiral further, a letter was found wedged beneath the castle's towering front doors.

In neat, elegant writing, it read:

I do hope it was not you, Paedyn Gray, who attempted to infect my kingdom. This is said in jest, as I knew you

494

truthfully believed the roses to be a gift. No matter — I sensed what awaited in that box before you ever stepped foot off my docks. Alas, I have little use for your Plague, but I suppose your king thinks differently. Perhaps he should have tried polluting another kingdom. Then again, I hear he is no longer with us. My condolences.

Any further attempts to infect my people will result in an unpleasant retaliation. Do not take my overlooking of this crime as a sign of weakness. I know the laced roses were not your doing. But I do wish for us to have a fruitful relationship.

Your fellow queen,
Z

I promptly looked over at Kai. 'How the hell did she know?'

We spent the rest of that day receiving condolences from the grieving castle. Without a plagued kingdom to worry about, Kai strode stiffly through the hall, his gaze vacant and words scarce. The entire palace had been draped in a sheet of darkness — black curtains covering windows while black clothing draped every body.

Scholars nipped at our heels like shadows, calling after Kai to discuss his coronation. 'I am not king until Kitt is laid to rest,' he would say, more toneless than the time before. I knew that he meant it, just like I knew that he was stalling. He did not wish to be king.

We spent that night in the arms of those closest to Kai.

'My boy,' Gail had wailed when he walked into her kitchen. 'My sweet boy.'

She held him long enough to burn what food simmered on the stove and cried hard enough that she didn't care. Jax sobbed against his brother's chest, mourning the loss of their other half. It was when he started hiccupping that Andy joined, her body shaking with sobs. A few traitorous tears had escaped my burning eyes before Gail pulled me in and wrapped her arms around us all.

The third and fourth day were more of the same. Berating Scholars, a castle in mourning, gossiping Ilyans, grief, tears, sobs.

When we could stomach the conversation, solemn Healers circled us in a dim room to swap hushed details of the king's slow demise. They spoke of his insistence on taking the Plague despite knowing the ramifications, then more hesitantly of his unraveling mind soon after. He was easily agitated, often caught speaking to the empty air or wandering around at all hours of the night.

Kitt was dying long before he forgot to dodge his brother's advance, we discover. The Healers could not save him, and suddenly, this makes sense after learning the truth of Elites' limitations. His body was rejecting another dose of the Plague. It was only a matter of time until the sickness unraveled all that he was.

Within the long stretches of sorrow, we spent much of our time in the study, simply staring at everything exactly as he left it. All but the bloodied rug remained. Jax and Andy would sit with us, partly in silence but, occasionally, more boldly in reminiscence. They would swap memories, each one bleeding into the last and lending a smile for fleeting moments.

And that was something.

By the fifth day, that emptiness occupying Kai's gaze had lessened slightly. Still, we held each other, just as we had for the past several days. And when he pulled away, he spoke soft gratitude against my skin. 'Thank you, Pae. For everything.'

I would smile – it was always sad. 'It no longer surprises me when you say that.'

'Good.' His nose brushed mine. 'I want you to grow so used to my gratitude that you're sick of it.'

That night, I slipped the wedding ring from my finger.

And on the sixth day after Kitt's death, we read his letters.

CHAPTER 71

Rai

Dirt smears my sweaty face.

The shovel is slick in my hands, peppering each palm with splinters. Dusk settles behind the willow's swaying arms as I carve out a patch of earth among its roots. Fresh soil piles beside me; memories surface with each scoop of the shovel.

Kitt was with me the last time I dug a grave beneath this tree. He was at my side, shovel in hand and muddy face mirroring mine. We reminisced about Ava until our laughter turned to tears.

Ava.

Her death was the doing of the man I called 'Father'. All because of Edric Azer's greed for power. He killed my sister with a dose of the Plague. He killed my brother with the need to be great.

My vision blurs. I blink past the anger and grief and urge to crawl into this grave myself.

My brother.

My brother.

My brother is dead.

The shovel slips from between my fingers to land in a cushion of dirt. My knees sink into the damp grass, shoulders shaking with the

weight of grief atop them.

His letters are fresh in my mind, each of them a stab in the gut before breakfast this morning. I wasn't there to protect him from his own thoughts, from the need for greatness that swallowed him whole. He was breaking before my very eyes, tearing at the seams from something more sinister than the stresses of being king.

I'm reminded of that odd shift in his power and curse myself for dismissing the feeling. Kitt's ability was the first I ever felt, one so familiar I could taste it on my tongue, but still, I failed him.

He had become a pawn to power, and I should have recognized myself in his gaze.

He took the Plague to be *more*. And I wasn't there to tell him he was enough.

I hear the footsteps behind me. She wanted me to hear them.

The familiar warmth of her embrace wraps around me from behind, holding together the broken pieces I've become. I stare at the shallow grave, allowing a tear to escape my empty gaze.

He's gone.

He's gone.

'I'm right here,' she whispers in my ear. 'I've got you.'

I turn slowly in her arms, watching that beautiful face come into view. Paedyn's eyes swim with tears, just as they have for days. For me. There is only so much grief she can have for the man who wished to kill her. No, this hurt is for me.

My eyes fall to the shovel at her side. Managing a sad smile, I lift dirt-stained fingers to her face. 'Have you come to help me dig, darling?'

'You've dug enough graves for me,' she breathes. 'I figured I would repay the favor.'

My sob is part laugh. 'I don't know how I would survive this without you.'

'Well, never again will you have to survive anything alone.' Her gaze grows determined. 'Cockroach, remember?'

I shake my head, forever astounded by her. 'No. You are strength. Life itself. That is why Death fears you.'

'All I do is fear Death,' she corrects. 'Fear losing you.'

It hurts to smile. 'Death knows better than to try and drag me from you.'

We hold each other in our gazes, gentle but sure. Sniffling, she stares down at the shovel she brought and clears a tightening throat. 'Once he's buried, they will make you king.'

'So let's sit here a little longer,' I mutter. 'Please.'

We do.

Leaves rustle all around us as I breathe in the smell of freshly turned soil. Paedyn leans back on her palms, eyes shutting when a soft breeze whispers through her hair. Chattering birds muffle the stream of screaming thoughts in my head for a few blissful minutes.

'You will make a great king.'

The reminder of my looming future shatters the short-lived peace. 'That was supposed to be Kitt. Not me.' My head falls into shaking hands. 'But he was so focused on his father. On greatness.'

His father. Not mine. Perhaps not even before I discovered the truth of my birth. That king was never my family.

Distantly, beneath the growing ache of grief weighing on my chest, I wonder for the man meant to be my father. Perhaps he wasn't worth knowing. Perhaps I'll find out for myself one day.

'Kitt was obsessive.' Paedyn gnaws on her lower lip. 'Sick with the Plague.'

'He tried to kill you,' I say numbly.

'He wasn't himself. I . . . I don't blame him for it.'

'I killed him.'

I barely hear her words. 'It wasn't your fault. He was already dying, Kai. The Healers told us so.'

'I still killed him, Paedyn.' My voice breaks. 'I killed my brother!'

She hooks her arms around my neck, pulling my shaking body against her own. 'Shh. It's not your fault, Kai.'

I bury my face into her scar. 'I couldn't save him. I told him I would save him.' My voice is choked. That formidable power running through my veins had *failed*. 'He was supposed to dodge. We were supposed to keep our promise.'

'You will,' she whispers. 'You will see him again. Just like I will

499

see my father. Adena. Mak.' There are tears in her eyes when she pulls away to clutch my face. 'Your promises are not broken. They are just awaiting you.'

I can hardly breathe. 'I need him, Pae. I need my brother.'

'Shh.'

'I can't do this without him.'

'Shh. I'm right here.'

'I did this to him!' Each sob is a painful shake of my body. 'I couldn't save him. I couldn't save my brother . . .'

Paedyn holds me until grief's tide pulls away long enough for me to catch my breath. This is not the first time she has saved me from drowning.

A shovel is quickly pushed into my hand, followed by a string of stern words. 'It's time for Kitt to rest.'

A weight seems to lift from my chest.

Rest. Not death.

He is at peace, and that is all I have ever wanted for my brother.

Stiffly, I stand to my feet, pulling Paedyn up with me. My shovel meets the torn earth beside us. I push through the pain still lingering in my voice. 'Think you can keep up, Gray?'

'Are you seriously making this a competition?'

I plunge steel into the ground, freeing dirt from the base of Ava's willow. 'Kitt always had a knack for making anything enjoyable.' My lips twitch into a smile I force myself to find just for him. 'I figured he would want his death to be no different.'

Her grin has my heart stuttering back to life. 'Then you better start digging, Azer.'

CHAPTER 72

Paedyn

My arm strains against the taut bow.

We stand in the very same spot we had during the Purging Trials, facing a faded target and competing for bragging rights. It's been nearly two days since Kai buried his brother beneath the willow tree, and this is one of the many distractions I've forced upon him.

There was a quiet walk through the garden, interrupted only by the occasional reminiscence of the boy buried so near. Our trip to the kitchen was filled with soft laughter and warm sticky buns – Jax sought comfort in his brother's arms while Gail kissed the top of Kai's head. I've urged him to write like Kitt had, relieve his mind of the many swirling thoughts within. His hands are still stained with ink.

Every night has been spent in a pool of moonlight. Blankets litter the floor of my room, layered into a makeshift cot beneath the row of windows. Kai prefers it this way, and I happily oblige. It is as though we have created our own little fort to feel closer to those we have lost. We hold each other before drifting into the nightmares that plague us. But with each sleepy sun that peers down on us, Kai wakes more like himself.

I let the arrow fly. Allow myself a smug smile when it sinks just beside the bullseye.

This is my latest distraction for the future king.

'I would understand if you wished to forfeit now,' I offer.

Kai's fingers brush mine as he pulls the bow from my grip. 'Don't play nice, darling. I can handle losing to you.'

I raise a brow. 'Did you already admit defeat?'

His lips twitch. He looses an arrow quickly, unfazed by the several inches separating it from the center of the target. 'This is meant to be a distraction, is it not? So, I don't need to win.' I swallow when he steps in to me. 'I just want to enjoy it.'

Normally, I would scoff at his arrogance, but I've missed it enough to settle on a slight tilt of my head. 'And what is there to enjoy in losing, Malakai?'

'That.' His dimples steal my breath away. 'Your company. Your taunting. Your lips forming my name.'

I nock an arrow. 'I don't need to be winning to insult you.'

With a deep breath, I fire.

'No,' Kai says slowly. 'But you need to be winning to smile like that.'

I realize then that I'm beaming at the bullseye I've struck. Taming the triumph on my features, I turn towards the seemingly casual Kai. His hands are tucked loosely in his pockets, hair tousled, and eyes bright in the fading sunlight.

He is beautiful.

The thought isn't a surprise. And yet, I'm unable to tear my gaze from him. Such stoic strength seeps from him like the shadow clinging to his heels. This is a boy who has known little more than hardship his whole life, wounded by the man who raised him and left by the brother who loved him.

The brother who hated me.

'What is it?' Kai's voice is laced with concern.

Frustrated, I wipe at the emotion welling in my eyes. 'It's nothing. I'm sorry. This is supposed to be a distraction for you and . . .'

'Talk to me, Pae,' Kai urges. He pries the bow from my sweaty hand before tossing it aside.

I shake my head. 'It's just . . . I hate that he hated me.'

'He didn't. He wasn't himself, and you were just . . .' His gray gaze falls from my face. 'In his way.'

That gnawing numbness I've suppressed over the past several days comes rushing to the surface. 'I cared for him. And this is all my fault—'

'No. We read his letters.' Kai grasps my hands. 'You know what he said in that study. None of this was your fault. Kitt was sick. Both physically and mentally. He only wanted to prove himself.' His voice grows rougher with every word. 'Did I make him feel that way? Why did he take that Plague? Did he think I needed him to be anything more?'

'No, Kai.' I cut off the dangerous thought before it can fester. 'He wanted you at his side because you never made him feel inferior. You were the good in his life. The anchor he clung to.'

'Kitt was the good brother,' Kai murmurs. 'Not me.'

'Good. Bad.' I shrug a shoulder. 'We are all just shadows of what we believe to be true.'

Kai's scoff is pained. 'Kitt certainly believed in something.'

'And you?' I prod. 'What does the future king of Ilya believe in?'

He ponders this for a moment. 'The inevitable. You.' His fingers tickle my cheek on their way to tuck a strand of hair behind my ear. 'I think we got it wrong in Dor. You are the Flame. And I . . . I am the Shadow falling at your feet.'

Eventually, we fire the rest of our arrows at that target.

Unsurprisingly, I gloat thoroughly at my predestined victory.

Delicately, we visit the willow tree and those buried peacefully beneath.

Admittedly, I fail to be a diversion from Kitt's death.

Foolishly, a poet tells me I am never not his distraction.

CHAPTER 73

Kai

There is still dirt under my nails when the crown is placed on my head.

It is a silver tangle of steel, sharp and swirling among my black hair.

Kitt's golden crown remains with him, still gently resting on his brow beneath the willow tree's base.

I stare out at the court from the very dais my brother once stood upon. But startlingly, I don't feel that gaping absence of him anymore. No, he stands at my side, a warm hand on my shoulder and smile in my very soul.

From Enforcer to king. Monster to redeemed.

'I will continue what my brother started,' I inform the court, though they hadn't known the truth of his plans. And they never will.

I have a promise to keep.

My first decree is steady and sure. 'Our borders will remain open. Ordinaries will be welcomed into our city once again. Together, we will rebuild Ilya like Kitt wished.' I swallow the lump in my throat. 'And he will be remembered as the greatest king in our history.'

The throne room echoes with applause, but my eyes are on her. I

step from the stage, pushing through my people until I meet the only one I truly wish to call mine.

Hand in hand, I pull Paedyn out the castle doors and into the courtyard beyond. That bed of forget-me-not flowers still blooms beside the staircase, family to the one I tucked behind her ear so long ago. And I gladly repeat history now.

Pae laughs as I present her with the bouquet, the petals matching her piercing blue gaze. 'Forget-me-nots—' I slide a stem into her hair, '—because you always seem to be forgetting who I am.'

She smiles, and I wonder at how something can be so perfect. 'You're the king of Ilya.'

'And what am I to you?'

I tip her chin up so I can watch the words form on her lips. 'My fool.'

My fingers flick the tip of her nose lightly. 'Don't forget "cocky bastard".'

'You wouldn't let me, even if I tried,' she says sweetly.

I grin – wider when her eyes flick greedily between my dimples. 'And you are forever my undoing, Paedyn Gray.' My knee meets the cobblestone, and her mouth opens in a gasp. 'Marry me, Pae. I'm already on one knee, but I'll get down on both and beg for you, if you like.'

I lift that ring towards her, the one Kitt pressed into my palm with a dying wish.

'Love each other for me.'

Tears well in those blue eyes above. She knows of Kitt's final moments, every word uttered, every hope laid bare. Now the sight of that familiar ring is freeing. I can see the flood of relief washing over her features, because Kitt Azer – the boy she cared so deeply for – did not hate her in the end. The hurt she felt when he aimed a sword at her chest has begun to melt away beneath the truth of his motives.

'Pae,' I breathe. 'I'll kneel here all day, so long as your answer is yes.'

A hand falls from her mouth to reveal a wide grin. 'Good. I quite like the sight of you beneath me.'

'Vicious little thing,' I murmur with all the admiration she deserves.

Her voice grows choked as she spits my own words back at me. 'You forgot the "my" in front of that endearing nickname.'

And then she is falling to her knees before me.

Her hands shake against my face before a pair of smiling lips have found mine. She kisses me like forever is fleeting in the face of this moment. My hand finds her hair, tangling in the uneven strands I'd cut in that cave. Her lips taste of love and longing, and I beg for more.

'Is this—' I kiss her deeply. 'Is this a yes?'

She laughs against my lips. 'This is inevitable.'

I slip Kitt's gold band onto her thumb, opposite that steel ring of her father's. 'I'll get you something better—'

'No,' she insists. Her eyes shine as they take in the rings hugging each thumb. 'It's perfect. *This* is perfect.'

'Good.' My rough palms graze the sides of her neck. 'Because I love you, Paedyn Gray. And I will happily spend the rest of my life trying to deserve you.'

'I love you,' she says, suddenly stern. 'And I will spend the rest of my life shouting it until even Astrum hears, because it is Death who should fear *me* if he ever tries to take you away.'

We hold each other atop that uneven cobblestone. Forget-me-nots blow in the warm breeze, encircling us in a hug that feels like our past meeting our forever. Tears sting my eyes for the bittersweetness of this moment.

Paedyn Gray is finally mine. But only because my brother is no longer here.

'We will love for him,' she whispers in my ear.

A tear slips down my cheek.

'You and me.'

CHAPTER 74

Paedyn

$\mathfrak{I}$ dream of Adena on the eve of my wedding.

Kai has slept at my side every night since slipping that ring onto my thumb, warding off a month's worth of nightmares. But tradition chases him from my chambers on the eve of our union, and I am left to my hauntings alone.

When Adena takes my hand, I feel the faintest tug of fear in my drifting body. I had hidden from this nightmare, shielded myself behind Kai's comfort, because I couldn't bear to watch Adena die all over again.

But that is not this dream.

What lurks within my resting mind is something sweet. Soft. So like the Adena who once lived and breathed that I awake with tears staining my cheeks. It is all a hazy memory when the sun pries my heavy eyelids open, but I remember the feeling Adena left me with:

Peace.

I had said goodbye.

Or rather, a good way to say bye until I see my A next.

Ellie alone helps me prepare for my final, inevitable wedding.

Dark clouds crowd the sky beyond my windows, threatening rain with an angry rumble. This only makes me smile.

'It's good to see you happy on your wedding day,' Ellie says softly. Her fingers thread through my hair to weave thin braids within it. They hang down among my wavy hair, elegant in its simplicity.

I gnaw on my lip to busy my smile. 'This is what I've wanted for longer than I even realized. And I'm letting myself enjoy it.'

'You should enjoy it,' Ellie reassures. 'You both deserve that.'

My smile is tainted with the sadness that typically accompanies thoughts of Kitt. But my grief resides with the boy he was, and the brother he left behind. Despite Kai's resilience over the past several weeks, I know that he wishes to celebrate today with Kitt, just as I wish to with Adena.

Stepping behind the dressing curtain, I slip into a simple stretch of fabric. The gown is made up of a thin, billowing material that lands just above my ankles. Its strapless bodice hugs me closely before white fabric cascades from my waist. There is little about the dress that makes it particularly interesting, and that is exactly why I chose it.

Adena's vest captures the attention, its faded, olive fabric snug around my bare shoulders. After days of a seamstress painstakingly mending it, I'm eager to be reunited with my piece of Adena. I stand before the mirror and admire precisely what I had always envisioned for my wedding day.

This moment couldn't be more different than the one I had stolen before marrying a man I didn't love. Then, panic prickled my heart and crowded my mind. Now, I'm glowing with happiness, flooded with peace. I've already done the grand wedding day and want nothing of the sort. I simply want *our* day.

A confident knock at the door has my gaze flicking to Ellie.

She reciprocates my confusion before peeking into the hallway with a soft gasp falling from her lips. 'Your Majesty, it's bad luck to see—'

'Bad luck is far less concerning than Pae is with an empty stomach and a dagger in hand.'

Annoyingly, my lips twitch into a smile. 'If you're afraid of me, Azer, just say so.'

Kai's voice is touched with awe on the other side of my door. 'You know I would be a fool not to be, darling.'

I have to plant my feet to keep from running to him.

'I'm sorry, Your Majesty,' Ellie sympathizes through the cracked door. 'You really shouldn't see her until the wedding.'

There is a grin burrowed between his words. 'So I won't look.'

The door swings open.

Ellie's protest dies in her throat as Kai strides into the room, his head bowed slightly with a hand shielding his eyes. I press a palm to my mouth and smother the laugh tickling my tongue as the king walks towards me. His gaze is on the shifting feet beneath him while mine is on the bowl of porridge clutched between his fingers.

When Kai stops before me, I look down into the soup of oats speckled with fruit. He can't see my smile. 'You added blueberries.'

'It pained me greatly.'

'Your bravery is inspiring,' I croon.

His hand drops from that beautiful face beneath to display dark lashes aimed at the floor. 'And selfish.' Dimples frame his curved lips. 'I want something in return.'

I cross my arms. 'And what would that be?'

'A "yes" at the end of that aisle today.'

The words are quick, a rush of uncertainty I'm so unused to hearing in Kai's voice. My heart aches at the veiled worry he wears. After finally letting himself feel for someone, he fears I'll walk away. A king stands before me, stripped bare, and back to the boy who was forced to believe love was a weakness.

Gently, I slip the warm bowl from his fingers and set it on the floor beside me. Then his face is in my hands, his brow creasing at the feel of my touch. 'At the end of a blade, I would love you. Until it pierced my throat, I would say "yes" to you.'

The tear that slips down his cheek coaxes one from my own eye. Kai's voice is rough with emotion as he murmurs, 'You're quite the poet, darling.'

I laugh, my vision blurring with the scrunching of my brimming gaze. 'Some fool inspired me.'

We spend the next several moments basking in this limbo between our present and the future awaiting us at the base of a willow tree. We laugh. We pretend not to cry. We say our goodbyes – one due to the temporary distance Ellie insists between us, and the other in memory of our final moments before forever.

Long after Kai strides from my chamber, and Ellie has fussed with my appearance for the final time, a second knock sounds at my door. Lenny asks if I am ready. I don't hesitate before taking his arm.

'All this time I've been calling you "Princess" . . .' Red hair ripples with the slow shake of his head. 'Who the hell would have guessed you were one.'

I throw him a playful glare. 'Yes, how very shocking.'

It felt good to share the truth with him and those closest to me. But I keep the secret of my royal blood tucked close to my heart, hidden from the kingdom who has already begun to accept me. I say nothing of the forgotten princess I am, so as not to draw Kai's legitimacy into question.

My whole life, I have been Ordinary. And I no longer feel the need to change that.

'Look,' Lenny continues, undeterred, 'I'm more interested in the fact that I might actually be Psychic. I mean, how did I know to call you that?'

I snort. 'What next, are you going to discover I'm truly a cockroach?'

'Very funny, Majesty.' He shakes his head at me, even while wearing a smile. We step out into the blooming garden and begin our stroll through the winding paths. Passing the fountain I now look at fondly, Lenny asks, 'This is the wedding you want, P? Right?'

I glance over at my friend. He returns the smile lighting my face and flushing my cheeks. My admission is bold and freeing and daring Death to make me regret it. 'Desperately.'

CHAPTER 75

Rai

She walks towards me, looking like a dream I wish to never wake from.

Her fingers clutch a collection of twining stems. Above, poppies' red petals bleed into pink roses while the deep blue of dainty forget-me-nots weaves between.

I stand beside the willow's mighty trunk, beside my brother and sister. I'm swallowed in the swaying branches, lost in a tangle of slender leaves.

It is only me, and the ghost of those I love, awaiting Paedyn beneath the willow. She, too, steps into our future alone, but not entirely.

Her slippers pad slowly across the stretch of soft grass. Adena hugs her tightly atop the plain dress she wears; the memory of a father encircles the thumb wrapped around her bouquet.

Time slows long enough to let me bask in a moment I've only ever dreamed of.

She is my dream.

She is my piece of paradise.

She is my inevitable.

My composure begins to crumble with every step she takes towards me. Tears well in my eyes, but I smile for her. Always for her.

Thunder rumbles beyond the willow's embrace, but Paedyn's gaze never leaves mine. Happily, I drown in it.

A bead of water splatters Paedyn's nose. She laughs. Rain drips from the canopy of leaves to sprinkle us in the brewing storm. Damp hair curls atop my forehead. Jax lifts his palms towards the crying sky. Ellie stares lovingly at her queen. Gail's tears mingle with the rain while Andy rests her head on the cook's shoulder. Lenny winks at the drenched bride who passes.

This is no grand wedding. We wear no crowns or jewels. This is the gathering of loved ones, and the spirits of those left behind. This is a union of souls that ache to be stitched together.

Lightning cracks through the sky behind Paedyn. Her steps do not falter.

When she stops before me, I nearly fall to my knees.

I am forever awed by the mere presence of her.

She passes her bouquet to Ellie. I grab her hands, willing to let her lead me wherever she pleases.

There is no rambling Scholar, no lengthy vows exchanged.

It is simply us, standing before fate and defying the odds.

Pae's commitment to me lacks any hesitancy. 'I do.'

My heart stutters. It is broken and healing and missing Kitt beside me. But it is full.

She is what my scarred heart beats for.

I tilt her face towards mine before clutching it in my trembling hands. 'I do.' My voice is heavy with emotion. 'In every lifetime, I do.'

Her lips find mine, sealing the promise between us.

Thunder claps alongside our family.

I breathe in my bride. She tastes like my forever.

We walk from beneath the willow's canopy, hand in hand.

King and queen.

Shadow and Flame.

Poet and muse.

Tears fill the eyes of those around us, accompanied by clapping and followed with laughter. The small group parades behind, wet branches grasping at our clothing as we push through the leaves. Lightning is quick to greet us. We step into the clearing beyond, damp grass beneath our feet and a raging storm above.

'I have something for you,' I murmur against Pae's ear.

She smiles up at me. 'Oh?'

Jax hands me the dripping crown with a beaming grin. I hold the twining circlet of roses between us, watching Paedyn's gaze widen. Then I'm placing that delicate crown onto her damp hair.

She gapes at me in shock. 'You finally did it. You made a flower crown.'

'I just needed more practice.'

Water drips from her lashes with every astonished blink. 'All that hard work for me?'

'For my queen,' I correct with a soft kiss to her lips.

And then we dance.

Paedyn is spinning in my arms, laughing in the spitting rain. The hem of her dress is muddy, but she can't seem to take her eyes off me long enough to notice. I push wet hair from her face, straighten her crown of roses, hold the hand that now wears my brother's ring. We cling to each other while shadowed figures dance around us. Laughter envelops our swaying forms, warming us despite the chilled rain.

I hold Paedyn against me.

My wife.

My eye in the storm.

She slips a hand into one of the many pockets of her vest before shouting through the rumbling thunder. 'You're not the only one who brought a gift.'

I track the movement, blinking in the rain as she pulls a stem of forget-me-nots from the soaked fabric. Paedyn Azer's smile is dangerous as she reaches up to tuck the flowers behind my ear.

'So you don't forget who I am,' she whispers against my lips.

'And what am I?' I trace my thumb along her bottom lip. 'A fool? A cocky bastard?'

Her voice is steady. 'You are mine, Malakai.'

Water drips from my lashes, some from her nose. 'I always have been,' I murmur. 'Until . . . whatever the hell.'

The laugh that spills from her soft lips has my breath catching. She tips her head back to smile at the storming sky, unburdened by the mention of Adena. 'Until whatever the hell,' she echoes, letting that piercing gaze fall back to me.

Beads of water trail down her bared neck as I greedily take in the curve of her mouth. Like a reflex, reverence softens my gaze, coats my voice. 'There is that smile I have been waiting to memorize.'

Paedyn blinks up at me in the rain, grin widening. She twines slick arms around my neck before her cold nose is brushing mine. 'And you have all the time in the world to admire it.'

CHAPTER 76

Paedyn

5 YEARS LATER

I breathe in the fresh air, sun soaking my skin.

A blue sky hangs above the yawning stretch of crops. I shield my gaze with a hand, determined to find the end of this daunting cornfield.

'Somewhere more interesting.'

Kai's voice is a drawl beside me. My eyes flick to him, combing over the stubble clinging to his strong jaw. 'What?' I ask, fearing the answer.

'Somewhere more interesting,' he repeats with a sigh and crossing of his arms. 'That is likely where this field ends.'

I scoff before I scold. 'Tando has been good to us. That being said—' I glance around the nearly deserted brick road we stand on, '—let's settle this year's trade agreements and get the hell out of here.'

Kai takes a step towards me, blotting out the sun with his broad shoulders. 'Admit it, darling. You hate it out here more than I do.'

I'm spinning the rings that hug each of my thumbs.

'What makes you say that?'

'The quiet.' He brushes a long strand of hair from my face. 'The open space. The lack of handsome strangers to rob.'

I give him a flat look. 'You're right. Not a single handsome face for miles.'

'Easy, Azer. Don't hurt your foot with such a blatant lie.' He flicks the tip of my nose gently. 'I said *strangers*, and we both know I am nothing of the sort.'

'No, you're not.' I grab his hands and pull him close. Then I'm murmuring, 'But that doesn't mean I can't still rob you.'

I lift his wedding band between our close faces.

It was simple, really, snatching the silver ring from his thumb. He wears his symbol of our union on the same finger I do – a reminder of our love, and the love of a lost brother.

Kai shakes his head at me before grasping my hand. 'Still as vicious as ever.'

'You love it.'

'I love you,' he murmurs. 'Foolishly.'

He kisses me, and still my heart flutters at the brush of his lips.

Pulling away, I glance over at the field of corn waving beside us. 'You still feel her, right?'

Kai's lips twitch into a smile. 'She's on her way back.' Then he raises his voice towards the sea of corn. 'Did you find it?'

A small body tumbles from the maze of crop to scurry towards us. That shock of gray hair blows around her face, obscuring the excitement displayed there. With a large ear of corn gripped between tiny fingers, she runs into her father's awaiting arms.

'That's the one you were looking for?' Kai asks, examining her loot. 'You're sure this is the best corn in all of Tando?'

'I'm sure, Daddy!' She shoves the vegetable into his hand and promptly reaches for me. I pull her into my arms, trying to ignore how big she has gotten in the last three years. Resting on my hip, she runs her small fingers through the hair falling down my back. Her own is an ashy blend of Kai's ebony waves and my silver strands. With gray hair and muted blue eyes, our little girl is a messy mixture of two strangers who fell in love.

'What else did you find on your adventure?' I ask while straightening her rumpled clothes.

'Bugs,' she states indifferently. 'Big, fat ones.'

Kai nods. 'I'm sure. Now, did you bring anything else back?' He inches closer, making her giggle. 'Maybe some new freckles?'

She knows this game. And Kit loves it.

Kai presses his lips to the bridge of her nose, over and over until she is squealing. Once he has finished peppering our daughter with kisses, he turns to me. 'Is it time for that recount?'

I roll my eyes. 'Is that not what you did last week?'

His grin has my cheeks flushing. 'One can never be too sure.'

The first soft kiss is to my cheek.

'One,' he murmurs.

The second is on the bridge of my nose.

'Two.'

The third is when I lift my chin and press my lips to his. I smile against his mouth. 'Your recount will have to wait. Let's get the hell out of here, remember?'

We head down the quiet road, Kit's hands in each of our own. The cottages here look lonely between the fields that accompany them. It is quiet in Tando, eerily so, and I'm grateful when we finally step into the city's market. Though it is certainly not the bustling Loot I'm so accustomed to, the relief I feel at the sight of milling bodies is shocking.

Kit skips between us as we point out the muted colors all around. Tando's banners are a soft yellow that seeks no attention. The market is docile and brimming with kind individuals. I quietly envy those so content in such quaintness.

But Loot is my home, and Ilya is thriving around it. The kingdom is open, our borders welcoming of trade and travelers. Ordinaries live alongside their Elite neighbors, growing bolder despite their lack of abilities. It was all I ever wanted to see as a powerless girl.

The slums are my current project. Crumbling buildings are being restored, allowing more shops and homes to border the alleyways. Feasts are held regularly at the castle to welcome the people of Ilya into our home. The once crushing divide between Elites and Ordinaries is slowly smoothing into something promising.

I take in the quiet street, the uniformity between each sturdy brick shop. This is certainly not my kingdom. My Ilya is lively and drenched in color. It is worn and healing and *home*.

'Kit, honey, stay close!' I call after watching her tear down the street, brandishing an ear of corn.

Kai stares after her with a shake of his head. 'She looks just like you. Only, someday soon, that corn will be replaced with a blade.'

I smile sweetly at him. 'And she can practice using it on you.'

'You have prepared me well,' he reminds.

His arm tugs me close. I rest my head on his shoulder. We watch our daughter skip in the pooling sunlight.

Until a flash of lilac has my gaze flicking to a shadowed corner of the street.

I stare into the face of a ghost. She stares back.

Scarred flesh climbs up the side of her neck. Mutilated skin stretches across her features before disappearing into that lilac hair. Only one half of her sharp face bears the remnants of my hatred.

I can still feel her soft skin beneath my palm, feel the heat of that raging fire I forced her into.

I expect that rage to resurface now. I expect to crave that revenge on Adena's behalf and ache to finish what I apparently did not the first time. Blair seems to anticipate the same, because I watch her shoulders tense beneath the cloak slung over them.

But I feel nothing. I do nothing.

We stare at each other for several beats of my clamoring heart.

In another lifetime, she was my enemy. Here, she is a stranger.

I do not wish to avenge Adena any longer. I wish for her to rest.

So, with a slight nod of my head, I let Blair go.

She returns the silent peace offering with a dip of her chin.

'Mommy! Daddy! Look what I found!'

Kit steals my attention with a flurry of limbs and the waving of what must be the best rock in all of Tando. Kai scoops her into his arms, feigning astonishment for the gift she sets in his palm. I, too, look impressed by Kit's finding as I smooth her wild hair.

And when I finally glance over at that shadowed corner, the ghost is gone.

Kai catches my flitting gaze. Holds it gently. Tilts his head.

'Not-so-vicious little thing,' he murmurs endearingly.

Of course the Wielder knew she was here.

I blow out a breath before stealing our daughter from his arms. 'Don't get used to it.'

'I wouldn't want to.'

We continue down the sun-drenched street.

Onward, always.

A king. A queen. A princess. A rock and an ear of corn.

Those we have lost walk alongside us, their memory warming our scarred hearts.

We are those we loved.

I tilt my face to the sky and let the sun brush warm fingers over it. The soft rays are a comfort I embrace like an old friend.

My husband stands at my side, just as he always has and always will.

He smiles, and it's the one meant solely for me. Kit copies her father, though only one stolen dimple peeks out on her right cheek.

I flick them both lightly on the nose. This draws a giggle from Kit and that ceaseless look of reverence from Kai.

I smile back, just as Adena taught me to.

This life is sweet.

Like honey.

EPILOGUE

Kitt

There is no flash of light.

No bang or slow fade.

Kitt feels cheated. That is what he has always been promised, after all. Some great entrance into the world beyond the one he has drifted from.

But this is none of that.

This is nothing at all.

The first time he opens his eyes after Death has closed them, Kitt tries desperately to make something of the void before him. He squints at it, walks within it, tries to grip it between his fingers. But nothing is nothing, and the lack of something is frustrating. It is like the void that occurs behind one blinked eye – no color, no shape, no anything.

Nothing. And that was not the death he had anticipated.

The former king wanders in the empty afterlife, not quite conscious but never entirely aware. He often wonders – there is little else to do here – if he is meant to wait for someone. Perhaps his brother. Perhaps Paedyn, if she ever wishes to see him again.

So when Death arrives, Kitt only feels comfort. Not fear or

confusion like a saner mind might.

No, Kitt recognizes the face of Death. Knows her by name.

'Mara.' The dead king reaches for the woman who dragged him into this abyss of nothingness. Because he only feels relief at her presence.

Death stands before him, her form so unlike the ominous tales humans so like to spin. For starters, she is just that – a she. Despite an eternity of stealing souls, not one of them anticipates Death to be a woman. There was once a time when this vexed Mara, but she has since grown accustomed to a dying face drenched in disbelief.

Is it so shocking to feel anything but warmth from a woman's touch? Can a pretty face not drag you into the afterlife, all the same?

'Hello, Kitt,' Death says curtly. 'I warned you of this fate.'

'I know,' he answers earnestly. 'But this isn't the Mors. Where am I?'

Mara sweeps a strand of chestnut hair from her dark eyes. No, she doesn't look like Death. 'This is your peace.' Her voice is chilled. This shouldn't surprise Kitt. 'It seems you accepted your fate long before dying.'

The king frowns. 'I guess I did.' Then he attempts a weak 'But I'm happy you're here. I . . . I didn't think you would want to see me.'

'I can't stay long.' Mara takes a breath before feigning politeness. 'How are you enjoying peace?'

Kitt sweeps his green gaze over the expanse of darkness. 'I'm still lonely.'

'You didn't have to be,' Mara spits. 'This is your own doing.'

Before drifting back into the darkness, Death leaves the king with a veiled goodbye. The broken words are nearly swallowed up in the nothingness. 'But I'll let you go gently.'

Alone once again, Kitt thinks on a life left behind.

He does not blame Kai for the unfortunate end he met (after all, it was he who was meant to dodge the Enforcer's strike) or Death for her help in it. Neither does he let anger fester towards the girl who stole his brother from him. Resentment tends to be cumbersome in the afterlife. Since relieving himself of it, little by little, death has felt far more freeing.

In fact, without the Plague muddling his mind and stealing his sanity, he now finds his last few weeks among the living seem wasted. He wishes, futilely, to try it all again. Perhaps he wouldn't let power consume him this time around. But this is wishful thinking, and regret is what keeps the dead rolling over in their graves.

He does ponder — frequently, remember — how this is meant to be peace. Is he a monster worth such gaping loneliness? Kitt often shouts into the void, pleads his case to this shunning afterlife. But it gives no answer. Death does not return. And this gives him none of the peace he was promised.

Kitt never sits in the same spot of eternity. In fact, he never knows where he is or where he is going. Still, he stares up — assumably — into the nothingness. There is no ground beneath his feet, but he reclines all the same. And just as he has for however long he's been dead, Kitt wishes for company.

A soft light above startles the dead beneath.

Kitt squints up at it, finding two shimmering dots among the sheet of nothingness. They wink down at him like stars plucked from the sky above Ilya.

'Hello, Kitt,' a light says softly. It's a female voice, as warm and bright as the glow she emits.

At the startling sound of his name, Kitt stands to blink up at the oddities. 'Who are you?'

It seems a silly question to ask, as he has little use for the information. But that gentle voice graces him with something that is not quite an answer. 'We thought you might like some company.'

Kitt nods. 'I would. Thank you.'

Death has been kind to him.

There is a long pause.

'Do you think I'm a monster?' He isn't sure why he feels the need to ask a pair of stars.

The female's voice is sad. 'No. You are your father's sins.'

'You're not alone in that.' This reassurance comes from the second star, in a deep voice.

'But I am alone here,' Kitt says solemnly. 'You two have one another.'

The softer star informs, 'Life ripped us apart.'

'Death brought us together,' the rougher one finishes.

There is something so vaguely familiar about the pair of glowing orbs. Kitt doesn't ponder this absurdity further. Instead, he sits once again, folding his legs beneath him. 'Would you . . .' He feels oddly shy. 'Would you stay with me awhile?'

Kitt could have sworn it looked as though the stars were smiling at him. That warm, bubbly voice fills the void between them in response. 'Until you see your brother again, if you like.'

The deep voice rumbles above him. 'We are all waiting for someone.'

Acknowledgments

Here we are again, at the end of another book and the beginning of my typical procrastination. This is where I struggle to find the words for a proper farewell. I'll sit here for a while, staring at a blank page meant to be filled with my acknowledgments while desperately clinging to the remains of this story. Because, in truth, I cannot imagine a world in which I didn't dare to create this one. Paedyn and Kai hold more than my heart, they clutch my passion between these pages, cradle the little girl who had big dreams of becoming an author. This series has been so gentle with me as I've grown into myself and my writing – I only hope to repay the favor by doing this finale justice.

Writing *Fearless* at the age of twenty-one was one of the most daunting ventures I've faced in my young career. This book challenged me, my writing, my sanity (kidding – kind of!). In fact, I have been dreading this bittersweet farewell since the publication of *Powerless* – only then I never dreamed of having the privilege to continue writing for so many people. I was (and still am) equally honored and terrified by all the anticipation surrounding this release. The pressure I felt to appease every reader, to write the perfect finale, weighed heavy atop a story born in my childhood bedroom for myself alone. But *Fearless* forced me to push aside all the noise, all my worry, and simply write the conclusion I always envisioned for this series. In its own (albeit, sappy) way, this book taught me to embody its title. What a beautiful thing, the creator being molded by their creation. And I hope you too, dear reader, have walked away from this series more powerful, reckless, and blazingly fearless than before.

Now, it's time to bring my procrastination, and this chapter of my life, to an end. There are so many incredible individuals who helped me make it to this acknowledgment page in the first place. But it only seems right to begin my gushing gratitude with the two incredible editors who made this book what it is. Nicole Ellul and Yasmin Morrissey never fail to amaze me. This duo is one to be reckoned with – their constant support and invaluable input has shaped this series into something I am immensely proud of. Nicole, your insight and readiness to jump to my aid is not taken lightly. You are my designated left brain! Thank you for grounding me when my head is in the clouds – this book would look very different without your brilliance. As for Yas, you are the bravest of souls for putting up with my rambling voice memos and stubborn self-criticism. There is never a dull moment with the two of us – I love scheming up new ideas with you! I so appreciate how gentle and supportive you've been with me since the moment I stepped into this crazy publishing world. I'm honored to work alongside the both of you (and have your numbers on speed dial).

As I've bragged about before, I have the privilege of working with not one, but two incredible Simon and Schuster teams. This has allowed me to build relationships with so many wonderful people across the globe, and I am forever awed by the delicacy in which the UK and US handle my work – their care and dedication is commendable.

That said, I will begin spewing my admiration for the team closest to me (geographically speaking, of course). There are several individuals from the US crew that I have the honor to thank, starting with Justin Chanda and Anne Zafian as my two Publishers. As for Nicole Russo and Anna Elling, we all have you to thank for the amazing US tours and every surreal opportunity to share my book. Erin Toller, Brandon MacDonald, and Shannon Pender do a fabulous job in marketing while Kendra Levin, Jenica Nasworthy, and Jessica Egan manage all things editorial. With Chava Wolin as Director of Production, Lucy Cummins as Art Director, and Hilary Zarycky as Designer, I am in very good hands. Thank you for everything you do.

As for the UK team, you all deserve a crushing hug I can't currently give from Detroit, so it seems I'll have to settle for a general thank-you. Rachel Denwood and Laura Hough – my Managing Directors – thank you for all your hard work. Danielle Wilson has championed my work with UK retailers while Loren Catana, my in-house Designer, came up with the gorgeous cover design for *Fearless*. Thank you to Alex Forrest – my Illustrator, Alesha Bonser – my Marketing Director, and Miya Elkerton – my Digital Marketing Manager. Finally, Ellen Abernethy as my wonderful Publicist and Sophie Storr as Senior Production Controller. Thank you to every other member of this team who made *Fearless* possible.

By now, I'm sure you're quite sick of reading my ramblings and would instead like to stare at the gorgeous artwork displayed at the front of this book. Patrick Knowles, thank you for bringing my world to life!

To my unflinching attorney-agent, Lloyd Jassin, I must give my obvious gratitude. Thank you for helping navigate me through this world of publishing – I cannot imagine tackling any of this without you. You are a pleasure to work with, and I hope to continue doing so for many years to come.

Besides the incredible S&S teams who helped assemble *Fearless*, there are several others at work behind the scenes. And I happen to be related to those individuals. Firstly, I can humbly admit that none of these dreams would have come true if it weren't for my parents. Mom and Dad, I've said it before, and I'll say it yet again — you have supported me every step of the way, believed in me when I found it hard to believe in myself. Thank you for trusting your little girl enough to let her pursue this passion. I am so blessed to have you both, but especially a mother who happily juggles being my confidant, assistant, and bookkeeper.

Being the runt of the family, I suppose there are a few older siblings to acknowledge. Jessie, Nikki, Josh — you have all supported me in your own ways. I deeply appreciate every encouraging text and proverbial pat on the back. Thank you, Foos.

Aside from my family, it was my friends who ensured I stayed sane during this writing process. I would like to give a general thank-you to every person who had to put up with me rambling about this book. Each of you have helped and encouraged me in your own way, and I am eternally grateful for your unending support.

Now onto the daunting task of attempting to express my admiration for a certain fiancé. Zac, I cannot thank you enough for your encouragement and willingness to help. Whether it's cooking me a meal or offering a shoulder to cry on, I can always rely on your comfort. Thank you for being exactly what I need.

As stated in the back of *Powerless* and every book following, I'd like to thank the One who gifted me my love of words and the desire to write. I truly would not be where I am today without my Lord and Savior, and I thank God for the opportunity He has given me.

Now to thank the very, *very* many people who made my dreams possible. That would be you, dear reader! I am honored to be on this journey together, and even more so that you took the time to read my story. You are my inspiration, my reason for every word. And I hope to hold your attention for many years to come.

Here's to more dreams, and the stories they create.

XO, *Lauren*

About the Author

When Lauren Roberts isn't writing about fantasy worlds and bantering love interests, she can likely be found burrowed in bed reading about them. Lauren has lived in Michigan her whole life, making her very familiar with potholes, snow, and various lake activities. She has the hobbies of both a grandmother and a child: knitting, laser tag, hammocking, word searches, and colouring. She's the author of the Powerless Trilogy, and she hopes to have the privilege of writing pretty words for the rest of her life. If you enjoy ranting, reading, and writing, Lauren can be found on both TikTok and Instagram @laurenrobertslibrary or her website laurenrobertslibrary.com for your entertainment.